Strebor on the Streetz

EVERLASTING

STREBOR ON THE Streetz

EVERLASTING

STACY-DEANNE

STREBOR BOOKS

NEW YORK LONDON TORONTO SYDNEY

Strebor Books
P.O. Box 6505
Largo, MD 20792
http://www.streborbooks.com

ISBN-13 978-1-59309-187-3
ISBN-10   1-59309-187-7
LCCN 2007924151

First Strebor Books trade paperback edition October 2007

Cover design: www.mariondesigns.com

10 9 8 7 6 5 4 3 2 1

Manufactured in the United States of America

For information regarding special discounts for bulk purchases,
please contact Simon & Schuster Special Sales at 1-800-456-6798
or business@simonandschuster.com

DEDICATION

For my mother, Elva, and father, John,
for always standing by me.
For my Aunt Linda and my cousin Brenda,
Rest in Peace
This one is for all of you.

CHAPTER ONE

"So. Another dead body. What a surprise." Juan Alonso watched his three friends.

The four young men stared at the muddy corpse covered in New York Assassin tattoos. Dead bodies were the norm on this side of the world. The gang life ruled the streets. The Bronx Gangstas claimed another NYA victim. Juan knew his brother's gang would retaliate very soon. And there wasn't anything he could do to stop them.

✠✠✠

The Bronx was known for busy days and long nights. The rest of New York passed the Bronx residents by. Everything within the Bronx moved in slow motion. At least it seemed that way for Nina Sagastume. It wasn't enough that she'd been jerked away from her regular life within only a few days' notice. She'd expected to swallow the hazardous rituals of gang life brought on by a cousin she hadn't seen since she was six years old.

She knew it was unfair judging Tajo's lifestyle before he had a chance to defend himself. But what sane sixteen-year-old girl wouldn't be disgusted by the overwhelming tides of crimes that turned the Bronx from a once-productive community to a place you couldn't walk around at night. At least, that's how Nina saw it.

She'd never had trouble adapting to change. She was brought up to be wiser than her years and she vowed to follow her dreams. She never let anyone get in the way of what she wanted. So when her mother's cancer took a bad turn, forcing Nina to move to Edgewood, she promised she'd do whatever she could to adapt. From now on she'd live with her cousin, Tajo—the only family she had outside of Mexico.

Many things had rescued her from the burden of watching over her mother for the last eight years. The doctors claimed it was a miracle that Michelle Sagastume had lived this long, liver cancer wasn't usually so prolonged. Michelle hadn't been the best mother in the world. She'd resented being saddled with Nina at an early age. Nina felt Michelle could have been more sympathetic to her. It wasn't easy being the daughter of a woman only fifteen years older than she was.

It wasn't only embarrassing, but also vicious. Throughout school the kids always pointed out how much younger Michelle was compared to other parents. They commented on how hip Michelle acted. How hot Michelle looked. That same "hotness" had always gotten Michelle into trouble. Her wild side had subsided since the cancer. She finally had no choice but to confront the normality of motherhood.

Nina appreciated that her parents had given her beauty and talent, at least. Nina's beauty outshone Michelle's. She'd inherited Michelle's trademark full lips and her luscious black hair. Nina's exhilarating skin made her lovely eyes radiate. Her beauty stunned most, yet she never paid her physical blessings much attention. Michelle had used her own good looks to get through life easily. Nina felt having talent was the most important thing.

She was thankful to her dad, whoever he was, for giving her the talent of art. She painted finger portraits that sang to everyone who looked upon them. Michelle couldn't draw a stick figure let alone paint a picture. It had been relatively easy for Nina growing up in a decent neighborhood. She hadn't expected everything in Edgewood to be so different.

She'd only been in the neighborhood for a few hours. She counted out a thousand variations. It was funny to her. The entire Edgewood community was made up of Latinos so she assumed she'd fit in. Edgewood's dwellers had the power of sensing when someone didn't belong. She hoped with it being Saturday night they'd go about their business and not inquire about the "new girl on the block."

Tajo lived in a two-story house that was inherited from a distant uncle of his and Nina's. She was happy to see he'd kept it up. The home had been in the family for years, back when Edgewood was predominantly Italian. The Latino population had grown significantly, proving how much everything had changed since she'd last visited. She had been told to wait on the porch for Tajo's crew to show up.

Nina scanned the neighborhood. She sure as hell didn't want to be caught sitting alone at night. She'd been a tough broad in her own neighborhood, but the folks of Edgewood watched her every move. Especially the girls across the street. *Rucas*, if she'd ever seen them. Oh yeah, she knew gang girls. And these were the roughest-looking chicks she'd ever seen.

A long brown car Nina couldn't immediately identify stopped in front of Tajo's.

Mexican guys poured out of the car like rice. The four in the front seat cackled boisterously. The eight in the back were silent as corpses. Nina gripped her purse. She stood, straightening her jeans.

"Yo, pass that shit, homes!" The driver reached for a joint

from the backseat. He took a couple of hits, then turned the car off.

"All right, time for some bullshit," Nina whispered.

"Hey, don't wet the shit all up, motherfucker." A younger guy reached over the backseat. He yanked the joint from the driver. He didn't have it for ten seconds before the guy sitting on the side of him snatched it away. "Yo, quit playin', Spider."

"Man, fuck that shit. I'm trying to get my weed on and I don't have time to be waiting."

"Talking shit, little man." The driver rubbed his goatee. "You're still a baby gansta."

"That's right." The second one snatched the joint from Spider. "Which means you can't claim shit until you smoke somebody. Dumb-ass motherfucker." They laughed.

"Oh, so it's like that? Well, when the time comes, y'all let me know."

"You can bet on that, motherfucker." The second guy continued puffing. Nina wondered if they even noticed her.

"Yo, man, check her out." Spider made sucking noises to Nina. He waved his hands toward his pants. "Hey, baby! How you doing? Spider love you long time, man!" He cackled.

"Spider, sit your skinny ass down." The driver shoved him. "She wouldn't be looking at your young ass no way. Fuckin' thirteen years old and still watching *Blues Clues* and shit."

"Ah, ha!" The guys in the back high-fived.

"She wants a real man," the driver replied. He peered at her. "Yo, snap. That must be Nina, man."

"What?" One of the guys in back took a quick peek. "*That's* Tajo's cousin? No way, homes."

"It's her. I met her years ago. Damn, milk must do a body good." The driver laughed.

"Man, she is so fine." Spider squeezed his skinny body out of the back window. The others slumped out of the car. "What's up, baby?" Nina stood back. "Hey, I said what's up, baby?" Spider stepped up to her.

The driver chuckled. "Spider, back off her, man. Breath smelling like tuna fish."

They laughed. Even Nina managed a quick chuckle.

"Homes, how you gonna play me like that?" Spider glared at Nina. "Don't tell her shit about me, let her make up her own mind. What's up, Nina?"

"What's up?" she groaned. Spider was only thirteen with a body so thin he wore two belts to hold up his sagging pants. They all wore the usual gang wear—long white socks, sleeveless T-shirts, and the latest sneakers.

"You know you are so fine, Nina. You wanna get with me? I know I'm young but you could teach me everything I need to know." Spider smirked.

"Spider, chill." The driver pulled him to the side. He licked his lips, checking her out also. "I'm Shorty-Five." He took her hand. "It's nice to meet you, Nina."

"Nice to meet you, too." So far he was the best-looking guy she'd seen in Edgewood. He played the gangsta role well. His body was covered in BG tattoos from his legs to his neck. He sported a large, gold crucifix on his chest.

"Hi, Nina, I'm Paz. It means 'peace' in Spanish." He took her hand.

"I know. And you seem to be proud of that." She chuckled.

"I'm Juice, Nina." He smelled of weed but Nina did her best not to let on. "So when's the last time you been around here?" He shoved his hands in the pockets of his oversize Adidas wear.

"About ten years." Spider licked his lips. Within seconds his eyes went from her lips to her breasts down to her thighs. And she could feel every inch of it. "Things have changed around here."

"You know it. I'm Cannon." The guy with the dark cap stepped up.

"Cannon?" She couldn't believe someone had a name she recognized. "What, no G name?"

"Yo, snap, she put it on you, homes!" Spider laughed.

"Cannon *is* my G name as you call it. Cannon like in *gun*."

"Oh." Nina backed away. "I hope I didn't offend you."

"Don't worry, baby. As fine as you are, you're welcome to offend us all night long." He laughed. The others howled.

"Last but definitely not least, I'm Bone." Bone was obviously the player of the group. The way he carried himself showed Nina he was not to be taken lightly.

"Nice to meet you, Bone." She shook his hand. "You guys got the key to let me in or what?"

"Uh…" Spider looked around. "Who has the key, man?" They patted themselves down.

"I think it's in the car. Hold up." Juice galloped back toward the car. He dug in the front seat. Nina prayed he'd find it before Spider finished undressing her with his eyes. She assumed he was halfway done and about to repeat the task.

"So, you can think of us as your protectors." Bone adjusted his shirt. "Any family of Tajo's is family of ours. You're in our hood now and we take care of our own. Now this ain't Kansas no more, Nina. No matter what you think you know about thug life, you don't know as much as what you can learn here."

"That's right." Shorty-Five yawned.

"Do you know when my cousin will be back?"

"He'll be back in a while." Juice opened the door. "Ladies

first." He held the door open. "You, too, Spider." They laughed.

Nina strolled around the living room. The house was not immediately familiar, yet it was one she'd never forget. Just the way Tajo had the furniture rearranged proved he was in charge of everything around him. Except for a few stacks of old newspapers, the room was completely intact. The living room was a lively peach color, which blended masterfully with the dark carpeting.

Nina felt she was in a museum that showcased Spanish and Mexican decor. Some of the walls were covered in dusty-brown wallpaper. A small glass table in front of the television was covered in shoe prints, which proved Tajo let visitors rest their feet wherever they pleased. A computer sat behind the television stand with a screensaver of a bikini-clad Latino girl wiggling her hips to an instrumental song Nina recognized but couldn't name.

"I didn't imagine the hallway would be that long." Nina squinted at the hallway that led from the living room, past the kitchen, and to the bedrooms.

"Tajo sleeps back there, when he's around." Spider shrugged. He hopped on the couch with a wrinkled magazine.

"Does this bring back any memories, Nina?" Bone squeezed beside the computer, watching her with his arms crossed. She suddenly became aware of his tattoos.

"Something wrong?" He noticed the stare.

"Nope. Okay, if I'm going to stay here, then we have to get along, right?"

"Right." Juice squatted on the glass table. Cannon returned from the kitchen with a glass of soda.

"What's right?" Cannon asked.

"You guys say I'm your family, too, don't you?" Nina twiddled her fingers. "I want to be as honest and forthcoming with you as I can."

"Shoot." Juice tilted his head.

"What's with the tattoos? I know it's a gang thing, but what's really with them?"

"Oh, looks like a little schooling is in order, huh?" Bone grinned. One by one he pointed to the tattoos on his arms and legs. "Our tattoos put us on a different level. See, Juice and I are *veteranos*."

"Veteran gangsters?" Nina sat in the small chair, huddling up to her purse.

"Yeah. As of now we are the longest members next to Tajo. He's the leader so nothing can surpass him unless he's snuffed out or smoked. Then either Juice or I take his place."

"And how is that determined?"

"Simple," Cannon broke in. "Whoever smokes the person who smoked the leader automatically takes his place. See, everyone has to smoke someone high up in another gang to move up."

"Yeah." Spider stood in front of her chair. "See, once someone smokes the leader of a rival gang, the person who did the hit automatically moves up in status." He gleamed.

"And the Bronx Gangstas' rivals are…" Nina blinked heavily.

"The NYAs, New York Assassins. You didn't know that?" Spider grimaced.

"No, apparently that information hasn't become available nationwide." She rolled her eyes. Bone and Juice laughed.

Spider shrugged. "Seriously, we just thought you knew since you were Tajo's cousin. No one's schooled you on BG fundamentals?" Spider chuckled. "I guess that will be my job."

"This neighborhood is Bronx Gangstas territory *only*." Juice smirked. "NYA territory is on the other side of town, past the park. I know it's complicated but you'll get used to it, Nina."

"And you're all happy with being in a gang? Even though you know the madness never ends?" she asked.

"When I was five I watched three of my brothers get smoked by NYA bastards. Since that day I haven't cared about *shit*." Bone shrugged. "It's a hard-ass life, Nina. If you're looking for morality and peace talks, you're not going to find it here. We're a crew of over a hundred now and we work hard every day to honor the lives of our homies and families who've died because of the NYAs."

"That's right." Cannon winked.

"And all of you have witnessed people you cared about getting smoked?" Nina looked at them back and forth. They nodded. "And have all you murdered, too?"

"It's part of the game." Cannon sipped his drink. "It's the life we live and the life we need to survive. It's not like you can snap your fingers and not be a G no more, Nina. Once you're in this it's forever. Even if we moved away, we'd still be Bronx Gangstas, and no matter how far we go, there's someone out there who wants to even the score. Most of all, the New York Assassins."

"Us Bronx Gs, our honor is thicker than blood. Shit, I'd kill damn near anybody for my homies." Juice looked at the others. "That's just the way it is. You got to be down for your brother and he has to be down for you no matter what gets in the way. If it's time to throw down, he needs to be ready to throw down with me. Know what I'm saying? If it's time to bust some caps, my brother has to be down for me on that. And I have to be down for him."

"True dat, true dat." Cannon and Juice bumped fists. "Ain't nothing I wouldn't do for these motherfuckers. As far as I'm concerned, *this* is my family. I need no one else."

"Does this scare you?" Spider asked. "Because if you can't hang with this maybe you should go back to where you came from." Everyone looked at her.

"My cousin's the leader." She shrugged. "Why should I be afraid? I know my back is saved. And do the NYAs come over here?"

"Disguised. See, we know everyone in the neighborhood so whenever a stranger appears, we already got the shit straight. They come down here, and it's our job to be ready for them," Shorty-Five said. Nina had forgotten he was in the room. He seemed to be the mini leader when Tajo wasn't around.

"Ready." Juice lifted up his jersey, showing his gun. "And willing."

"So I'm protected by all of you? Are there any ground rules?" Nina straightened in the chair.

"The only one you need to know is to stay away from the NYA crew. Everything else is like butta, baby." Shorty-Five smirked.

"Who are the girls across the street?" Nina grinned.

"That's Gloria and her crew. Them Bronx G bitches. They do whatever we need them to do and they protect the streets and score blow, shit like that." Juice shrugged.

"Another pair of hands, huh?" Nina asked.

"Exactly." Juice smiled. "You're kinda smart, huh? Got all the shit up there." He pointed to her head. "I like that."

"Me, too." Spider flirted.

"See, Spider here is a baby gangsta. He hasn't popped his

cherry yet. On his fourteenth birthday, which comes up soon, he's going to have to kill an NYA member of our choice. He will automatically move up in status." Shorty-Five hit the back of Spider's neck. "Right now he doesn't have many privileges. He's proven himself to a point, but he ain't a real gangsta yet. So he can hang with us but he can't bang with us. There's just some things baby Gs can't do."

"He's not even promised protection from us yet." Bone stared at Nina. "See, until he's jumped in, he's nothing but a fake-ass buster. He hangs with us at his own risk."

"How do you feel about that, Spider?" Nina wondered why she cared to ask.

"It's all good." He smiled wildly, showing off a silver tooth in the back of his mouth. "I'll be a real G soon. And when I am… the world better look out." He waved his gun around the room. He put it away after noticing Nina's odd expression.

Bone sighed. "Look, Nina, what we do has nothing to do with you, all right? You can still have your little friends and your own life. Just remember we only ask for one thing, complete honor. As long as you don't go against your cousin, everything's fine with us."

Loud rap music exploded outside. A car door slammed, followed by deep footsteps up the porch. The door seemed to open in slow motion. She wondered if the way she saw things in this part of the Bronx was a sign. Nothing was common, yet everything struck her as oddly familiar. She'd never dealt with such a fickle feeling. Tajo Munez stood in the door, blocking everything behind him.

Nina gulped. He was huge. He had to weigh over two hundred and fifty pounds. He wasn't muscular, yet he wasn't flabby, either.

His solid, five-eleven frame had no trouble holding his weight. His goatee and bald head could fool anyone into thinking he was older than twenty-eight. In fact, he looked more like thirty-five. His firm arms were covered in dark Bronx Gangsta symbols. "*Asesinato*" was tattooed on the back of his neck in Gothic-style letters.

"*Comó estás*, cuz!" Tajo held his stout arms high. Nina ran toward him like a magnet.

"*Comó estás*, Tajo?" Nina fell into his arms in laughter. She remembered how much Tajo loved swinging her around like a puppet. He picked her up as if she weighed two pounds.

"How are you, girl? Damn, you look good. Don't she look good, y'all?" The guys moaned in agreement. Especially Spider, who hadn't stopped drooling since he'd met her.

"I'm fine." Nina swept her hair from across her shoulder. "How are you doing?"

Tajo tilted his head. "You know me, I do whatever I have to. So how's Aunt Michelle? How are the treatments going?"

"We don't know yet. Mind if I don't talk about it?"

"That's cool." He held her close. He smelled of expensive cologne. By the look of his jewelry and clothes he had money to spare. "So you like the place or what? It's all that, huh?"

"Yeah. You look good, cuz. Put on some weight, though." She smacked his belly. The others laughed.

"Oh, so you're gonna play me like that, huh? Yeah, I put on some weight here and there. But when you got as much cheese as I do it don't matter. I got women all over me, cousin. You'll see."

Nina gleamed. "The place does look nice, Tajo."

"So, what's up?" He walked around the room. "You want something to eat or drink? Have the guys gotten you anything?"

"No, I'm fine. I ate before I got here." They sat on the couch. The others watched in amazement while Nina and Tajo quickly caught up on old times. "Where you been? How come you didn't see me by yourself?"

"Oh uh…" Tajo looked at the others. "I had some business to take care of. You know how it is."

"Would this business be anything illegal?" She gaped.

"Come on, Nina. Why you gonna play me like that?"

"Because I'm worried about you, Tajo. I want to make sure you're all right. Now spare me the bullshit and tell me how you're really doing."

"Kind of uppity for a sixteen-year-old, isn't she?" He grinned, pulling her from the couch.

"Yeah." Bone shrugged.

"Damn, Nina." Tajo turned her around once more. "Shit, you better be glad we're related or I'd be all up on that booty."

"You couldn't handle it, fool!" Nina laughed. She slapped the top of his head.

"Really, you doing okay? Let's catch up."

Tajo nodded. "Sure thing, I thought you'd never ask. Let me make a phone call, then we can talk." He left the room.

❊❊❊❊

Juan Alonso despised the boredom of Sundays. He felt the day went to nothing after morning church. Needless to say, he was not your average seventeen-year-old. Juan indeed knew how to have fun, but lately he spent time thinking about future plans. Being ambitious proved to be a bitch where his brother was concerned. The only thing Rico Alonso supported was the NYAs.

Juan figured it was only because Rico was the leader. Rico didn't seem to give a damn about anything that didn't make the road of life easier for him. Their relationship was like most brothers'. Rico had showed him the ropes of life early on. With a thirteen-year age difference it was easy for Juan to stray from Rico's policies about life and growing up as a Latino male in the Bronx.

Rico, on the other hand, always blamed others for his short-comings. When he was in high school he didn't make the track team because of his discipline problems. He attempted to sue the school for discrimination. It probably would have worked if the school hadn't been primarily Latino in the first place. Juan still chuckled when he thought about that one. Rico barely slid by enough to graduate. He never had an honest job in his life.

Juan reflected on that one *seemingly* honest waiter job Rico had for an Italian restaurant that used to be on the corner. It turned out Rico only worked there long enough to case the joint out and rob it. Ever since then he'd been preaching the "word of the streets." No matter how many times Rico assured Juan the world was out to get them, Juan refused to give in to his way of thinking.

"Hey, Juan, man." Homicide, an NYA member, bumped Juan's elbow, jolting him into reality. "What's up, cluck?" Homicide blew weed smoke toward Juan's ears.

"You're dead to the world, huh, man?" A short bald guy billed Tray-Eight, after his favorite gun of choice, leaned against the front door watching the neighborhood cuties stroll by.

"Nah." Juan noticed a smudge of dirt on his new sneakers. He wiped them against the porch pole. "Just thinking."

"You're always 'just thinking.' When you going to have some fun? When you going to come over to our side once and for all?

Rico won't be having more of this attitude you been springing."
Homicide walled his eyes.

"That's right. He's been letting you get away with the lip and
that's going to change, Juan. I mean, look around." Tray-Eight
raised his muscular arms. "We own this shit, motherfucker. We
own these people, these stores. We're gods, fuckin' kings. You
telling me you don't want a piece of all this, man?"

"I've said it, screamed it, cursed it. You want me to write a
fuckin' letter?" Juan's ex-girlfriend walked past. She didn't
speak and neither did he. "See, this gang shit ain't for me. I got
dreams and plans. I want to be somebody. I'd like to be the
only male in my family to not have been in jail."

"You're always trippin'. You think you're too good for us?"
Homicide stood against Juan as if to challenge him to fight.
Juan's icy stare dissuaded Homicide's intentions. "You're our
brother, all right?"

"I'm Rico's brother. And sometimes I wish I wasn't."

"Fine, be that way. You're full of shit." Tray-Eight lit a joint.
"But you don't know what you're missing, man. You can get
anything you want if you're down with us. We get free pussy,
free blow, free anything." Juan walked away toward the front
door. "You mean to say you don't want any of that?"

Homicide pointed at Juan. "You owe us your life, man. If it wasn't
for us, your punk ass would have been dead a long time ago."

"Yeah, yeah." Juan scoffed. "I'm going inside."

"It's a great fuckin' day, man." Homicide shook his head, disgusted. "You think school is going to help you out? Let me tell
you something, it won't. Know why? Because it won't change
who you are. Society is not going to let you in because…"

"You mind not breathing your skunk breath in my face?" Juan
shoved him away.

"Spare me the 'I'm Latino, so I can't do anything with my life' bullshit. It's just an excuse suckers like you use when life gets too hard."

"Look, street smarts is all you need to survive around here, Juan. I don't know what you plan on doing with your life, but this right here is what you should be focused on."

"If I become part of your so-called life, Homicide, I won't have one for long."

Juan went into the house. He found his mother studying a recipe in the kitchen.

"*Hola*, Ma." Juan hopped on the kitchen countertop.

"*Hola*." Florence Alonso was attempting her latest recipe from her cooking class.

"What's wrong with you?" She shook a pan of boiled noodles into a colander.

"What makes you think something's wrong?" He grabbed an apple from the fridge.

"Why are you not out there with your friends?"

"They're not my friends, Ma. You know how I hate them always hanging around. Why do you let Rico run this house? It's your house, for God's sake."

"Your father left Rico the house, may I remind you." She sliced a sausage.

"You're still our mother. Rico barely contributes and when he does it's with drug money. Ma, how can you, of all people, go along with this?"

"Rico is thirty years old, Juan. He may not be a saint but he's all we got. I'm barely making enough at the supermarket to cover the bills, let alone anything else. Rico's bringing in the bigger half." She sighed. "I hate what he does and I hate how he is but it's the best we can do. Did you forget I got three other babies under you?"

"Ma, I would be happy to get a job."

"No." She leaned against the counter. "I want you to concentrate on school, Juan. College is important."

"*You* went to college. It doesn't seem so important now." He finished the apple before he noticed how deep his words cut. "I'm sorry, Ma. I didn't mean that."

"College doesn't always get you what you want in life, Juanito." She chuckled. "I was going with the major I wanted but didn't realize how hard it was for women to break into certain fields back then, especially Hispanic women. I was the only one from my neighborhood to even think of going to college. I made bad choices. My concentration wore out, I started partying and screwing up." She stared in space. "I couldn't fulfill what I wanted in life."

"I want to go to college, but not if it hinders me. No disrespect, Ma, but you went to college and you've been working at the grocery store for years. If I go to college I'd like to know the knowledge I pick up works for me."

"And it will. This is a different time, a different place." She caressed his jaw. "You can do whatever you want. Don't listen to your brother." She kissed him.

"Rico wants me to join the Assassins, Ma."

Florence froze in place. Juan nearly suffocated from her stare. She'd never looked at him so gravely before.

"Like I said, don't listen to your brother."

CHAPTER TWO

On Monday Nina was ready to conquer new experiences and a new school. She'd heard a lot about Roosevelt High's extracurricular activities. The school wasn't strong in sports but made up for it by offering advanced classes. Many of Roosevelt's students went on to decent colleges already equipped with the knowledge of life's hardships. Roosevelt High wasn't as educationally awarding as her previous high school, but Nina could overlook its faults.

Roosevelt offered a boastful art program. As of now, it was all that concerned her.

"Nina?" Tajo tapped on the bedroom door. Even though she was forced to stay with Tajo, she could still appreciate the effort he'd made to make her comfortable. Nina admired the glorious room she'd been offered for the hundredth time.

"Is Claudia here yet?" Nina checked her backpack for the third time. Tajo observed her actions from the doorway.

"Yeah, she's waiting with that tacky-ass convertible." He chuckled. "Don't be nervous, cousin. Roosevelt's just another school." He walled his eyes.

"I wasn't nervous until you came in." She checked herself in the mirror. She looked stunning but in her mind she could use more freshening up. Too bad she lacked the time.

"Sure you don't want *me* to take you to school?"

"Positive." Nina sighed. She appreciated the offer but the last thing she needed was to arrive at a new school with the leader of the Bronx Gangstas. She wanted to blend in, not start controversy.

"At least you get to hook up with Claudia again now that you're going to the same school. You're happy about that, right?"

"Pretty much." Nina smiled. "I'm nervous as hell, though. It's going to be rough being the new girl." She chuckled.

"If it gets *too* rough, you let me know."

She hugged him. "Thanks for taking me in, Tajo. I don't know what I would have done if you hadn't."

"Hey." He ran his stout finger across her forehead. "What's family for?"

She left the room smiling.

❈❈❈❈

"Hey! Hey, Rico!" Juan ran through the house holding a bath towel around his waist. The house was alive with raging gangsta rap. The living room was flooded with the smell of weed. Rico sat at a table surrounded by NYA thugs, sipping beer and playing poker. The guys took a look at Juan, waved their hands, and laughed.

"Check this fool out, man! Yo, Rico, do something with your brother, man!" Gil ripped shades off the top of his head. He grabbed a handful of poker chips.

"What's up, Juan?" Rico hobbled toward Juan, supporting his bad foot. He wore an oversize red jersey and baggy jeans with his NYA tattoos alive and kicking. "Did you lose your pants, bro?" Rico laughed.

"Yo, I am trying to get dressed. Isn't it enough that you play this shit all night long? You got to play it in the morning, too?"

"*Hola*." Florence walked through toward the kitchen.

Juan gripped his towel. "Rico, just because you think you own the neighborhood it..."

"I *do* own the neighborhood. Why the fuck you tripping anyway? No one's bothering you."

Juan exhaled. "The music is so loud I can't hear myself think!" A DMX song replaced a Jay-Z single. "Can you please just give it some rest? I'll be gone in a few minutes." He stomped back to his bedroom.

Florence glared from the kitchen doorway. "Rico, can't you turn this down? We don't all won't to hear this mess."

"Anything else I can't do in my own house, Ma?" He smacked his lips and went back to his seat.

"Little fool." Florence headed to Juan's room with his breakfast. He stood in front of the mirror tinkering with his necklace. He didn't acknowledge her presence. At times like these Juan couldn't tolerate Florence's endurance of Rico's behavior. "Juan, are you all right?" She sat on the foot of his chaotic bed. "What's bothering you?"

"You know exactly what's wrong, Ma." He straightened his jeans and threw on his blue T-shirt. It took the smallest amount of effort for him to look good. Florence drifted into memories of Juan's father. Even years after Peter Alonso's death, no man compared to him in her eyes.

Juan had storybook beauty. He was tall, dark, and handsome with a hint of a newly sprouted goatee. It wasn't that noticeable, but added grandeur to his handsome face. Peter hadn't been book smart but he'd possessed common sense. His traits fed into his sons in different ways. While Juan had gotten Peter's looks, Rico had been blessed with Peter's strength to carry on a good argument. In Rico, this was a dangerous attribute.

"Juan." Florence waved him toward the bed. She took his hands. "I love you."

"I love you too, Ma. But I don't like how Rico disrespects this house and you. I know he makes most of the money, but how can you settle for that? As soon as I'm out of school I'm leaving and I ain't coming back." He grabbed his backpack from under the bed.

"It saddens me to hear you speak like that, but I guess I cannot blame you. Can't you see my side of things, or Rico's side? Come on, Juan. In his defense, he doesn't have what you've got. He doesn't have your good looks and your book sense."

"Ma, that's no excuse."

"Juan, being good-looking is a plus and people are drawn to you because of the way you speak. You've got beauty inside and out. Rico only has what he knows, violence."

"You can accept that?" He slipped on his backpack. He turned his white baseball cap backward. Needless to say, Roosevelt High hardly enforced the standard dress code. "Well, I can't accept it, Ma. I can't see throwing your life away on drugs, crime, and murder. I don't know how Rico can justify that. And I sure as hell don't know how you can accept it."

"Juan, *please*."

He exhaled. "Good-bye, Ma. I'll see you after school."

Florence struggled for any word that would comfort him. She realized there was nothing more to say.

Claudia Olmos sped through the Bronx streets blasting her favorite rap music. Claudia was everything Nina wanted to be. She was wild, crazy, and knew how to have fun in any given situation. Nina wasn't built that way. She played life by the book, but lately she found it quite boring. Claudia and Edgewood could be the change she needed.

"Woooo!" Claudia swerved her sky-blue convertible in and out of traffic as if she were blind to street signs.

"Jesus, Claude. That was a red light. How could you do that?"

"Chill, Nina, no one was watching." Claudia jiggled in the seat.

"But that was a red light." Nina chuckled. Claudia's fun-loving attitude had the potential to damage their health. "I hope you don't do this all the time."

"Chill, Nina. I don't do that all the time." Claudia played with the radio. "Ooh, that's my jam!" DMX's latest hit bounced along the airwaves. "Man, this nigga is all that! You *got* to like DMX."

"He's all right." Nina struggled in her seat. She wasn't into hip-hop of any kind. She was more old-school R&B and modern Spanish songs. Claudia started shouting the lyrics.

"So how am I dressed? Does this outfit look all right?" Nina tugged on her little T-shirt.

"Yeah," Claudia muttered in between rapping. "How do *I* look?" She wore a tight T-shirt cut halfway up her stomach, a tiny diamond stud in her navel, jeans, and her hair was in shiny, thick braids.

"Great. You sure they won't say anything about your stomach being out? Your shirt is halfway up your chest." Nina grinned.

"No, they don't care. Roosevelt is a cool school. Other than a few teachers to get in your ass, the school's the easiest around. People don't bother you about dress codes and shit."

"Why not?" Nina watched an ugly green motorcycle pull up beside them. The driver winked underneath his helmet, then increased his speed. "Why not, Claude?"

"They got too much else to worry about. They got to worry

about how the grades on the tests have been going down, as well as teachers leaving, and that sorry-ass football team."

"How's the enrollment? I tried to check on the computer last night. I couldn't find a website."

"And you *won't*." Claudia laughed. "Roosevelt is stuck in the nineties as far as technology and shit. We were the last school to get a Coke machine. Now, what does *that* tell you?"

"That this is probably going to be a long school year."

"But a fun one, homey. I promise you that." Claudia pulled into the parking lot of Roosevelt High.

❖❖❖

To Nina, all schools seemed the same. Each one was equipped with honor students, troublemakers, and losers. Then there were overachievers such as herself who worked hard at being better than everyone else only to prove that what they wanted to be wasn't enough. Nina wasn't a big fan of her old school, but Roosevelt seemed too undisciplined for her own tastes. The disorder in the halls alone showed her that the school district could care less about any high school in this part of town.

Claudia howled through the halls, shaking hands and talking to girls who showed as much skin as swimsuit models. Nina felt odd all of a sudden. She thought she'd fit in, but the lack of respect shown by the nonchalant dress code proved how far off base Roosevelt was. If the school suffered from an absence of discipline, it had to be missing a few strings elsewhere as well.

She quietly followed Claudia down the tight, dark hallways. Claudia had so many friends, it was impossible to tell them apart at first glance. Claudia introduced Nina to everyone, then escorted her to the end of the first hallway. She was issued a schedule in the counselor's office and instructed to go to the main office and inform them she was new. Everything about Roosevelt seemed backward. Nina was beginning to think the same way.

"So anything you need, you let me know." Claudia wrapped her hands around Nina's shoulders. They walked down the hall. The late bell rang. Surprisingly most of the kids listened except for two black guys, who huddled at a locker. Nina wasn't surprised that Claudia knew them, too.

"I could use your help with this schedule." Nina tucked her backpack underneath her arm. She ran her finger down the little card. Within seconds, Claudia outlined the entire school. The description was so informative Nina second-guessed that she hadn't been on a guided tour. "I got to go to the main office now, right?"

"Yeah." Claudia pointed past trash cans to a large room with glass doors.

"What class you got first?" Nina asked.

Claudia yawned. "Girl, get this, they gave me wood shop. Can you believe that shit?" Nina laughed. "I mean, what the fuck am *I* supposed to do in woodshop? It had my manicure all fucked up. I only went three times. I guess I'll take a smoke around the back."

"It has to be an easy A, Claude. Would it hurt you to spend forty minutes in wood shop? I'm surprised you would mind."

"Why you say that?" She popped her bubble gum.

"I thought you'd like being in a class full of cute guys." Nina winked.

"Girl, please. It's like they put all the dumb ugly motherfuckers in there." They laughed.

"Then come to the main office with me."

"Oh no, girl. I've been in the principal's office so much this year he knows my number by heart."

"School's only been in six weeks and you've already seen the principal?" Nina shook her head.

"I'll see you later, girlfriend." Claudia hopped down the hall.

❉❉❉

"Nina Sagas...tu..." Mr. Phillips, the secretary, examined Nina's card closely.

"*Sagastume*." Nina smiled.

"Oh, I've never heard that one before. You transferred from Reagan High School, huh? May I ask why?" He looked over her folder.

"My mom's sick. I needed a guardian so I had to move in with my cousin, Tajo. It's been hard adjusting on such short notice."

"I can imagine." Mr. Phillips passed her the card. "Well, let me escort you to your first class." He smiled.

❉❉❉

It took Mrs. Garrett ten minutes to quiet her class each morning, then longer to call the roll and retrieve excuses for absences. She was one of the veteran teachers of Roosevelt. Unfortunately she'd been rewarded with a hectic schedule of teaching history and algebra to unappreciative juniors and seniors.

"Class, can we settle down, please? Okay, everyone take out your homework."

Before Mrs. Garrett could gather the homework, Mr. Phillips

entered with Nina huddling behind. The male students took one look at the gorgeous fresh meat and began howling.

"Settle down, boys," Mrs. Garrett scolded.

The girls probed Nina from head to toe, sizing up the competition. Hands down, she was the most beautiful girl in school. She easily put the prettiest in the class to shame. The boys sat in their seats with imaginary tails wagging. One way or another everyone was mesmerized by the new arrival. Especially Juan Alonso.

Mrs. Garrett bid good day to Mr. Phillips, then introduced Nina to the class.

"Class, this is Nina Sagastume. She's a transfer student from Reagan High." The boys' eyes widened while their tongues roamed their mouths. "Nina, say hello to everyone."

"Hello." She awkwardly held onto her backpack. She did her best to ignore the curious stares.

"Nina, we were about to check the homework from last night and do a book practice. Since you don't have a book, you can look on with someone. Uh, would anyone mind sharing his or her book with Nina?"

The guys jumped from their seats with their hands raised. For some reason, as if it were fate, Mrs. Garrett led Nina to the quiet, handsome guy in the center row.

"Juan, would you mind if Nina shares your book for today?" Mrs. Garrett's eyes gleamed.

"Uh, no." Juan took a deep breath. The other guys mumbled their jealousy.

"Good. Nina, this is Juan Alonso. Juan, this is Nina."

"Nice to meet you, Juan." Nina felt a rush of heat within her body. She thought she'd faint from being the center of attention.

"Nice to meet you, Nina." Juan pulled the empty desk beside his. She slid beside him. He pushed the book in the middle of the desks with one half on his side and the other on hers.

"Well, good. Now we can get started." Mrs. Garrett took her place in front of the class. Nina took a deep breath as Juan observed the mystifying beauty beside him.

* * *

By lunchtime Nina was tired of being the "babe on display." Any other girl would kill for the attention the guys generously threw at her, but Nina was happy being left alone. Claudia and her friends were eating outside on the patio with the other juniors and seniors. Claudia explained how the freshmen ate in the cafeteria and the sophomores gathered by the parking lots.

Claudia had given Nina the shakedown on her friends during class breaks. The chubby girl with the nose ring and dyed hair was Rosa Tomás. She lived in Nina's old neighborhood but didn't go to Reagan because she had twelve cousins at Roosevelt. Lisa Flores sat on the side of Claudia while Claudia sat beside Rosa, spewing jokes about ugly guys and homework.

Nina liked Lisa instantly. Lisa was a cool chick who kindly took to strangers. She seemed to be the only girl who didn't see Nina as competition. It said a lot for her character.

"Sit down, girl. We wondered what took you so long." Claudia grinned. Lisa brushed leaves from the bench. She held Nina's tray for her.

"Thanks." Nina smiled. "The lines were so long in the cafeteria."

"You got to learn the system." Rosa sucked a blue lollipop that turned her mouth purple. "We always ask our third-period teacher if we can go to the bathroom. Then we meet up and go to the cafeteria early, get our lunch, stash it, and return to class. That way we're ahead of everyone." Rosa winked at Nina.

Nina stared at the groups of kids in the courtyard. "I don't necessarily mind the long lines, but…"

"You don't seem to mind much of anything." Rosa walled her eyes. Nina caught the friction. She looked at Claudia. Claudia shrugged, ignoring Rosa's rude behavior.

Lisa picked lettuce from her sandwich. "Enjoying your classes, Nina? Can I see your schedule?"

"Sure." Nina passed it to her, then continued eating her burger.

"Yo, you got Mr. Jones. The black man with the funny hair." Lisa laughed. "I loved his class. I had him last year for elective. You'll have fun in art class."

"I believe I will. I'm an artist myself."

"I don't think stick figures count." Rosa moved her flabby arm, showing a tacky, black tattoo that Nina couldn't make out.

"I don't do stick figures." Nina dug in her backpack.

"Yeah, she's a *real* artist." Claudia nodded. "She's talented. Show them your stuff."

Nina pulled out a thick blue binder with blotches of paint as decorations and handed them to Lisa. Within minutes they were hypnotized and Rosa was eating crow. It was satisfaction enough for Nina that she let Claudia do all the bragging.

"You did these, girl?" Lisa thumbed through the pictures that were held neatly within the binder. "These are fantastic. Mr. Jones definitely has to enter you in the showcase."

"What showcase?"

Rosa finished the lollipop. "Every semester there's an art show-case here at the school. The best artist students get to show off their work. People pay two dollars to get in and the proceeds go to the school."

"Last year they made five hundred dollars. That's pretty good and it helped us get better sporting equipment, too," Lisa said.

"It's a shame they couldn't get better players." Claudia grinned.

Lisa chuckled. "Seriously, Nina. It may not seem like a big deal, but one of the girls who showcased her work got the attention of the community center. They paid her big bucks for her picture and now it hangs for everyone to see. She goes there and paints on the walls every weekend. People watch her like she's God or something."

"God, huh?" Nina moaned in mental relaxation.

"Yeah, and her paintings weren't half as good as yours." Lisa flipped the binder upside-down to take a better look.

✦✦✦✦

Carlos twirled around in a circle, threw an apple up in the air and caught it behind his back. Juan, Tony, and Dell looked on curiously. Carlos reclaimed his seat on the edge of the school roof. He looked at the lunch crowd in the courtyard below.

"And that really happened, Carlos?" Tony chuckled. He'd known Carlos long enough to know he was full of shit. So did the others.

"Yeah. I kicked his ass and he left me alone."

"I would have just walked away." Juan pulled plastic wrap from his tuna sandwich.

"You can afford to walk away. Your brother is a gang leader. You could start shit with anyone and you'd be safe. We're not so lucky." Carlos rolled his eyes.

"You think I'm lucky to have a brother who's a gangbanger?" Juan scoffed. "I don't get how everyone seems to think the gang life is so damn cool. I'm ashamed of it. I'd lie before I claimed Rico as my brother, if I could."

"He's still blood, no matter what you think of his lifestyle." Dell bit into a soggy beef sandwich.

"All I'm saying is that I want more out of life. No one seems to get that."

Tony winked. "We understand you, chief." He patted Juan's shoulder.

"Enough about that. Have y'all seen the new chick?" Carlos sucked his lips.

"Man, she is fine! She's the best-looking girl in this school. Her body is bangin', man, like the chicks in them videos. I mean, the titties are luscious, man!" They laughed. Carlos backed up his description with vibrant hand gestures. "Her ass is like boo-ya, baby! She's the prettiest girl in this school."

"That ain't saying much in this kennel." Dell laughed.

"Seriously, man, she's dope. I think her name's Lena." Carlos ripped open a bag of cheese chips.

"It's Nina." Juan smirked. "She's in my first period. She shared my book today."

"You lucky dog." Carlos hit him. "Go ahead with your bad self!"

"Level with us, Juan. Is this girl as fine as Carlos says she is? Or is this another one of his stories?"

"Dell, if you're asking that question you definitely haven't seen her." Juan gathered his trash. "Now, let's get down from here before we get caught."

"Shit, we've been doing this since the ninth grade and we ain't never got caught before." Tony sniggered.

✠✠✠

When they got inside, they waited until the hall monitor passed, then collectively continued down the hall. The bell was about to ring in five seconds so they were confident they wouldn't get caught. As Tony pointed out, they never had before.

"I wish I had seen this girl." Dell exhaled. "If she's as hot as you all say she is."

"She's that and more." Juan pitched his trash in a wastebasket. "She's beautiful, for sure. She seems smart and she smells good."

"Seems like someone's got the flavor for the new girl." Tony chuckled.

Juan sighed with a broad smile. "You should have seen how the guys were acting when she walked in. We were all speechless. She had them wagging their tails like dogs, practically rolling on the floor."

"You included?" Carlos snickered.

"No, I kept my cool. But I wouldn't mind getting to know her a little better." Juan's beautiful brown eyes produced a familiar twinkle. He rubbed his hands together.

"There's something about her that's different."

"So you're interested in her?" Dell raised an eyebrow. He brushed roof soot from the back of his jeans.

"Maybe."

Carlos shook his head. "Forget it, Juan. I heard she turned down half the football team this morning."

Dell smirked. "So did the college scouts." They laughed. "What's your point, Carlos?"

"My point is that Juan may be handsome and cool when it comes to other girls around here, but there's no way in hell he's gonna get close to Nina. Everything about her is made from every man's deepest fantasies. Besides, I may want to talk to her myself."

"Oh yeah, you're a much better choice," Tony jeered. Juan and Dell laughed.

Carlos smirked. "It doesn't matter who goes after Nina. Juan won't have a chance with her."

Juan stopped at the end of the hall. His friends formed a circle around him.

"I happen to think I do have a chance with her. She didn't only share my book today, she talked to me, too. In between Garrett's babbling we got some good conversation in."

"Did you get the digits, though?" Carlos rubbed his hands. He stuck his head in the air.

"I didn't ask, for your information. I don't believe it's appropriate to go up to a girl when she's new and ask her number. She was already uncomfortable. I didn't want her to think I was sweating her, man."

"Sounds like the cluck of a chicken to me." Carlos put his hands on his hips and clucked mockingly.

"I happen to have been raised a gentleman. Girls don't like to be pressured into anything. It's tacky for a guy to be pushy. You got to get to know them, show them you really care."

"But we *don't* really care; we just want the booty." Carlos walked off.

Tony shook his head. "Don't listen to him, Juan. And he wonders why girls don't talk to him. Honestly, do you like Nina?"

"I felt something when we met. Like a spark." Juan shrugged. "And she's the most incredible-looking creature I've ever seen in my life."

"Then it's your job to find out if she's digging you, too." Dell winked.

"But it's too soon, isn't it?" Juan pulled at his shirt. "What am I saying? I'm behaving like a wimp."

"You sure are. I say make your move, homey." Tony winked. "The worst thing she can do is not like you."

"That's what I'm afraid of." Juan sighed.

✠✠✠

"So did you have a good day at school today, Juan?" Florence viciously stirred the sauce for dinner. "Juan, call your brothers and sister in here, please."

"Guys, get your asses in here!" He grinned. Florence playfully slapped his arm.

"Wise guy." She removed his cap and kissed his forehead. "Each day you remind me of your father."

"And who does Rico remind you of?" He played with the floral tablecloth. Juan's younger twin brothers strolled in with his little sister, Cynthia, lagging behind.

"Let's just drop it, all right, Juan?"

"Why? The family can hear this." He looked around the table. The thirteen-year-old twins, Jorge and Benny, shook their heads, hoping their older brother would abandon his intended speech. "I'm not saying anything that doesn't merit talking about, am I, Ma?"

"I said drop it, Juanito." She filled his bowl with fish soup, then dumped two stuffed tomatoes on his plate. Though Cynthia found Greek food oddly tasty, she got her satisfaction from watching Juan suffer. He hated fish.

"What the hell is this?" He sniffed the bowl.

"Eat it, it's good for you, Juan." Florence went around the table until everyone was served. "It's good Greek cooking. I'm the top in my class."

"Good for you, Mamá." Cynthia winked. She turned toward Juan. "What are you waiting for, big brother? Eat it."

"Yeah." Jorge chuckled with a mouth full of tomato. "Don't want to hurt Mamá's feelings, do you?"

"Go on and eat it, Juan," Florence said.

"Ugh." He groaned through two sips. His siblings laughed. "Come on, Mamá. Now why couldn't you have taken some soul food class? Anything but *this*. I bet we're the only Mexican family eating Greek cuisine."

She chuckled. "You'll get used to it."

"You say that every night. I never do."

"Mamá, I got an A on my math test," Jorge shouted with a mouth full of soup. "Benny got a B."

"So, it's still a good grade." Benny fiddled with his baseball cap. "It's still passing."

"Yeah, but which twin has the real brains?" Jorge laughed.

"Jorge, there's nothing wrong with Bs as long as Benny tried. And Benny, you know you don't wear baseball caps at the table."

"Right, dumb-ass." Juan reached from behind Cynthia. He seized Benny's cap.

"Mamá, look what he did!" Benny hit the table.

"Juan, stop teasing your brother. Everyone just eat."

"Mamá, guess what?" Cynthia slurped soup. "There was this cheerleading scout from one of the high schools. She told us about the games and stuff. I think I want to be a cheerleader when I get in high school."

"Ha!" Juan laughed.

"What's so funny, horse face?" Cynthia scowled.

"*You* a cheerleader? Right."

"What are you trying to say, huh? Trying to say I'm not pretty enough?"

"I didn't say that." Juan finished his second tomato. "*You* did." Cynthia hit him.

"All right, all right, settle down!" Florence sighed. "Juan, why are you tormenting everyone today?"

He laughed. "No reason. Just my wit coming to a head, that's all. I had a pretty good day at school. We got a new girl. Her name's Nina."

"Is she pretty?" Jorge asked, licking soup from his spoon. Juan didn't know how to answer. He believed when someone was as attractive as Nina you didn't have to say it. Florence dished up dessert before he could object.

"Ma, mind if I skip dess... What the hell is this?" Juan examined the flat cake. "Let me guess, another Greek recipe?" Florence nodded happily. Juan moved from the table.

"Where you going?" Florence held her hips.

"To the library. I got some homework to do. Mrs. Garrett's loading us up like she's the only teacher in the school."

"Well, when will you be back?"

"I'll be back around nine or ten." He kissed his mother while tugging Cynthia's ponytails. "See you guys later."

"Yeah." Florence sighed.

CHAPTER THREE

Nina struggled through the packed aisle of the library. An elderly librarian walked back and forth between the elementary kids' tables supervising. The place was silent except for a college student asking about Shakespeare books at the front desk. Nina shuffled her way through the shiny floors. She observed a young couple sharing the computer.

She heard coughing from behind the mystery section. Juan Alonso sat in the middle of a small table with an empty chair across from him. He searched his history book with one hand leisurely on the top of his baseball cap and the other flicking pages. Nina experienced a vibrant chill. Her heart pounded from anxiety. This was stupid. He was just a guy.

A very handsome guy, but still a guy sitting at a table. It was a public library so no one would accuse her of coming on to him. Of course, it was all so silly. Why was she even thinking this way? She hardly knew Juan. When they first met in Mrs. Garrett's that morning, the most they'd spoke of was the traffic on the way to school. Juan explained how he drove through the back way every morning to skip school zones.

Nina had found Juan's charm hilarious. They'd shared the type of innocent, harmless conversation between two students of the opposite sex. Why did she feel so weird about stirring up another harmless conversation? She walked toward the table, with Juan staring straight at her. His mouth spread into the same inviting smile he'd shown that morning. He gestured to the chair across from him.

"Hi, Nina. Uh, I didn't think you'd be here." He smirked. Why wouldn't he? He hardly knew her.

"Oh yeah, well, I had to do this homework for Mrs. Garrett. I had other homework but I finished it already. May I sit down, if you don't mind?"

"Of course. I don't own the library." He chuckled. He watched every move she made.

She straightened in her seat. "It's very quiet in here. Is it always this crowded?" Juan nodded. He continued reading. "There are more kids than I thought in this neighborhood. I didn't like the looks of the library where I'm temporarily staying. So I caught the bus here."

"Where are you staying?" Juan drew anxious breaths.

"Ed…" She stopped. There was no way in hell she was going to tell him where she was staying. Everyone and their mother knew Edgewood was Bronx Gangsta territory. It would scare him away for sure. "I just moved out here so I don't really know the place yet."

"Oh." He turned toward the window behind him. He pointed to the pool hall across the street. "It's disgusting, isn't it?" It took Nina a while to realize he was speaking of the graffiti-covered bricks. "You think a pool hall that sells liquor wouldn't be this close to a library. There used to be strong politicians who cared about the neighborhoods. Now all they care about is fame and making headlines." He exhaled.

"I don't think that's completely true." Nina looked at the scratched-out symbols that were impossible to interpret. Obvious gang signs. "They do the best they can. Remember funding comes into the picture, too. Sometimes certain neighborhoods don't get such good treatment."

"I got cousins who live in peaceful, respectable Latino neighborhoods. I don't believe it has anything to do with funding. Just lazy-ass politicians. When I enter the running, you can bet I'm going to do what's right for everyone. Little kids shouldn't have to grow up around this mess, Nina."

"I agree." She shrugged. "Not to argue with you, because I see your point, but minority communities don't always have the strong backing other communities do. For instance, where do your cousins live, Juan?"

"New Jersey." He crossed his arms. Nina almost choked, hiding her grin.

"What's so funny?"

She tapped the table. "Juan, come on. This is the Bronx, not New Jersey."

He cackled. "Well, my cousins, to name a few. Okay, I see your point. But I can't stand people using their race as an excuse or crutch. As minorities, we need to rise above that. Every race needs leadership. How are you going to get that if no one stands up or at least cares enough to fight? The people around here don't try. They just give up and join gangs. It's the easy way out, if you ask me."

"Some people are forced into a gang, Juan. Maybe you should take a closer look at someone who's in a gang before you judge."

"Whoa." He sat back, grinning. "Did I hit a nerve? Is someone's boyfriend in a gang?"

"No. But you have no right to make assumptions about something you know nothing about."

Juan left it alone. He could have easily spent the next twenty minutes talking about the rise of the New York Assassins. How they'd been at war with the Bronx Gangstas for thirty years. How Uncle Jonah started the gang on a Thursday and by Saturday had over eighty members. He could have explained how living with a brother who was the leader of a gang had hindered Juan.

How he hated being associated with the NYAs and Rico everywhere he went. How much he hated Rico being treated like a god when he was nothing but a disrespectful killer with no remorse or drive to do anything but hurt people. And last but not least, he could have told her how the Bronx Gangstas killed Uncle Jonah and Rico took his place at an early age. Yeah, so much he could have said.

"Did I offend you?" Nina sighed.

"No. Why would you say that?" He hooked his pencil between his fingers.

"Well, you'd gotten so quiet. What were you thinking about?"

"I was thinking about how it doesn't matter how good-looking you are or how smart you are. When you're growing up around all of this, it just doesn't matter. That's why you've got to get out."

"I did offend you." She sighed. Before they both knew it she was caressing his hand. He could have stood the treatment all night. Later Juan would rewind the moment she decided to touch him over and over in his head. Juan took another look into her fiery brown eyes.

"You could never offend me, Nina. Hey, you mind if we stop talking about gangs? It's creeping me out."

"Deal." She smiled.

"I'm glad you decided to come to the library today." He flirtatiously cocked his head to the side. "What luck, huh?"

They concentrated on their work. Nina hummed a Spanish tune a man sang on the bus ride over. She shut up when she noticed Juan watching her. "Before you get any ideas, I am here to *study*, Juan."

"Hey, you never know where it may lead."

"*Seriously*," she whispered. She did her best to avoid his inviting eyes.

He chuckled. "How come people say 'seriously' when they don't mean it?"

"Well, *I* mean it."

"You never said what gang he was in." He rocked his long legs under the table.

"What?"

"Your boyfriend. You never said what gang he was in. Obviously he's in one, the way you launched that defense just now."

"I have a mind, don't I? I commented because it was what I thought. My boyfriend isn't in a gang." She stared at her book.

"Well, what is he in, then?"

"He's not in anything," she snapped.

"He has to be in *something*. What's the deal? What does he do and stuff? What's he like?"

"He's not like anything." She irritatingly flipped the pages.

"Huh?" Juan leaned back in his chair, gawking. His cunning smile annoyed and enticed at the same time.

"What I mean is, I don't have a boyfriend." Her voice trailed off. Surprisingly, she felt relieved that he knew she didn't have a boyfriend.

"I see." Juan concentrated on his work for five seconds before resuming the conversation. "I can't believe that, Nina. You have to have some boyfriend you left at Reagan somewhere."

"Well, I don't." She twirled her hair.

"I don't believe it."

"Well, it's the *truth*," she snapped again. She shyly looked down when a woman at the other table turned around. "I don't have a boyfriend, Juan," she whispered.

"That shouldn't even be allowed."

She flipped through her book, noticing more missing pages. "This book's for shit. Mind if I look on with you?"

Juan couldn't hide his amusement. This was one time he thanked Roosevelt High for having crappy books. Pages were missing out of his, as well, yet he wouldn't have mentioned it in a million years. He slid his chair beside hers. He gentlemanly opened the book in front of her.

"How's that?" He beamed. "Anything you need help with just ask me, I'm your man."

Nina loved the sound of those words and that electrifying voice. She also loved how good he smelled close to her. His chest produced warmness. When he held his arm behind her chair, it was as though he belonged there. She'd never had a boyfriend or anything close. Everyone assumed she had hundreds of guys, but the truth was she'd never even been kissed. She'd never felt so open to a guy. Especially one she'd just met.

"You all right?" Juan asked, amused at her wide-eyed expression.

"Yeah." Nina smiled.

"So you need a ride home?" Juan stopped beside his car while Nina tried to find the bus stop in the dark. She spotted it a few feet past the sidewalk.

"No, I'm going to take the bus."

"Nina, it's dark. No matter what you think you know about the Bronx, that would be stupid." She shrugged. "Come on. Let me take you home."

"I'm a very independent person, Juan."

He leaned against his brown Toyota. He was glad to wait with her. He couldn't have forgiven himself if he left her to the tribulations of these dark Bronx streets. He knew she could take care of herself. The way she'd ridden the bus to the library and automatically fit into a new school showed that. Still, he felt he needed to be even more convinced. Or else he just needed an excuse to stick around.

"When's your bus supposed to come?"

She checked her watch. "Should be a few minutes if the schedule is right."

"I really don't feel right having you catch the bus, Nina. I can take you home in a few minutes."

"Nah, I stay a ways from here."

"I don't care. I don't have anything to do. By the time the bus gets here you can be lying in your bed comfortably." He cocked his head to the side. "Come on." He opened the passenger-side door for her.

"Juan, I don't mind waiting. I really don't want you to drop me off. The neighborhood isn't that safe and I wouldn't want you there at night."

"Do I look worried?" He jiggled the door. Just when Nina made up her mind to take him up on the offer, her bus came down the street. It halted to a peaceful stop. She waved to show she was on her way. Juan's face squealed disappointment.

"Looks like I won't be needing that ride after all." She straightened her backpack on her shoulder and walked off.

"Damn." Juan chuckled.

❈❈❈

"Spider, get your ass in here!" Tajo banged the refrigerator with a pot until Spider came barreling into the kitchen.

"No, Tajo, it's all right!" Nina covered her face.

"Yo, what's up?" Spider pulled up his sagging pants.

"You left my cousin fuckin' stranded at the library? You're supposed to keep an eye on her! Do you know what could have happened? If you fuck up like this again it's your ass."

"I wasn't stranded, Tajo." Nina sighed. "I took the bus. Did you forget I'm a grown girl? I'm older than he is, for God's sake."

"Nevertheless." Tajo slammed the pot in the sink. He cursed in Spanish.

"Spider is in charge of showing you around and looking out for you. Besides, he has a gat and you don't."

Nina smirked. "Tajo, were you worried about me?" She rubbed his belly. "I think that's sweet."

"My job is to keep an eye on you, Nina. There are some things you can't do all right. I'm the leader of a set." She wrapped her arms around his neck. "Which means it's not safe for you to go some places alone. There are a lot of people who want to fuck me up."

"I don't think going to the library poses a threat."

"Are you listening to me, cousin? Just be wise and careful. You're not in Kansas anymore. You have to keep in mind what I am and what I do. This ain't no game, Nina. I do whatever I have to to survive in this life. I don't want you caught up in that."

"Relax. No one knows I'm your cousin. I won't spread it at Roosevelt. It's nowhere close to this neighborhood anyway."

"But a little too close to NYA territory," Spider said.

"That's right. They won't hesitate to kill you or any one of us, Nina. Please remember that. I love you, baby girl. I don't want anything to happen to you." Tajo held up his arms, show-casing his BG tattoos. "That's honor."

"Nothing's going to happen." She moved away from him, hit hard by his realistic words. He'd told her exactly how gang life was and she appreciated it. She had to be cautious. She hadn't understood that before. "Do you mind if I have some privacy in my life, though?"

"No. Just remember that you're one of us now, Nina. No matter if you want to be or not."

She nodded.

❖❖❖

Juan lay in bed, thinking of the night's events and what led up to them. His mind kept shifting to Nina, though he had more important things to think about. He turned over on his left side. He stared out the window. It had been bolted since he was ten due to numerous break-ins, but he still enjoyed looking through it. Nothing was more beautiful than watching a dark street, though this one was covered with hoodlums, Rico in particular.

Rico's voice echoed down the street. Juan grimaced at every curse word he shouted. He was with his homeboys yelling something about jacking a stash. Juan swore he heard the Bronx Gangstas mentioned, too.

Florence entered the room with a glass of milk and some cookies.

"Hola, hijo. Tienes problemas?"

"No, nothing's wrong. What's with the milk and cookies?" He scratched his naked chest.

"I wondered if you were mad at me, Juan." She sat her chubby frame on the chair beside the bed and crossed her legs. "I don't want us to keep fighting about Rico."

"*Si'?*" He stuffed in a chocolate chip cookie.

"*Si'*," she sighed. "Baby, I love you so much. But I can't turn my back on him. I feel like everything's bad enough as it is."

"Why don't you just kick him out?" Juan clenched his ears as Rico shouted again. "Don't use money as an excuse. I'll be out of the house soon. You can't like this, Ma. You know what he does to people."

"I don't want to hear it, please, Juan."

"And he wants me to become a part of it, Ma. What do you say to that?"

She moved the chair at the end of his bed.

"Good night, *miel*." She blew him a kiss and left.

✠✠✠

Rico gestured toward the main five of his crew. They huddled into a circle around him. He sipped from a bag-covered beer bottle, chuckling. He'd come up with the dirtiest scheme of the century.

"This way we can stick it to those Bronx *faggots* for sure. We get to their stash first and they won't know what hit them."

Double Deuce AKA Double D. licked beer fuzz from his top lip. "Sounds good to me, homes. That stash has to be worth, what? Eight hundred?"

The four-hundred-pound OG by the name of Jelly nodded. "That's what I heard. But we can double it to some sucker down here."

Damian removed his sweaty red headband. He replaced it with another one from his pocket. "They think they're so fuckin' smart. We'll get Leon to do it. He's baby gangsta, so he has to stand up now."

"And if he refuses we just kill his punk ass." Rico finished his beer.

❊❊❊

That night Nina awoke to loud chattering. She peered into the living room. Thirty Bronx Gangstas sat at attention. Tajo sat in the middle of them, shining his gun with a dark green bandanna. The Bronx Gangstas' primary color.

"We got to be careful." A gangbanger laid his leg on the couch. He rocked back and forth. "Moving that much rock. We have to be fast as hell."

"Yep." Tajo nodded. The others watched his every move. Nina had never seen such respect. She couldn't fathom him hurting a fly. Of course, this demeanor had been for her benefit. She knew he wasn't innocent on the streets. So what *had* he done?

For the next ten minutes they talked about a stash of crack rock valued at eight hundred dollars. She couldn't make out their connections or their suppliers. She thought they stole it, but that was impossible. Where would you find eight hundred dollars' worth of crack unless it wanted to find *you*? The tone of the conversation turned from fierce to lightweight within minutes.

They spoke about someone named "Box." She didn't know what the G-word meant and she didn't want to. They mentioned that it would be time to jump him in soon. Nina overheard the address where the event would take place. It would be so stupid to follow them there. For some reason she had to get a taste of Tajo's life first hand. She walked back to the bedroom. Already she knew she'd regret it.

"Nina?" Juice stood in the hallway with a forty. His eyes hauntingly probed her. His mouth curved into a menacing scowl. She'd been caught. What would they do to her? She turned around slowly, gripping her white nightgown. "How long you been there?" Juice walked up to her.

She chuckled. "Been where?"

"You know what I mean." He slumped up to her with a gangsta limp. "You were listening, weren't you?"

"I didn't mean to listen." She hoped her smile dissuaded his curiosity. "I didn't hear much, Juice."

"Maybe you should get on to bed."

Nina followed the command without hesitation. Juice made his way back into the living room.

"What's up, homes?" A gangbanger noticed Juice's worried expression.

"Tajo, man, Nina heard us. I think she heard everything."

"It's cool." Tajo smiled. "She's family, she won't say nothing. She don't know anyone anyway."

"She may be a blabbermouth, *ese*." A guy with a green bandanna pasted around his tattooed neck puffed a joint.

"She's not." Tajo rocked in the chair. He only pulled the chair out for meetings such as this one. It made him feel like a king, reminded him who was in charge.

Juice paced. "She looked freaked out, Tajo. How do we really know we can trust her?"

Shorty-Five raised an eyebrow. "Yeah, how can you be sure

of her loyalty, man? Women freak out with shit like this. I like Nina, but if she fucks this up..."

"I said, she won't." Tajo looked at everyone individually to make sure there wasn't conflict. If so he'd have to illuminate the friction by reinforcing his power. "She is my blood, okay? Just like you all are. Just stick to getting the stash and don't worry about nothing else. I will take care of my cousin, all right?" He performed a hand symbol that stood for Bronx Gangsta loyalty. The others repeated the gesture.

Juice was not convinced.

✠✠✠

Nina tried to keep a straight face in art class Tuesday evening. She felt Mr. Jones was a good teacher and that his skills were fine for high school, but he obviously didn't know the main principles that went into certain forms of art. What he didn't know, he covered with his enthusiasm for teaching. He reminded Nina of one of her old elementary school teachers who glowed when she talked.

Jones went over some basic techniques before the bell rang to dismiss class. He'd expressed his admiration over Nina's paintings the first time they met. He'd asked her to bring another sample and she gladly did. She brought her recent collections that dealt with Michelle's illness. After Michelle's diagnosis Nina had turned to her talent obsessively. Her latest work became the best she'd done.

"Ooh, exquisite, Nina." Jones salivated as if he were looking at a naked woman.

"Your form and technique is genius. You have a God-given

49

talent, don't you?" He smiled, looking like a tall Sherman Hemsley with red glasses.

"Thank you." She twiddled her fingers. Little instruments of the heart, she called them. "Do you like these as much as the ones yesterday?"

"More. I mean, they're all lovely." He moved to the back table. "But this one speaks to me. It does everything you want it to." She explained about Michelle's condition. He seemed to appreciate the pictures more. "I do hope you pursue this talent, Nina."

"Hopefully. But only as a hobby because it won't bring in the money."

"It could if you had backing and promotion."

"Mr. Jones, do you realize how hard it is for an artist to get noticed in their own city, let alone nationally? You can't make it in this business unless someone wants to buy your work."

He took off his glasses. He slyly smiled. "I think I know a thing or two about the art world marketplace, Nina. Stop comparing yourself to everyone else. Some artists don't make it because they don't have anything original to say. Some are just in it for what they think they can gain."

"The more famous artists didn't become recognized until death." She played with his pencil sharpener.

"Yeah, but it was worth it to be known centuries afterward, don't you think?"

Nina looked around the room at the walls filled with student paintings and colorful construction paper. "I want to enter you in the showcase, Nina." He jotted her name down. She wanted to dispute that, but he was so enthusiastic she couldn't have stopped him.

Afterward she met up with Claudia and the others at Rosa's

locker. They hadn't gotten a good sentence in about the show-case before Juan walked up. He hoped Nina got the sign that he wanted to meet her at the library again. By her despondent attitude, he wasn't sure.

"What's up, ladies?" His eyes automatically searched Nina's. "Hi, Nina. How you doing? You were quiet in first today." Nina didn't speak. Claudia and Lisa grinned. Rosa searched her locker for her car keys. The halls emptied immediately. The last bell was of hardly any use.

"Hi, Juan." Nina turned away from him, knowing he would make her smile and she didn't want to smile. She didn't want him getting any ideas.

"Well, see you around, okay?" He stood behind her for a moment, then walked down the hall to Dell's locker.

"Wow, Juan Alonso." Lisa gasped. "Man, every girl has tried to get with him. Why didn't you want to talk to him, Nina?"

"Yeah, girl, he was giving up mad signals," Claudia said.

Nina looked back to see him staring at her. She turned away when he waved.

"I just didn't feel like talking to him."

"No, it seems like more than that." Lisa grinned. "I think you like him a lot. That's why you were giving him the cold shoulder."

"No way." Nina grumbled but couldn't hide her amusement.

"See, she likes him, Claude." Lisa laughed.

"Could you all stop babbling long enough to help me find my keys?" Rosa dug in the top of her locker. Lisa went to help.

"Level with me, girlfriend. Do you like Juanito? Because he definitely seems to like you."

"It's too early to say. I hardly know him, Claude."

"Fuck 'too early,'" Claudia scoffed. "You need to loosen up and have fun. You ain't never had no boyfriend. I bet you still haven't been kissed."

"Shhh!" Nina grimaced at her. "Announce it to the whole fuckin' world, why don't you?"

Claudia laughed. "This is me, homes. I know all about you, all right? Anyway, tonight we're going to that hot club on Fifth. I'll pick you up at seven, okay?"

"Claudia, I got loads of homework. I can't afford to mess this up. With everything in my life I need a..."

"*Break*, exactly, Nina. One night of fun won't hurt. You'll be back before eleven. You need to have some fun. Get your mind off of your Mamá."

"I don't know."

"Got 'em!" Rosa's keys fell from her locker. "So we're meeting at the club tonight, right?" she asked.

Claudia looked at Nina, hinting with her eyes. "*Are* we?"

"All right, all right. I'll go." Nina grinned.

"Good, girl! You won't regret it." Claudia wrapped her arms around Nina's shoulders. The girls gossiped for a few more seconds, then disappeared down the hall.

Juan stood against the lockers, smiling. He'd heard every word.

❉❉❉

"You look good, girl." Claudia sped through Edgewood that night as if there were a fire. "We're gonna be the best-looking chicks at the club!"

"I don't know." Nina looked down at the white lace top and matching miniskirt she'd picked. "My ass is too big to wear this."

"That's the beauty of it, girl. You need to show that little butt off. I show mine's off." Claudia opened her black denim jacket, showing off her little bra top and spandex skirt. Nina shook her head. No matter what she wore, it wouldn't have compared to the MTV attire Claudia always draped herself in.

"Rosa and Lisa are meeting us at the club, right?" Nina looked through the rearview mirror. She wrapped her hair around her fist and held it in a big lump on top of her head. "Should I?"

"Leave it down," Claudia commanded.

"I'm still edgy. I can't believe Tajo had sex while I was in the house." Nina shook her head, dismayed. "I don't think I'll be able to eat for a week. And you should have seen that girl Lexi. Major slut if I ever saw one." Nina leaned her arm over the side of the convertible.

"You're still weird about sex, huh?" Claudia smirked.

"It's gross." Nina fiddled with her seat belt.

"Nothing's wrong with sex. You need to realize that. Nina, you're sixteen."

"I know how old I am." She glared at Claudia.

"My point is you got to get laid this year, Nina. How long until you do? Girl, you don't know pleasure until you've been with a man."

"Unlike you, Claudia, I have to like a man before I fuck him." Nina grinned.

Claudia playfully shot her the bird. "Tonight needs to be the night you just let go. That's why you're always so uptight."

"I am not uptight. And you need to pay attention to the street signs." She pointed.

"My ex-boyfriend taught me how to drive, I'll have you know." Claudia slapped Nina's thigh.

"How old is he, two?" Nina pulled at her skirt. "I'm nervous. What is this gonna be like?"

"*Fun*. Something you don't know anything about." Claudia pumped up her favorite rap station. "So how come you were all dazed this evening when I brought you home? Would Juan Alonso be the reason?" Nina ignored her. "So you getting all quiet on me now?"

"I'm thinking about something else. I heard the Bronx Gangstas talking about some stash last night. I'm worried about Tajo. There has to be some way to stop all of this."

"Are you living in a fairy tale, Nina? These are gangs you're talking about. Just because Tajo's your cousin doesn't mean he's not as hard as anyone else out here. How do you think he got to be the leader if he wasn't?"

"Is that supposed to make me feel better?"

"No." Claudia lit a cigarette. "I'm just telling you like it is, girlfriend."

❈❈❈

"Oww, asshole!" Lexi grinned as Tajo bit the tips of her fingers. She pinched his chest. He retaliated by nibbling her arm. "Stop it." She laughed. "That girl really your cousin?" She moved her long hair from her chest, exposing her plump, tattooed breasts.

"Yeah." He laid his arms behind his head on the pillow.

"You sure? You ain't just telling me that and fucking her on the side, are you? Because I'll cut your ass if you are."

"You ain't cutting nothing, bitch." He forced her toward his chest. "On the real, she's my little cousin. I got baby pictures to prove it."

"Oh, all right." She lit a joint. "She's cute. Does she know everything you do here?"

"Of course. She's family."

"Can she be trusted?"

"Can *you* be?"

"You know I can be, baby." She rubbed his stomach. "You know where my loyalties lie."

"I know you're one dirty little bitch who'll screw anyone for a hit off the pipe or anything else you're hooked on at the moment."

"Maybe." She watched him, exasperated. "I'm also someone who gives you the lowdown on people who plan to fuck you up. Don't forget that."

"Shut up." He turned over. "Go get me a Coke, bitch."

"Remember it, Tajo." She left the room.

Being naked was second nature to Lexi, so she had no qualms walking to the kitchen in rare form. A crowd of guys yelled through the front door. Lexi slipped on an apron with just the front of her thighs to her neck covered, then answered the door.

"Damn, girl." Bone pulled at the apron. "I can see what Tajo's cooking for dinner." He laughed.

Shorty-Five glared at Lexi. "Why don't you get the fuck out of here and tell Tajo we need to see him?"

"About what?" She held her hips.

"Move it, bitch!" Juice shoved her. Lexi took her time leaving the room. A second later, Tajo slumped in with his arms crossed.

"What's up?" He glared at them.

"Get ready to torture some motherfuckers, man." Shorty-Five sucked a cigarette.

"I think we should line them up and shoot all their dicks off, Tajo."

"What's going on, man?"

"They got our stash, *ese*." Bone bit his lip. "Fucking NYA motherfuckers got our stash."

"Hold up…" Tajo rubbed his head. "I know this can't be fucking true. You telling me those pussies got our stash that's valued at over eight hundred dollars?" he yelled.

"Damn right. They wrote all on the fucking walls of the hideout and left this note." Juice passed it to him.

Tajo read it and balled it up. "Oh, it's on. Where are the rest of the fellas?"

"They're still over there. I said we needed to check with you. We already got the car heated, ready to go," Shorty-Five said. "Just say the word, man. And we'll pop a cap in all them motherfuckers now."

"True dat." Bone nodded. Lexi stared at Tajo, who was smiling maliciously by now.

"No, fuck that. We ain't doing shit tonight so don't call nothing on," Tajo ordered.

"What?" Juice looked at the others.

Shorty-Five furiously shook his head. "Tajo! We got to get these motherfuckers, man! I'm so sick of the NYAs I don't know what to do. Let's go kill all those bitch-ass niggas right now. What the fuck is your problem? We need to get out there and take care of business!"

"You better back the fuck up off me." Tajo stared him in the eye. Shorty-Five remembered his rank and stood back.

"All right." He sighed. "You're the fucking leader."

"That's right. We can't get them tonight because they'll be expecting something. I want it to be a surprise. So we hit them when they least expect it. Just like when we smoked that other motherfucker. I'll let you know when the time is right. Then we'll pop a cap in those motherfuckers one by motherfucking one."

"I like that." Bone moved from side to side. "Yeah, we can get busy like that. Let them stir a little bit."

"Right." Juice grinned.

"But please, let me do it." Shorty-Five rubbed his belt. "I haven't shot a NYA in a while and my trigger finger is itching. I'll pop so many holes in those motherfuckers, they'll look like colanders."

"Yeah, boy!" Juice yelled. He bumped fists with Shorty-Five. "But break me off some of that NYA action, too."

"Don't worry. There'll be enough to go around." Tajo sneered.

CHAPTER FOUR

lub Calina was a fortress for misbehavior. Although fairly new, it was the perfect addition to an already hostile environment. Nina didn't frequent the teen club scene and she wasn't enthusiastic about making Calina her first choice. But Claudia was more than persuasive and had the gift of making Nina feel guilty for not having fun. Besides, Nina was curious about the spicy side of life.

They arrived at Calina along with a crowd of rowdy regulars. They had a five-minute wait in line, then broke through the door with the others. Calina could have easily been mistaken for a library from the street. The only outside decor was brown brick walls and tinted windows, but the inside was an enchanted universe of uninhabited fun. They walked up a large platform leading to five steps toward the dance floor.

On each side of the club were long rows of crowded tables. Security stood against the walls in case things got out of hand. Nina shielded her face from bright red and green lights that swarmed the club. She had a tough time finding her way behind her friends. Rosa and Lisa swayed to the music. Claudia screamed to kids she knew. Nina hadn't ever felt more out of place. She imagined herself sticking out like an eight-foot root and all eyes seemed to be on her.

A gorgeous waiter greeted them at a table. He took their

orders for beverages, then went on his way. Nina's stomach was in knots. She'd never been so uncomfortable. She noticed a table of guys staring her way. She quickly avoided eye contact. She wasn't about to give any guy in Calina encouragement.

"Now, Nina." Claudia arranged the tiny napkins in front of her. Rosa and Lisa held a conversation of their own. "Is this more than you imagined?"

She had to admit it was remarkable. The dance floor gained more people as they all partook in the latest unison dances. The waiter returned with four pineapple drinks. Claudia had recommended them, claiming they tasted like liquor.

Lisa was the first to sip her drink. "Damn, this is sweet." She licked her lips.

"What did they do, dump a bucket of sugar in it?"

"I thought you said it tastes like liquor, Claudia." Rosa sucked her lips to drain as much flavor as possible. "Six dollars for *this*?" Rosa shook her head.

"I like it." Nina sipped.

"You would, Little Orphan Annie." Rosa walled her eyes. "Claude, we could have gone to that other club by my house. We already got the fake ID's and everything and it would be no sweat to get Nina in, too. Let's cut out of here."

"Sit down and stop complaining. If the drinks are what you have a problem with then relax." Claudia took out a tiny bottle of whiskey. "Here's the solution. Pass me your drinks."

"All right, let's get this shit on!" Rosa passed Claudia her drink. Claudia poured a few shots in hers and Lisa's. The girls gulped them down.

"And there's more where that came from, ladies. Nina, give me your drink."

"No," she snapped, appalled. "Claude, I can't believe you're doing this. We're not supposed to drink. We're underage."

"Girl, what planet are you from?" Rosa handed Claudia her drink for more whiskey. "Haven't you ever done nothing spontaneous? I bet you can't even shit without having a schedule."

"Ha, ha!" Lisa laughed, already tipsy.

"You're a fucking teenager. Live a little bit," Rosa mumbled.

Nina glanced around the room. "I realize that *you* all could care less about how to act. But I choose to go a different path and not be so damn wild. And another thing," When Nina turned around, Claudia dashed her drink with whiskey. Rosa nodded in humorous approval.

"You're right, Nina." Claudia pretended to be affected by the holier-than-thou routine. "We shouldn't be so wild. Go on and drink your pineapple thing."

"I don't mean to be a downer but there's a time and place for everything. Why you want to grow up so fast?" She sipped. Claudia and Rosa nearly died from laughter.

"What's up?" Lisa asked. She'd been concentrating on the dance floor and hadn't witnessed Claudia's trick.

"Oh, you'll see." Claudia winked.

Before Lisa or Nina had a chance to ask what that meant, four guys with skullcaps and Nike jumpsuits walked up. The whiskey went down Nina's spine like acid. She felt an intense hotness all over her body. She started laughing for no reason at all. Claudia and Rose winced. They hadn't expected it to kick in so fast.

"What's up, ladies?" The guy in the blue jumpsuit gazed at Rosa.

"I feel so weird and hot." Nina fanned herself with the napkin.

"Did you say 'hot,' baby?" The guy in the red jumpsuit leaned in beside her.

"What's that smell? Ooh, you got drinks over here!"

"Shut up!" Claudia snapped. "What is it to *you*? Why don't you take your ass back where you came from?"

"So it's like that?" Red Jumpsuit rolled up his sleeves. "I wasn't talking to you anyway. I was talking to this one over here." He pointed to Nina. "So stay the fuck out of it."

"Fuck you. She'll *have* to be drunk to look at *you* twice," Claudia snapped. His friends laughed.

Red Jumpsuit stared at Nina. "Slow down with the drink, baby. You want to dance?" He took her hand. The club announcer instructed everyone to get on the dance floor.

"They're gonna do that 'blindfold' shit." The guy in the brown jumpsuit looked at Lisa.

"What's that?" Lisa asked. He helped her out of the seat.

"It's a dance where the girls are blindfolded and turn in a circle. Then you dance with a guy and you have to try to get back with your partner and if you don't, you have to sit down and the last four couples left get prizes. Last time I won Master P tickets. It's off the hook." He chuckled.

"Sounds corny to me." Rosa muttered but took Blue Jumpsuit's hand anyway and followed him. Nina unintentionally joined Red Jumpsuit seeing how she was halfway drunk and didn't have a clue what was going on. She wobbled to the dance floor.

"Hold up, baby." He got a scarf from the club attendant and blindfolded her.

"Not so tight, shit." Nina laughed. Overbearing music drowned the club.

"Sorry, baby." Red Jumpsuit took her hand. His cologne was

louder than the music. She wouldn't have a problem finding him each time. She wiggled her hips wildly. Red Jumpsuit held on for the ride. "Got a little flavor in ya, huh?"

"You better believe it. Dancing's my thing." Nina swayed.

"I can see that." Red Jumpsuit wrapped his hands around her waist.

As the game swung into motion, all the girls struggled to find their partners. Gradually mismatched couples came together. Woozy, Nina tried to keep up with the fast music. Red Jumpsuit grabbed her in a way that seemed different from how he'd held her before. His touch was almost *magnetic*. He twirled her to a rhythmic stop. Claudia and Rosa dropped out of the game from fatigue.

It wasn't until they got back to the table that they could see Nina and the guy who had his hands all around her. Red Jumpsuit was nowhere to be seen.

"Holy shit." Claudia laughed. "Rosa, look."

"I see." Rosa covered her mouth. "I fucking see it, Claude."

"What is he doing?" Claudia squinted.

"What does it look like?" Rosa gaped.

His arms drew Nina closer. She felt his chest against her breasts. She knew this wasn't the guy in the red jumpsuit. The smell of this person was extremely familiar.

His warm lips took hers without warning. Nina nearly suffocated by an overwhelming need to experience more. His tongue probed her lips until her mouth accepted his.

Distant, erotic thoughts crammed her head.

Was this like in the movies? Had she caught the eye of some handsome stranger so compelled by her he couldn't control himself? Her heart shut down the longer he kissed her. Her body jerked. She thought her legs had fallen off and run away. Her arms went limp. Her restless mouth silently begged for the sensation only his could provide in return. It was such a delicious kiss. Like chocolate and vanilla ice cream combined.

He let go of her without warning. He snatched off the blindfold. Had she taken a trip to the moon? Wasn't she dreaming? This couldn't have been happening. But it *had* happened. And she wasn't ready to deny or accept the reality of it. Juan Alonso smiled as though he'd won the Olympic gold medal for stealing kisses. Shit, she had enjoyed that kiss. Yet she'd never been so confused and agitated.

That kiss had affected her in ways she couldn't ignore. She'd enjoyed his lips on hers. She longed for him to repeat the task. Though she begged for more like people begged for breath, all Nina could do was slap him. Once she did, everything stopped. The music died. Everyone stopped dancing. They glared at the kids in the center of the dance floor.

"Uh-oh! Looks like we got a problem on the dance floor." The announcer laughed. He ordered the spotlight on Nina and Juan. Suddenly Nina wished she could erase the present humiliation. Juan looked pissed, as well. He rubbed his swelling jaw.

"You." He lowered his voice to escape the solid gazes from around the club.

"You didn't have to hit me."

"The hell I didn't." Nina exhaled. Someone in the background whistled at Juan's romantic gesture. "You had no right to do that. You think I'm your property that you can just take?"

"Nina?" He grabbed her arm. She yanked away. She had so much to say. All she wanted to do was assure him that she enjoyed the kiss. Hell, she wanted more of it this minute! But she couldn't bring herself to look him in the eyes. Without even a whimper, she ran out of the club.

"Uh-oh, ladies and gentlemen! Looks like some guy couldn't keep his hands to himself! Ha, ha!" the announcer shouted.

Nina didn't breathe until she got outside. She frantically searched for an area to vomit. She ran toward the alley behind the club, catching the eye of a curious security guard. She threw up in the grass. She held her stomach, frantically gasping. Juan blasted out of the club. Nina took off in the opposite direction.

She thought she'd made it away from Juan and the humiliation until the guard drew attention.

"Are you all right, young lady?" the guard called out. Juan rushed to her. Nina shielded her eyes from the guard's flashlight.

"Yeah, she's okay." Juan fanned him off. He took her into his arms, examining her tired expression.

"Maybe you two should get inside or go home. Is she sick?" The security guard shined the flashlight in Nina's eyes.

"I'm fine." She coughed. She moved from Juan, leaving him more confused than he'd been in the club.

"Okay. Maybe you two should be getting home. You need to call your parents or something for a ride?" The guard slowly lowered the light.

"No, but thank you." Juan waved. The guard went on his way. "It's ten-thirty, Nina. You need a ride home?" She turned away. He walked around to see her face. She turned around again. He walked in circles around her until she was trapped. "Nina? Okay, I shouldn't have done that." He tugged on the arms of his light jacket. "But can you blame me?"

"You are the biggest asshole I've ever met." She wiped her mouth. "And I'm feeling sick."

"Well, you smell like Jack Daniels. I didn't know you drank. And where did you get the stuff anyway?"

"I *don't* drink. Someone, namely Claudia, slipped some whiskey into my drink. I hadn't figured it out until I was dancing and my excitement turned into nausea. Then I saw your face and the nausea multiplied."

Juan smiled. "Not how I pictured you'd react after our first kiss, but I'll take it over nothing." She rolled her eyes. He was gloating. He'd shocked her. He'd pulled the wool over her eyes. Nina was angry but couldn't deny that he was one of the most exciting people to have ever entered her life.

He rested a hand on the wall beside her. She stood in pouting mode until curiosity forced her to look at him.

"I'm sorry, okay?" he whispered ever so sweetly. Nina couldn't ignore the racing of her heart. She felt his radiating eyes drawing her in once more. This time *she* controlled the moment.

"What are you doing here anyway?" she asked.

"My friends come here sometimes." He smirked. Nina watched him doubtfully until he came clean. "Okay, I overheard you and the girls saying you would be here. So I decided it wouldn't harm anything if we accidentally met here tonight."

"But it wasn't 'accidental,' was it, Juan? The first thing I want you to know about me is that I don't succumb to someone by force." He sighed. "You can't bully me into doing something you want me to do. You may be able to run that on the girls at Roosevelt, but not me."

"Okay. Uh, my bad?" He grinned.

"You're damn right it's your bad." She said some less-than flattering words in Spanish, then walked away.

"Hey, Nina?" He rushed after her. "Nina, wait up."

"Just leave me alone, Juan." She furiously waved him away.

She gathered with her friends, who were searching the front of the club to find her.

"What happened to you, girl?" Claudia brushed a leaf from Nina's shoulder. Nina just grimaced at Juan in return.

"So where did you go?" Lisa asked.

"I felt sick so I had to throw up." Nina glared at Claudia. "Thanks to someone who I thought was my friend."

"Hey, I *am* your friend. That's why I tried to loosen you up. You were so damn uptight. You can't go through life being uptight, Nina."

"Save it, Claude." Nina knocked Claudia's arm off her shoulder. Juan was still watching pitifully. "I hope you aren't too drunk, Claude, because I need to get home."

"No, I'll take you, girl." Claudia bid Lisa and Rosa good-bye. Nina sat in the passenger's seat with her head back. They were gone before Juan could further persuade Nina of his apology. He walked up to Rosa and Lisa.

"God, she could have cut me some slack, huh?" He walked off toward the parking lot.

"You know." Rosa belched. Lisa frowned at her. "That was kind of dumb, right? I mean, humiliating a girl like that is one surefire way to make sure she hates you."

"Oh, I don't know." Lisa watched Juan get into his Toyota. "I thought it was kind of romantic." She followed Rosa to her car.

❖❖❖

Juan reflected on the incident all night. He refused to believe he'd misread Nina's signals. He turned on his side in bed. Women were known to confuse men to a capacity that left them deaf, dumb, and stupid. But he knew Nina liked him. During the kiss she'd reacted in a way that couldn't have been denied.

❈❈❈

The next evening he met Nina at the library. She smiled as if nothing had happened. Any other guy would have rolled with the punches, thanking God she wasn't angry. Not Juan. He had to know the if, why, and but of everything that came his way. She hadn't spoken to him at school so he wasn't surprised she said nothing now. God, she was so beautiful. As breathtaking as a storybook princess.

Sometimes Juan questioned if she was real. She took out her history book.

"I'm sorry I hit you, Juan. But you, you can't do things like that to people. It took me off guard in a bad way. I got embarrassed and everyone was staring at me. I hated the feeling." She flipped through the book.

"I really am sorry, Nina. When I saw you out there, I couldn't take my eyes off you. Who am I kidding?" He chuckled. "I can't take my eyes off you in class and I can't stop thinking about you, either. I know it sounds like some lame shit, but it's the truth."

"I know. Something about you tells me it's the truth." She sat up in her chair. "But you have to back off, Juan."

"Why?" His eyes widened. He reached for her. She moved away.

"Because there is too much in my life right now. I'm into my schoolwork and getting into a good college. I got so much shit to deal with in my family. I don't have room for anything else."

"You mean like a boyfriend?" His voice cracked from sorrow.

"Yes. I don't have time for that. I've never had time for that." She looked at her book.

"So we can't get together or go on a date? We can't even hang and get to know each other better? Can't we even be friends?"

"I'm just afraid that it will turn into something I won't be able to handle." She played with her watch.

"You've never had a boyfriend, have you, Nina?" She didn't answer. "I won't hurt you or embarrass you ever again. But to just close the door on me is stupid. You like me."

"I never said I liked you."

"You didn't have to." He gleamed.

"You can wipe the smirk away, Juan." She crossed her arms. "I don't like you. I just want to be left alone."

"Then why did you come to the library then? You know I come here every evening."

She scoffed. "I came because I had a lot of work to catch up on. I'm a new student. I've missed a lot of work and the teachers are loading it on."

"Uh-huh. Why sit with me then? It's not crowded today. You could have easily sat somewhere else. You could have sat in the front and I wouldn't have even seen you. But you came through all those aisles to sit by me. How come?" He tapped his fingers.

"I..." She smiled at a passing librarian. "For your information, I was checking out a book from the shelf over there." She pointed in back of her. "It wouldn't have made sense to go all the way back to the front of the library."

"Face it, Nina." He shook his head, silently mocking her. She hated every minute of it. "You like me. And it's okay to like me."

"You are the most arrogant boy I have ever met."

"But you like me, right?" He grinned, clasping his hands behind his head.

"You wish." Nina turned away.

"Yeah, you like me." Juan laughed.

Nina smirked.

❖❖❖

For the next few hours, Juan and Nina studied every aspect of history. During the studying, Juan schooled Nina on Roosevelt. He gave her the lowdown on the teachers. They became so overcome with each other they lost track of the time. By nine they found themselves waiting for Nina's bus. They felt the time couldn't pass slow enough. If they had the power to stop it, they would have.

"It's cold tonight, huh?" Nina rubbed her shoulders.

"I don't know. Maybe you should try wearing thicker clothes." Juan draped his jacket around her.

She smiled. "If you got it, flaunt it, right?"

"Hey, you'll never get no complaints from me." He scanned her curvaceous frame. "You got any brothers or sisters, Nina?"

"No. I always wanted a sister when I was little. My mom couldn't have any kids after she had me. She had me very young." Nina was happy he didn't ask how young Michelle had been. She wasn't comfortable sharing such details and never had been.

"Who you staying with again?"

"My cousin."

"What happened to your mom? Didn't you stay with her?"

"Yeah, but she has cancer and she had to be taken out of our home."

"Jesus. I'm sorry, Nina." She shrugged. "Are you all right?"

"Yeah, I've had time to get used to it. I mean, it bothers me and I worry, but I know God will make things go the way they're supposed to. Do you have any brothers or sisters?"

"Yeah. I got one older brother. I got younger twin brothers and a little sister. We stay with my mother. My father died a while back."

"I'm sorry. It must have been rough, your mother not having help with finances and things, huh?"

He hunched his shoulders. "Yeah, of course. But my brother Rico helps out. I believe he could do more, but…"

"What did your father die of?"

"He had a heart attack." Juan looked across the street at the men gathering in the dirty pool hall. "He used to get so mad sometimes. One day he was yelling and something busted in his heart. He died in an instant." He turned to her. "And that's the end of the story."

"How did you feel about it?"

"Shocked at first. Then I felt very bitter toward God. I blamed a lot of people, including my mother. She didn't deserve that. I eventually got over it."

"My mom and I aren't close, but I don't know what I'd do if she died, Juan."

"Something tells me you could handle it better than you think." He smiled. "So what's up with *your* dad?"

"I never knew my dad." She relaxed against his truck. "I never cared to know him, either. I'm thankful to him for one thing."

"What's that?" Juan lit up.

"My talent for art. I know I got it from him because my mother can't do anything. The woman burns water."

Juan laughed. "My mom's a good cook, it's just that I wish she'd give up on this Greek shit. One day a week is all right, but I can't take any more fish soup." He shook.

Nina chuckled. "She likes Greek food or something?"

"No, she's taking this Greek cooking class so she's become obsessed with it. I tell you, I miss regular meals and pizza."

"God, I couldn't live without pizza." Nina moaned.

"So…" Juan licked his lips. "An artist, huh? That's why you spend so much time with Mr. Jones?"

"The man has leashed me. He thinks I have some great talent that can change the world. Yawn." She grinned.

"What's so bad about that? I'd love to see your art sometimes."

"Sure." She handed him his jacket. "My bus is here."

"Oh." He gently cradled the jacket in his arms. It seemed like it would take a thousand arms to break his stare. "Well, I had a nice time studying with you, Nina."

"Me, too." She flicked her hair behind her ears.

"I don't mind taking you home." The bus came to a slow screech at the sidewalk.

"That's okay." She started walking. "See you at school tomorrow, okay?"

"Yeah." He watched as she got on the bus and left. He sniffed his jacket, sucking in the reminder of her sweet smell.

Art class kept Nina focused. Every other time she found herself daydreaming about Juan. He vowed he wouldn't give up on her and he hadn't. She found herself entranced by the idea of him. She intended to stand her ground, but the idea of losing

Juan's interest terrified her. She was incredibly obsessed. His smile made her shiver. His touch made her body produce a warm ache she'd only experienced watching the sexy guys on soap operas.

She started staying after school in Mr. Jones's room to work on her art. Though he admired her previous work, he wanted her to cook up something special for the showcase. That meant more work for Nina, but it was also a chance to dabble in her creativity. Claudia started staying late with Nina. She didn't find it safe for Nina to be in the halls alone.

"I forgot how you got into this finger-painting stuff." Claudia sat on top of one of the front desks studying Nina's ritual.

Nina bent over the large table in the back of the room with her hair looped into a messy ponytail. She'd finished applying a loud shade of pink to the grayish-blue canvas. She called it "Waterfall."

"I don't know. I just started it one day. I picked up some ketchup, scooted it on a napkin, and before I knew it, I had a picture. I didn't think much of it until the lady in the restaurant held it up and swore I was a genius." She chuckled.

"Let me guess." Claudia popped her bubble gum. "Your mother didn't say shit about you playing with your food, huh?"

"Nope." Nina momentarily reflected on the odd relationship with her mother.

"She didn't say shit." She stood back as if she'd reinvented the "Mona Lisa."

"Whoa." Claudia raced to the back of the room. "Nina, it's amazing. You've outdone yourself, girl. I love it."

"Oh, you always love my work." Nina leaned with her arms behind her back.

"No, I really do."

"Well, it's not finished yet. I have so much more I want to do with it. Honestly, I don't know the direction." Nina stared at the waves of different paint types and structures. "Mr. Jones says I can be someone, Claudia." Nina moved a loose strand of hair from her face. "You think so?"

"Yeah." She shrugged. "You got talent, girl. Don't sell yourself short."

"Thanks." Nina got her purse from the table. "I hate getting my hopes up only to find out nothing happens the way it should."

Claudia turned the light off while Nina wrapped up her belongings. They strutted down the hushed hall. "You always think on the negative side, Nina."

"You would, too, if you had as much negativity as I have."

"Whatever." Claudia danced down the steps behind Nina. "You can't be like this forever, girlfriend. Maybe if you had a man you wouldn't be so bothered."

"It's just like you to think that a man can solve everyone's problems. My life is uptight because my mom is dying and my life has never been more confusing."

"Nah." Claudia's grinning annoyed Nina more. "That's not it. And I'm tired of trying to change you." They passed the second-floor entrance until they reached the steps to the first floor. "Would you just go out on *one* date before you're fifty?"

Nina stuck her nose in the air. "I'll date as soon as I find someone worth dating."

"What about Juan Alonso?" Claudia lit up. "Is he worth dating?"

"How come you bring him up all the time?"

"Because you like him." Claudia watched as Nina abruptly stopped at the first-floor doors.

"I heard something," Nina whispered.

"This *is* a school. There's bound to be other people around. And don't try to change the subject. Now, Juan is…"

"Claude, I heard something." Nina gaped at her.

"It's probably the fuckin' janitor."

"No, the janitors can't use these entrances. And the kids are practicing by the gym." Nina crept backward. Her caution didn't faze Claudia, who calmly reached for the doors.

"Nina, you're tripping. There's no one here but…" Claudia was swung from the stairs and forced inside the stairwell.

Before Nina could scream, a hard hand pressed against her mouth. Someone swung her toward the stairs in the same fashion. Two guys in dark T-shirts who appeared to be as young as Claudia and Nina looked them over. They wore ski masks that hid every inch of their faces. They felt them up, searching for money and other valuables. They ripped off Claudia's gold necklace. They snatched Nina's purse.

"Claudia…" Nina inched her hand against the wall to Claudia. Claudia signaled for her to be cool. Claudia had been in similar situations before. Staying calm was the only insurance for safety. One flipped Nina's purse upside-down. A package of Kleenex, two pens, and her billfold fell on the floor. Claudia's purse was given the same treatment. She cursed as they looted her fifty-dollar bill.

"Twelve dollars?" One frantically held up Nina's purse. His voice was incredibly stuffy. He definitely sounded young. A drug head perhaps.

"That's all I have." Nina shook. He threw the purse to her feet. Pissed, he stuffed the money in his pocket.

"Claudia, I know you got more money than this," the second

guy said. Him knowing her name hadn't surprised her. She knew they went to the school. His familiar voice struck a chord. "You drive that bad-ass car. Come on." He moved toward her. "I know you got more money."

"Leave her alone!" Nina yelled.

"Stupid bitch." The first guy pulled out a knife. He held Nina's chin until her head plunged into the wall. "What else you got? You got some jewelry? You got something!"

"No, I don't have anything!" Nina cried.

"Get off her!" Claudia shoved him. The other one slapped her to the floor.

"Claude! Leave her alone!" Nina shrieked.

"Money!" The second one yanked Claudia's hair until her neck bent backward. "Money, bitch!"

"Nina, is that you?" Juan and Tony stood at the doorway. The thieves jostled the girls. They ran out the doors and down the hall.

"What the fuck?" Tony screamed. Juan rushed after them. "I'm going to go find security! You girls stay here, all right?" Tony ran off.

"Nina, are you all right?" Claudia asked.

"Yeah." She examined her clothing, then picked up what was left of her purse. "I can't believe you can't be safe in your own school."

Claudia brushed dust from her legs. "Sorry to say it happens more than you think."

"And you aren't scared? Claude, I know this is the Bronx, but no one is *that* brave." Claudia searched the floor for anything that slipped from her purse. "They probably hold up students at every chance."

"'Course they do, Nina. That's probably their game. They probably do this every day. I'm sure no one bothers to report it."

"And why not?"

"Because that's how it is around here."

"But toleration doesn't make things *right*!" Nina flipped her ponytail from her right shoulder. "When is everyone going to stop settling for violence and start doing something to stop it?"

"Anyone ever told you you're living in a fairy tale, Nina?" Claudia didn't mean for the question to be condescending. Normally Nina would have taken it that way, except Claudia wasn't the first person to ask that question.

"There they are." Tony led a pudgy, short security guard toward the girls.

"You two all right?" He took measured steps around the area. "The guys ran this way?" He pointed toward the doors. Everyone nodded. He spoke through his walkie-talkie, then replaced it on his belt. "Are you two okay?"

"Yeah. Juan Alonso ran after them," Nina shouted in a tone that hinted she was impressed by the action.

"He had no business being so stupid. Did they have weapons on them?"

"One had a knife," Claudia whispered. "I'm not sure what the other one had. They stole my money and took my necklace. They stole twelve dollars from Nina, too."

"Did they do anything else? Did they hurt you?"

"No, sir." Nina took a deep breath. The security guard spoke through his walkie-talkie again. Afterward he stared at the girls. "Can you identify them? The young man here said they had on ski masks."

"I thought I recognized their voices." Claudia cleared her

throat. "But I don't want to say anything and get someone into trouble. I want to be sure first."

"Okay, just wait here for a minute." The security guard stepped outside the doors. He stayed there for a few minutes, then disappeared.

"What happened?" Tony gazed at Claudia.

"They just grabbed us and jacked us." Claudia shrugged. The security guard returned with his partner. Juan staggered from behind.

"No such luck." The chubby officer sighed. "They got away. Do you have any idea how dangerous it is for you two girls to be in here after school? This is about the fifth time in the last three months someone has been robbed after school. We repeatedly tell you kids to be careful. Next time the crime may turn from robbery into something else. If you have to be in the building this late again, take the central exit, all right?"

"Yes, sir," the girls mumbled in unison.

"I still think it's safer for you not to be here at all. But take the central exit and don't lollygag. Get out of the building and stay away from dark corners. This is a big place and we won't always be able to rush to help," the second guard said. "Please take that into consideration."

"What's going to be done about them?" Nina stuffed her belongings back into her purse.

"The only ID we have is what they were wearing." The chubby guard shrugged. "If they are students in the school, they'll probably do it again and hopefully we'll be ready for them."

"Well, is it the same people doing this, you think?" Nina gripped her hips.

"This is not the safest neighborhood and we do our best," the first security guard said. He gave them another warning and left with his partner.

"So that's it?" Nina scoffed. "We get robbed, could have even been raped or stabbed, and they just say, 'We do our best'? How is someone supposed to be comfortable at a school when they don't know if they're going to be grabbed or God knows what?"

"You may not agree with his words, Nina." Juan walked up to her. "But this is how it goes. I don't like it any more than you do. Hey, the world is a great place to live in if you can accept its beauty and faults equally."

"That doesn't comfort me, Juan. It only makes me more agitated."

"Juan, we got to go, man." Tony tapped the doors.

"Nina, do you need a ride somewhere or…" Juan reached for her.

"No." She slipped on her purse. "I'll ride home with Claude. But thanks anyway."

"Sure." Juan found it impossible to tear himself away from her. He needed to always be sure she was okay and right now he wasn't. "What were you guys doing here anyway?"

"Mr. Jones gave me an after-school pass for me to work in his room for the art showcase. I hadn't thought anything of it until now." Nina whipped her ponytail around so quickly it brushed Claudia's face. "What were *you* doing here?"

"We were watching the kids practicing outside. We came in to get a drink of water and we heard you guys from the hallway."

"Yeah." Tony nodded.

"The guards were right. If you're going to be doing this every evening you should use the central exit." Juan adjusted his backpack. "And I'd love to take you home myself. We could talk."

"Uh, nah." Nina would have enjoyed the ride, but she wasn't ready for him to learn her big secret. Juan would know Bronx

Gangsta territory immediately. Damn, she'd have to find a neutral place he could drop her off one day. She planned to give into his charms, but on her own terms, of course.

She wobbled with a lovesick gaze. Juan didn't think he could move if he wanted to.

"We got to go, man." Tony gestured to the doors. Juan kept his eyes on the gorgeous artist against the wall.

"Will I see you at the library, Nina?"

"Uh." She looked at Claudia. "Yeah." She shrugged.

"Cool. 'Bye."

"Yeah, 'bye." Nina hadn't noticed she was staring at an empty doorway until Claudia bumped her elbow against the wall. "Ow!" Nina scowled.

"Why didn't you let him take you home?"

"You know *why*. The minute he sees where I'm staying he'll freak and know I'm connected to the Bronx Gangstas."

"How the hell he gonna know that just because he takes you home? All streets look the same."

"I'm sure Juan knows about Edgewood just like anyone else. Shit. I got to think of some place he can start dropping me off." Nina grinned. "My damn bus is always late after we finish at the library and Juan has to wait with me anyway."

"Uh-huh." Claudia marched to the doors.

Nina rushed behind her. "Seriously! It's not like I *want* him to take me home."

"Oh yeah. I know." Claudia winked.

"Claudia, he's just like you, a friend."

"Well, in that case, can I be honest here? I hope you don't look at *my* ass that way when I leave a room." She laughed.

"Oh, shut up." Nina chuckled.

CHAPTER FIVE

"So you really think she likes me?" Juan was too busy searching for Tony's expression to pay attention to the road. A man honked for him to make his left turn. Finally, Juan glided down the street.

"Yeah. Didn't I say that like, what? A million times already?" Tony lounged in the passenger's seat fiddling with his CD player.

"Yeah, but how do you know? I mean, I think she likes me. But it's hard to tell because you know how girls trip." Tony nodded. "And I didn't want to come off as a straight sucker and just assume it. I didn't want her to think I liked her and she might be trying to play me. You listening?"

"Yeah." Tony clicked off his CD player. "Nina doesn't seem the kind to play anyone. She's pretty cool and if she likes you, well, you're damn lucky. I can name fifty guys trying to get with her. Me included." He mumbled the last part wondering if Juan heard. "Then she slapped you at the club, remember?"

"So?"

"Well, she wouldn't have slapped you if she didn't like the kiss you laid on her. My man! That was smooth!" Tony howled.

"Hold up, wouldn't she have slapped me if she *didn't* like me?"

"Yeah, but she does like you, so what's the point?"

Tony's reasoning wouldn't have made sense to Juan if he hadn't been so desperate for advice. Tony was a true friend and knowing that, Juan could put up with Tony's unique outlook on life.

Even if it didn't make sense. "Besides, she's fine as hell, too! Ooh, I mean *fiiinnnneeee*! She's so fine she got to know it. She's so fine her shadow looks good!"

Juan laughed. "I can't disagree with that."

Tony nodded. "And Claudia is fine as hell, too. Been trying to get with her for a while…"

"What stopped you?" Juan looked at him.

"My girlfriend would kick my ass, that's what stopped me. But Nina is, man, she's just too damn fine for her own good. Got ass for weeks!"

"Yeah, she *is* fine. So I should strike while the iron is hot, huh?"

"You don't want no other sucker grabbing her up, do you? You need to play on the fact that she meets you at the library every night even when she doesn't have homework."

"Right, right." Juan turned another corner. He honked at a friend from around the way.

"You say you two don't just talk about school and work anymore, right? And you guys hang when you wait on her bus with her. Shit, you guys already going steady." Tony laughed. "You're doing more for Nina than I do for my lady."

"That is the truth, isn't it?" Juan smirked.

"So why you tripping over it?"

"Trying *not* to trip, dog. The thing is, she got me trippin so hard I can't even sleep at night." Juan rubbed his head. "I want to get with her and it's killing me. But Nina ain't having it."

"Did she say that?"

"She keeps saying she needs to focus on personal things. For some reason she doesn't think she can have a boyfriend and still have a life of her own. Does that make any sense?"

"Hell no. And girls never make sense anyway. I don't know

why we go through the trouble." Tony clicked the player to its highest volume.

"Because we're horny bastards and they're fine as hell." Juan sniggered.

❊❊❊

Tajo looked up from his phone conversation when Nina arrived home. Juice and Spider greeted her from the couch, then went back to watching an old black-and-white western. Tajo finally hung up the phone. He adjusted his diamond earring, deep in thought. Nina wondered if he even noticed she'd witnessed the call.

"What's up, baby girl?" Tajo gestured for her to approach his seat. When she did, he kissed her forehead like he used to when she was little. He checked the clock.

"Comin' in here kind of late, Nina."

"Was that about that ripped-off stash?" She pointed at the phone. Spider and Juice stared wide-eyed.

"No." Tajo gazed at her. She knew he was lying but not about to question him about it. "You look funny, by the way." He took her hand.

"I had a little problem, but I'm fine. I'm going to finish my homework, then go to the library." She headed down the hall.

"Hey!" Tajo gestured for her to walk back. "Was there any problems at school today? Did you have detention or something?"

"No, it had to do with this art showcase. I lost track of time."

"Ah." Tajo held her hands. "Is that why you're shaking like you stole something? Come out with it, Nina. What happened?"

"It was no big deal, but..." She looked at Spider and Juice to confirm they were listening. They were. "Claudia and I were jacked after school."

"Say what?" Spider stood.

"Yeah. It was by two guys who probably go to the school. They had a knife and they stole our money. It's no big deal."

Tajo twirled her around to make sure she was visibly all right. "Who were the assholes, huh?" He rubbed his chin.

"I don't know. Some guys in ski masks. Apparently it's been happening for a while. I think Claudia says it was the fifth time. Might not even be the same guys."

"Son of a bitch. Man, I wish I could get my hands on those punks. They'd wish they'd never thought about messing with you."

"It's cool, Tajo." Nina sighed, not in the mood for confrontation. "They didn't hurt us. They took a total of sixty-two dollars. So it's no big deal."

"It is to me. If you can't be safe in a fuckin' school, where can you be safe? From now on I'm putting a gangsta on your tail. I want to make sure you're protected."

"No, Tajo. I don't want someone following me around like I'm some baby. I can take care of myself." She kissed his cheek. "Now, I'll eat after I come back from the library, all right?" She went to her bedroom.

"Funny attitude your baby cousin is developing, man," Juice commented.

"Why do your homework at home, *then* go to the library? What's up with that?"

"I was wondering the same thing." Tajo crossed his arms. "She goes to this library like it's church or something. Anyway,

I don't want her spending time after school and not be protected. Juice?" Juice sat at attention. "I want you to keep an eye on Nina. Be there after school, but don't let her know you're there. Just be there in case something goes down."

"Sure, homes. She won't even know I'm around."

Screams erupted from outside. The impact of people running down the street vibrated the front door.

"What the fuck?" Spider ran to the window. The street was crowded with spectators. A group of young men stood on the front porch.

"Tajo, open the door, man!"

A Bronx Gangsta stormed in with Box bleeding and gasping in his arms. Nina ran to the living room. She stopped in her tracks when she saw the scene. Before she knew it, over fifteen of the gangstas stood in the living room. They scrambled into the kitchen for ice. One person held Box's leg up while another held his head. Tajo held Box's hand against his chest.

"Box! Box, can you hear me?" He smacked Box's face, forcing his eyes open. He had four gunshot wounds in his stomach making the size of a football. Blood seeped onto the carpet. He'd also been shot twice in his left leg.

"Box!" Spider jumped around like a little fly. The blood alone made Nina want to hurl. She stood by the walls, shaking. No one noticed her so far.

"Box! Box, can you hear me?"

"Tajo, we got to get him to the clinic, man." Shorty-Five's forehead was covered in sweat.

"No, I don't think we should move him, man. Nina call nine-one-one! He's bleeding too much to be moved. Shit, how did this fuckin' happen?"

"The park. We were just kicking it at the park!" the guy who'd brought Box in said. "And the next thing we knew a van of NYAs blasted through, *ese*. They had to be aiming at Box because before we got our shit together they shot him. We couldn't do nothing, man! It happened so fast."

"Fuckin' NYA motherfuckers!" Bone kicked the coffee table. He watched Nina jump. Secrecy wasn't an option tonight. "I say we need to go now, Tajo! They took our stash! They got Box. We need to go now!"

"Chill!" Tajo held his hand up. "I say when we go and when we don't. Now I got it under control and you'll know when it's time to make the move."

"Tajo, it's time now!" Shorty-Five yelled. "Look at Box! He's as good as dead! This is our homey!" Everyone silently observed Box, who'd gone into convulsions. Tajo's lap was saturated in blood.

Tajo exhaled. "Haven't you learned anything? *Surprise* is the key! Tonight they will be expecting us, and will be ready for us. Which means we probably won't accomplish shit. Now, we will retaliate when those motherfuckers least expect it and we can kill them one by one. Does anyone have a problem with that?"

They mumbled. Spider stood stiff as a mannequin. Tajo repeated the question until they all agreed.

✠✠✠

Nina had forgotten about her library date with Juan. She didn't remember until she and Tajo got home around midnight from the hospital. Tajo called Box's parents and informed them of his death. He hadn't spoken to Nina on the ride home. She couldn't even guess what he thought.

She was surprised. She thought since violence came with the territory, Tajo would just move on. But he'd taken it as though someone in his own family had been shot. In his eyes, that was exactly what had happened.

"Would you like me to make you something to eat?" Nina asked. Tajo sat at the kitchen table with a glass of warm water.

"No. You'd better go to bed because you got school. I don't want your grades going to shit."

She understood, but couldn't leave him. "Tajo, do you want to talk about it?"

"Nothing to talk about." He slipped off his gold watch. He slid it across the table. "This is part of the life, right?"

"I guess so."

"Nothing more to say, is there? It hurts every time you see your brother smoked, Nina. And every time it's like your heart is being chipped away. I know it's hard for you to see that. I know we're nothing but a bunch of thugs to you. And maybe we are. But at least we know where we all stand. And you don't get that in the best of blood families." He sighed.

"Tajo, if I misjudged you, I'm sorry. But there are a lot of things about this life I don't understand. I probably never will because I'm not built on violence. I can't understand how any-one can justify killing each other just to prove a point."

"Then I see you don't understand. It's okay, Nina. All I ask is that you respect me the way I respect you. And I'm cool with that."

"Okay." She kissed him. "I'm sorry about Box, Tajo." He took her hand as she walked away. Nina slightly fell over his chair, but held her balance.

"I'm leader for a reason, Nina." Despite the events of the evening, Tajo's eyes hadn't lost the severity she'd become accustomed to. "Do you know what that reason is?" He let her go.

"No," she whispered. "But whatever you have to do, I hope you'll come back in one piece."

"I…"

"Please, Tajo. I'd rather not hear your plans and I hope you don't want to know my opinion about all this. We will never see eye to eye."

"So you don't believe in family loyalty, Nina?"

"Why are you talking like you're the godfather?" She chuckled nervously. Even the way he sat in the dim kitchen was similar to Marlon Brando's infamous character. Tajo's stance confirmed Nina's opinion that people in gangs were nothing but dumb kids hoping to find a place to fit because society turned on them. She still found it pathetic and sadistic.

"I asked you a question, Nina. Because I don't need anyone around here who isn't loyal to me. I know you don't understand and don't like what this is, but all this shit is me. Can I trust you? Can I trust that you're loyal to me?"

"Of course. Why do I suddenly feel like I'm on trial here?"

"I'm sorry, baby girl." He kissed her hand. "Have a good night."

"Yeah." She left him to think over his options in private.

❖❖❖

Mrs. Garrett was becoming a bitch. She kept assigning homework as if she expected a brick to fall on her head and kill her the next day. Mrs. Garrett issued over eighty percent of Nina's homework. When she didn't assign any, she made damn sure she made up for it the next day.

Thursday was the coolest day so far. Bronx mornings were

peacefully embracing the fall weather. Nina loved the fall because the holidays were her favorite time of year. They helped Nina escape the conflicts she dealt with. Fifteen minutes into first period, Mrs. Garrett gave a pop quiz on the homework. Nina finished the quiz quickly. Juan finished a few moments after her.

Juan was the kind of person who checked over the same answers a hundred times before finally accepting it was over. Nina worked on instinct. She never checked over her answers. She felt second-guessing yourself was not a smart decision. She was an A student, after all, so the theory worked.

"Five more minutes," Mrs. Garrett called out from her desk.

Juan jiggled in his seat. Nina turned toward him, scribbling a pencil drawing in her notebook.

"What's up, Nina?" He tapped her wrist. "What happened to you yesterday? I waited at the library almost two hours," he whispered, keeping his eyes on Mrs. Garrett at the same time.

"I..." Nina waited to make sure Mrs. Garrett wasn't looking. A girl got up to ask her a question about the quiz. She was so big she blocked Mrs. Garrett's view perfectly.

"I'm sorry. Something came up and I couldn't do anything about it."

"How come you didn't just tell me that when I came in this morning?"

"Because I didn't think I had to," Nina snapped. Juan watched her, puzzled.

"Are you angry with me, Nina?" He saw the big girl going back to her seat. He didn't care if he was caught disturbing the class. This was more important. "Did I do something to you, Nina? Are you mad at me? Is that why you didn't show up?"

Juan reached out to her. "Nina?"

"Juan?" Mrs. Garrett stared at him. Half of the class followed suit. "You want me to rip up your quiz?"

"No, ma'am." He faced the front.

"Then leave Miss Sagastume alone and do your work."

"I'm finished. I was just…"

"Then sit there and be quiet and don't disturb the class." She called for the quizzes.

Juan tried to read Nina's distant expression. It burned him that she wasn't speaking to him. He had to know. He always had to know how she was feeling and *what* she was feeling. She generated so much interest within him since the moment they'd met. He was falling in love with her.

"Will you be there today?" he whispered. A boy in front of him chuckled at Juan's courting attempt.

"I don't know, Juan." Nina copied the work from the board.

"Well, can you tell me something so I won't waste my time waiting?" He rolled his eyes.

"I didn't ask you to wait, did I?"

Juan scoffed. "No, but you knew damn well I was waiting on you. Here's my number." He scribbled it on a corner of notebook paper. "Whenever you can't make it, let me know and…"

"Juan!" Mrs. Garrett jumped from her desk. "One more warning and it's the office. Do I have to move you?"

"No, ma'am," he grumbled. The kids chuckled.

"I want it quiet in here now! Juan, if you speak one more time I will take points off yours and Nina's quiz." Nina flashed Juan a burning frown. "Now, no more talking! That goes for everyone in here."

Juan waited for an explanation from Nina. She didn't even look his way.

✠✠✠

Being robbed hadn't deterred Nina from staying after school. She constantly dreamt of her chances in the showcase. She wouldn't let two petty thieves ruin it.

"How's it going, girlfriend?" Claudia waved from Jones's doorway.

"Fine." Nina appreciated Claudia's support toward her art, but today she had hoped to be alone.

Claudia sensed Nina's need for solitude. She agreed to wait elsewhere until Nina finished. Then Claudia suddenly bolted over into the doorway. Juan gaped at Nina from the hallway, wondering whether or not he should enter the room. Once Claudia saw him, he had no choice.

"Nina, your friend's out here." Claudia teasingly twirled her hair.

"Who?" She rushed toward the door. Juan walked inside. He kept his distance. He'd let Nina make the first move. "Juan. What are you doing in here?"

"Uh..." He looked around the room. "Just chilling, you know? I was here after school again and I figured you'd be, too. I saw Claudia's car in the parking lot."

Claudia winked. "See you, Nina. I'll be outside waiting."

"No, Claude!" Nina grabbed her. Juan chuckled at Nina's blatancy. "You don't have to go." She winked.

"Oh, you got this, girlfriend." Claudia laughed.

"Claude! Claude!" The door nearly slapped Nina in the face. She stood there for a few seconds, then headed over to "Waterfall." Juan had the picture neatly clasped in his hand by the time she got to the table.

"Well." He looked at her. "No wonder they call you the next Picasso."

"Jesus, is everyone saying that now? It's bad enough Mr. Jones says it."

"You should be proud." Juan rubbed against her. She enjoyed the closeness but didn't acknowledge the flirtation.

He slipped up onto the top of the table to watch her work. The way she dipped her delicate fingers in the paint aroused him spiritually. Before he knew it, an entire world opened up. "How did you make these streaks up here?" Juan pointed to the grayish black lines in the corner of the painting.

Nina dipped two fingers in two different paints and demonstrated.

"Why don't you use brushes?"

"Not comfortable with them. I like using my hands. I can get into it better, touch it, move around. I feel like I'm truly creating something as long as I can feel it. You can't feel with a brush."

"I see." Juan's eyes sparkled. He leaned beside her. His chin touched her shoulder. His breath caressed her ear. "I agree with that. Sometimes touching is the only way." He rubbed his hand up and down Nina's back until her eyes automatically closed. She moved her body with his. Juan became hypnotized by Nina's sensuous mouth.

"Juan?" She moved her body against his so slowly it should have been illegal.

"Yeah?" He brought his mouth closer to hers. He gripped her neck for leverage.

"If you don't get your hands off of me..." She pushed him away. "Nice try."

"Hey, you can't blame a guy for trying." He guffawed. "The kiss at the club, didn't you enjoy it?

"No. I washed my mouth out eight hours after that."

He played with his backpack straps. "Yeah, right. I bet you

never knew it could feel like that, Nina. I bet you've never had a boyfriend. Tell me I'm wrong." He took her hand.

She snatched away from him. "You're wrong."

"If you have, they didn't kiss you like I did." He bent toward her again. "Guess what? No man ever will." He pulled her close. He kissed her before she had a chance to object. His mouth forcefully examined the newfound territory. Juan's tongue searched hers until their mouths managed on their own.

"Stop." She pulled away. She held "Waterfall" next to her chest. She wiped her mouth. "I thought you were going to respect my wishes and not push me. Every time I turn around you're in my face, Juan. What's it going to take to get through to you?"

"Sue me, Nina. I like you, all right? And I have a feeling you feel the same way. But for some reason you think I would jeopardize your future. I would never do that. I care about you, Nina. It may be hard to see, but I do. I saw something in you that I never saw before. The first day we met, it was like, shit, I can't even explain it. You're all I think about. I like being with you and I like the way you make me feel."

She looked away. "I've got work to do. I'm not supposed to be in here alone with a boy. Mr. Jones trusts me, Juan."

"Okay, can you just honestly answer this? Do you like me? Is that true?" He desperately anticipated the answer. She nodded. "I like you, too, Nina. So why can't we just hook up and let things go from there?"

"Because I know guys like you, Juan." She sighed. "You only want one thing. Once you get it, you're gone."

He snickered, moving even closer to her. "Now, I don't know who you've dealt with, but I am not like that, all right?"

She shrugged. "Did I offend you?"

"Look at me, Nina." She did. "I am not a dog and I am not a

player. As long as you're honest with me I will be honest with you. There are a lot of girls who want to get with me. But I could give a shit about them because all I want is to get with you. Didn't the kiss at the club prove that? You think I do that with every girl I meet?"

"Maybe." She shrugged. "How do I know you don't?"

"You like me, Nina. Don't try to disguise it."

"I..."

"Tell me I'm lying." She looked off. "You can't, can you? Come on, Nina, give me a chance." He scooted toward her. "You gonna leave me hanging like this? My heart exposed? I'm lying here, bleeding and vulnerable." He grinned. "I'm a slave to your kingdom. It's your world." He rested his head on her shoulder. "Look at this face." He made his best puppy dog expression.

"Begging doesn't seem your speed, Juan." She chuckled.

"Then go out with me and I won't have to beg."

She laughed. "Is that your best tactic?"

"Well, I could follow you home and kidnap you. But I think this one is a little better than that, don't you?"

"I really like you, Juan." She patted his cheek. He closed his eyes, memorizing her forbidden touch. "But I don't think going out is such a good idea."

"Okay, then what *is* it?" He moaned. "I look good! So it can't be that."

"Yeah, you look good." She nodded.

"Then what is it?"

"It's just me. I'm not ready for a boyfriend right now. I got too much to worry about."

He dropped his head. He was too tired to continue friendly persuasion. "Okay. You done here?"

Nina was surprised he'd given up so quickly. "Yeah."

"Well." Thwarted, Juan strapped on his backpack. "I'll walk you outside."

❊❊❊

"I don't believe this!" A few minutes later, Nina stared at the empty school parking lot.

"Hold up." Juan rubbed his face. "Where's Claudia?"

"That's what *I'd* like to know! She did this on purpose so I'd have to ride with you. I cannot believe this!"

"Remind me to thank her tomorrow." Juan laughed.

Nina finally took Juan up on his offer to take her home. She definitely wouldn't direct him to Tajo's. She knew that whenever a strange vehicle entered Edgewood, the residents circled like bees over flowers. She didn't know what her relationship with Juan had become but she wasn't going to let her cousin's way of life dictate the outcome.

She liked Juan's taste in music. He liked slow jams and old-school R&B the same as she did. They talked a while, then he turned the radio to one of Nina's favorite stations. She bobbed her head to the music until she noticed Juan watching again.

"If I didn't know you, I'd assume you were a creep by the way you're always staring at me." She dug in her purse.

"Nina, you're a good-looking woman, all right? What guy wouldn't stare at you? Do you know you're the finest girl in the school?"

She chuckled. "Don't tell Claude that or she'd flip."

"All kidding aside. What was the real reason you didn't show up at the library last night?"

Nina had no idea why she wanted to open up to him. She knew she could tell him anything and he'd understand. He was perfect to talk to about Box. She knew Juan wouldn't be judgmental. And he liked her a lot, which meant he'd give her his most thought-out opinion. Besides all that, she just enjoyed talking to him.

"A friend of my cousin's got killed last night."

Juan jerked the steering wheel, causing his tires to squeal. "Nina, I'm sorry."

"He was in the park with his friends and some guys gunned him down. He nearly died right there in my cousin's living room. Juan, I couldn't sleep. All I thought about was how he looked with that blood running out of him. I will never understand gang violence." She bit her lips. "Shit." She'd caught the slip.

"*Gang* violence?" Juan shook his head in agreement. "So the guy was in a set, huh?"

"It's so sad that all these people think to turn to violence before anything else. It's like they want to give up before they start."

"This may seem rather cold, but I can't feel sorry for the guy," Juan declared. Nina looked up. "You have people who die because they can't help it. Take my dad, for instance. He died because of health reasons. Then you got kids who are healthy and they want to kill each other. Am I supposed to feel bad for a guy who's been shot when he put himself in that position?"

"*Society* put him in that position, Juan." Nina gawked at him.

"Oh please, Nina, spare me!" He hit the steering wheel. "Baby, I thought you were more intelligent than to believe that bullshit."

"Juan, it's not bullshit. You can't always blame the gang life on the members. Put the blame where it belongs. When society closes the door on these kids, where can they go? What can they do?"

"I can't believe you were just jacked yesterday and now you talk as if you're the poster girl for criminal kids. I'm not buying the society argument, Nina. And neither should you."

"I am not saying it's right, Juan. All I am saying is that, look, I know it's hard not to judge, but you are lucky compared to those kind of people. I am, too. We have the strength up here." She pointed to her head. "They have what they know on the streets."

"Yeah, selling drugs and killing people. That's worse than what society's *supposedly* doing to them, isn't it? Society doesn't close doors on people just because they're Latino, black or Asian, Nina."

She laughed. "Juan, that's ridiculous! Of course society does! Why do you think we're in the predicament we're all in? Because we want to be? Juan, you're talking more and more like a, dare I say it?" She turned away.

"Go on and say it."

"A *Republican* politician."

He smiled. "You're half-right. But I'm a Democrat. But I do want to be a politician, by the way."

"You don't talk like a Democrat." She exhaled.

"Well, I am." He sounded offended but quickly got over it. "All I am saying is if our race held us back, how come you have people before us who made it? These are excuses minorities are using and I won't put myself in that category."

"*Put* yourself? Juan, when people look at you that's what they see. You think those white folks you go up against in the candidacy are going to only see your *views*? Please. Some may look past what you are once they get to know you, but they'll always see you as a little Latino guy trying to live a big dream." He scowled. "No matter what you think about society, you're never going to truly be included."

"Then what's *your* opinion on gang violence, Nina? Since you know so much."

"I never said I knew so much. I'm just saying that if you believe race doesn't hold you back at some point, you are wrong. We wouldn't need affirmative action or scholarships for minority students if that were true. Even with status, race is always a factor. A poor white guy, a bum on the streets, is accepted before a rich Latino or a famous black man. Why don't you think hard about that when you're working on your campaign?" She sighed. He didn't say another word.

She stopped him at a corner store and gathered her books. He didn't look at her, he just pouted like a five-year-old whose toy had been given away to charity.

"Juan, look at me." Nina stepped out of the car. She walked to the driver's side to face him. His brown eyes blinked with urgency. "There are real problems in the world, Juan. You can't say there aren't."

"I didn't say that! I said that just because you have problems it doesn't make them eligible excuses to fuck up your life. Nina," he turned toward her, "there are thousands of people who die from gang violence." She impatiently exhaled. "No, listen to me. And think about innocent people who are caught up in the situation. Think about those little kids in the crossfire when some gang decides to do a drive-by. That's what I'm thinking of. That's what I'm *always* thinking of. I want to make things better."

"I don't think we're going to see eye to eye on this, Juan. I understand what you're saying and I agree to a point. But I still think there's only so much some people can do. That's how the world is."

"I think people should push themselves." He shrugged. "And I still think being in a gang and doing crime is a cop-out."

"Guess so." Nina sighed.

Juan pointed to a little boy riding his bike down the street. "Just like that kid. He seems like he's doing all right. He may be one to make it far."

"Why? Because he doesn't *appear* to be in a set? Juan, do you always judge people on first glance? That's a very shallow way to live."

"I don't know. I judged *you* on first glance, Nina. And so far my assumptions have turned out to be right. I'll see you, okay?" He drove off.

Nina had a couple blocks to walk before reaching Edgewood. She used the time to think over the argument she'd had with Juan. He'd taken it so personally. She smiled at some of the people walking her way. She found herself looking at them through Juan's eyes. She evaluated her thoughts on what they'd discussed. Juan talked as if he knew the gang life firsthand. Did he?

Nina hadn't truly felt his point until she reached Edgewood. The tattered buildings, graffiti-stained walls, liquor stores, wobbly signs, and the built-up trash on the streets sickened her. Where were the libraries? Where were the community centers? For every pool hall and bar, Nina couldn't see one place for kids to escape to. Her argument had been against society, but now she was puzzled.

Was it society's fault entirely? Couldn't the people of the community clean up their own neighborhoods? Couldn't they demand child-friendly businesses and ditch the additions of liquor stores, drug-dealing, corner stores and gun shops? Reassessing herself made her stomach hurt.

Was Juan right? Had everyone given up? Deep down wasn't everyone born with a brain and the opportunity of an education? 'Course they were. Juan had been right! It *was* what you chose to do and how you chose to do it.

She passed trashy-dressed high school girls who draped every car that turned the block. She could have been like them. She'd spent her life using her mind instead of her body. She had goals and desires. No one had that anymore, at least not in Edgewood.

She'd defended these people to Juan. The truth was she'd been defending her own cousin. Maybe if Tajo hadn't been a banger she wouldn't have thought twice.

Maybe if she wasn't standing on his side, but on the side of someone he'd killed, perhaps on the side of the relatives of the Bronx Gangstas' victims, she'd feel like Juan. She knew the gangs were to blame, but she just couldn't find it in her heart to crucify the mice inside the trap.

❖❖❖

That evening Tajo had a gang-related errand to run. Nina wondered if it had anything to do with the missing stash. She didn't plan on seeing him any more that night. Studying at home was peaceful. She wasn't in the mood to catch the bus to the library and she needed time away from Juan. She gathered by the living room window to take a break from her grueling homework.

The streets were full of kids and teenagers. Every now and then, a Bronx Gangsta came by. Tajo had instructed her not to open the door for anyone else. Time passed hastily as she stared out the window. Before she knew it, 7:30 had arrived. She was rescued from facing homework alone. Claudia called to invite her to a hot little eatery the girls went to. Nina eagerly agreed to meet them. A little time with her girlfriends would be exactly what she needed.

CHAPTER SIX

The eatery was the coolest joint this side of town. Sitting across from the mall, it attracted people from miles around any day of the week. People had the choice of dining in or outside. Nina found her friends joking around at one of the outside tables. Claudia was too busy laughing and spitting Coke to notice Nina had arrived.

"What's up?" Nina squeezed beside her friends.

"What's up, homes?" Claudia held up her arm for a high-five.

"I am so pissed at you, Claudia."

"What did I do?" She grinned.

"You know what you did. Pretty clever that you left me at school this evening and I had to ride with Juan." A waiter slunk over. Nina ordered a burger, then waited for Claudia's explanation.

"Did I?" Claudia chuckled. "Sorry, girlfriend. I must have forgotten." Claudia waited until the waiter served Nina's order before she continued. "Hey, I was trying to help you out. As slow as you're moving, you'll be eighty before he asks you out."

"I don't need your help with getting a boyfriend."

"Looks like you needed help to me."

"All right, calm down, you guys." Lisa chuckled. "Nina, Claudia wanted to help because she didn't want you to be lonely. I'd appreciate it if someone as fine as Juan wanted to get with me."

"Who wouldn't?" Rosa agreed. "But this is Nina, the queen of uptight."

"Hey, I can be just as spontaneous as all of you and I resent you guys saying I can't." Nina snatched her burger from the waiter. He mumbled, then went on his way. Rosa left to get another drink. Lisa and Claudia contemplated Nina's outburst.

"Only *you* could make liking someone complicated, Nina. I know you like him. We *all* know it," Claudia grinned. Lisa nodded in agreement. "What is your fuckin' problem?"

"Claude, just be my friend on *my* terms, all right? I don't need you fixing me up with guys. I can do that on my own."

"Fine. I was just trying to help. Since it happened, what did you talk about?"

"Yeah," Lisa grinned. "What?"

A sly smile swept Nina's face. "He asked me to go out with him again and I said no."

"But…," Claudia gasped.

"I don't want to hear it, Claude." Claudia sighed. "Just respect my decision."

"To be an old maid? Shit, if that's what you want to be, fine. But I don't have to like it." Claudia declared. Rosa ran to the table with a forty-ounce of 7UP spilling over her cup. She laughed so hard she doused Lisa's arm.

Lisa wiped the mess from her arm. "What's wrong with you?"

"Guess who I saw in the line, Nina? Juan Alonso," Rosa grinned impishly.

"Shit." Nina touched her forehead. Once again she had an instant fever.

"How is it that he always ends up where I am?"

"Maybe it's fate." Claudia winked. She motioned behind Nina's chair. Juan and his friends came around the corner with their food. "Too late to wonder why, Nina."

"Shit." Nina motioned to Rosa, who sat across from her. "Rosa, switch seats with me." Nina pulled Rosa up by her flabby arms.

"What? Why?"

"Just do it! I need to see and I don't want Juan looking at my butt."

"But you wouldn't mind him staring in your face while you gulp down burgers and Tater Tots?" Claudia asked.

"Shit!" Nina shrieked. They laughed at her outrageous behavior. Nina stopped Rosa before she switched seats. "Never mind, Rosa. I'll stay in this seat." Mumbling, Rosa reclaimed her original chair. "Okay, how do I look?" Nina asked as she tugged her hair.

"Why do you care? I thought you didn't like him." Claudia teased. Nina returned the gesture.

Juan, Tony, Carlos, and Dell purposely picked the closest table beside the girls. Doing his best to seem unconcerned, Juan sat down with his friends.

"What are they doing? Are they sitting down yet?" Nina whispered.

"Yeah." Lisa slurped her soda. "Damn, Juan looks good in that shirt."

"What's he wearing?" Nina blurted out.

"Clothing. Why are you tripping now, Miss I Don't Need A Man?"

"Cut her some slack, Claudia." Rosa gulped a handful of fries. "You'd be acting the same way if it was someone you liked."

"What is he doing?" Nina impatiently tapped the table.

"He's looking right at you." Rosa chuckled.

"Shit." It looked like Nina was attempting to eat though her hands which shook violently. She could circle the globe a million times before figuring out why Juan made her so edgy. "Is he still looking?"

"Uh, no." Lisa leaned back, squinting. "Wait, he's looking again."

"Oh shit." Nina exhaled.

"Hey, ladies." Tony waved. "Everything all right tonight?"

"Fine." Lisa winked. Tony looked at Juan, chuckling.

"Hey, Nina." Juan spoke. His voice hit her like a sword through the heart. Unsuspecting and fierce.

"Uh, hi." She didn't turn around. She waved her hand over her shoulder. He shook his head in amusement. He continued talking with his friends.

"Girl, you are pitiful." Rosa sighed. "Do we have to catch *and* gut this fish for you? Are you not going to stand up and do something for yourself?"

"What's going on now?" Nina asked.

"They're talking and giggling. And looking at you," Claudia said.

"Fuck. Laughing *or* giggling, did you say?" Nina slightly turned in the chair, hoping to catch some of the conversation.

"I said, giggling." Claudia pointed to the boys. "Juan's still looking at you. He's smiling. Now he's whispering something into Dell's ear. Now Dell's looking at you."

"Shit, I hate it when boys do this. Do they know how embarrassing this is?"

Rosa shrugged. "We do the same thing to them."

"But they don't know that," Nina said. The girls guffawed. The guys looked to see what was going on.

"She must have said something about me." Juan took a tiny bite of his foot-long. He shook the ice in his Coke. "They're laughing."

"Girls always do this shit." Carlos peeled a fry from his hot dog platter.

"Wonder if they know how much that burns us?"

"You were right, Juan. Nina *is* fine." Dell whistled.

Nina wiggled in her seat. "Who was that that whistled? Was that Juan?" she whispered.

"No, it was Dell. Look, I'm getting sick of this. You are too old to act like some middle school kid." Claudia forced Nina's arm from her face. "Stop hiding and talk to him."

"Yeah." Rosa gestured toward the table.

"Hold up. She may not have to." Lisa watched Juan scribble something on a piece of paper. He passed it to Tony. A few seconds later, a note popped over Nina's shoulder. She turned around. She needed to see the look on Juan's face at that moment. The guys stood at the table, sliding their chairs in place.

"See you all at school, ladies." Juan waved. Nina gaped at the note. The guys left.

"You see how he tried to be all cool and shit?" Rosa scoffed. "See how he didn't acknowledge Nina personally? Guys can never put their shit on the line first."

"What the fuck difference does it make, Rosa? Nina, open the letter." Claudia moved her chair closer to her.

"Hey, I didn't say I was going to read it to y'all." Nina grinned.

"Look, you owe us, now read," Claudia ordered. Nina unfolded the letter and proudly began. When she'd finished the heart-drawn love letter, her friends were dumbfounded. Nina died for more.

"Holy shit." Lisa gasped. "He is so damn romantic! What other guy would be able to come up with a poem like that? And the way he described your hair and your smile, Nina you better get with him *now*. Because if you don't, I sure as hell will try."

"Shit, me, too." Rosa sipped her drink.

Nina stuffed the note in her purse. "No one's ever said such beautiful things to me before. Guys don't do that anymore. Wonder why he's so romantic?"

"He's always been considerate and caring. He's a true gentleman. We didn't finish the end, did we?" Lisa asked. She pulled the note from Nina's purse. "Cool, he's invited you to his sister's birthday party next Friday. He says we can come, too."

"I'm not going to go." She hoped her friends would let her get away with the decision. So much for wishful thinking. "Okay, I *may* go. But I don't think you guys should."

"Hey, he invited us, too!" Rosa plopped her drink on the table.

"Yeah, Nina. It will be off the hook if we come. You need our support." Claudia wrapped her arm around Nina's shoulder. "What would you do all alone with Juan without us to give you pointers, hmmm?"

"Yeah," Rosa and Lisa added.

Nina couldn't very well disagree.

❦❦❦

The next evening Box was laid to rest. Nina hadn't planned on going to the funeral but Tajo claimed he would never need her as much as he did now. Naturally, Nina couldn't refuse. She always daydreamed at funerals. She remembered the first funeral she'd attended. Till this day, that first funeral stuck in her mind. Back then she'd been incapable of understanding death. Now she lived with it on a daily basis.

She strolled around the funeral grounds, dodging loose conversations from people she'd just met. The Bronx Gangstas looked terrific in their matching black suits. They wore their bandannas tucked in the side of their pants. They stood silently to give respect the way a true family would. Box's parents hadn't minded the BGs wearing gang colors. Nina wasn't sure how they could accept their son's gang so openly, but it wasn't her place to question why.

"Hi," a guy said.

"Hi." She held her hand up to shield the sun.

He adjusted his shades. "You're Nina, right? Tajo's little cousin? He said you're quite the artist."

"Yes. Who are you?"

"Chino." He kissed her hand. "I was watching you over there. You look dazed." He was gorgeous. His seductive brown eyes ignited his smile. He had thick black hair that twirled together in waves. His full lips stood in a deeply mysterious pose.

"*Dazed*? How come I look dazed to you?" Nina crossed her arms, careful not to wrinkle her black outfit.

He shrugged. "I don't know. You looked as though you were thinking about something far off."

Chino intrigued Nina. He had a style to admire. He was suave and confident. He seemed like the kind of man that followed his own rules and ignored everything else, no matter the consequences. Even his voice was a sign of vigor.

"I was thinking about the first funeral I'd been to." She leaned against the table.

Chino leaned with her. "All I remember was all the black

people had on. I can't remember what anyone said or did, but I can remember what they had on. The blackness stuck in my mind." She shrugged.

"That's probably because you're an artist and colors are receptive to you."

"Receptive?" Nina laughed. "Hold up, where did you put the *real* Bronx G that this outfit belongs to?" She pulled on his suit.

"Hey, just because I'm a G doesn't mean I can't speak or know about art. I'm cultural, too, Nina." He flashed his pearly whites. "I asked Tajo about you when you were at the hospital the other night."

"Yeah, I remember seeing you there." She sipped ginger ale.

"I hope you can be objective when forming an opinion, Nina." She watched him. "We're just like other people."

"I doubt that. Now, if you'll excuse me I..."

"Hold on." He blocked her. "I meant to say, don't condemn all of us for the actions of some. We really do believe this is a family. We loved Box. We were about to truly make him one of us when this happened."

"Do you know why the NYAs shot Box?"

"Do they need a reason?" He looked away.

"I think so. I mean, he wasn't even in the Gangstas yet. Why would they target him?"

"They just did." He took a deep breath. Nina realized he was annoyed.

"I'll see you, okay, Chino?"

"I meant what I said, Nina. We are all different. Don't judge a G by his cover." He slipped his shades back on. When Nina looked back around, Chino had taken his place against the tree beside his brothers.

✦✦✦

After the funeral, the Bronx Gangstas threw a party in Box's honor. Tajo rented an upscale hotel ballroom. The hotel employees weren't thrilled to host gang members, but as long as they had money they were treated like royalty. Nina stayed to herself for most of the time. She toured the hotel grounds while the others celebrated. Some hotel guests mistook her for a hotel employee because of her outfit. She enjoyed the unique attention.

She returned to the ballroom. Tajo sat alone at a huge table in the back of the room behind a fancy cake. He nonchalantly looked at the guests. Nina figured he kept an eye on things in case the New York Assassins got wind of the party and decided to pay a visit. She caught Chino staring as she joined Tajo. She looked off, but Chino didn't budge an inch.

"How you doing?" She sat beside Tajo.

"Fine," he whispered. "I appreciate you being there for the BGs and all, Nina. I know it wasn't easy. I'm proud that you're making an effort. It means a lot to me."

"I'm sorry about Box, Tajo. This is all so wonderful. It was great for you to do this for Box and his family."

"I should have done more. But I will." His eyes darkened. Nina knew he spoke of retaliation. She was glad he didn't go into details. "You enjoying yourself?" He leaned back in the chair.

"Who wouldn't love a classy hotel with people waiting on us hand and foot?" She smiled at a waiter with a tray of champagne. "A beautiful ballroom. It's magical. I bet the prom won't be as great as this."

"Prom." He chuckled. "Ain't heard that word in a while."

"I think I'll walk around some more."

"Hold up, Nina." He sipped champagne. "What do you think of my boy Chino?"

She grinned. "Where did that come from?"

"Just wondering. What's up? He digs you and I was wondering if you felt the same way." He tapped her chin.

"He's nice, I guess. I don't know him that well. I only spoke to him at the funeral. What did he say about me?"

"He says he thinks you're fine and very pretty. Wanted me to see if I could hook you two up." He smirked.

"Oh, *no*." Nina held up her hand. "No, Tajo."

He laughed. "Why not? You don't have a man."

"He doesn't need to know that."

"Come on, cuz. What's wrong with my man Chino? Can't be tripping on the fact that he's a G. You get a G and you got protection." Nina rolled her eyes. "Nina, he got mad bank, baby girl. He can buy you what you want. He drives this fat-ass car. He's twenty-two and already he's set to inherit his father's business."

"I don't care, Tajo. I am not interested in Chino, all right?" She left the room.

Tajo waved Chino toward the table. "What's up, Chino? Sit down."

Chino sipped champagne. "What's up with your cousin? What did she say?"

"You just got to let her get to know you a little better, man. She'll come around."

He licked his lips. "You think so?"

"Yeah. But don't sweat her too much, man. Don't forget, she's only sixteen. Just, you know, chill and let her get to know you."

"Okay." Chino thought over the option. "I think it would be in your best interest if Nina gets to know me better, too, Tajo. This could help us all. You don't have a problem with me getting with Nina, do you?"

"Shit, my cousin and one of my boys *together*? Hell yeah, I'd want it to happen. But it's not fully my choice." Tajo grinned.

"You can put in a good word for me, can't you?"

"Yeah." Tajo grinned. He loved to be reminded of his power.

"And no one goes against your word, do they?" Chino smirked.

Tajo sipped his drink. "Not if they know what's good for them."

✦✦✦

A week later the Bronx Gs sat in a circle in Tajo's living room while he went over the nature of their attack.

"I want Juice and Shorty-Five in the back of the van, aimed and ready. Bone and Chino," Chino twirled the joint behind his ear, "You're back up. If Juice and Shorty-Five miss getting one of those motherfuckers, it's your turn."

"We won't miss, Tajo." Shorty-Five chuckled. "Do I ever miss?"

"The party's going to be at Rico's aunt's house tomorrow night."

"You sure about that, Tajo?" Bone cracked his knuckles.

"Well, if Jay got his info wrong, then we're killing his ass for being stupid." They grinned. "On the real, it's his little sister's birthday party. Now we let them party and get as high as they want to get." Tajo laughed. "Then around ten or eleven, we blast through there."

"And get everyone. We don't give a fuck!" Shorty-Five howled. The others followed suit.

"That's right. No matter who's in the way. Just don't stop shooting until you get all them motherfuckers." Tajo rubbed his hands.

"So what if they're ready for us?" Chino popped bubble gum.

"How the fuck they gon' be ready?" Bone asked him. "Unless someone in here opened their big mouth, they shouldn't know shit."

"I'm just saying that the NYAs aren't fools. You know when they have a party going on they'll be watching the streets to make sure no shit goes down. Now, is this going to be a drive-by or a street blazing?"

"You scared, Chino?" Juice teased.

"Hell no! I just want to know before we go out there. I don't want to think I'm sneaking up on these fools then they blast us right back. What's the point in that?"

Shorty-Five winked. "They don't know shit. They'll be so high and drunk by the time we roll through there, it won't be nothing they can do." Nina walked in. She watched the gangstas one by one.

"What's up, cuz?" Tajo gestured her toward the table. Chino smiled at the sight of her again. "How was the community center thing?"

Fine." She looked around. "You guys look so guilty."

"What, *us*?" Shorty-Five pointed to his chest.

"Yes. What's going on?"

"Is it me or am I mistaken?" Bone stood. "I don't remember ever jumping you in, Nina." She gawked at him.

"Chill, Bone." Tajo sucked his lip. "Nina, it's all right. We were just talking about business."

"Tajo, is this business that can get someone killed?"

The others looked away.

Tajo kept his cocky grin. "Business is business. Nina, some things you don't need to know. Why don't you go do your homework or something?"

"I'm not some little dumb kid you can just dismiss, Tajo." She went into the kitchen. She got a glass of milk, then heated up the dinner she hadn't finished. Chino gazed at her from the doorway. He got a soda from the refrigerator. Nina hadn't noticed him until he sat beside her.

"Hey." He smirked. "You mad? Why you tripping?"

"I'm tripping because this isn't right, Chino. In subtle hints, I try to persuade Tajo to go against his violent ways. I knew you guys were planning something." Chino sipped his soda and listened. "It has to do with that stash, doesn't it?"

"Like Bone said, Nina, we haven't jumped you in. Now you're putting your nose where it doesn't belong. You could get hurt that way."

"Are you threatening me?"

"No. I'm just saying that people who we're against may target you. You need to start showing some loyalty for your cousin." He lightly touched her wrist. "And your family. Like me, for instance."

She jerked away. "Don't touch me, Chino."

"And why not? You think you're too good or something? You think you're better than me? Well, you're not." He stared at her chest. "I want to go out with you."

She finished her milk. "No chance." She stood. Chino pulled her against him.

"You'll change your mind, won't you?" He rubbed the back of her legs. She jerked away.

"I thought you were the one with sense and manners. Guess I was wrong."

"Don't let your nosy state get you into trouble, Nina. But if you ever need a helping hand, look to me." He rocked back and forth. "I'll be there to help you out of a jam." Someone called him from the living room. Nina followed. She listened to another one of the gangstas' whispery conversations. When they left, she started back on Tajo.

"Tajo!" She rushed behind him in the hall. "What do you plan to do?"

"Nothing." He changed his shirt when he got to his bedroom. "I'm going out.

Don't answer the door and don't eat up all the donuts."

"Tajo, I'm serious! You guys were planning a drive-by, weren't you?" Tajo listened, then exhaled impatiently. "Can't you let this go? It's not worth it!"

"You listen to me!" He grabbed her. "I know what to do! I know my place here! Don't you ever tell me what to do!"

"All right, you're hurting me, Tajo!" She pulled away. He embraced her.

"I'm sorry, Nina. I just don't like what I'm seeing here."

"What *are* you seeing?" She rubbed her arms.

"That you don't think I know what I'm doing."

"Tajo, please don't do this. Can't you for once let it go? Just move on."

"Nope." He walked past her and out the front door.

❈❈❈

Florence spent Friday morning fixing up her sister Mercedes's home for Cynthia's party. Mercedes was a retired interior decorator who spurted creative ideas just by mention of a party. Cynthia wanted a formal, traditional Mexican fiesta with the boys in white shirts and black pants and the girls in frilly light-colored dresses. Florence felt nothing could go wrong. They'd even prepared for unexpected guests.

By 3:00 p.m., colorful piñatas hung in the back of the house for the smaller children. The den had been turned into a lounge for relaxing. Mercedes walked in the living room an hour later, scratching off the guest list. A few people wouldn't be able to show up, but they would hardly be missed, considering the "sure-things."

She tended to dress up for a party hours ahead, so Florence wasn't shocked when her older sister walked out in a fancy blue top, crisp black slacks, and her church heels.

Florence grinned at her sister's promptness.

"How do I look, Flo?" Mercedes kept her hair long, unlike Florence, who'd been cutting hers since college. Mercedes's locks whooshed down her back like grayish-black water, hitting the end of her wide buttocks.

"Mercedes, you know you're going to be out of those heels before the guests come. Why don't you just admit that you're in your early sixties?"

"Just because I'm sixty-two doesn't mean I can't dress like I'm forty-two."

Flo grabbed a pink balloon. "I want everything to go well for my baby's party tonight. But I keep getting this feeling that something's going to go wrong. I don't know." She blew up the balloon half way, then continued talking. "I've been feeling antsy lately."

"How's work and all that?" Mercedes twirled in front of the mirror, examining her hair.

"All right. Money is getting better. You know it set us back when I got the house fixed up after that leak." Mercedes nodded. "Juan wants to get a job."

"I was wondering when he was going to start."

"No, I don't want him to have a job." Florence tied the end of a balloon.

"He needs to work on his education if he plans on being a politician."

"Unless you're expecting a million dollars to drop in your living room, Flo, he's going to have to work sometime to hold him over. He can't start out with nothing and end up rich."

"I don't want him working *now*." She sighed.

"Check the economy, Flo. He's doesn't necessarily have a choice."

"Maybe, but Rico's helping out and..." Florence noticed Mercedes's scowl. She didn't want to get into the same old argument. She knew mentioning Rico's name in Mercedes's house would cause the conversation to escalate.

"I don't want that thug in my house, Flo."

"Mercedes, he's your nephew."

"I know who he is," she snapped. "Which makes it sicker to think of him and what he's doing. Florence, how can you go along with this? He's a murderer. Do you know what he does?"

"Mercedes, please," Florence mumbled in Spanish. "He's my son."

"He can be your son. But you don't have to tolerate every-thing he does and accept it. If he was my son, I'd..."

"I know, I know." Florence stood. "You'd kick him out of the house! Would have years ago. Well, I'm not like you, Mercedes. I can't just turn my back on my son."

"It's not turning your back and you know it, Flo. You just keep saying that to make yourself feel better for allowing him to do what he does."

"Don't you think it kills me to know what he does?"

"Then do something about it, damn it! Kick him out of your house and don't tell me you can't! And I don't want to hear that lame shit about him helping with the bills either. Because it seems to me that he spends the money he steals on those gang-bangers and himself. I've yet to see one dime flow your way."

Florence exhaled. "Mercedes, he loves us. He loves *you*." Mercedes watched doubtfully. "I know he doesn't always show his love, but he loves all of us. He won't do anything bad tonight."

"I'll have to watch everything."

"He won't take anything." Florence sighed again.

"Yeah, but what about those thugs? I don't want them huddling around in a group, plotting all night. And I want them dressed like the other people and no bandannas and tattoos showing or whatever else they've got."

"Rico knows the ground rules and he'll keep his friends in line. If Cynthia doesn't have a problem with it, you shouldn't, either. Lighten up." Florence waltzed toward her. She wrapped her arms around Mercedes's waist. "Just don't start anything with him tonight."

"Start anything? Flo, I don't even want to *look* at him." She left the room.

✠✠✠

The front door opened. Rico peeked inside. "Mamá?" He walked around the living room, doing his best not to touch anything. He always stayed on his toes around his aunt. Mercedes's wrath reduced his gangsta appeal to that of a frightened kitten. She was one tough lady. "I came to see if you needed some help setting up."

"Wow. Are you really my son?" She chuckled.

"Come on, Mamá." He took a deep breath. He twirled a skullcap in his hands. "What I do has nothing to do with you. I told you that. Damn, you don't ever give me the benefit of the doubt."

She glared at him. "You know what I want from you, Rico."

"No way. NYA is my blood. It's from our family, Mamá. You know it goes back generations. I can't just leave the set. I'm the leader. What do you expect me to do?"

"What's right!" She pounded the coffee table. "For yourself and for the rest of us. Rico, do you know I shake for an hour before I go to sleep every night? I listen to every damn thing. My ears are trained like a dog. I'm always worried that some rival gangbanger is going to come up and shoot you, Cynthia, or the boys."

"That won't happen."

"You don't know that! You're still a kid in mind, Rico. You need to get an education and stop worrying about how tough and mean you can be on the streets. You still want to be a gangsta when you're forty years old? You want to be like those old gangbangers in jail, out of jail, in jail, out of jail?"

"If that's what it takes."

"You're thirty, Rico. Why don't you live up to your name, son? Be a noble leader. Make a difference. Turn your life around before you get sucked in any deeper."

"Still don't understand that this is my world, Mamá. Shit it ain't how it used to be around here." He circled the couch. "I can't just go out there, snap my fingers, and expect to change my life."

"That's right. It takes time."

"Time." He chuckled. "Time is something I don't have, Mamá. Who's going to give me a job? I've been in prison. I sling rock and I ain't gonna stop. So who's going to give me a job on top of all that? Do you know someone who will give me a hand? No, you don't. So don't stand here and tell me what I can do. It's not that easy."

"Lord have mercy. How did I raise a bag of excuses like you?" She looked at the ceiling. "Boy, get some pride. Go out and work and stop worrying about what you *can't* get and worry about what you *can*. You just don't want to do any better."

"I got nothing but what I know on the streets, Mamá. I can't sit in no classroom and work out of no science book knowing damn well they won't let me be a doctor. To me, that's wasting time."

"Getting an education is never wasting time. Even if the person is one hundred years old, an education is always valuable."

"You think just because you went to college that means something?" He scoffed. "It doesn't mean shit. Look at you, Mamá. You went to college. You got a job. What has that done for you? Nothing. You still down there in that neighborhood with us."

He rubbed his hands. "You talk about me changing my ways, yet I'm the one with the hundred-dollar bills in my pockets." He pulled out four. "What did college give *you*? Can't even pay your damn bills. You *still* down here with me. Do the fuckin' math, Mamá. I'm where you are now and I didn't go to college."

"Don't you dare speak that way to me again!" Florence waved her hand. "You're gonna get killed, Rico! If not for your set, then for your dumb attitude!"

He opened the front door. "Maybe so. But it's my life, isn't it, Mamá?"

He left.

✠✠✠

"Which apartment is Lisa's?" Nina asked when Claudia parked beside a run-down building with kids playing jump rope in the front. A group of guys in baggy clothes whistled at them as they passed Claudia's convertible.

"The one beside that old garbage pail." Claudia lit a cigarette. Rosa sat in the back struggling with her makeup. "I'm glad you decided to go to Juan's party, Nina. I hope this is a night you won't forget. Here, I got you a little present." Claudia presented a package of condoms from her purse. "Use them in good health."

"Claude!" Nina stuffed the condoms in her purse. "I can't believe you did this."

"Believe it. Nina, don't you want to say you have lived? You don't want to be the only virgin in the school, do you?" Claudia rolled her eyes. "If you don't lose it tonight, when will you?"

"Once again, at my own pace, when I feel it's right. It may be when I'm sixteen, seventeen, or may even be when I'm thirty. No guy is going to pressure me into something I'm not ready for and neither will you."

"Okay, fine." Claudia looked straight ahead. "I won't bring it up again unless you need pointers. But you haven't lived until you've felt a man in his natural form. Ain't that right, Rosa?"

"That's right." Rosa dabbed on face powder. "Nina, I lost my virginity when I was fourteen to my first boyfriend."

"And how was it?" She turned to look at Rosa.

"It was heavenly. Oh sure, I'd heard about how bad the first time can be. But it was nice. I cared for him a lot so I can see what you're saying about waiting. I miss him." She sighed.

"What happened to him?"

"His family moved." Rosa stared into the night air. It was the first time Nina looked beyond Rosa's exterior to see the person inside. At first glance you'd think Rosa was just mouthy, rude and selfish, but something was different in her eyes when she doted on her first time. Nina realized that Rosa had been in love. And this guy would always hold a special place in her heart. "Why you staring at me?" Rosa chuckled.

"Oh, I just can tell you really loved him, that's all." Nina smiled.

"Enough with the chitchat. Here's Lisa." Claudia unlocked the doors. Lisa ran up the sidewalk in a black dress that showed off her fabulous hips. She greeted the girls quickly, jumped in, then began touching up her makeup. Claudia took off.

"Don't drive too fast, homes! I don't want my hair to go flat."

"Lisa, you got a bottle of hair spray on the shit." Rosa grinned. "Is that what took you so long to come out?"

"I had to get ready, didn't I? Anyway, I started my period and the dress I wanted to wear was white so I had to change."

"You look good in black, Lisa," Nina smiled.

"Thanks." Lisa leaned over the seat to see what Nina had on. Nina looked amazing in her slimming pink dress and white scarf. Her makeup looked as though a professional had applied it. "Yo, Nina, I love that outfit! I have to borrow it." Lisa gawked.

"Girl, you are going to have Juan kissing your feet as good as you look."

"I didn't wear this for him."

"*Right*." Claudia grinned. She swerved between two slower cars. Nina exhaled. "I didn't. It *is* a formal party and I didn't want to look out of place."

"In that dress everyone will be looking at you, Nina. Shit, we all look good tonight." Claudia tugged on her short dress. She wiggled to the music on the radio.

"Aren't going to embarrass us tonight, are you, Claude?" Nina watched her from the corner of her eyes.

"Now, would I do that?" She laughed.

CHAPTER SEVEN

"Damn, homes." Carlos looked down the hall from Mercedes's guest bedroom. The party hadn't officially started but the guests entered in clusters. "I didn't know this many people would be here for a little girl's party."

Juan checked his hair. He could put any male model to shame. As he smiled in the mirror he visualized himself giving his first press conference as senator. He wondered if he'd be as confident then as he was now.

"My family knows how to throw good parties."

Dell flinched at a group of kids running through the hall. "How many people are here, man?" he asked.

Juan waved his hand. "Cynthia's friends, relatives, kids from the neighborhood, Rico and some of his friends, a bunch of girls I don't know." Juan grinned. "Shit, I don't care who's here as long as Nina shows up. How do I look?"

"Suave, homes." Carlos peeled a banana.

"You guys look sharp, too. It's almost seven, huh?" Juan checked his watch. He grabbed a key off the dresser and he locked the bedroom door behind them.

"What's up with that?" Carlos asked. They followed Juan down the hall.

"Mercedes locks everything she can in case someone has sticky fingers." Juan slipped the key into his pocket. They strolled toward the living room. Carlos and Dell went into the den with the other teenagers. Juan and Tony headed into the kitchen to check on the food preparations.

"Something smells good in here." Juan and Tony squeezed between a group of female guests fixing the trays. Florence was at the stove preparing something a scientist couldn't identify.

"*Hola*, honey." She kissed Juan, then checked out his snappy attire. "Sharp."

"How do I look, Mrs. Alonso?" Tony did a little dance and stroked his collar.

"Magnificent. Would you like a cookie?" She passed him a chocolate chip cookie that quickly took his mind off other matters.

"Ma, when are we eating the cake?"

"Juan, we haven't even sung 'Happy Birthday' yet. All the guests aren't here, honey."

"There's not room for anyone else." He scanned the food items. Mercedes's platter of enchiladas and beef burritos could make a corpse's mouth water. Juan reached for a burrito. Florence took his hand.

"Not yet," she whispered with a grin.

"Mom, I'm starving." He eyed the plate with the homemade corn chips.

"All right, *one*." She smiled.

"I'm looking for something special." Juan winked at his mother. "Something only my Mamá could make. Where are those little bacon-baked potatoes you make that I love so much? I've been aching all day to get my hands on one."

"It's all he's been talking about." Tony stole another cookie. A fast Spanish song began to play in the other room. Guests gathered in the living room to dance.

"I didn't make the potatoes this time, Juan. I made something else." Florence pulled out a tray of stuffed mushrooms and a pot of stew. "Doesn't it smell wonderful?"

"What the hell is this? Oh no, Mamá. *Greek* food? Mamá...I got Nina coming here! Nobody's going to eat this stuff! You trying to embarrass me?"

She scoffed. "Since when did this get to be your party? Cynthia was happy with the idea."

"Mom, this was supposed to be a traditional *Mexican* party. No one's going to eat this Greek shit."

"Watch your mouth." Florence spooned some of the lamb stew. "You've never even had lamb. Taste some."

"And I don't want any now." He pushed the spoon away. "I wanted everything to go perfectly. The bacon-baked potatoes are what I live for, Mamá." He pouted.

"I'll fix them for *your* birthday, I promise." She kissed him and went back to setting up the trays.

"Hey, hey, peoples!" A short Latino man with high curly hair, a tacky suit, and old-fashioned leather shoes strode in. Florence turned away, giggling. "How's my favorite girl?" The man threw up his hands.

"Oh no." Juan sighed. Tony grinned.

"What's up, Juan?" Roger Vasquez slapped Juan on the back, something Juan always hated. Roger pulled him into a bear hug that forced Juan's nose into his armpits. "How you doing, Juanito, huh?"

"Fine, Roger." Juan did his best to ignore the musty odor under a bottle of cologne. "What are you doing here?"

"Well, Flo invited me. Come here, you big sexy thing you!" He grabbed Florence and kissed her.

"Stop it, Roger!" She laughed. Juan sighed. "Go on out with the other guests, Roger."

He cackled. "She's trying to get rid of me already. I'll check you young bucks later. And Florence, you and me get the first slow dance. You know how I like to do it."

He danced out of the room.

"Mamá, what the hell is he doing here?"

"What do you have against Roger? He's a good man."

"He's a slimy insurance salesman and I think you can do a lot better. He's a gigolo, Mamá. Everyone knows that. And you do, too."

"Maybe I do." She lowered her voice when the women walked through to take the trays into the living room. "I am not with Roger for love, Juanito, but more for companionship. I accept the terms and so does he. We like spending time together. We're not getting married."

"How come it's all right for you to mess around with Roger, but I always have to tiptoe around you about the girls I date?" He crossed his arms.

"Because I'm grown and you're just a child. Now, I like Roger and he likes me. Case closed."

"I don't trust him, Mom, and I never will." Juan sighed.

✦✦✦

Mercedes blocked the front door like a rigid gate. "Those are the rules, Double Deuce. I'm not about to argue with you in my own house. You are not smoking that shit in my house."

"Man, we ain't gonna do nothing, lady." Homicide purposely blew smoke in her face. He cooled his temper when Rico walked to the door.

"Yo, Aunt Mercedes, step off."

"You tell *them* to step off, Rico. Now, I am not having any disrespect in my house." Homicide and Jelly chuckled. Double Deuce stepped aside for more guests to walk through.

Rico turned toward his homies. "Okay, you know what's up. No weed and no shit, all right? You want that, you got to smoke it outside. Respect my aunt's house."

"Thank you." Mercedes trotted to the kitchen.

Homicide shook his head. "Man, what is up with your aunt, Rico? She acts like she's Jesus' mother and shit." They laughed.

❖❖❖

It seemed everyone in the world was at Cynthia's party. Cars were parked on both sides of the street. People swarmed around the card tables in the front yard. Groups of teenagers gathered on the front porch. A circle of twenty-something's drank sodas on the lawn. Little girls jumped rope by the fence. One little girl stood out from the rest. She wore a lovely pink taffeta dress.

The other kids circled around her like she was royalty. Nina squinted through the darkness. She noticed money pinned to the shoulder of the girl's dress.

"That must be Juan's little sister." Nina smiled. Claude squeezed her car behind a blue pickup truck parked on the street.

"Damn." Rosa whistled. "There has to be, what? A hundred motherfuckers here?"

"Hey, look at *him*." Lisa pointed to Homicide. He walked from the side of the house behind a group of NYAs. "He's fine!"

"You think everyone's fine," Claudia whispered. She slapped on thick auburn lipstick. "How do I look?"

"Like a net getting ready to catch some fish." Rosa laughed. Claudia was the first out of the car. The girls slowly followed, snickering at the way she walked in four-inch heels. They ran up the porch, with Lisa gawking at Homicide along the way. He lifted his head, giving her the usual gangsta flirtation vibe, then sat with the other guys to play cards.

"Man, I think he likes me," Lisa whispered once they'd made it inside. They checked out the living room. Except for a few balloons, the atmosphere and music suggested the party would turn into one of an adult nature at any moment. Three teenage girls stared at Nina and her friends. They turned away when Claudia gaped at them.

"Guess they can tell we're not from the neighborhood," Nina whispered.

"Any of these bitches comes with an attitude and it will be her last." Claudia grabbed a bowl of chips. The gawking girls whispered in Spanish, then walked off.

"Don't let me start nothing in here," Claudia said.

"Cool it, Claude. They're just looking because they don't know us. They might be in Juan's family." Nina passed the scattered guests. She peeked around the corner and inside the den. Teen-agers hogged up the area with the usual juvenile conversations. The lavish talk always bored Nina so she didn't bother going inside.

"Looking for someone?" Claudia watched Nina with a sinful grin.

"No," Nina jeered. They walked back into the living room.

Nina noticed a chubby woman setting up an odd centerpiece. Nina appeared to be the only one who actually noticed how the table looked, let alone could understand why the woman had arranged her display with the darkest flowers leaning out over the brighter ones. She stood behind the woman, studying the centerpiece.

"You arrange centerpieces on a regular basis, don't you?" Nina asked the lady.

"Quite right." Florence unhooked her apron, showing off her lovely outfit. "Most young people wouldn't have noticed anything here but the food."

"You've got a good eye. That's how I knew you must do it often. I notice anything with colors. I've been painting since I was a child. At the risk of sounding goofy, I think of it as my calling." Nina chuckled.

Florence gleamed. Nina had a naive way of looking at things. It reminded Florence of how she used to be. It was refreshing to meet a young person into culture instead of the usual juvenile interests. Florence politely took Nina's hand. She escorted her to the display for a closer look.

"I bring these home from my job all the time. I work in a food store and it's pretty cheery. Sometimes at home, nothing's on the up and up. So I get these to lift people's spirits."

Nina looked around to see where Claudia had gone. She didn't see her, so she continued the conversation. "I'm Nina Sagastume."

"Nina?" Florence balled over in giggles. She tightened her grip on Nina's hand.

"I'm Florence Alonso! I'm Juanito's mother."

"You are?" Nina looked her over carefully. She tried her best to ignore the painful embarrassment that accompanied moments like this. "I had no idea! I mean, well, I figured you'd be here but, *wow*."

"Are you all right?" Florence grinned.

"Yeah. Uh, it's just that I expected Juan's mother to be something other than human."

"Ah." Florence crossed her arms. She grinned. "I see my son's been making an interesting impression on you. He talks about you all the time."

"Does he?" Nina nonchalantly flicked her hair from her shoulder. She hoped Florence didn't notice her fidgeting. "I'm glad to be remembered, I guess."

"*More* than remembered, Nina. Can I level with you?" Nina nodded. She stepped closer to the shorter woman. "Juan never babbles and he never rushes to school or skips dessert. But that's all he's been doing since he met you. So if he gets on your nerves, just realize he's doing it because you make him crazy." Nina sighed. "I didn't mean to embarrass you."

"No." She exhaled. "Your son is amazing, Mrs. Alonso. He's smart. He's got a good head on his shoulders. He has great plans and he's attractive. I don't have anything personal against him. I just, I have a lot of things on my mind."

Florence sighed. "*Goodness*, I hope I haven't given you the wrong impression, Nina. Juan didn't tell me to say these things to you."

"He didn't?"

"No. I just wanted you to know." Florence smiled. "If you need anything, I'll be in the kitchen."

"Oh, okay." Nina gawked. Florence offered some people more drinks, then left the room.

"Who was that?" Claudia munched chips.

"Juan's mother. She was so sweet. She was telling me how Juan's been acting since he met me. He's nuts over me, Claudia!" Nina hysterically gripped Claudia's wrists.

"So now that's a good thing? I thought you didn't like him that much."

"I'm just saying, it's good to be watched from afar." Nina glowed. The lights slightly dimmed. The fast-paced Spanish song was replaced with the Dramatics' "Be My Girl." "Oooh, Claudia, I love this song!"

"I know, I know." Claudia chuckled. Two of Juan's well-mannered cousins asked the girls to dance. Claudia took the offer but Nina declined. Juan was the only person she wanted to dance with tonight.

"She's here? She's really here?" Juan flew past Florence out of the kitchen. She grabbed him, causing him to tumble backward. "She said she would come, but I wasn't sure she would! With Nina I can never tell what she's thinking or how she's feeling. I guess that's part of the attraction." Juan grinned between babbling.

"Haven't I taught you anything about being smooth? I know I'm not a man but even *I* know you shouldn't run up to a woman. You got to take it easy, Juan. Women don't like to be charged."

"Oh, Mamá, I'm just so excited. This girl is wonderful! I'm not exaggerating. She's fantastic. I've never met anyone like her before."

"She *is* beautiful," Florence declared. "If someone were perfect, I'd say it were her. So don't blow it. I also took the liberty of doing some positive talking in your favor. Hope you don't mind."

"As long as you didn't show her my nude baby pictures, I could care less." He kissed her and rushed from the kitchen. He stopped long enough to see Jorge cuddling with a girl by the doorway. Big brothers loved to tease and Juan couldn't resist.

"Jorge?" Juan circled the unsuspecting girl. He stared at his brother. "Who is this?"

"This is Alexandra. She goes to my school. Now bug off."

Juan grinned. "Is this the girl you've been having those perverted little dreams about?"

"What?" Alexandra stared at Jorge.

Jorge bit his lips. "Juan, I'm going to kill you."

Chuckling, Juan went to find Nina.

✠

"Juan, where are you?" Nina whispered. She moved between the swaying couples dancing in the living room. She was about to give up her search when someone tapped her shoulder.

"I'm behind you." A slick whisper coerced her ear. Juan stood confidently, as if he knew he was the best-looking guy in the room.

He pulled her close without hesitation. His body felt amazing. His skin was so hard and firm against hers. She thought of that club kiss. Every time she looked at him she wanted the action repeated. Too bad he had too much pride to kiss her for risk of being slapped again.

"I love this song. Is that why it's playing?" she asked with an eyebrow raised.

"I know you like old-school R and B and this is from my mom's prized collection. When she was in college she had a small job and she'd put so much of her money toward her college fees and save enough to buy one record a week. It's expanded to about one thousand records."

Nina rocked against him. "One thousand?"

"Yeah." He licked his lips. "You look beautiful, Nina."

She twitched. "You look good, too."

"I hope so." He watched her hand caressing his shirt. "I'm glad you came. I thought you'd get cold feet."

"Claudia wouldn't have let me." She grinned. "This isn't what I expected for a little girl's party. I saw your sister playing in the yard. She's pretty. She looks just like you."

"Did you see my twin brothers, Jorge and Benny?" Juan pointed to Benny, who stood behind the food table talking to a group of boys. Jorge escorted Alexandra to the dance floor.

"And this is Jorge, the bad twin." Juan laughed. Jorge pulled Alexandra close. "You didn't tell me you could slow dance! You go, little man!" Juan teased.

"I guess I could teach you a thing or two, huh?" Jorge gazed at the lovely woman in Juan's arms. "Is this the babe you've been drooling over, big brother?" Nina looked at Juan, who'd just about turned a dark red.

"I haven't been drooling," Juan muttered.

"Can't take it when it's on the other foot, huh, big brother?" Jorge smiled at Nina.

"I'm Jorge. Nice to meet you."

"Nice to meet you, too."

"Word of advice, forget you ever met my brother. He's not worth it."

Juan exhaled. "If you want to continue living, I suggest you dance across the room." Juan gestured. Jorge and Alexandra moved across the room.

Nina chuckled. "He's cute."

"Don't tell him that." Juan grinned. Another old-school slow song began to play.

Homicide and Rico had been standing at the front door for minutes, staring at Juan and the strange girl he danced with. Homicide squinted to get a better look at her.

Rico calmly sipped soda, enjoying how tempting Nina looked in her dress.

"Shit, man. She's off the chain." Rico snapped his fingers. "Never seen her before. Must not live in this neighborhood."

"She came with them other bitches in that convertible. I think they go to Juan's school," Homicide said. Juan swung Nina around the dance floor.

"Wouldn't mind getting me some of that." Rico's eyes narrowed.

Homicide grinned. "Don't go there, Rico. Shit, you got enough problems with the bitches your own age. Leave the kiddie pussy alone."

Rico gazed as Juan whispered something into Nina's ear.

"Pussy is pussy. That's the way I see it." Rico rubbed his hands.

"But going after *that* pussy will get you put in jail and we ain't got time for that shit, Rico. Get your mind out of the gutter."

"Shit, no teenager got no business having a body like that. Wonder if she's broken it in yet? She would be broken with me. Fuck the dancing, shit, I'd get straight to pounding the booty. Something tells me she'd like that, too." He smirked.

"Looks like there's only one Alonso who's going to get close to trying and that's...Juan."

"Girls always fall for the punk asses. I swear, if Juan wasn't my brother, if I didn't love him, I'd be all up on her before you could say 'doggy style.'"

Homicide laughed. "Wonder who she is, though. How come Juan never mentioned her? There's something weird about this, man. Something that makes me think we ought to make sure Juan is handling things."

Rico yawned. "It's my little sister's party. I ain't thinking of nothing tonight but relaxing. Let's leave Juan to his precious little date." They went into the kitchen.

"You okay, Juan?" Nina noticed his change of behavior. He turned her loose.

"I really want to talk to you."

"You *are* talking to me."

"I mean alone. Let's go for a walk. There's a park just a minute away."

"Uh..." She didn't see any of her friends. "I should let Claude know that I'm going with you."

"Think she's going to leave you or something?" He laughed. "No more excuses, Nina. We're going to take a short walk and then we'll be back before your friends miss you."

"Will we?"

"Yeah." Juan held her arm around his. "Tonight, you're mine."

Nina followed him outside and to the back of Mercedes's house. Mercedes lived smack dab in front of a small park. Nina could still hear the chatter of Cynthia's party after they reached the woods. They walked along the dark path hand in hand, doing their best not to ruin their shoes. They made it to a lovely little bench lit by streetlights. Nina hadn't seen anything so romantic.

Juan gestured toward it, its metal glittering underneath the moonlight. Like a naive peasant girl, Nina followed his every move. Juan jiggled his feet, smiling arrogantly as usual. She figured he had her right where he wanted her. She wasn't sure if she'd fallen for his line or if her heart had given in to his charm. All she knew was being with him felt good. The feeling was so enormous she failed to compare it.

"Well?" Juan let his eyes trail down the curve of her back. She strolled behind the bench, looking up at the moon. "You gonna sit down or what?" He sensuously rubbed the space beside him. Nina unhooked the scarf from her neck. To no surprise, he was staring at her.

She sat down. "Why do you always do that?" She looked around to confirm they were alone.

"Do what?" Juan tilted his head to the side. He pulled her close.

"What are you doing, Juan?" She enjoyed the gesture but wasn't sure what he had in mind.

"What does it look like I'm doing? I'm taking control." He rested his finger underneath her chin.

Nina's heart raced. She swore Juan's would bust from his chest, too. He inched toward her with his eyes closed. Nina wouldn't dare look away. The way he looked when he kissed her thrilled her beyond reality. She'd been aroused before by the handsome men in the soaps, but no one duplicated that until Juan. His tongue gently tugged at her lips until her mouth swelled with passion.

Before Nina could reflect on the kiss's perfection, Juan pulled his mouth from hers.

"God, Nina." He held his hand to his mouth. "You got me hooked, girl." He chuckled. "No one has ever made me feel this way. I don't know how to convince you it's true, but it is. I want to be with you."

"I met your mother. She's something else."

"Yeah, she told me you guys talked." Juan sat back, grinning. "She's kind of strange, huh?"

"Oh, not at all." A strand of hair caught on her lip. Juan gently brushed it away, jumbling her thoughts even more. "You look just like her."

"Really?" He stared at the sidewalk. "Most people say I look like my dad." He pulled out his wallet. He handed Nina a picture of a handsome man around fifty. If it hadn't been for his gray hair he could have passed for younger. Nina gazed at the picture. Even the dimness of the night sky couldn't hide the similarities between Juan and his father.

"God, Juan, your dad was so handsome." She stared into Peter Alonso's bright eyes. "You're right. You do look like him by the nose and the eyes." She handed him the picture.

"Sorry you didn't know your dad." He put his wallet away. "I bet you look like your mother. She must be quite the knockout. Got a picture of her?"

"Maybe we should be getting back. You know I haven't even eaten yet." Nina rubbed her stomach. "That platter *was* calling my name." She chuckled.

"Hold on, Nina. I'm not stupid. I got the feeling something was up about your mom before." He sighed. "Why don't you like to talk about her? Is it because of her sickness?"

"How come it's so damn hard for me to lie to you, Juan?"

"What does that mean?" He stared at her.

She pulled her mother's picture from her purse. It was a glamorous shot of Michelle in a black-and-white bikini and her name and the date were written on the back. One of Michelle's beaus had suggested she and Nina accompany him on a little trip to Palm Springs. Even though Nina and Michelle spent most of the time together during the vacation, Nina hadn't been lonelier. She remembered how isolated she'd felt after that trip.

From that day on she didn't fool herself when it came to the so-called mothering instinct of Michelle Sagastume. In Nina's opinion, it didn't exist.

"I thought you were an only child." Juan turned the picture upside-down. He studied it as if it were some laboratory experiment.

"I am." Nina sighed.

"Then who is this?" He gaped at her.

"That's my mother, Juan. Michelle Sagastume is my mother."

"Hold on." He grinned. "Now, I'm not blind, Nina. And the back of this picture is dated to about four years ago. This woman looks like she's barely twenty. What kind of game are you running?" He playfully tapped her knee.

"I wish it was a game." She exhaled. "My mother was fifteen when she had me, Juan." Juan gaped at Michelle's picture. Nina continued. "We'd gone to Palm Springs with one of her boy-friends when this was taken. I was hoping we'd get closer. Of course, it didn't work out."

He sighed. "Another piece of the puzzle, huh?"

She took the picture. "So what do you think? Do we look alike or not?"

"Nina." He sighed into his hands. "God, no wonder you didn't want to talk about her." She looked off. "I always assumed you had a wonderful childhood. I guess now I see why you're so dis-tant with people. It's hard for you to trust someone new, isn't it?"

"God, all I ever wanted was a mother, Juan. I wanted a real mother who was there. Michelle was never there. You know, she sort of raised me as her sister for a while." Tears swept Nina's eyes. "She never once said she loved me. She never once even really talked to me. She never spent time with me. You know how someone can be there but they're not really there?"

Juan thought of his brother. "Story of my life." He pulled her close. "She still needs you now, Nina. No matter how she was in the past, you've got to be there for her now." He wiped her tears with his finger. "You are so beautiful."

"Oh, please." She sighed.

"No, you are. No one has ever made me feel like you do." His lips parted. She wanted so much to climb inside his warm arms, feel the tingle of his body against hers. But once again she pulled away. "What's wrong?"

"Juan, there's a lot of things that are happening in my life. There are a lot of things you don't know about me." She thought of Tajo. "Maybe we should be getting back now." She leaned from the bench but he pulled her back down.

"No, wait. I'm not going to let you run away from me, Nina. I know this can be something special. Don't you feel the same way?"

"I do." She sighed, relieved. "But I can't give in right now. I don't want to end up like everyone else."

"What is this hold on you? I mean, what is it that's really stopping you from being with me, Nina? Is it me?"

"No."

"Is it school?"

"No."

"You said you don't have a boyfriend." He exhaled. "Then what could it be?"

"A lot of things, all right? Juan, everything isn't black and white. Compared to my life, yours is a gem. I am not going to fall for your sweet lines and end up like the girls that have no future and no prospects."

"Nina, what the hell are you talking about?" He growled.

"I'm talking about..." She slowly lifted her head to find his stern eyes. "I'm talking about getting pregnant." She shook from embarrassment. "Shit, I can't believe I said that."

"How would you get pregnant when we haven't had sex?"

"Well, if we start going together, I know we'd end up going further. Juan, I've never been that way with a guy before." He contemplated her explanation. "This is scary and new. And I am not..."

"*Ready*?" His voice cracked. She nodded. "I'm in love with you, Nina." He looked at her. "That's not going to go away anytime soon."

"That's understandable, Juan. I wouldn't want you to hide your heart."

"So how do you feel about me then?" He rested his elbows on his thighs. He propped his head up with his fists.

"I deeply care about you, Juan." She kissed his cheek.

"You think that if we get together and start being intimate you'll get pregnant and your life will be over, right?" She shrugged. "Nina, you think I'm trying to get ass from you? Do you think I'm trying to score with you just to up and leave?"

"I don't *know*," she snapped.

"Bullshit. You knew the moment we met how I felt about you. I knew how you felt about me."

"Juan, please."

"Nina, even if we did make love and you got pregnant, I would never ever leave you. Look at me." He led her hand to his lap. She found his eyes once more. A barking dog in the distance temporarily stole their attention. "I would marry you." His voice shook. "I swear to God I would." He kissed her hand.

"I'm in love with you, Juan," she confessed. Tears flooded her eyes.

"I know." He pulled her into another kiss.

✠✠✠

"Hi, guys." Lisa grabbed a plate of food. Rosa and Claudia gathered beside her at the food tables. Carlos popped open a soda while Tony and Dell filled their plates with food.

Carlos held his chest. "Are you speaking to *us*?" Tony and Dell laughed.

"I can't believe such goddesses are speaking to three peasants like us."

"What's your problem, Carlos?" Claudia held her hips.

"My problem is that you're nothing but a bunch of stuck-up tricks."

"Excuse me?" Rosa walked toward him.

"Yeah, that's, right." Tony chewed a chip. "At school y'all think you too good to speak to us. Now you're so far up on us we can't even move. What's the deal?"

"Whatever." Lisa rolled her eyes.

"You look nice, ladies." Dell waved at them. The girls smiled, paying him equal compliments.

"Looks like one guy here knows how to treat a lady." Lisa glared at Carlos and Tony. "Anyway, we came here because Juan invited us. We can't find Nina anywhere."

"I know where she is." Tony sipped soda.

"Where?" Rosa crossed her arms.

"On Juan's jock!" He and Carlos laughed. Dell made the decision to act like he had some common sense.

Claudia scowled. "Very funny. If anyone's on someone it's Juan. He's been stuck to Nina since she got to Roosevelt."

"Please, Nina should be glad Juan even looked at her." Carlos grinned.

Claudia scoffed. "Juan should be happy Nina even *thought* about him twice."

"Please, she's not that fine."

"Uh, I can't side with you on that, Carlos." Tony grinned. "Nina is one of the finest girls I've ever seen. Ain't she, Dell?"

Dell swallowed a chip. "Oh yeah, man."

"Sellouts." Carlos glared at his friends.

"It doesn't matter what we all think anyway because they like each other. Maybe we should try to get them together," Lisa suggested.

Carlos looked at his friends. "If Nina wants to be with Juan, she can step up to him like a real woman instead of leading him on all the time."

"Nina doesn't lead guys on, okay? She's not like that."

"Come on, Claudia." Carlos gaped at her dress. "She's a tease just like you all are."

"We are not teases, shithead." Rosa held her hips.

"*All* girls are teases, it's a fact." Tony smirked.

"I am *not* a *tease*," Lisa shouted.

Tony dumped onion dip on a cracker. "You go all the way?"

"No."

"Then you're a tease." He laughed.

"I don't know why we bothered talking to you." Lisa looked at the others.

"Let's go, ladies." They walked off.

"Nice going, you guys." Dell shook his head. "I'm sure they're loving us now."

"What do they know? Juan's not that wide open for Nina." Carlos crossed his arms. "I know my man wouldn't go out like that."

"Yeah, they don't know what they're talking about." Tony watched the girls scamper to the living room. "Man, they're fine as hell, aren't they?"

"Yep." Dell and Carlos nodded.

✦✦✦

Nina and Juan stayed in the park for hours. All her life, Nina had been convinced she'd never find the right guy. Each time she looked at Juan, listened to the message behind his words, she knew no one else would ever come close. He'd taken her from a hovel of misery to a cloud of happiness since the day they met. She was still afraid to admit his charm overwhelmed her, but she wasn't ready to let go of the one person who seemed to make all her troubles disappear.

By the time their rendezvous was over, Nina felt like Cinderella. When they returned to Mercedes's it was past time to leave. Claudia, Lisa, and Rosa were headed toward the car. Lisa and Rosa giggled at Juan and Nina holding hands. Claudia noticed Juan wearing most of Nina's lipstick. She managed to keep quiet about it. Juan helped Nina in the car.

"I meant what I said," he whispered into her ear. "I want to be with you more than anything."

Nina blew a kiss in return. "Good night, Juanito."

Within seconds, she was gone.

CHAPTER EIGHT

"Hey, man!" Carlos slapped Juan's shoulder. Tony and Dell stood beside him with their arms crossed. "Missed you for a couple of hours." Carlos raised an eyebrow.

"Oh yeah." Juan rubbed his hair. Realizing the girls were long gone, he focused on his friends. "Let's just say I had some business to take care of." He grinned.

"Business you probably don't intend on telling us about, right?" Dell chuckled.

"No, I'll tell you at the right time. It's just that I don't want to jump the gun and say anything before I know the mission's been accomplished."

"So you *are* wide open for Nina, aren't you?" Carlos sighed. "Look, Nina is fine. I can understand if you want to hit that, but getting involved is a different story."

"Yeah, you hardly know this girl, Juan." Tony squinted.

Juan studied their twisted expressions. "What the hell is with you guys tonight? You act like I'm getting married or something." He laughed. He became alarmed when his friends didn't. "Guys, it was a joke." He blinked wildly.

"Yeah." Tony looked at the sidewalk. "Man, we got your back. We just want to make sure you don't get hurt. I know you like Nina, but just don't let that cloud your judgment."

"'Cloud my judgment'? I thought you all supported me. Tony,

you were the one telling me Nina liked me." Tony looked away.

"Carlos, you were the one challenging me to get her." Juan rolled his eyes. "What about you, Dell? You're the romantic one who has an insight into girls. What do *you* think?"

"Juan, you know I'm with you no matter what you decide."

"But what do you think?" Juan sighed impatiently.

"I think you shouldn't rush into anything. Make sure she feels the same way before you open your heart." He took Juan's hand. "We'll see you."

"Yeah." Tony patted Juan's shoulder.

"Later." Carlos waved.

✠✠✠

Juan watched until his friends were out of sight. Florence and Mercedes said good night to departing guests. A few of Cynthia's friends stayed. Their parents gathered them inside for leftover cake and ice cream. Juan enjoyed the stillness in the air until he noticed Rico's intense gaze. Curiosity forced Juan to give in to his brother's provocation.

"Something wrong?" He swaggered to the porch.

"No." Rico sipped soda. "Nothing's wrong as far as I can see." He pointed down the street. "What the fuck would be wrong, baby boy?"

Juan sighed. "I don't have time for your shit, Rico."

Rico blocked him. "So it's like that, huh? Shit, I can't even talk to my baby bro now, huh? You too good to even chew the fuckin' fat with me?"

"What do you want?" The last thing Juan wanted was an argument in the middle of someone else's block.

"That fine-ass chick you were with in there, man." Rico winked. "Who was she, homes?"

"Just a girl. I can't have friends now?"

"It's hard to believe she's just a friend. You can't be friends with a woman that fine."

"Seems to me you've been paying an awful lot of attention to Nina, huh?"

"Nina?" Rico grinned. "Nice name. It fits her, man. You like her, don't you? How about I make sure you get her?"

Juan shoved Rico's hand from his chest. "I plan on getting her, don't worry. But not in the way you mean. I care about her, Rico. If you try to come between us, I swear you will need *all* of the NYAs to save your ass."

"Is that right?" Rico sucked his bottom lip.

"That's right. Nina's none of your business. Remember that, hear me?"

"It's just weird to me because she popped out of nowhere. And come to think of it you've been acting strange for a while now. She seems important to you. I've never seen her around the neighborhood."

"She's not from our neighborhood, all right?" Juan exhaled. "She's new to the school. She stays with her cousin. It's no big secret, for God's sake."

"Who's her cousin?"

"Why the fuck you want to know? Stay out of my business!" Juan shoved him. Rico lost his balance down the steps.

"Shit!" Rico wiped soda from his pants. Homicide and Double Deuce laughed.

"You know I'm trying to look out for you, Juan. I get a feeling I don't like about this girl. You better watch your back."

"Whatever, man." Juan stared at a van down the street with blinking headlights.

Rico waved Homicide and Double Deuce to his side. The three of them scrunched down, doing their best to see the mysterious vehicle.

"What's that, homes?" Homicide glanced at Rico. He walked toward the street to get a better look.

"I don't recognize the car," Rico whispered. Juan held his eyes steadily on the headlights. They blinked faster.

Juan sighed. "It's probably nothing. I think we should be going now." Rico held his hand up to keep Juan from moving. "What is it, Rico?"

"Don't move." Rico lapped one foot carefully in front of the other. He stopped near the street. Slowly he lifted the ends of his shirt. Juan's heart raced when he saw Rico give the warning signal. Homicide and Double Deuce held their breath, ready to move. "Juanito, go inside," Rico ordered.

"What the hell's the matter with you? It's just a truck."

"It's a van we don't recognize. A van I ain't never seen before. Now go in the fuckin' house!"

Chino shifted in the passenger's seat. Juice and Shorty-Five stood in military-style poses at the back of the van. Bone lightly pressed his foot on the gas. It was light enough to not move the van but powerful enough to stroke the motor. Chino snugly held an Uzi in his lap.

"They see us." Chino grinned. He shifted a toothpick back and forth in his mouth. "We don't want those motherfuckers running."

"I got that bitch Rico locked in my sight." Bone pointed to his right temple.

"We're going to get that motherfucker. Shorty, Juice, you guys ready back there?"

Juice removed his baseball cap. He stuck his head through the curtain in the back window.

"We've been ready for the last fifteen minutes. What's up with this shit, Bone? You scared?" Juice held two semiautomatics to his side. "I need to pee, dog."

"On the count of four." Bone gripped the steering wheel. Juice and Shorty-Five glared from the back of the van. Bone counted.

"One." He roared the engine. Chino kept his Uzi pointed to the van floor. "Two."

Shorty-Five held his gun toward his head, aimed to the sky. Juice pressed his body against the back doors. Bone eyed Chino. Chino nodded with a callous smile. "Three." Bone slammed the gas. The van exploded down the street.

"Oh shit!" Rico ran up the porch steps. Homicide and Double Deuce pulled guns from their pockets. They took refuge beneath the card tables and barbecue pit.

"Inside, Juan! Go inside!" Rico rolled underneath the porch, cradled in darkness.

Bone jerked the van still. Chino rested with the Uzi held to his chest. Juice and Shorty-Five jumped from the back of the van. Standing with bent knees and guns held at eye level, the two fired.

"Drive-by!" Juan ran inside yelling. He grabbed Cynthia, Jorge, and Benny. They huddled underneath the kitchen table. Mercedes and Florence took handfuls of children into the back rooms. The other guests found their own places to hide. Deafening screams overlapped through the house into the streets.

"My baby! Rico!" Florence ran into the living room. She reached for the front door.

"Florence!" Mercedes threw her sister to the living room floor.

"I've got to get him, Mercedes!" Florence pounded the carpet. "He's out there!"

"All we can do is call the police!" Mercedes could barely control her shaking hands. She dialed for the police.

"Juan!" Jorge yelled as he rested in Juan's arms next to Benny and Cynthia.

"What's happening?" Jorge exhaled.

"It's a drive-by, idiot!" Benny yelled. He buried his head underneath his hands.

Juan checked on Florence and Mercedes in the living room, then ran back to the kitchen.

"Juan?" Cynthia stood, gripping her dress. "Juan, what about Rico? Rico's out there! He could be killed!"

"No one's going to be killed, all right?" He shivered. "Just stay in here. I'll be right back!" He ran into the living room. Florence scrambled across the floor. She snatched him. "How are the children?"

"Everyone else is safe, Ma. I think it's over." He peeked out the window. "Oh my God." He ran out the front door.

"No, Juan! Don't go out there!" Florence covered her mouth.

The porch dripped with blood. Two NYAs lay dead in the front yard. Juan didn't freak or blink an eye. He'd been used to the destruction of gang violence for years. He heard moaning from the side of the porch. Double Deuce struggled on the ground, encased in blood. Juan bent beside him to get a better look. Double Deuce tried to stand but only gripped dirt in his hands.

"Son of a bitch!" He spit. "Oh shit, Juan?"

"Jesus Christ. God, man, you got hit."

"Twice in my legs."

"Jesus. Where are the others?" Juan took a deep breath. Hysterical neighbors scurried through the streets. Florence peered from the porch. She ran back inside.

"Rico, he, he and the others chased the motherfuckers." Double Deuce coughed.

"Shit! See, I told him this life is not worth it! How many people have to be killed, Double D? How many times do we have to go through this?"

Double Deuce looked up. "It's the life, Juan. We can't change that. And we sure as hell won't." He grunted in pain.

"Double Deuce, you are shot in the fuckin' legs, man! You might not ever walk again. What does that mean to you?"

"It means that the NYAs have work to do."

"Work?" Juan rubbed his head. "More killings, right? More, uh, more retaliation? When the hell will it stop?"

"The Bronx Gangstas did this shit! And you can stand here and lecture *me*, man? You're a fuckin' punk. You talk all that tired politics shit but you ain't never there to actually help, are you?"

"What do you mean by that?"

"I mean be there, damn it!" Double Deuce pounded the ground. A crowd of people watched from the sidewalk. Others gathered around, inching closer to Double Deuce's horrific misfortune.

"What happened?" someone asked in the distance.

"I don't know." A woman gripped her robe. "Thought I heard gunshots."

A little black boy with thick curly hair pointed to Double Deuce. "Look at all the blood, Mamá." The lady hugged him close.

"Give him room!" Juan accidentally hit someone's legs. "Please, people."

They moved toward the street. "Deuce, what did you mean, be there?" Juan asked.

Double Deuce leaned up. "Do whatever you got to do to show you belong, Juan. You got to become one of us, man. There is nothing else for you."

"We've got to get you to the hospital." Juan ran back inside.

***

"Here." Juan passed Rico a cup of coffee. They sat away from the others in the hospital waiting room. Rico angrily eyed everyone who passed. Juan couldn't read his brother's violent mind. He vowed he wouldn't try to. Rico circled the Styrofoam cup in his hand. "Rico, we've got to talk about this." Rico took a deep breath. He turned away. "How much of this can *you* take? I'm not talking about the NYAs. I'm talking about you, bro."

"You know, sometimes when I'm alone I sit and wonder what my purpose in life was. Then I wonder what the fuck I would be doing if not the leader of a set. I picture myself being like you, Juan. I've set a path I can't get out of. You just don't understand my position. On one hand it feels good to be a bad-ass gangsta. I get respect. I got clout. I got money. I got followers.

Rico stared at his brother. "I'm like fuckin' Jesus in this neighborhood, *ese*. People look up to me. Little kids, six or seven, want to grow up to be like me." Rico grinned. "No matter what else I decide to do, I won't get half the benefits with something else as I do with this."

"I guess I'll never understand you, bro. To me you're throwing your life away and you don't even care. Don't you want to get married? Don't you want to have kids?" Juan asked.

"Right." Rico tugged on his ear. "Me married to a bitch?"

"I think the first step is to stop calling them 'bitches.'"

"Why get married when I can get any woman I want *now*? If you got money and power you got everything, Juan. I got just as much as some white executive on Wall Street sitting on his ass. It's a damn good feeling."

Juan grimaced. "That was Cynthia's party, Rico. She could have been killed."

"Wouldn't have happened." He sipped. "I have always protected you guys. I always will."

"Like you protected Double D? Now he's going to have to have surgery to remove bullets from his legs. Who are we kidding, Rico? Look at what this is doing to all of us. The life you chose affects the entire family. You've dragged us into this and it isn't fair."

"I didn't choose this life, all right!" He slammed his cup of coffee on the table. "This is fate, Juan. I can't choose my own path. We are put on earth to do everything we're doing now. NYA goes back to our family, man. Seems to me you're the one turning on what's important."

"I don't believe that." Juan clenched his jaw. "I think I'm a bigger man than you'll ever be."

Rico stood. "But are you a *better* one?" He walked away.

Florence stood in front of the central hall water fountain with her hands crossed. Juan could tell she'd been praying and perhaps crying. Double Deuce didn't have a family to look after him. Juan admired Florence's ability to look beyond Double Deuce's faults to be there for him. He took his mother's hand. She pulled him into a weak hug, then went back to daydreaming.

"I can't take this anymore, Juanito. Rico won't change. It's time we accept that."

"Is that what you really want?" The desperation in his own voice shocked Juan. Had Florence given up on Rico? If *she* didn't believe in him, how could Juan?

"I want you to promise me that you will be all you can be, Juan. Don't be a stereotype. Don't be like your brother."

"I believe I've already made that choice." He lightly chuckled.

"Listen to what I'm saying, Juan." She took his hand. "For your father, for your little brothers, for your sister, be what you said you will. Become a positive politician and make a difference. Give kids hope so they won't become like Rico."

"Mamá."

"Promise me." She jerked his hand. "It's the last thing I'll ever ask of you."

"Okay." He rested his hands on her shoulders. "I promise I will be all I can. But you've got three others to think about, too. We won't let you down."

"I love you, Juanito," she whispered.

Burning with envy, Rico watched them embrace from the end of the hall.

✠✠✠

"What am I doing here?" The next day Nina stood at Mercedes's door. She shoved some loose change she'd found on the

156

bus into her jeans. She couldn't ignore the odd atmosphere. Just the night before there had been a huge bash. Now everything seemed deserted. Mercedes's neighbors peeked from behind curtains. The postman greeted Nina, slipped two envelopes into Mercedes's mailbox, then hurried down the sidewalk.

"Mercedes, I can't do that." Florence shoved a bowl of cereal across the kitchen table. She stared at her sister for moments, desperate for the right words. It had been years since her excuses about Rico comforted her.

"Flo, you got to! If you don't, you won't have a life at all. You raised him already. You no longer have to feel you owe him a damn thing. You need to kick Rico out of your house. And if he won't go, you should call the police." Mercedes crossed her arms. "That's what I'd do."

"Got all the answers, don't you, sis? It's easy to advise when you're not in my shoes. Mercedes, I have to question you even care for Rico sometimes."

"You know damn well I love him. But I don't agree with this gang shit and you shouldn't put up with it! God, woman, what will it take for you to take a stand? Cynthia, your little baby girl, her party ended in horror. Jeez, Flo, I keep thinking what if she had been out there? What if Juan or you or I had been out there? We could have all died. How can you sit here as a mother and condone this?"

"He's my son, Mercedes. I can't give up on him."

"No one's asking you to! All I'm saying is you need to stop taking the blame for his mistakes. You seem to think just because Rico came from your womb you owe him a fuckin' house on the hill, but you don't. He's using you, Flo. You have to get away from him. It's abuse!"

"He has never laid a hand on me!"

"I mean," Mercedes sighed, "emotional blackmail, Flo. Rico knows your weak spot and he's using it to his advantage. You have to..."

Someone knocked at the front door. "What *now*?" Mercedes muttered.

Florence shrugged. "Might be the cops again to ask more questions about last night." They went to the living room. Mercedes checked the peephole.

"It's the girl from the party last night. The one Juan was with." She shrugged.

"Oh, Nina?" Florence opened the door. Nina passed her the mail. "Hello, Nina. How are you?"

"Fine, Mrs. Alonso. I know you don't stay here and I guess I took my chances, but I came to see if Juan was around. When I didn't see his truck I was going to leave. but I wanted to, well..."

"You can come in if you like, Nina." Mercedes smiled. The women stared at Nina as if she hung in a museum. "Uh, would you like some breakfast? I've got cereal. Out of everything else." Mercedes shrugged.

"No, I ate already. I forgot to tell you last night that you have a lovely home."

"Thank you, Nina." Mercedes glanced at Florence.

Florence moaned. "Nina, I'm sorry you wasted a trip. Juan isn't coming over, I don't think. You want to try our house? He has errands to run on Saturday but he should be home until noon. Our address is..."

"No, uh..." Nina shuffled her feet. She wanted to see Juan more than breathe but something kept her from showing it. "I guess I'll be going."

"Nina?" Florence walked toward her. "Is there something wrong?"

"I don't know why I feel so weird. I just do."

"The teen years are the worst." Mercedes shrugged. "It's been a while since I was one but I remember how awkward I felt."

"Don't you mean how awkward you *looked*?" Florence chuckled.

"Forget you." Mercedes grinned. Nina smiled.

The front door opened. Juan's eyes automatically found Nina's. His smile lacked its usual brightness. With just one look at him, Nina felt like the sun had invaded her body, warming every inch of her.

"Nina." He passionately sung her name.

"Hello, Juan." She didn't care how desperate she looked. She was just glad to be near him again. "I wanted to talk to you."

"I'm glad. I wanted to call you as soon as I got up."

"I wanted to call you when I got home last night." She chuckled.

"You look pretty." He pointed to her peach blouse. "I guess it is fate that I came here, huh? I started not to."

"Why *did* you come here, Juan?" Mercedes asked. He pulled out a package of floppy discs. Mercedes snatched them. "Oh, thank you, Juan. You found what I wanted."

"Yeah, I got them for you this morning. You'd been asking me to hook you up with some powerful computer tools. "

"Thank you." Mercedes smiled at Nina. "He's very reliable, Nina. Kind of like a collie." She left the room, chuckling.

Juan jiggled his keys toward Nina. "Do you want to take a ride with me?"

"Sure." Nina bade Florence good-bye. Juan pulled her close the moment they got outside. The heat of his body nearly suffocated her.

"God, I missed you so much." He caressed her hair.

"I missed you, too. Why was the air so stuffy in there? And why does the neighborhood seem so strange?"

"Something terrible happened last night." He sat down on the porch. "But I don't want to dampen the day talking about it."

"You can tell me anything, Juan." She rubbed his shoulders.

"There was a drive-by here after you left."

"What?" She watched two women jogging up the street.

"That's all I want to say." Juan waved at the jogging women. Nina smiled when they passed.

She took his hand. "Did anyone get hurt? My God, is everyone okay? Did someone die?"

"Two guys were killed."

"Oh my God," Nina shrieked. "Did you get hurt at all?"

"No, I was in the house. Shit, Nina, I couldn't stop thinking about you and what could have happened if you had been here."

"You mean," she said pressing her small fingers into his large palms, "through all of that you were still thinking of *me*?"

"I think about you all the time. God, Nina, I hope I don't fuck this up with you."

"You won't." She kissed the back of his neck. He playfully howled like a baby coyote. "I don't want to run from you anymore, Juan."

"You don't?"

"No." She wrapped her arm around his. "Someone made me see that I have to start living my life sometime."

"Whoever that person is, tell them I'll buy them a BMW." He chuckled.

"I want to be with you, Juan. I always did." She laid her head on his shoulder.

"Since you said all that, I guess I owe you something, Nina."

"Huh?"

He laughed. "Come on, Miss Sagastume. I want to introduce you to *my* world."

❈❈❈

"Can I take my hands from my eyes now?" Nina tried to peek through the gaps in her fingers. Juan made her swear she wouldn't look until they got to the location. After what seemed an eternity, Juan stopped the truck.

"Keep your eyes closed." He helped her out of the truck. Her feet landed on a rocky surface. "Just a bit farther, then you can look." He slipped his arm around her waist. Nina couldn't ignore the thunderous, erotic feeling she got from his touch. Did he realize the effect he had on her? They took brisk steps upward until they reached a smoother surface.

Nina laughed. "Okay, now! I can't wait any longer, Juan."

"Okay, okay. You can look."

Nina assumed she would open her eyes to a beautiful little lake filled with swans and ducks. Instead they stood in front of a rusty, paint-chipped door of a rundown shack. The windows were covered with tape to hold up the millions of cracks. The front door was dirtied with shoe marks. Nina couldn't find a blade of grass. The yard was covered in small rocks and weeds.

Juan stood with his hands folded. He smiled as if he'd brought her to a five-star restaurant.

"Well?" He lightly kicked the door.

"Well *what*?" Nina groaned.

"I told you I would show you the *real* me." He tugged on his black T-shirt.

"Yeah." Nina scratched her head. She looked the place over a third time. "And if this is the 'real you', Juan, I don't know if I want any part of it."

He sniggered. "This is where I spend some of my extra time. When I'm not in the library with you, of course. I come here mostly on weekends."

"On purpose?" Nina kicked a beetle from her shoe.

He took her hand. "Follow me. I see you don't understand the bigger picture."

The inside reminded Nina of a small church. Four tables stretched from one side of the room to the other. An uncovered light bulb dangled from the ceiling to give overhead light. Two little boys sipped soup at the front table. A teenage girl in tattered clothing sat in the back. Nina tried to catch a glimpse at what she ate but didn't want to appear rude.

Nina wouldn't have been caught dead in a place this filthy if she didn't care for Juan so much.

"Juanito!" A chubby Jewish lady with huge, gaudy earrings ran toward them. Nina found it hard to keep her eyes off the girl in the back. She held her arms around her soup bowl as if she expected someone to steal it. "How are you today, Juan?"

"I'm fine, Ms. Goldstein." He looked around. "Kind of an empty house today, huh?"

"Looks like it." She flung a dish towel over her shoulder. "I suspect more will show up." Ms. Goldstein lit up when she saw Nina. "Is she someone who needs our help too? Where did you find her?"

"Oh no." Juan laughed. "She's with me. She's a friend of mine. Ms. Goldstein, this is Nina Sagastume. Nina, this is Ms. Goldstein."

"I am so sorry, Nina." The lady abruptly took her hand. "I thought you were part of the lunch crowd."

"It's perfectly all right. I am hungry, though."

"Let me fix you both a bowl of soup and some juice." Ms. Goldstein wobbled toward the tiny kitchen.

"Juan, is this a mission of some sort?" Nina whispered.

"You can call it that. It's a secret little thing Ms. Goldstein started five years ago. She cooks for and feeds runaways. Like the ones you see now." Juan pointed to the boys at the front table.

"Wait a minute. Okay, if this is for runaways, how come the place looks so bad? Shouldn't the state funding help out?"

"There is no funding, Nina. Ms. Goldstein isn't supposed to be helping runaways like this. She is supposed to inform their parents or others where they are."

"Yet she doesn't?" Nina shook her head. "I'm completely confused."

"Nina, Ms. Goldstein helps kids who can't go home and who do not want to go into the system. These are street kids and what she's doing is actually illegal. She started this after her husband died. The word passes through the streets that kids can come get a meal from time to time."

"So they don't stay here?"

"Oh no, there's only enough room for them to eat. If anyone found out about this place, Ms. Goldstein could get in a lot of trouble."

"About how many runaways show up here?"

Juan shrugged. "Sometimes three. Sometimes one hundred."

"A hundred? Where do they sit, in the sinks?"

"At times it's hard to deal with. She gets extra help from outsiders she trusts."

"Like you?" Nina smiled.

"Yeah."

"And you would never tell?"

"Nope."

"Why not? I mean, how did you come across this?"

"Let's just say Ms. Goldstein did a favor for me and this is how I repay her. What do you think? I know this isn't as impressive as a day in the park, but..." Before Juan could finish, Nina grabbed him into a kiss. The boys whistled.

Ms. Goldstein brought out two large bowls of homemade chicken and broccoli soup, juice, and crackers. They sat at the last table. Nina watched the girl finish her soup and leave. She thought about her moments after she left. It was a picture she couldn't easily let go of. Juan gulped the soup like he hadn't eaten in years.

"God, I love this stuff. She makes the best soup."

"It smells delicious. So do you ever get the same kids around here?"

"Sometimes. Most times they're glad to get a meal once a week." He shrugged.

"A lot don't come by more than once because they're afraid their parents might show up. Kids in this predicament cannot trust many adults."

"Yeah." Nina blew on her soup. "You really want to make a difference, don't you, Juan?" He looked at her. "In everything you do and say, I know that's the truth. You got that drive in you that many people don't have. You see things in different ways. You don't accept the easy way out."

He smirked. "Something tells me I have impressed you." He touched her knee.

"But the day's just begun."

"Well, if the second half is as engaging as the first, I'm all yours." Nina flirtatiously sipped her soup.

❖❖❖

That night Juan had the house to himself. He showered and made a sandwich he didn't eat. He heard gunshots in the distance. He pictured Rico blasting some poor kid's head off for stepping on his toe. He rested on his bed with his arms cradling his head. He wanted to change everything in so little time. Nina's face stole his thoughts. He rubbed his muscular chest. He imagined her lying beside him.

Would they ever get that serious? Could it be that real? The doorbell rang.

Nina watched the neighborhood activities from Juan's porch. A few kids tossed a football through the darkness. A teenage couple kissed two houses down. They gave Nina dirty looks. She quickly turned away. This was gang territory. She knew that the moment she got off the bus. She didn't see a barrage of gang members standing around like in Edgewood, but she knew.

"Nina?" Juan stood at the door holding his naked, bruised stomach. She gazed at the bruises. A mountain of fear raced inside her. She wouldn't forgive herself if anything ever happened to Juan. She touched his face. He allowed her inside. Juan's family had good taste when it came to decoration. Plants accented the corners of the living room. Portraits of flowers hung over the furniture. Wide, antique lamps sat on fashionable, vibrant end tables. Crème-colored furniture glorified the regal, gray carpeting. Nina couldn't help but love a house that smelled like flowers at every turn.

She glanced down the hall toward the middle-size kitchen. She imagined Florence and Juan having heart-to-heart talks at the huge table sitting against the blue cabinets. Juan's home reminded her of bread baking on a Sunday afternoon. It was as old-fashioned as it could get.

"Are you okay? What happened?" Nina asked. Juan rubbed his stomach.

"Played a little football with the guys earlier. They really kicked my ass. What are you doing here?" He didn't seem thrilled at her arrival. In fact, he was damn near angry. Had she done something wrong?

"I came to see you." She shoved her Metro card in her pocket.

He limped toward her, rubbing his swollen chest. "You thought you'd show up without warning? How did you get my address?"

"It wasn't hard. Did I do something wrong?"

"Yes, you did. You had no right coming down here like this, Nina. I didn't want you to come here. If I had, I would have invited you."

"I'm sorry." Taken aback, she brushed her hair from her face. "I got this feeling you needed me."

"Is this how you always are? Will you be going behind my back, being nosy if I don't tell you every little thing?"

Tears filled her eyes. She wanted so much to play it off but she couldn't. "I'm sorry. You don't have to worry about me coming back here again. In fact, don't worry about me at all." She ran to the door. Juan blocked her. "Move." She trembled.

"I'm sorry, Nina. God, I just didn't want to expose you to this."

"So what if you live in a shady neighborhood? It's no different from my cousin's. You don't have to be ashamed of that."

"I'm not ashamed. I just didn't want you to know this part of me." He hobbled to the couch. He never looked so radiant. The bruises hadn't hurt his looks a bit. Nina settled in beside him.

"What's going on, Juan?"

"I was trying to play this 'knight in shining armor' thing for you." He scoffed.

"It's been blown, hasn't it?"

"Well, I'm not a princess, either. I don't want you to be something you're not. I like *you*, Juan. The entire package. Don't you like everything about me?"

"Nina, I don't know anything about you. You won't tell me anything." She looked away. "I mean, how come you don't let me go to your cousin's home? What's the deal with you being so secretive?"

"You know all you need to know. You know I want to be with you." She touched his chest.

"Someday I expect to know more." He groaned in pain as he leaned up. "You came because you were worried, huh? Funny, I was just thinking about you," he flirted.

"Oh, really?" Nina leaned toward him. "Where were you thinking of me?"

"Back there." He pointed to the hallway. She shook beyond control. She wanted to explore all options with Juan. Every time she learned something new about him it made her high. "What's back there?" She touched his thighs through his warm-ups. He flinched from pain.

"My bedroom. Would you like to see it?" He smirked.

"Already, huh?" She stood. "I guess guys *are* only after one thing." She went to the door.

"Wait, Nina!" He hopped toward her. "I want you to see my *room*. I don't want to have sex with you."

"You don't?"

"Well, I do." He laughed. "I just didn't mean that when I suggested you see my room. Come on."

"Maybe we should wait until your mother gets home."

"Nope." He took her hand. "I promise I won't bite you, girl." She reluctantly followed. He stopped her when they got to the doorway. She tried to look around him but he held his ground. "Just let me freshen up a bit. I never had a girl in here." He dashed inside.

Nina's curiosity was in full effect once Juan shut his door. She saw his mother's bedroom. Florence's room appeared tiny as a wasp's nest until Nina walked inside. They had much in common when it came to creativity. Little flower baskets sat on Florence's chest, arranged with an artist's eye. Art books sat on her hamper. The colors in Florence's room were so amazing. Nina became tempted to touch everything in sight.

She left the room before she overstepped her bounds.

"I'll be right out!" Juan yelled.

Nina loved what he went through to impress her. He seemed to be the only boy these days who practiced chivalry. Rico's door was wide open. Nina hadn't gotten a chance to meet Juan's elusive older brother at the party. She became extremely curious about him. She didn't even know his name. Rico's room was a haven of explicit photos of half-naked women. Clothes covered the floor. Trash and empty food containers fell from the bed in clumps. She got a chill the moment she walked inside. She noticed the unique symbols on his wall. They were exactly like the ones she'd seen down the street.

"Hey." Juan walked inside Rico's room with his arms crossed. He appeared uneasy about her being in his brother's room. Maybe she *had* overstepped her bounds.

"Jesus, what a mess. You don't need to be in this hellhole. Let's get out of here." He took her hand.

She sighed. "Oops. I was snooping again. Nasty little habit, huh?"

"Not at all. In fact, nothing you could do would offend me." He took her hand. His fingers slid between hers as they walked to his room.

"You sure about that? You were ticked off that I came here tonight."

"Let's just say I got over that." Juan closed the door behind them. Nina strolled around his room, looking for nothing in particular. She tried not to notice how sensuous Juan looked shirtless. He sat on the bed with his back against the headboard. He stared at her like she was a piece of meat. Nina wasn't frightened. She wasn't offended. She was *aroused*.

CHAPTER NINE

"How long is it gonna take for you to stop staring at me?" Nina sauntered to the bed. She wanted Juan. Foreign feelings she couldn't comprehend muddled her mind.

"What are you thinking about?" He pulled her on the bed.

"I'm thinking this is too good to be true." She took a deep breath. He pulled her toward him. He kissed her neck. "I never knew something could feel so good. Something could feel so real," Nina whispered. He trickled his fingers down her blouse, causing her to wiggle. "But it's too soon, Juan."

"Is it?" He sucked her neck.

"Yeah." He brought her body even closer to his. "We can't do this, Juan."

"Why not?" He looked at her.

"Because you said it yourself. We don't know each other well enough yet. Juan, I want my first time to be special." He scooped her hair into his palm. "I want it to be when I won't have any regrets. When I feel in my heart that it's right."

"I respect that. I'd wait for you forever, Nina." He stroked her hair. "I love you."

"What?" She moved away. His mouth puckered, begging for more of her tenderness. "Juan, you can't possibly mean that so soon."

"I do." He took her hand. "I love you, Nina. I've never been so happy. I never want to let you go." They started kissing. Once again, Nina stopped it.

"I do want to, Juan. But when the time is right."

"As long as it's with me, I don't give a damn how long you make me wait. I don't want to be with any other girl. I don't want you to be with another guy." She smiled widely. "I only want you to be with me. I promise to give you that in return. If you want it."

"Are you *kidding*?" She hugged him. "That's all I've wanted!"

"Juan?" Florence headed down the hallway.

"Oh shit! Jesus, uh." Juan threw on a shirt.

"Oh no, your mother." Nina gaped at the door. Florence busted into the room. Her faced filled with shock. Juan stood by the window, tugging at his shirt. Nina hid her face in her palms.

"What in the world is going on here?" Florence held her hips.

"Uh, Ma, I can explain. It's not what you think."

"Mrs. Alonso, we weren't doing anything."

"Is this something you usually do, Nina? Seduce young boys when their mothers aren't home?"

"Ma," Juan snapped.

"I, uh..." Nina stood. "I got this feeling something happened to Juan and I came by. I know it was wrong to be here without an adult, but nothing happened. I assure you I am not that kind of girl, Mrs. Alonso."

"I like you, Nina. But I want to tell you something before you and Juan step over the boundaries. If you two want to see each other, you have to respect my rules. I don't want you here when I am not around. It's not that I don't trust you, it's just that too many things can happen."

"We weren't doing anything, Ma. Instead of lecturing me you should be saving some of that for your other son." Juan leaned against the dresser.

"Nina, I think you'd better go." Florence moved aside to let her pass.

"I really am sorry, Mrs. Alonso. Next time I will respect your rules." Nina smiled at Juan.

"Nina, I'm sorry about that 'seducing' crack." Florence exhaled.

"Nina, I'll take you where you need to go. It's not safe for you to be here at night. Wait for me in the living room." Nina nodded and left the bedroom.

"Happy, Mamá? For your information, Nina's my girlfriend now. So you can expect to see a lot of her. You had no right to treat her like that."

"Oh, *I* had no right? It's just *my* house. How dare I try to make rules since I pay the bills?"

"How come you're on my jock?"

She hit his chest. "Don't talk to me like that, Juan. Now you are getting out of hand. You haven't acted normal since you met that girl."

"I'm acting happy for once, aren't I? I know you aren't used to seeing me this way. I'm a man now, Mamá. You *can't* control my life."

"You know you're not supposed to have girls in your room. Don't act like it's something I just invented."

"I didn't invite her here to fuck, Ma! She came over *here*. What was I supposed to do?"

Florence stepped toward him. "Watch your mouth! You don't break the rules! I am *not* arguing with you about this. I think Nina's a lovely girl, but that doesn't give you two the right to do whatever you want. If I catch you two in this house alone again I won't allow you to see her!"

"*Allow* me?" Juan laughed.

"Did I stutter? Say something smart right now." She tapped

her foot. "Go on, you won't see her now, either, if you do." Juan fell over on the bed. "Now go to bed!"

She slammed the door. A second later she popped back in. "What the hell happened to you?" She rushed toward him.

"I'm fine." He pushed her hands from his face.

"You're all bruised up. Did you get into some trouble with somebody?"

"No! Look, you don't need to worry about me. I won't end up like Rico, if that's what you're thinking."

Florence leaned away from the bed. "I can't help it, Juan. You're changing."

"Yeah?" He glared at her. "Good."

✠✠✠

Nina couldn't believe her eyes when she got back to Edgewood. Spectators crowded the elementary school parking lot. People moved from side to side struggling to see. Police roped the areas off, urging the people to stay behind the yellow ribbons. Two more cop cars sped through the street, honking horns to make a passage through the gaping citizens. Nina stopped beside two women who were conversing in Spanish.

"*Hola*," Nina spoke.

"*Hola*." The first lady smiled.

"Uh, what in the world happened?" Nina made way for a group of curious teenagers.

"There was a murder. A young man was killed from the neighborhood." The lady struggled through her accent. "We don't know when. I was coming home from work and my friend told me." She pointed to the lady beside her who didn't speak English.

174

"A murder?"

"My friend said it was a big fight earlier. That some gang-bangers from the New York Assassins did it." She shrugged.

"Oh my God. The person who was killed, he was a Bronx Gangsta?" Nina's stomach turned. The image of Tajo lying in a pool of blood polluted her mind. She'd warned him that his life would lead to death. She hoped to God that hadn't happened. Someone grabbed Nina's arm, whisking her from the crowd.

"Let me go!" She struggled, not realizing who held her.

"Be quiet, all right?"

"Chino?" She rubbed her arm. "What are you trying to do?"

"Do you have any idea what went down tonight, Nina?" He eyed her suspiciously.

"No. Why the hell would I?"

"Sure is funny, things start happening when you show up."

"Yeah." Bone stood behind her, chewing an apple. A crowd of Tajo's best circled her.

"I don't know what's going on, guys. Please tell me Tajo's all right!"

"He's all right. He's mad as hell, but he's all right," Shorty-Five said. "Nina, you got some explaining to do."

"I didn't do anything!"

"How come you were at that punk-ass Rico's?" Juice raised an eyebrow.

"What? I don't know what you're talking about."

"We're talking about you being chummy with Rico Alonso. Don't act like you don't know who he is."

"I don't, Chino." She tried to break from Shorty-Five's grasp. "I don't know anything! Could you please tell me what's going on!"

Shorty-Five tightened his grip. "What's going on is you were in NYA territory and we want to know why."

"Guys, please. I don't know what you're saying!"

"Lay off, fellas." Chino smirked. Juice and Shorty-Five hesitated but gave in.

"Someone this beautiful doesn't lie." Chino caressed her face. "You really don't know a thing about this, do you?"

"All I know is that the New York Assassins are your rival gang. But I don't know what that has to do with…" She covered her mouth. "Alonso?" She looked away. "Rico *Alonso*?"

"Rico is the leader of the New York Assassins, Nina." Bone crossed his arms. "Don't play this shit like you didn't know."

"I swear, I…" She broke into tears. "I didn't know. Oh my God. This can't be happening."

"Are you all right?" Chino took her hand. "We didn't mean to scare you. We just needed to know. Anyway, the New York Assholes were just here and pulled a train on Cannon."

"Wh, what?" Tears danced in Nina's eyes.

"Look, you don't want to know what they did." Chino sighed.

"They cut off his balls and beat him to death," Juice blurted out. Chino winced at Juice's interference.

"Oh my God." Nina fell against Chino's chest. "This can't be true! This can't be true! He can't be connected to the Assassins. He can't be!"

"Hold on. Who are *you* talking about, Nina?" Chino turned her loose.

"I'm talking about *Juan*! I'm talking about *Juan*!" She ran away.

"Who the hell is Juan?" Chino looked at the others.

"Juan Alonso is Rico's little brother." Juice walked off.

Shorty-Five cracked his knuckles. "Obviously, Nina had something going with him. Once we tell Tajo, it's over for sure."

"Isn't that a shame?" A devious smile spread across Chino's lips.

"You're full of shit." Bone laughed. "You know damn well you're happy about this."

Chino grabbed his crotch. "Well, Bone, you know me, right? Maybe a little..."

Chino tip-toed into Nina's bedroom moments later. "Go away, Chino." She sniffled.

"Hey, are you okay? Nina, I know this may be hard, but it's for the best. If Juan is Rico's brother, then he has the same beliefs toward us as we do them."

"What do you mean?" She sniffed again.

"I mean..." He sat on the bed. "He's going to hate you when he finds out. He's not going to want anything to do with you."

"That's not true. You don't even know Juan. We love each other. We have a connection nobody else has." She cried into her palms.

"I know it's hard. But the truth is, you can't see him again. If you do, we'll have to kill him. You understand?" She looked up. "Juan Alonso isn't the man for you, Nina. But I can be." He leaned to kiss her. She turned away. "When you can't be with the one you love, love the one you're with." He walked to the door.

"Chino, wait." She stood. "Juan has nothing to do with his brother's life. We can still be together. I love him."

Chino left without another word.

❖❖❖

"There's nothing she *can* do," Rosa declared during lunch the next day. She followed the others to the last table in the school cafeteria. "She has to quit seeing him."

"But why? Tajo shouldn't make that decision. It's Nina's life."

"Wake up, Lisa." Rosa drowned her fries in ketchup. "If Nina and Juan even think of getting together, Juan's family can start planning his funeral."

"Not to mention what would happen to Nina." Claudia sighed. Nina finally looked at the trio. She actually had to remind herself she was the subject of their conversation.

"What could happen to me, Claude?"

"Think about it. Not only would Tajo want to hurt Juan, Rico would want to hurt you. It's a no-win situation. You got to find someone else."

"I can't just find someone else." Nina shoved her tray across the table. A group of kids from the other table stared. "I've never felt this way about anyone else. Do you guys understand that I am in love with Juan? I can't just cut him out of my life."

"I support you, Nina." Lisa touched her hand. "You should follow your heart."

"Yeah, if she wants to send Juan to an early grave. Nina, do you have any idea what you've gotten into? This isn't some little game you can talk your way out of. Do you want to be with Juan or save him?" Rosa sighed. "It's your call."

"Rosa's right. I have no choice."

"No, Nina."

"Lisa, please." Nina held up her hand. "We can't possibly be together. You have no idea how thick the hate is between the Bronx Gangstas and the NYAs. I don't want to turn on Tajo. He's my cousin." She played with a napkin. "Family is more important than anything else."

"So what do you do about Juan?" Claudia asked.

"I have to tell him, right?" She stared at her friends. Rosa and Claudia nodded.

Lisa shook her head in objection. "Lisa, I can't string him along."

"How are you going to tell him?" Lisa gaped.

"She might not have to tell him the truth. She can just say she doesn't want to be with him. Just dump him with some feeble excuse. Guys are dumb as ticks, he'll buy it."

Rosa chuckled.

"Juan's not dumb at all. He won't believe that I don't want to see him all of a sudden. I'll just tell him the truth. That way it can keep him from bothering me about it. I'm sure once he finds out he'll hate me anyway."

"Don't worry, Nina. I'll be around for moral support."

"Thank you so much, Claude." Nina hugged her.

"I still think you should be with Juan and stand up to your cousin." Lisa dug into her lasagna.

✠✠✠

Carlos returned to the table with a bag of chips he scored from a scared freshman. Dell and Tony were too busy making cheat sheets for their next class to eat. Juan stared at the last table in the cafeteria. Carlos chuckled when he noticed Juan gazing at Nina.

"What's up, homes? Got a lot on your mind?" Carlos asked.

"Huh?" Juan watched Claudia whisper into Nina's ear. Carlos finished his chips by the time Juan answered him. "Did you say something, Carlos?"

"Yeah, about twenty minutes ago. What's your problem today?"

"I don't know. Something's not right with Nina. She's acting strange."

"How?"

"She's avoiding me big time. Every time I try to say something to her she runs the other way."

"Maybe it's your breath." Dell laughed. Juan ignored him.

"She did that about three times today. Then I saw her and Claudia talking outside the restrooms. I called her name over and over and she just walked off. Why is she treating me like this?"

"Because you were dumb enough to tell her how you felt." Tony played with his pizza. "Juan, you don't ever tell a girl how you feel unless you know for sure she's down for you."

"Yeah, didn't we school you?" Carlos asked.

Juan played with a French fry. "I told you that playa shit don't work on Nina. She's different. She can see through an act a mile away. Something happened and I wish I knew what it was."

"Probably those three hens over there." Carlos gestured to Nina's table. "You know how girls are when they get with their cliques. They probably did everything they could to show Nina you're no good."

"But why?" Juan frowned.

Tony shook his head. "Don't you know anything about women? Shit, if they're single they want their friends to be single, too, so they can all have something to bitch about. They probably spent the entire time talking you down to Nina."

"Nina has a mind of her own. She's strong. That's what I like about her the most. Shit, maybe she has a man and lied." Juan scratched his arm. "You know girls love to pull that."

"They sure do. How come girls can't be more honest and open, like guys?" Tony gulped soda.

"Tony, dog shit has more brains than you." Dell rolled his eyes. "Juan, Nina cares about you. Even I see that. Why don't you go and ask her what's wrong instead of staring like some stalker?"

"No. Maybe I'm tired of running after her. If she wants to talk to me she can come to me herself."

Carlos grinned. "Something tells me you'll be waiting here until the year three thousand and two."

Dell sighed. "Ignore him, Juan. Go over there and talk to her. She's your lady."

Juan stood.

"Hold up." Tony accidentally spit pizza across the table. "How come the *man* always has to go and ask what the deal is? Let her come to him. Sit down, Juan."

Dell waved off Tony's opinion. "Forget Tony, Juan. You can talk to Nina if you want to."

Juan stood again.

"Juan, sit your whipped ass down." Tony grabbed him. "Shit, if you go over there now she *knows* she's got you where she wants you. Every time she snaps her fingers you gonna go running?"

Carlos snickered. "Tony, do you see how fine Nina is? Shit, if she snapped her fingers, *I'd* go running."

Dell laughed.

Tony shook his head. "She ain't that fine that she can be treating people like she is. Shoot, there's more honeys in the sea. I'm telling you, Juan, make her ass come to you. Don't go out like a punk."

"Juan, would you rather be a punk with a fine, beautiful woman on your arm or would you rather be stubborn and single?" Dell asked.

"Sorry, Tony. You lose." Juan headed to Nina's table.

Tony shook his head. "Man, he's so whipped he should change his last name to 'Cream.'" The others laughed.

"Nina?" Juan tapped her shoulder. She didn't turn around. She knew seeing his face would make her break down. She wouldn't be able to handle him for a second. She decided to let her girlfriends take care of the situation.

She looked at her friends. "I'm going to the bathroom. Lunchtime is almost over anyway. See you guys later." She left without laying an eye on Juan.

"Nina, wait!" He started after her. Rosa blocked him.

"Hold on, Juan." She crossed her arms. "Maybe you'd like to spend some time with *us*."

Claudia smirked. "Yeah. As Nina's friends, we'd like to get to know you a little better."

"Not *now*," Juan growled.

❈❈❈

Nina needed to think. She'd been up all night worrying about this situation. Nina knew Tajo's gang affiliation affected the family, but she didn't conceive it would ever affect her love life. She stared into the crooked mirror of the girls' bathroom. The symbolism terrified her. Did the mirror represent her life? Why did she feel she had no control all of a sudden? She was cornered once again.

The doors flew open. She didn't hear the usual girlish chatter that invaded the bathroom. She noticed a shadow. She wondered why the person wouldn't move. She smelled men's cologne. Juan walked in, holding his breath.

"Hi." He stood in the center of the bathroom. Nina hurried to gather her things.

"Juan, get out of here. This is the girls' bathroom."

"I know what it is." He looked at the pink and beige stalls. "It's pretty nice in here. You should see our joint. It's filthy." He walked around. "Damn, you even got soap in here?"

"I don't want to talk to you." She tried to pass him. He tugged her arm.

"I want to talk to *you*."

"Let me go, Juan!"

"Not until you listen to me, Nina. Now, what's going on?"

"I don't want to talk to you, all right? I don't want to see you ever again!" She pushed him.

"That's bullshit! What the hell changed? Just tell me the truth!"

"What part of 'I don't want you' do you not understand?"

Claudia, Nina and Rosa entered the room. "Are we interrupting something?" Claudia asked.

"Juan, this is the girls' bathroom." Lisa pointed at the stalls.

"I know, Lisa. Nina wouldn't talk to me so what choice did I have?"

Another group of girls entered. They chuckled at the handsome young man. Some opted to wait outside until he left. Others pretended to apply makeup just to witness the teen drama unfold.

"Get out of here, Juan!"

"No, Nina. I demand you talk to me right now."

"'Demand'? Who the hell do you think you are?"

"I don't know. Shit, I thought I was your boyfriend! I know something's up. People don't just change overnight."

Nina eyed Claudia. "Maybe I decided you weren't the guy for me after all."

"Or maybe someone else did it for you." He looked at the others. Claudia shrugged. "Did you guys have something to do with this?"

"No. I made up my own mind. Isn't it possible for you to think I have a mind of my own?"

"Don't give me that shit, Nina. What's going on?"

"Leave me alone!" She shoved him.

"Funny, you weren't saying that last night in my bedroom, were you?"

"What?" Rosa busted out laughing. Another group of girls walked in.

Nina looked at Juan. "You planned to embarrass me? Mission accomplished."

"Nina, wait." He grabbed her shirt.

"Get off me!" She pushed him against the sink and ran out.

"Claudia, what's the deal?" Juan sighed. "Does she think I did something to her?"

"Juan, you have to take it up with Nina. As her friend, I can't go behind her back and tell her business. Why don't you try talking to her later on?"

He scoffed. "Is she going to run off then, too?" He headed out of the restroom.

"Juan?" Lisa stepped toward him.

"Yeah?" He accidentally bumped into some girls when he turned around.

"You're the best thing that's happened to Nina. I wanted you to know I think you belong together. I'm cheering you on."

"Thanks, Lisa, that means a lot. And I hope you're right." He left.

❉❉❉

"I must admit, Tajo, you're handling this better than I would." Chino handed Tajo a crisp joint. They sat on Tajo's porch gazing at a car full of women who turned tricks for twenty dollars.

"Why does it surprise you, homes?" Tajo wasn't a fool. He knew Chino's agenda was to have Nina for himself. He didn't object to that possibility but didn't like the feeling he was being played. He handed the joint to Chino, careful not to let on his suspicions.

"Think about it. Juan Alonso with his shitty hands all over your little cousin. Her being in the midst of our rivals, man. It's enough to make me sick."

Tajo grinned. "Really? It's settled. Nina knows so she won't see him again."

"You believe that? Man, she was crying like her daddy died when I spoke to her last night. I don't know if you can trust her so much. Remember, you haven't seen her in years. You got to get to know her again."

"Nina would never step over my loyalty. She knows the Bronx Gs are just as much a part of her as me."

"Okay, fine." Chino passed the joint. "What about Juan, huh? You think he's going to let her go?" Tajo contemplated the question. "No way, man. Tajo, he's going to keep pushing her and pushing her until she gives in. You want your cousin fucking that piece of trash?"

Tajo crushed the joint until it fizzled, leaving a mark in his palm. The pain didn't faze him. After being stabbed and shot numerous times, his body was immune.

"If Nina doesn't know the deal, I will make it clear for her. And if I have to I'll make it clear to Juan Alonso, too. But you can't fault him, really. Nina's a fine one." Tajo chuckled.

"She sure is. Why don't you let me keep an eye on her when I can?" Chino licked his lips. "Just to make sure she's as loyal as you say."

"Spider's already doing that. How you think we found out she was at Rico's?"

"I mean..." Chino scratched underneath his baseball cap. "I would keep an eye on her to make sure she don't have nothing to do with Juan. If I see them together *once*, I'll tell you and we can take care of him."

"No."

"But Tajo, you got to take control, man. Nina is not going to stop seeing this guy."

"Just keep your ass out of it, Chino. I can handle her." Tajo went inside. Chino stared into space.

***

"I want to see you, Nina," Juan whispered into the phone that night. He covered it every time Florence passed the hall.

"Juan, what is it going to take for you to get the hint?" She walked around the living room in her nightgown. Tajo was gone on an all-night errand. She was happy to have the place to herself. She prayed she could get through one night without thinking of Juan. His call destroyed that option. "How many times do I have to tell you I don't want to be with you? It was just a fluke." She timidly chuckled. "I realized we don't have much in common after all."

"Bullshit." He took the phone into his bedroom. "Why are you doing this? What's happened, Nina?"

"Nothing! Look, it's almost nine and I want to go to bed. I haven't been feeling well."

"Probably all the lying you been doing." He sat on his bed. "You think I'm buying this, then you're crazy. Anyway, Claudia said there was something you should tell me. Now, what's going on?"

"I don't have to explain my decisions to you." She sat on the couch. "I don't want to be with you. Why don't you get over it and find someone else?"

"You're talking so much bullshit I can smell it from here."

Nina sighed. "You won't let this go, will you? Believe me, it's all for the best." She said the words, although being away from Juan killed her already. "I don't want to be with you, Juan."

He looked at his dresser. "You paused."

"What?"

"You paused. You paused and now I know you're lying."

"Juan."

"I knew it." He grinned. "You care about me as much as I care about you."

"No, I don't."

"You still want to be with me, Nina. I can feel it. I know you better than you know yourself."

"Really?"

"Yes." He walked to the window. "Meet me tonight. We have to talk about all of this."

"Are you kidding? How many bricks have to fall on your head for you to get the idea, Juan? Leave me alone!"

"If you don't meet me, I'll be forced to take other options."

"Do whatever you have to, just leave me alone." She hung up the phone. He rubbed the receiver underneath his chin. "Okay, Nina. If that's the way you want it."

❉❉❉

Even a few dollars could get information from a best friend. Juan used his last ten dollars to bribe Claudia for Nina's address. After finding out she lived in the notorious Edgewood, he wondered why he risked his life just to see a girl who'd pushed him away. He tugged on the steering wheel. He couldn't allow himself to believe Nina for a moment. Something was terribly wrong. He knew she loved him. He could see it in her eyes, every touch from her spilled eternal passion. He reluctantly turned down the trashy, graffiti-stained streets of Edgewood. Groups of boys his age sat on every corner, guzzling forties and smoking weed. Heads turned to witness the strange vehicle entering the area. Yep, Juan had to be in love. He'd never put himself in such danger for any other reason.

Car lights shined through the living room window. Nina needed something to take her mind off her impending anxiety. She couldn't determine the make of the car in the darkness. Someone knocked on the door. She remembered Tajo's rule to not let anyone in. A girl could never be too careful in Edgewood.

"Nina, are you in there?" Juan pounded the door.

"Jesus." She leaned against the door, shaking.

"Nina?" He shook the knob.

"Juan, you shouldn't have come *here*. Do you realize what you've done?"

"Yeah, maybe." He looked down the street. A group of guys milled toward him. "Could you hurry up and open the door before I'm killed out here?"

Trembling, she unlocked the door. He breezed in like a breath of fresh air her body craved. His eyes wandered down her chest to her thighs. She'd forgotten she was in her nightgown. "Maybe I should put on something else."

"No, maybe you should talk to me."

"Juan, you don't know what you've done. Being here is extremely dangerous. God, I was trying to protect you! Why did you come here?"

"Because you didn't want to speak to me otherwise. And I'm not about to buy this change in attitude, Nina. I know you still care about me." He scoped Tajo's living room. "Your cousin has taste. Where is he, anyway?"

"Out, and for your sake you'd better hurry up before he gets back. We can talk about this at school." She shoved him to the door. He pulled away.

"No. Now I risked my life, bribed Claudia for your address, and I intend on getting some answers!"

"God, you're stubborn," she scoffed. Still, she couldn't help being flattered. He laid his jacket on the back of the sofa. Nina sat on the couch. Juan stood in front of her with his arms crossed. She'd never seen him so serious. "Sorry if I treated you badly at school today. You didn't deserve it."

"No, I didn't." He sat beside her. "I've rushed you, haven't I? Damn, I didn't want to do that. I wanted everything to be slow and easy."

"And it *has* been." She took his hand. "Juan, I never thought I could meet anyone like you. I was so closed off to the world before we met. Just being with you has opened my eyes to so many things."

He laid his arm on the back of the couch. "Then what happened, Nina?"

"I fell in love with you, that's what happened." She sighed into her hands. "And I wanted to break up with you before you broke up with me."

"Broke up with, Nina, what are you talking about?" he pleaded.

"Didn't you notice the neighborhood on the way here? It's Edgewood, Juan."

"Yeah, so? So you were ashamed of where you stayed, too. But that's no reason to push me away."

"Juan, I wasn't ashamed of staying here. Juan, this is Bronx Gangsta territory."

His eyes widened. "I know you know this." She gaped.

"Okay." He sighed. "But what does this have to do with *us*?"

"Juan, you have no idea what you've gotten into. I found out something last night. I just can't see you anymore. It's too dangerous for the both of us."

"Hold on." Juan sighed. "Maybe I am going crazy, but I don't have any idea what you are trying to say! Could you just spit it out, please?"

She looked at the ceiling. "We can't be together! Why can't me saying it be enough?"

He grabbed her. "Because it isn't. Look into my eyes, Nina."

"No."

"You don't want to because you won't be able to lie any more. Let me tell you something, okay? I've spent my entire life doing the right thing. Other people have been able to fuck things up at will, but I was always expected to rise above everyone else. I usually give up everything I want to please other people. Well, I'm not doing that anymore, Nina. I want you and I am not going to give you up, no matter the reason."

"Please go, Juan." She went to the door. "Just go before it's too late."

"No." He walked toward her. "No, I'm not going anywhere."

"Juan, go!"

"No. I came to talk and I intend on talking. I'm not leaving until you come straight with me, Nina."

"Get out! Get the fuck out!" She slapped him. "Get out! Don't you care at all what this is doing?"

"Nina, calm down!" He grabbed her wrists.

"Let go of me! Get out, Juan!" She pounded his chest. He threw her on the floor. "Get out!" She wiggled. "Just go, Juan! Just go before it's too late!"

"Stop it, Nina!" He held her arms down.

"Get out of here! Get out!"

"Stop it!" He got on top of her. She settled down when she looked into his eyes.

"Just stop it." He took a deep breath. He realized he was on top of her. Nina never felt so helpless. She never thought she could enjoy the feeling...until now.

CHAPTER TEN

Juan clamped his lips over hers. No matter how hard Nina tried, she couldn't get her body to reject what she'd been wanting all day. He brought his arms down to her waist. His tongue deeply pursued every avenue her mouth offered. He'd never had a chance to feel her like this. Either she'd stop or he'd stop. But no one stopped at this moment.

He leaned against her thighs. One hundred horses couldn't pull him away. She rested on the carpet. He waited for the parting of her sweet mouth, anticipated any word.

"Nina, can you feel how much I want you?" He touched her thigh.

"Yes."

"Do you know how much I care for you?"

"Yes." She stared at the ceiling.

"Do you want *me*?" He brought his mouth toward hers. Her warm breath hit the tips of his lips. The teasing nearly killed him.

"Yes."

"Then tell me what's wrong. And let me decide how we'll handle it."

"I know your brother Rico leads the New York Assassins."

"God." He shut his eyes.

She kissed him. "But I would have accepted that. Juan, I'd accept anything to be with you."

"Nina." He kissed her neck. "That's not me. I'm not into that life. I don't agree with it."

"I know, Juan. But it's more complicated. It's not about who your brother is. It's about who my cousin is. Juan, my cousin is Tajo Munez. Does his name ring a bell?"

Juan felt his blood rushing all over his body. For a moment he doubted he'd heard her correctly. At least he wanted to believe he hadn't. She leaned up. "It does ring a bell, doesn't it?"

He sighed. "He's the leader of the Bronx Gangstas. Maybe the world *is* too fuckin' small after all." He pulled his legs against his chest. "And I feel like crawling into a hole and never coming out." He stuck his head into his thighs.

"It's amazing that all this time we had no idea." She rubbed his back. "Juan, I love you. But how can we possibly be together now?"

"I don't know." He mumbled into his thighs. "All I know is that I won't be able to be happy without you." He took her hand. "Nothing has changed in my heart, Nina. I hope it hasn't changed in yours."

"You still want me?" She fell into his arms.

"I'll always want you, Nina. No one's ever gonna take your place. Here." He took off his gold chain. Nina gazed upon the four-leaf clover pendant that dangled from it. He slipped it around her neck. "This binds us, Nina. As long as you have this, nothing can touch us. It will be a symbol of our love. No matter how corny it sounds." He laughed.

"Want to see *my* bedroom?" She stood. He couldn't ignore how the nightgown tangled between her thighs.

He brushed lint from his pants. He retrieved his jacket. "No, I'd better be going. If we go to your bedroom we may not come out." He gripped the doorknob. "I can't believe this is happening."

"That we're connected to rival gangs?"

"No. That we're alone, you're in your nightgown, and I'm leaving." He shook his head. "I must be crazy."

"I know I'm crazy for *you*." She kissed him. "We'll be together."

He ran his fingers across her lips. "When the time is right."

He left.

* * *

"Say what?" Carlos did a one-eighty in Dell's backseat the next evening.

"Yep." Juan shrugged. "Nina is Tajo Munez's cousin. And I don't really care."

Tony leaned in from the backseat. "Yeah, we'll see how much you care when the Bronx Gangstas turn you into a Christmas ornament."

"I admit it's going to make the relationship difficult, but I love Nina. We aren't going to let anyone dictate our lives."

Tony stared out the window. "You really think you can keep this hidden from her cousin? Or better yet, from Rico?"

"Rico doesn't care what I do." Juan opened a bag of chips.

"Earth to Juan." Tony shook his head. "Rico hates the Bronx Gangstas as much as fire hates water. If he found out you even looked at a girl involved with them, you won't have to worry about Nina's cousin smoking you, Rico will take care of that himself."

"So what are you saying, Tony? I should give up on love?"

"I'm saying you need to live! Is this girl worth all of this trouble?"

"Tony's right, man." Dell made a right around a sharp curve.

"Dell, I would think you of all people would be cheering me on."

"Juan, that was before I knew who Nina was. You're my best pal and I want to save you from making the biggest mistake of your life."

"Hell, I wish you'd all make up your damn minds! Are you all saying I shouldn't see Nina anymore?" He looked at them one by one.

"Well, out of all honesty, it's hard to say. She's so damn fine." Carlos whistled.

"I'm serious. What do you all think?"

"Hell, what the fuck do we know about real love?" Tony grinned. "We're just here to save you from making mistakes."

Juan grinned. "So you all got my back if the shit goes down?"

"Of course." Dell sighed. "Hey, it won't be the stupidest thing you've ever done, will it?"

"Very funny." Juan stared straight ahead. "I saw her in her nightgown last night."

"What?" Carlos grabbed Juan's shoulders.

"Oh man, I wish I'd been there!" Tony took Juan's chips.

"I can't explain how I felt. There we were on the living room floor. She was looking up at me. You know how girls look at you when they want to." Juan chuckled. "And she looked so beautiful, man. It was like she wasn't real. We started kissing. Her body was hot as lava, man. My hands landed on her thighs, kind of under her gown."

"Yeah, yeah. I'm about to pop a woody right now," Tony whispered.

"Is that body as great as we think it is?" Carlos leaned up.

"More than you could ever dream. I think she wanted to,

though I can't be sure. You never can be too sure with girls. You know how they are. Anyway, I started kissing her neck. She kind of moaned." Juan closed his eyes.

"Go on." Tony licked his lips.

"Then I looked at her body, man. She wasn't naked but the gown was so sheer I could see anything I wanted to. She wanted it, too, man. My face brushed her chest as I leaned up."

"Yeah, yeah? Get to the part where the panties are *already* in a ball on the floor."

Dell shook his head. "Tony, you're such a pig."

"Like you weren't thinking it, too," he scoffed.

"Go on, Juan. How were the tits?" Carlos asked.

"And that ass, is it as glorious naked as it is in clothes?" Tony rubbed his hands together.

"I wouldn't know the answer to either question." Juan took his back. "I got up and left."

"Excuse me? I know you did not just say what I thought you said." Tony gawked.

"Yeah, I left. I really care about her. I don't just want to do her and leave her hanging. That wouldn't have been right."

"What the hell planet are you from, Juan, 'cause it ain't Earth!" Carlos crossed his arms. "You don't leave a woman when she's half-naked."

"Hell no. Especially when she's as fine as Nina! Do you realize you probably won't get that close again?"

"I believe I *will*, Tony." Juan beamed.

✳✳✳

Rico couldn't believe what he heard. Tray-Eight stood against

Rico's silver-gray Cadillac smacking gum. He rubbed his bald head. The last inkling of sun glared against his gold chain. Rico leaned from the driver's seat, exposing his handgun. He rested it on the dashboard. He beat the steering wheel until his thumb burned.

"Say that one more time, homes." Rico squinted.

"I say that girl your brother is so hot for is down with the Bronx Gs, man. I found out from one of the homies. This is bullshit, man. I know Juan's your brother but he needs to be taught a lesson. His loyalty is for shit, Rico. He cares more about that bitch than he does us. It ain't right."

Rico popped his jaw. "You say this Nina chick is Tajo's cousin?"

"Yep." Tray-Eight pulled out a sack of coke. "Where the fuck does Juan get off acting the way he acts? He has to learn to respect us, homes. He has to stay away from that girl."

"Oh, don't worry about that, *ese*." Rico gritted his teeth. "He won't be seeing that girl ever again."

"She sure is a pretty piece, though, huh?" Tray-Eight sniffed cocaine. "I guess you can't blame your brother for going after that. Shit, I wouldn't mind a piece myself."

"She's a Bronx G ho. She ain't worth dog shit on Juan's shoe. My brother has plans. He's got a future. He's going to make it out of here someday. I won't let him waste his life on some two-bit Bronx G bitch. I don't give a damn how fine she is. Thanks for telling me, man. Good looking out." They bumped fists.

"Whatever happens, you know NYAs got yo back." Tray-Eight laughed from his high. Rico massaged the thick ring on his middle finger. He always had a plan. This time wasn't any different.

❖❖❖

Nina felt like the dumbest girl in the world. She didn't even try to go slow with Juan, despite knowing who his brother was. He'd invited her to dinner with his family. Before he'd gotten the invitation out, she'd accepted. What worried her most was that she wasn't scared of Tajo or Rico finding out. Being with Juan gave her enormous strength.

She didn't think twice about the dinner after Juan assured her Rico wouldn't be around. On the way over, they did their best not to talk about the gangs. They listened to Nina's favorite radio station. They chatted about the upcoming showcase. From time to time Juan stole kisses at red lights. After a soothing ride, they reached Juan's house.

"I hope this beats the library." Juan escorted her inside. "We can study here if you want."

"You sure it's safe?" Nina whispered. She heard Florence digging around in the kitchen.

"Trust me." He kissed her. "I didn't tell anyone you're connected to the Bronx Gangstas and Rico will be gone all night. He's handling business." He took her hand.

"And you don't have to tell me what kind." She exhaled.

"So sit down, Nina. Get comfortable." Juan lapped his arm behind the couch.

Nina straightened the couch pillows. "I really like your house. I didn't get a chance to tell you before."

"That will mean a lot to my mother." Juan played with her hands. She giggled, reading his devious mind.

"Hi, Nina." Cynthia ran into the living room.

"Hello, Cynthia. I forgot to tell you how pretty you were at your party. How does it feel to be eleven years old?" Nina smiled.

"It's okay. I can't wait until I'm thirteen so Mom will let me start dating. She's so old-fashioned." Cynthia smirked at her brother. Nina laughed.

"Uh, Cynthia, go help Mom in the kitchen." Juan stared at Nina.

"She doesn't need any help."

"Well, I don't need someone spying on me, do I?"

She smirked. "Want to get fresh with Mom right in the kitchen? Guys are such pigs." She ran off.

Nina laughed. "She's adorable, Juan. You have an amazing family."

"I like your earrings."

"Thanks." She moved her hair to give him a better look.

"There's a smudge spot on this one." He wiped the silver stud earring with the tip of his finger.

"Thank you." She watched him with a strange expression.

"Wait, Nina. You got something on your neck, too."

"I do? What is it?" She leaned up.

"Hold on, let me get it. A little spot right *there*." He sucked her neck. Nina felt she would die, it was so ticklish.

"Stop, Juan!" She playfully hit him. He pulled his arms around her, forcing her closer.

"You got another spot right there." He kissed her chin.

"Juan!" Nina guffawed. "Your mother is right in the kitchen!" She pushed him away.

"Okay." He leaned back. "But after dinner, you're mine."

❖❖❖

"Wow. This looks great, Mrs. Alonso." Nina sniffed the tempting pork and beef noodle dish. "Smells delicious."

"Thank you, Nina." Florence glanced at Juan. "At least someone around here appreciates my cooking."

"I appreciate it." Jorge sliced a big piece of pork.

"Is it Greek?" Juan picked at the meal.

"Yes."

"What a surprise. I guess on this special occasion I can give it a try." Juan nudged Nina's elbow. She grinned. "Damn, this is good, Ma. That class is paying off."

"Yep. A few more weeks and I'll be a Greek chef." Florence spooned salad into Benny's plate. "Can you cook, Nina?"

"Yes. Things are kind of up in the air where I stay. It's just my cousin and me, so we grab our meals when we can. He's a great cook."

"Where do you stay?"

"Uh…" Nina looked at Juan. "I just moved, so I am not that good with directions," she lied. "It's not far from here."

"You like Roosevelt?"

"Yeah, it's cool."

"I bet a young lady like you has made a lot of new friends."

"My best friend, Claudia, goes there so she got me into the mix of things. I met these cool girls, Rosa and Lisa. It took me a while to get used to things but it's worth the effort." She looked at Juan.

"Mom, did I tell you Nina's an artist?" Juan sipped his juice.

"Only about four thousand times." Florence grinned. "Nina, he couldn't stop babbling about you the first day he met you."

"He spoke about me on the first day, huh?" Nina smirked at him.

"I wouldn't call it 'speaking,' Nina. The boy was practically jumping over the furniture. Had so much energy he could fly home." Florence cackled.

"That's not true. I barely mentioned her." Juan wiggled in his seat.

"'Barely' my foot," Jorge blurted out. "Nina, you got my brother sprung."

"Shut up, Jorge!" Juan kicked him underneath the table. Nina laughed so hard she nearly dropped her fork. "You guys on a campaign to embarrass me all of a sudden?"

"Are you two doing the wild thang?"

"Cynthia!" Florence stared at her.

Cynthia blew bubbles in her milk. "I just asked a simple question."

"No, we aren't," Juan growled. "Not that it's any of your business. What do you know about things like that anyway?"

"I know you two almost swallowed each other's tongues before dinner." She grinned.

"Cynthia, that's enough. I'm sorry about this, Nina."

"It's fine, Mrs. Alonso. This is the most interesting time I've experienced since I met Juan."

"Hey, Nina, got a little sister?" Benny raised an eyebrow.

"Nope, sorry."

"Anyone you could hook me up with?"

"Benny." Florence gestured for him to be quiet. "Sorry, Nina, these kids are a handful."

"Nina, are you a virgin?" Cynthia propped her elbows on the table. Nina turned away, sniggering. "I was just wondering because Juan's last girlfriend was a bit loose."

"Cynthia, I am warning you," Florence huffed. "I don't know

where you get off being so nosy. Where do you pick up these things?"

"Hey, I'm growing into a teenager practically. It was bound to happen."

The others laughed.

"You're just like Juan was at your age. Digging into things he had no business digging into." Florence looked at him.

"I was never like that." Juan mumbled.

"The hell you weren't. I wish I'd videotaped some of the things that came out your mouth. Talk about Kodak moments." Florence chewed a piece of beef.

"I think you all have accomplished your mission of embarrassing me beyond repair." Juan sighed.

"Don't feel bad, Juan," Nina teased. "It's your family's job to humiliate you."

The kidding ceased when Rico walked in. Nina noticed the hold he had on the family immediately. Jorge and Benny busied themselves with their meals. Florence's face contorted with a look that could only be described as disappointment. Juan exhaled. His sense of humor seemed nonexistent. Nina took a good look at Rico. He stomped toward the table like a king.

"*Hola*, Mamá." He threw his car keys on the table. Nina's hands shook. She found swallowing impossible with Rico's presence. He seemed the most intimidating, frightening person she'd ever come across.

"*Hola*, Rico." Florence spoke without looking up. Rico rambled in Spanish about his car needing a new paint job, then sat next to Nina.

"Rico, what are you doing here, man?" Juan took Nina's hand under the table. "I thought you had plans of your own."

"But Ma's always saying I should have dinner with the family. Something wrong with that, Juan?"

"No," Juan grumbled. "What would be wrong with that?"

"Whoa." Rico looked at Nina. "I didn't know you could grow flowers at the kitchen table. And you're the prettiest flower I've seen in a while." He kissed Nina's hand.

"Thank you, uh, that's sweet."

Rico glared at Juan. "You're Nina, right?"

"Yeah." She fidgeted. She got the feeling he knew more than he let on.

"I'm Rico Alonso. I don't think we were properly introduced at the party." He looked at Florence. "Ma, can I get a plate or will the food walk out here to me?"

"Be right back." Florence went to the kitchen. Juan shook his head in disgust.

"What's up, little brother? How you doing?"

"Fine." Juan made a fist. Everyone stopped eating. Cynthia kept her cool. Nina saw a lot of Rico in her. She didn't appear intimidated by anyone.

"Cynthia." Rico dangled a thin paper sack in front of her. "Look what I bought you."

"What?" She snatched the bag. "Oh, man! Lil' Kim!" She held up the CD to show Nina. "See, Nina?"

"Uh, I do."

Juan snatched it. "Lil' Kim? You bought a Lil' Kim CD for a child?" He threw it at Rico. "Take that shit back to the store."

"Hey, this fuckin' CD cost sixteen dollars! Anyway, she asked for it. She's my little sister so I buy things for her."

"You ain't giving her no gangsta rap shit while I'm around here." Juan slammed his fork down.

"And who the fuck do you think you are, *ese*?" Rico stood. "You think you all that now? You think you too good?"

"No, I don't." Juan stood. "But I'll be damned if I let you corrupt Cynthia by bringing her into your world. She's my little sister and I care about her."

"She's my sister, too! Where the fuck you get off making rules? Are you the one bringing the dough into the house now? Are you? You don't do shit but make noise. Motherfucking pussy!" Juan lunged at him. Rico threw his chair across the room.

"Stop it!" Florence stood.

Nina exhaled.

"What, huh? What you gonna do, little brother?" Rico grinned. He moved his shirt to reveal his gun. "What are you going to do?" Juan gaped. "What the fuck you want to do?"

"Stop it, Rico! The kids." Florence tugged his shirt.

"You gonna shoot *me* now?" Juan yelled. "Is that how it goes?"

"I wouldn't shoot my own brother. Man, why you tripping?" Rico pushed his chair behind the table. "You need to chill out, homes."

"Rico, take that trash back to the store," Florence ordered. "I don't want the kids listening to this kind of music."

"Fine." He looked at Nina. "You can all sit here and eat what you want with who you want. I'm out." Rico bumped Juan with his shoulder. Juan threw a fist into the air.

"Don't do it, Juan." Florence exhaled. "Please."

"*Do* it, Juan. Fuckin' pussy." Rico left, laughing boisterously.

"Welcome to my world, Nina." Juan slammed his chair underneath the table. He ran to his room.

"Juan, wait! Juan!" Florence followed.

Perspiration stuffed the air that night. It rained throughout dinner. The weather didn't seem to faze Juan. He kept his eyes steady on the car's lights ahead of him. He hadn't said a word to anyone since the fight with Rico. Nina stroked the back of his neck. Her hands lingered down his sturdy arms. She tangled her fingers around the steering wheel to force his attention.

"Stop, you're distracting me." He exhaled.

She chuckled. "Relax. You're so tense. You want to talk about it?"

"Nothing to talk about," he said moments later.

"You sure about that? You didn't say a word after the argument with your brother. Juan, you don't have to hide your feelings from me. I know how families can be. Nobody in my family gets along, either."

He scoffed. "You seem to think everything is so simple."

"I'm not a naïve child, Juan."

"How come you act like it sometimes then? Nina, everyone's problems can't be solved by poetry and pretty pictures. When will you realize that?"

"I know you're upset but I won't be your punching bag, Juan." She immediately regretted the words.

"I'm sorry." He touched her chin. "I hate him so much. I sometimes wish he was dead."

"Don't say that, Juan. You'd be the first one to rescue him if something happened."

"I don't think so, Nina. Look at the picture. Our world would be better off if he were gone. Mom's life would be better. My brothers' lives, Cynthia's life, and my life. *Your* life even." Nina looked at him. "His death would provide so many options."

"Juan, stop it, okay?" She sighed. "You're scaring me."

"I don't mean to. I'm just being honest."

"A little *too* honest, if you ask me. Hey, look." Nina pointed to a gathering on the side of the road. Juan leaned to get a better look. "Wonder what that was with all the people and everything." Nina wiggled to the loud music.

"People have all kinds of get-togethers in this area. That reminds me, you going to the festival?"

"What festival?" Nina chuckled. "I tell you, every time I turn around there's some jamboree."

Juan smiled. "I'm talking about the festival in Hariam Park. Teens from all around show up. It lasts all night. People usually camp out in their cars or get a room at the hotel across the street. There'll be booths, concerts, talent contests, bobbing for apples, relays. Claudia didn't tell you about this? Well, maybe she's not going."

"Claudia?" Nina straightened in the seat. "Juan, wherever there's anything that *looks* like a party, Claude is there."

"So will *you* be?" He raised an eyebrow. Nina returned a flirtatious glance of her own.

"Maybe. You?"

"Oh, you know it." He pulled up to Nina's regular drop-off spot outside of Edgewood. He peered out the front window. A boy sped through the sidewalk on a bike. "Sure I can't drop you off at home?"

"You know you can't. Especially now."

"You think I care about that?"

"You should." They kissed. "We got to be smart. We also have to figure out a way to see each other. I think Tajo's been having me followed."

"For real?" Juan shook his head.

"He's been sticking to me pretty close himself, too."

"Hmmm, how about we come up with some special meeting place? Somewhere no one can find out."

"Yeah, but where?" Nina sighed.

"I have no idea." He laughed.

"Damn you for getting my hopes up for nothing." She pretended to punch him. Juan grabbed her into another kiss.

❖❖❖

Nina threw her purse on the bed. "I told you, Tajo, I was with a friend."

"What friend?" He leaned against the doorway.

"A friend. Shit, why are you so nosy all of a sudden?"

"You know why." He walked inside. "You're only a kid, Nina. It's my responsibility to make sure you do what you're supposed to. You been going out all times of night, not telling me where you are. It's going to stop *now*. You won't be running around here like some strung-out ho."

"Like you're anyone to judge me."

He grabbed her. "Don't play with me, Nina. Were you with that boy?"

"What boy?"

"You know the one. Is that where you've been? Fucking in some car? Answer me!"

"No!" She tore away. "Tajo, what do you take me for? You know what kind of person I am."

"I know what kind of person you *were* before you hooked up with that bitch ass. He ain't no damn good."

"You've never met him!"

"He's a NYA, they're all alike!"

"Bullshit. And he's *not* one of them. He can't be blamed for what Rico does."

"You don't want to test me, Nina. If I find out you've been with that asshole I'm going to make sure you won't need to lie to me again." He slumped to the door.

"Are you threatening me?" She crossed her arms.

"No. I'm threatening *him*." He shut the door.

❊❊❊

"Yeah?" Juan's laughter erupted over the phone. He tried his best to keep the talk with Nina in his room but it spilled into the hallway. It was past 3 a.m. They could barely keep their eyes open but were dead set against stopping the conversation.

"Yeah." Nina sighed. "You're all I've been thinking about since I got back." She kicked her legs in bed. "I can't wait to see you at school tomorrow."

"I can't wait to see you, either. But we got to keep a low profile, remember?" Juan pulled his sheets. "Do me a favor, Nina?" He licked his lips.

"Anything." She moaned.

"Promise you'll dream of me tonight. Dream of us together with no problems. No one to stand in our way."

Nina chuckled at the request. "I'll do my best. Is that good enough?"

Juan blew a kiss into the phone. "See you tomorrow."

"You, too." Nina hung up.

"Juanito?" Rico shuffled into the dim room. He sat on the end of the bed. "We need to talk, homes."

"About what? I got to get up early for school tomorrow."

"Just shut up." Rico sighed. "About earlier, I wanted to apologize."

Juan gasped. "You never apologize to anyone."

"Just let me say it, shit. Look, you're my little brother, all right? I wouldn't want nothing to happen to you. You could be so much and you know this. People take to you. You got that star quality. I never had that. You can get your message out. I believe in you, man."

"You do?" Juan squinted.

"Yeah. And as your older brother I am gonna protect you, man." Rico held up the NYA hand signal. "I'm not going to let anything stand in your way."

"I appreciate that. But I can handle it. So if you don't mind, I'd like to go to sleep." Rico ripped the covers from the bed. Juan jumped out.

"Yo what's the deal, Rico?"

"What's the deal with you? Isn't there something you're not telling me, man? Something I need to know?"

"No! What are you talking about?" Juan shivered in his boxer shorts.

"I'm talking about Nina. I think you left out a big detail about her. What, did you think I wouldn't find out? I know everything."

"It's a lie. You just think you..."

"Don't fuck with me, Juan! I know she's Tajo Munez's cousin. So you can cut the shit."

"Come on, man." Juan stood against the wall. "You don't want to wake up everyone else."

Rico charged him. "I don't know who you think you are but you're not going to pull this shit on me. I'm too smart for the cops and I am too smart for you. Girls like that fuck up every-thing. They can mess up your life." Rico threw his hand up. "You can go farther than I ever could! But you got to make the decision *now*, Juan. I am not going to let some Bronx G bitch ruin your life."

"Nina isn't like that. I love her, Rico! You ever been in love? Of course not. You were too busy plotting murders."

"And what I do is my business."

"And what I do is *mine*." Juan snatched back the covers from Rico.

"Wrong, Juan." Rico leaned against Juan. "As long as you're seeing that bitch, it *is* my business. All this time you've been whining about a better life, fixing up the community for the kids. Now you want to throw it away on that little tramp?"

"It's not even like that!"

"And it won't be! You're gonna stay away from her."

"Fuck you!"

"Hey!" Rico grabbed him by the neck. Juan struggled to breathe. "You are not going to see Nina ever again except for at school. Then at school you're going to stay as far away from her as you can." Juan grunted in pain. "If you see her walking down the hall, you walk the other way. If she's lying in the street hurt, call the fuckin' police. Just don't go near her, ever! Make sure you keep your distance." Rico let go.

"And if I don't?" Juan coughed.

"You'll deeply regret it. And I promise, I'll make sure you wished I was never born." Rico clomped out the door.

"Too *late*." Juan rubbed his aching neck.

CHAPTER ELEVEN

The next evening Juan ran to Mr. Jones's room after school. A slither of sunlight spread through the blinds, creating white lines across the chalkboard. Nina sat at the back table fumbling over her latest painting. Juan slyly tipped toward her. She watched him from the corner of her eye. She expected him to lunge at her. Instead he put his arms around her waist.

"Miss me?" Juan caught the edge of her ear in his mouth. "All day, on the basketball court, at lunch, in class, all I thought of was you," he whispered.

"Really?" Nina pulled away, grinning. She dipped her fingers in paint. "How do I know that? You seem to me to have been keeping yourself pretty occupied."

"What are you talking about?" He shoved his hands into his pockets.

"I saw you at lunchtime talking to Kristen." She got a kick out of teasing him.

"Kristen?" Juan laughed. "She's just a friend of mine. Ask anyone." He followed her to the other side of the table.

"How can I believe that?" She stooped over the painting. "When you guys looked so cozy." He wrapped his hands around her waist.

"Nina, there is no other girl in this world for me."

"How about the 'loose girl' you went with before me?"

"If it were meant to be I'd still be with her, wouldn't I?" He leaned against her. "Rico knows who you are. I didn't tell him."

"Shit." She stared into space.

"I promise he won't hurt you. I will kill him before I let that happen."

"It's still so scary." She stared at her painting.

"But love's worth it, isn't it?" He turned her around. She folded her arms around his neck. "Nina, I refuse to let your cousin or my brother dictate our lives. I don't care what I have to do to be with you, I'll do it."

"You're too good to be true, Juan." She leaned against his chest. "I can't help but feel like we're doing something we will later regret."

"Nina, it doesn't matter if we're together. Don't you understand they'd find another excuse to keep up this bull? Honey, these gangs were fighting before we were born. This feud is bigger than both of us. If it wasn't you or me, they'd find something else to fight about. They have to have an excuse to keep going. Let's not give them that. Or hell, fuck them."

"Saying that's easy, isn't it?" She played with his collar. "Doing it's a bit harder. We shouldn't have to choose between each other and our families."

"I know, but we do. That's our world, Nina. That's why we got to look out for ourselves." He looked off. "For starters, if we're going to be together we got to find out how. I've been racking my brains all day and haven't come up with anything."

Nina bit her lip. "I'm stumped, too."

"Almost finished here?" Juan admired the painting.

"Yeah. I told Claudia to go on without me. You don't mind taking me home, do you?"

"Are you kidding? I'd take you to Spain if you wanted me to."
He kissed her.

"Hey, Juan? Maybe Claudia can help us with our problem."

"How?" He stared, wide-eyed.

✠✠✠

"Oh, *hell* no!" Claudia picked up wads of paper from her garage
floor. Nina followed, trying to persuade her to listen to reason.
Juan stood against the wall with his arms crossed.

"Come on, Claude. It's the perfect thing. Look at me, will you?"

"Nina, there is no way I am going to let you and Juan shack
up at my uncle's place to have your little love nest."

"He's dead. I'm sure he won't mind." Nina grinned.

"He left that place to my mother in his will. It's not my
responsibility to let you be there anyway. She has authority."

"Claude, listen. Juan and I just need a place to meet. We won't
stay long. Your mother won't know. You said it yourself, she's
scared to death of that place. She never goes to see it."

"Nina," Claudia sighed.

"You keep the keys, right? You're the one who checks up on
the place, right? No one else will know. Claude, we won't tell
anyone as long as you don't. It's the perfect situation."

"Nina, this is crazy."

"Maybe it is." Nina looked at Juan. "Claudia, I've never needed
you as much as I do now."

"So you're gonna use guilt on me, huh?" She looked at the
pile of dust beside her feet. "Okay." She sighed.

"Yes!" Nina kissed her.

"But there are going to be some conditions. I'm keeping the
key."

"That's fine." Nina jumped up and down. "I love you so much, Claude!"

"Sure, you love me when I'm doing you favors." She smirked.

※※※

"Get back, nigga!" Chino blew on his dice. "Get ready to give me all your motherfucking money."

"Then bring it home, nigga." Bone sipped a forty. Shorty-Five and Spider laughed at Chino's attempt.

Claudia skidded up to Tajo's house, getting the boys' attention. She gently tugged Nina's hair, silently reassuring her.

"Thanks for the ride, Claude." Nina paused when she saw Chino on the front steps. He waved his dice. "Shit."

"What's wrong?"

"Come inside with me, Claude. I can't stand this guy."

"Why?" Claudia stared at Chino. "Does he bother you or something?" They walked toward the house. Nina greeted the others without looking their way.

Chino lifted his arm. "Nina, blow on my dice for good luck." She ignored him and went inside.

Bone laughed. "When are you going to understand she doesn't want you?"

"She wants me. She just don't know it yet. I bet you she *will* want me. I bet you that shit." Chino dropped the dice. "Be right back."

"Yo, you can't hold up the game, man!" Shorty-Five yelled.

"Y'all losing any damn way." Chino went inside.

"Little bitch. He's always doing that shit," Bone muttered.

"Something up?" Claudia strolled around Nina's bedroom. Nina took out her schoolbooks for her homework.

"I can't stand that Chino guy."

"Why?" Claudia chuckled.

"He's always hanging around. He's always looking at me funny. One time I was in the kitchen and he started coming on to me."

"Well, did you tell Tajo?"

"No."

"Why not?" Claudia grabbed a green lollipop from Nina's nightstand.

"I can handle myself. I just wish Chino would stay out of my business."

Chino tapped his fingers against Nina's door. He walked in without an invitation.

"Hey." He kissed Claudia's hand. "Where have you been all my life?"

She flicked her hair over her shoulder. "Right here, baby. I'm Claudia Olmos."

"So you go to school with Nina or what?"

"Yeah. She's my homegirl from back in the day, though. We're tight as two butt cheeks." Claudia rubbed Nina's head. "Who are *you*?"

"Chino."

"You a G?" Claudia seductively sucked the lollipop.

He rubbed his hands together. "Why, you like gangstas, Mamá?"

"I like *a lot* of things." Claudia winked. Nina felt Claudia's flirting always came at the wrong time.

"Chino, is there something you wanted?" Nina tapped her pencil.

"Just wanted to see how you were, that's all. We're hanging later. You want to roll with us?"

"I got loads of homework." Nina shrugged.

"How about after the homework? You can roll out with us then, right?"

"Chino, I, I can't do it."

"Uh-huh." He gritted his teeth. "I bet if my name began with a 'j' and ended with an 'n', you'd want to go."

Nina threw her pen down. "Would you get out of my room, please?" He left, smirking. "Damn, he gets on my nerves, man."

"He got a little something-something, though, don't he?" Claudia stood in the hallway gaping as he went back outside.

"Maybe for you. I don't want to be hooked up with no gang-banger. What can a guy like that do for me? I just want him to stay out of my face."

"I hear you." Claudia checked her watch. "You need me to hang here a while?"

"No, you can go."

"I'll check you later, all right? It's going to be okay, Nina. Just hang in there."

"Yeah." Nina smiled.

***

"Uh-huh. Yes." Florence looked up from her phone call when Juan entered the kitchen. He grabbed a snack from the cabinet, trying not to be so nosy. She leaned against the sink with her eyes glued to Juan. "I see. No, he didn't tell me that." Florence watched Juan. "Thank you and have a nice day." She hung up.

"Something wrong, Ma?"

She loosened her apron. "That was Mrs. Garrett, Juan. She was concerned because you got a 'D' on your last history quiz."

He sat at the table. "Why the hell didn't I know about this?" He shuffled his feet underneath the table. "Answer me, Juan."

"I guess I forgot."

"You forgot?" She slapped the apron on the table. "Juan, you have an A average. You could graduate with honors. You want to lose that?"

"No, Ma." He rolled his eyes. "I'm pretty sure one 'D' on one stinking quiz won't hurt my average."

"Juan, she also says you've been despondent in class. You used to be full of excitement and turned in excellent work. She says you've been slacking off and you can't keep your mind on your business."

"Ma, it is no big deal, all right? Even Einstein got one 'D'." He chuckled.

"Do you see humor in my face?" He sighed. "You know Mrs. Garrett's not the only one seeing changes in you. Ever since you met Nina, you haven't been yourself."

"Here we go again."

"Juan, I don't want you slacking off. You're going to hit those books as hard as you can and keep up your average. You've made As all through high school. It makes no sense to mess that up now." She laid a dish towel on her shoulder. "I'm very disappointed in you."

"Okay, I'm sorry. I didn't tell you because I didn't want you to worry. I just got off track. It won't happen again. Uh, I wanted to ask you something."

"What?" She crushed black olives into the skillet.

"Uh, it's about, you know, that festival thing's coming up again."

"You mean that thing at Hariam Park that you beg to go to every year?" She made meatballs.

"Yeah. And every year you say no and I end up sneaking there anyway. Can I go?"

"I don't know, Juan. I mean, you haven't been showing me you deserve to go."

"Mamá, I promise nothing will happen with my grades. Hell, it was *one* D."

"It only takes one." She looked at him. "You know I won't tolerate bad grades when I know you can do better."

"I promise." He sighed into his palms. "I'll work so hard they'll have to invent a better letter than A to fit me." Florence chuckled. "Can I go?"

"I guess so. But I want you to be careful. People drink and carry on at those things. Hariam Park's not the best area, either."

"I was thinking of staying over at the hotel across..."

"Don't even think about it. You can go to the festival, but you better have your butt back here before two a.m. I don't agree with this all-night thing anyway."

"Don't worry, there's always tons of security to keep us children safe." Juan snickered.

"Is Nina going to be there?"

"I guess. She doesn't like crowds and things that much."

"Are your friends going to be there?"

"For sure. We're gonna shoot hoops, do all kinds of things."

"Well, make sure you keep your pants zipped."

"Ma." He held his chest, grinning.

"I mean it, Juan." She held her hips. "I hate that you're sexually active anyway, but since I can't stop you..."

"I practice safe sex." He popped in two animal crackers.

"I'd rather you practice 'no sex.' You keep your equipment in your pants. There are enough children around here."

"Nothing like that's going to happen. The last thing I want

is a baby. Besides, Nina is the only girl I want to do it with. And that's not happening anytime soon."

"Why not?" Florence stared.

"She's a virgin."

"Oh." Florence chuckled. "I knew she might have been one. You know, mothers can tell."

"So you can trust me, Ma. I'm going to be a good boy."

"Mmm-hmmm." She shook her head in doubt.

✠✠✠✠

Tajo slammed his cards on the table. Juice brooded over his struggling hand. Shorty-Five and Bone exhaled, realizing they'd lost and couldn't recover. Chino played with his stack of poker chips.

"Can we just play the game, Tajo?" Shorty-Five rubbed his head. "Can't you handle that other shit later?"

"Does it look like I can handle it later?" he growled.

Shorty-Five shrugged. "Whatever, dog. Handle your business."

"So she just gonna turn you down, huh, Chino?" Tajo rubbed his fist. "She acting like she too good to hang with the homies and shit?"

"Yep." Chino tugged his baseball cap. "Here I was trying to be nice and shit. She wasn't hearing none of it. I asked her to go out with us tonight. She turned me down. I bet she was with that bitch-ass Alonso before she came home, too."

Tajo glanced down the hallway at Nina's room. "She probably was. She's gonna learn I mean what I say."

"Who the fuck she think she is, turning down a Bronx Gangsta for that shithead?" Chino slapped a card down. "Yo, Tajo, I didn't want to say shit but your cousin needs to be put in check.

221

And I'm the one to do it. You know I don't take any shit. I *won't* take any shit."

"Hold up, asshole. She's still my baby cousin and nothing better happen to her. Y'all supposed to be protecting her."

"We try to." Shorty-Five shrugged. "But shit, we got lives, too. We ain't babysitters and shit. Your turn, Juice."

"My hand is fucked," Juice mumbled.

Chino sighed. "The point is she's disrespecting us. Worse than that shit, we look like pussies if we let Nina walk around with Juan Alonso. They'll be calling us the Bronx Faggots if we keep this up." Chino shook his head.

"Who are you trying to fool, *ese?*" Shorty-Five puffed a cigarette. "You just want Nina with you, that's all."

Tajo stared at Chino.

"Better with me than Juan Alonso. Shit, at least I know what the deal is. I can give Nina what she needs on the street—some protection. I'm just looking out for my boy here." Chino patted Tajo's arm. "We got to put an end to this now. People be stepping all over us if we don't take control. Shit, something needs to be done."

"And it will be." Tajo headed for Nina's room.

❈❈❈

"Chino." Juice laughed. "You're one sly motherfucker. Now Tajo gonna make her go for sure."

"That was the plan." Chino grinned. "Shit, if I'm lucky maybe he'll really get on her and I'll get some pussy tonight."

Shorty-Five shook his head. "She's only sixteen. That shit's nasty, man."

"It's not nasty to me." Chino rested against the chair.

"Just because she can't see Juan doesn't mean she's gonna want yo' sorry ass."

Juice sipped beer. "Deal, nigga," he told Shorty-Five.

Chino smirked. "She'll want me if Tajo *says* to want me. Shit, she'll want me if she knows this is all she can have." He rubbed his chest. "Once she gets a taste she won't be able to get enough."

"I think you got that backward, homes." Juice chuckled.

"Man, you've seen the way she looks at me, right?"

"Uh…" Shorty-Five glanced at Juice. "No!" They laughed.

"Fuck both of you, motherfuckers. I see things and just because you don't, don't mean it's not true. Besides, Nina's an artist. We got things in common."

"You gonna pull that cultural shit on her? Use that 'I'm an educated G' shit?" Juice laughed.

"Whatever it takes, dog." Chino stared at the hallway. "Whatever it takes."

✠✠✠

"You can't be serious." Nina slammed her algebra book shut.

"I am. You gonna roll with Chino tonight. If you don't like it, tough."

"You can't tell me what to do, Tajo. Now I appreciate you taking me in, but I am not going to let you disrespect me."

"You're the one disrespecting *me*, Nina! Going around town with that boy. I know you were with him. How many fuckin' warnings do you need? I told you if I catch you with him…"

"You didn't catch us, did you?" She smirked.

"Fine. Play with the motherfucker's life if you want to. I hope you still find Juan attractive once I pop a cap in his ass."

"Tajo." She shook.

"It's your choice. You want Juan to live a long and happy life? Then stay the fuck away from him!"

"Let me guess. Chino told you he *thought* I was with Juan, right? And of course he's your homey so you believe anything he says." She shook her head. "Tajo, we go to the same school and we have the same class. I can't avoid Juan even if I wanted to."

"You'd better find a way to."

"You don't care about me at all."

"Nina, I care about you more than anything. That's why I'm trying to protect you."

She moved when he reached for her. "From Juan? Tajo, he would never do anything to hurt me. Can't you just meet him at least? At least back in the other centuries the king would offer to meet the person before banishing them from their kingdom." She grinned. "Tajo, you claim you're a fair person. You're not being fair to Juan or me. Give him a chance. Seeing how much he cares for me should be enough."

"Nina, I don't have to meet a snake to know it's a snake. If you don't stay away from Juan I'll make sure he stays away from you."

"Tajo, he's not in the gang! He cannot help who his brother is."

"Maybe not." He shrugged. "But we're destined enemies and nothing's going to change that. Now you and Juanito can do your Romeo and Juliet shit if you want to, but I'm telling you right here that one of you will regret it."

"And what does Chino have to do with this?" She scowled.

"What's up with you and Chino anyway?"

"*Nothing*." She scoffed.

"Nina, I know you don't like Gs but you ain't giving my man a chance. And I told you before, Chino's different. He's not like the others. I think you'd like him if you opened your eyes.

Sometimes the one you belong with is right under your nose."

"I love Juan."

Tajo rubbed his forehead. "Loving someone doesn't mean you belong with them, Nina. Consequences play a role in relationships, too. In this life, the gang life, you just got to settle with what you can."

"This is *your* life, not mine."

"If you don't go out with the fellows tonight it'll give me reason to mistrust you, Nina." He looked at the tips of his fingers. "And you wouldn't want that, right? I know Juan wouldn't."

She sighed.

❖❖❖

Nina couldn't believe the card Tajo played. Would he dangle Juan's safety in front of her every time she didn't do what he wanted her to? She checked out the rowdy bowling alley. Teens huddled around the arcade games. Families bought burgers and hot dogs by the dozens, crowding the counters. Nina carelessly munched Fritos. What the hell was she doing here?

Bone, Juice, and Shorty-Five made it back to the table with trays of food. Chino sat two small hotdogs in front of Nina. He squeezed beside her, licking chili from his finger. Even the way he looked at her made Nina ill.

"Yo, look at this, homes." Juice pulled a mile-long string of cheese from his foot-long. It whipped around his index finger. Shorty-Five doused his food with ketchup. Chino topped his with the works.

"Jesus." Nina stared at him. "You can't open your mouth wide enough to put that thing in."

"Wanna bet?" Chino shoved the messy hot dog into his mouth. Nina laughed. She neatly attempted to eat hers. "Damn, girl. You don't know nothing about eating no hot dog." Chili flew from Chino's hand. "You can't be all neat and stuff. Look at her. She might as well be eating with a fork and spoon."

"Dang, girl." Juice chuckled as Nina tried to eat the hot dog.

"Man, I'm ready to get my bowl on." Shorty-Five wiped his mouth. "You bowl, Nina?"

"Nah." She finished her first hot dog.

"Chino, let's bowl, bitch." Juice and the others gathered their trays to take to the bowling lanes.

"I'll be there in a minute." He gestured toward Nina.

"Oh, I see." Bone grinned. He and the others dissolved into the crowd. They picked the lane beside the exit door.

Juan lagged into the congested bowling alley feeling like death warmed over. Carlos pulled him by his shirt. "Come on, Juan." He followed his friends to the counters to get bowling shoes.

"Man, I'd rather shoot hoops than bowl." Juan glared at the chaotic lanes.

"It's raining, asshole." Tony pointed to the windows. "Besides, you used to love to bowl."

Juan grumbled. "It's too crowded in here. There aren't even any lanes left."

"There's one over there." Tony pointed to the lane beside the soda machine.

"Loosen up, Juan. You used to like hanging with us." Dell fastened the tacky yellow-and-green bowling shoes.

"All right." Juan sat beside them. "Let's bowl."

Nina tried her best to distract Chino's attention. Whenever she looked at him she couldn't help wishing she were somewhere else. Chino didn't get the hint no matter how cold she acted. He slipped his arm behind her. The more she rejected him, the more turned-on he seemed.

"What are you doing?" She moved away. A parade of kids ran past the table.

"Nothing." He winked. "Let's not play any more games, Nina. You know I like you."

"I'm not playing any games." She popped in a chip.

"How come the best-looking girls are always teases?" He chuckled. "You know what's up, Nina." He licked his lips. "I think you're kinda fly. I think we'd be good together."

"Really?" She smirked.

"Yeah. I got money and stuff. I could hook you up with things. I could buy you things. You know, do all the things guys are supposed to do."

"The word…," she pulled his arm from her shoulders, "…is that I don't like gangbangers."

"Maybe you haven't found the right one yet." He touched her earring. She jerked away. "Don't play with me, Nina. You know what's up with us."

"Chino, I don't want to hurt your feelings but you don't get the point. I am not interested in you. There is nothing you can do to change that." He kissed her. She slapped him. "Asshole!" A family stared from the next table. "I want you to leave me alone, Chino!" Nina leaned up. He grabbed her before she could move.

"Come on now." He massaged her arm. "Give me a chance. Relax and you might enjoy it." He tried to kiss her again.

"Let go of me, Chino!" A table of people turned around.

"Don't be like that."

"I said, let go!" She hit him.

"Yo, who the fuck you think you are?" He pulled her arm.

"You're hurting me!" Nina screamed.

"Look at that." Carlos shook his head, getting into bowling position. "You can't go nowhere without a scene."

Juan pointed. "Hey, that's *Nina*."

Tony squinted. "Shit, it is."

"What the fuck does that guy think he's doing?" Juan headed toward Nina and Chino.

Dell blocked him. "Hold on, Juan. From the look of his colors he's a Bronx Gangsta. Just let it ride, man."

"Yeah." Carlos exhaled. "You don't want to get in the middle of some shit."

"I don't care who the hell he is." Juan shoved Dell from his path.

"Who the fuck you think you are, huh?" Chino lapped his hands around Nina's neck, forcing her lips to his again. She violently struggled. She wondered why no one helped. She held her lips together tightly to block his kisses.

"Hey!" Juan flung Chino from the table. "Yo, what the fuck you think you're doing?" Juan yelled. One by one, everyone took notice of the scene.

"Who the fuck are you, faggot?" Chino shoved Juan into the table behind him.

"Juan!" Nina covered her mouth.

"So this is Juan?" Chino laughed. "In fuckin' person, I see! Well, it's good to finally lay eyes on you. Now I know what you look like when it's time to kill your dumb ass."

"The only way you could kill anyone is with your breath," Juan snapped. Chino lifted his head. "I don't know who you are and I don't care. But if you ever come near Nina again I will bury your ass."

"Oh yeah, big boy?" Chino lifted his shirt. Juan's eyes rested on Chino's silver nine-millimeter. "So go on, homes. Fight for your lady's honor then. Let's see who's still standing. NYA piece of shit." Chino spit at him. Juan knocked him to the floor. Chino punched him.

"Stop it!" Nina screamed.

"Hey, Chino!" Juice pulled him off Juan. "Don't do this, man!"

"Get off me, motherfucker! I'm going to kill this pussy. I've been waiting to see his monkey ass. Get off me!"

"Chill, homes!" Bone held Chino by the chest. "This ain't the right time for this shit!"

"The hell it isn't! Let me kill this motherfucker *now*. Then there will be no need to worry about his ass."

"What are you waiting for, huh?" Juan wiped blood from his mouth. "Come on!"

"No! Stop it!" Nina shrieked. People huddled beside the tables.

Chino pounced at Juan. "Ooh, I can't wait to whip your ass, Alonso! I'm going to kill you! I'm gonna pop a cap in yo' ass, motherfucker!"

"Come on." Juan chuckled breathlessly. "I'm waiting for you."

"Stop it, Chino!" Nina yelled. He calmed down when he looked at her. He shoved Juice and Bone away from him. "Just go home." Nina held onto Juan.

"That's how it is?" Chino looked around the bowling alley. Two security guards rushed toward him. "Fine. It's cool. I won't waste my time. Because when Tajo finds out, your ass is dead anyway."

"I'm shaking in my boots," Juan muttered.

"*Juan*." Nina took his hand.

Chino chuckled. "Say good-bye to your Romeo, Nina. Because this is the last time you'll see this motherfucker alive! You're dead, motherfucker! I swear to God, you're dead."

"Come on!" Juice pulled Chino away.

"Nina..."

"Just go, Bone." She rested her head against Juan's arm.

"Do you have any idea what you're doing? This isn't smart."

"Bone, please." She held her hand up. He followed the others.

"Are you okay, Nina?" Juan rubbed her hand. The people went back to their business.

"Yes. Are you?" She looked up at him. She couldn't believe he could smile after the moment he'd had. "Juan, that was stupid. He could have killed you."

"Who was that fool?" He watched security usher Chino and the others outside.

"Chino. A member of my cousin's gang obviously."

"Well, if he wants trouble, that's just what he gets."

"Juan, you can't pretend to be brave around these people. They'll kill you. The only thing that stopped him was a room full of people. Juan, there's no way you're safe now. There's just no way."

"Do you see worry on my face?"

"There should be," she scoffed. "I'm worried. I love you but I don't want anything to happen to you just to be with you. What's the point in that?"

"I am not backing down anymore, Nina. We have a right to live our lives. They run everything. They are not going to run our hearts. I thought you agreed with that."

"I do, but..."

He touched her lips. "Then ride with this and trust that I'm gonna take care of you." He hugged her. "I promise." Nina relaxed in his arms.

Chino slammed the hood of Shorty-Five's car. "That punk-ass motherfucker!"

"Yo, ease up, man." Shorty-Five shoved Chino from his car.

"So that's Juan, huh? That's who she's so crazy about? And why? What the fuck does he have?"

"*Nina*, for one thing." Juice grinned.

"But not for long. I'm getting that motherfucker tonight." Chino rubbed his fist.

"You guys down?"

"Juan hasn't done shit to you," Bone said. "It's not his fault his brother is an NYA."

"Fuck you, man." Chino looked at the others. "You guys down?"

"Of course. Maybe it's our chance to give the NYAs a little surprise." Juice winked.

"I'm out. This shit makes no sense." Bone walked away.

Chino scoffed. "We don't need him. Come on." They got in the car.

***

"It's late." Juan pulled up to Nina's usual spot. "Why don't you let me take you all the way home?"

She smiled, hugging her purse. "You know that you can't."

"But I want to anyway." He caressed her thigh.

"Sorry about that argument with Chino." She touched his face.

"Why are *you* apologizing? He was manhandling *you*. I tell you, seeing you with another guy made me crazy. Especially with a thug like that. Were you scared?"

"No one else helped." She shrugged. "Yeah, I was very scared. At first I thought Chino was different than the others but he's worse."

"Why were you out with them anyway?"

"It's a long story." Nina wasn't about to scare him off by telling him the truth.

"He likes me. I can't get him off my case. He won't take no for an answer."

"Can't he find any women his own age? He looked damn near thirty to me."

She grinned. "He's only twenty-two."

"Anyway, can you blame him? That's what you get for being so damn hot."

❖❖❖

Nina closed her eyes. Her breasts tingled. Juan's damp lips clasped hers. She would have done it with him right then and there in his truck. But she wanted it to be special. She wanted the first time they made love to mean everything, to mean no turning back. Juan held her like he thought he'd never see her again. He rubbed his lips against her hair. He tightened his hands around her waist. His touch felt too right.

Nina looked at him for a few seconds, then got out of the truck.

"See you at school tomorrow." She smiled in a daze.

"I can't wait." He wiped traces of her lipstick from his lips.

"'Bye." Nina blew him a kiss. He pretended to catch it in his hand. She ran down the sidewalk.

"There that punk-ass motherfucker is, right *there*." Juice pointed from a corner down. Juan drove off. "Who the fuck do he think he is coming down to Edgewood any damn way?"

Chino gripped the steering wheel. "I told you we were right to follow his ass."

"Yeah, and all that shit he was talking." Juan made a right at a light. Chino followed. "He won't be talking at all once we get through with him. Ready for a party?"

"Yep, let's do this." Juice grinned. He bumped fists with Shorty-Five.

Chino licked his lips. "After we get through with him he's gonna wish he never heard of Nina Sagastume."

CHAPTER TWELVE

Nina grabbed the phone by her bed. "Hello?" she whispered. Silence swam through the line. She realized it was nearly 3 a.m. She struggled to adjust her eyes. Normally Nina would have hung up but something warned her against it. She heard a soft whisper. She begged for the person to speak again. She recognized his voice after the third try. "Oh my God, Juan?"

"Nina." He coughed into the phone. "Nina, I need you. Don't want anybody else…" His voice drifted. He rambled off a location. He hung up before she could get more information. She immediately called Claudia.

"Claudia?" Nina tiptoed to the hallway. She didn't give Claudia a chance to ask who it was. "Claudia, I really need your help. I need a ride."

"Who the fuck is this?" Claudia yawned.

"It's me, Juan, Nina. Wake up."

"Nina? It's three in the morning. What's your problem?"

"Claudia, I need you to give me a ride somewhere quick. Juan's in trouble."

"What?" Claudia yawned. "Are you on crack? You expect me to sneak out the house? And how the hell will you?"

"Tajo's not here. Look, I'll meet you out front in ten minutes. Claude, please hurry."

"Nina, what in the world is going on?"

"I can't tell you that now. I barely know. All I know is Juan needs me. Please, Claude."

"All right. Why do I put up with so much shit from you?"

"Claude, it's a matter of life and death."

"I'll be there in a few." She hung up.

✠✠✠

Claudia's convertible crept through the empty streets. They came to a barrage of tall weeds and dead trees. Nina saw movement behind a raggedy abandoned house.

"You see something?" Claudia slowed down.

"Over there." Nina held her breath. "Oh my God, Claudia." Claudia swerved beside the fence. Juan was lying face down in the dirt. He gripped the cell phone in his hand. They noticed his truck parked a few feet away. They ran toward him. "Juan!" Nina shrieked. "Oh my God, Claudia!"

"Oh my God." Claudia reached for her cell phone. "I'm calling the police."

"Don't." Nina struggled to turn Juan over. "He begged me not to call anyone."

"Nina, this is serious! Look at him. He was attacked!"

Drops of blood seeped through Juan's shirt. His eyes were swollen. His bottom lip was smashed. He couldn't open his left eye at all. Nina forced his head on her lap.

"Juan. Juan, say something to me. Please." She pressed her ear to his mouth.

"Nina." He coughed. "Nina, you came."

"Of course I did." She cleaned grass from his face. "Oh God, how did this happen? Speak to me, baby," she whispered.

"Bronx Gangstas." He swallowed hard. "They followed me. They forced me into…their car…made me come out here. They drove my truck so no one would get suspicious." He gripped his stomach.

"Jesus." Claudia shivered.

"I…tried to fight them. Just too many at one time." He coughed. "Just too many."

"Nina, we have to take him to the hospital. We can't just leave him like this."

"Juan, what do you want to do? We'll do whatever you want us to."

"I don't want to go home. I don't want to go home."

"You don't have to." Nina wrapped his arms around her shoulders. "Claudia, help me lift him up."

She scoffed. "Nina, are you *crazy*?"

"No. You heard him. We can't take him home. We got to take him somewhere to fix him up."

"Nina, this is crazy! We should call the police. Where the hell would we take him anyway?"

"Your uncle's place." They dragged Juan to the car.

"No way. I am not getting involved in this shit, Nina. He's *your* boyfriend, you take him to *your* uncle's place."

"How can you be so selfish, Claude? He needs our help!"

"You're calling me selfish? Are you fuckin' insane, Nina? What has happened to you? You act like Juan is the only person in the world you care about now. Is that the truth? He's just a guy."

"He's the guy I love!" Nina helped him into the car. "If you won't take us to your uncle's, let me know. I'll help him alone."

"How are you going to do that? What the hell can you do with him? If you take him to Tajo's you might as well leave him here because he'll be dead."

"That's right." Nina crossed her arms. "He *will* be dead. Claudia, I would never ask you to help me with something like this. I love you. But I don't have a choice. Juan doesn't want to go home and I can't question his reason now. All I want to do is help him so he can get better. I need him to tell me exactly what happened. Do you understand?" Nina took her hand. Juan squirmed in the backseat.

"Nina, this is…this is just getting out of hand. I'm scared for the both of you."

"So we're not your average couple." Nina shrugged. "Doesn't mean we don't belong together, right?"

"You don't even make sense when you speak anymore." Claudia ran her fingers through her hair. "Now you got me in this shit."

"I wish there was something I could say, Claude." Nina kicked her foot in the dirt. "I can't say if I'd help you if the shoe was on the other foot. I don't know. I just know I need you now." Claudia sighed. Nina wasn't sure what she'd decide. She'd never seen Claudia so confused.

"Do you know how much trouble we could all be in if this is more serious than we think?"

"Yes." Nina rubbed her eyes. "And right now I could care less."

Claudia got in the car. "Shit. Come on. I'll take you to my uncle's place."

✠✠✠

Juan didn't make a sound during the ride. He kept moving in his seat as if he didn't know where he was. When they got to Claudia's uncle's place, she rushed in to make sure the coast was clear. It took all the strength they had to pull Juan's strong body from the car and into the two-story home.

"Come on, Nina." Claudia moved the pillows off the couch. "Put him down here."

"Easier said than done." Nina struggled. Claudia took Juan by the arms. "Man, he's heavier than he looks, isn't he?"

Claudia grunted. "No shit." They plopped him on the couch.

"Oh my God, Claudia. He isn't moving."

Claudia checked his breathing. "He's conscious. I think he's just out of it."

Juan moaned. Nina's body grew warm with relief. "I'll get some water and towels to wipe his face," Claudia said.

"And check to see if there's any alcohol upstairs, Claude."

"I'll try. You know the supplies are dwindling. Since no one lives here we don't shop for the place." She went on her way. Nina gazed at Juan for a few minutes. She tapped his face. He shifted his body. He moved his head wildly, then became still again.

"How is he doing?" Claudia carried a small bowl of water, face towels, and alcohol. "Look at the stuff I found. We were lucky. What time is it?"

"Nearly five." Nina bent over to manage Juan's breathing.

"Nina, I really don't think we should be doing this."

"He's not dead, Claude." Nina soaked a face towel in the water. "As long as he's not dead we can fix him."

"What fantasy land are you living in?" Claudia shook her head. "We're not nurses."

"I bet Juan would much rather stare in *my* face than some fat nurse's." Nina held the cool rag to his lips. He jerked at the touch of something foreign. He opened his eyes. Nina was happy to see the swelling had gone down.

"Ah." Juan sucked his lips in pain.

"Thank God you're all right, Juan. We were so worried about you."

"Nina?" He didn't look at her. He focused on the strange surroundings. "Where am I?"

"My uncle's house." Claudia passed Nina the alcohol.

"Claudia?" Juan gulped.

"Juan?" Nina touched his hand. "Tell us what happened." Nina applied the alcohol to his face.

"Chino and those two other ones jumped me. I should have been careful. I should have known he wouldn't let it go."

"Chino?" Nina exhaled. "Damn him. Who the hell does he think he is?"

"A Bronx Gangsta." Juan chuckled. "And I'm his enemy."

"Not anymore. He won't be able to kick you around again. You said two others? There were four with me at the bowling alley. Did you hear names? One of them must have left." Juan described them. "Bone must have left," Nina said. "He always seemed to have more sense than the rest. I don't believe this."

"And why not?" Claudia scoffed. "Didn't you think it would come to this? You thought they were just playing? You're lucky they didn't kill him."

"Gee, thanks for your concern, Claude."

"Are you taking this seriously? For God's sake, Nina, it's only going to get more out of hand. I don't want to be dragged into this."

"Scared?"

"Hell yes! And you should be, too."

"Well, I'm not. Being frightened of them won't solve anything."

"Okay. Let's see if you're singing that same tune when the NYAs start to come after *you*."

Nina contemplated the possibility. "I'll watch my back, don't worry."

"Like Juan was watching his? You think they're going to let you know when they're coming after you, Nina? Wake up. What the hell are you going to do when you're cornered? When it's your turn?"

"I don't know, Claudia!" She stood. "But I know I won't run *away*. We love each other. What is it going to take for others to realize this? You say the gangs aren't playing? Neither are we! We'll do whatever it takes to be together. If you don't like that, maybe you shouldn't be here."

"Excuse me?" Claudia raised an eyebrow. "Is that how you talk to someone who just helped you?"

"Nina, don't say anything you'll regret," Juan whispered. "Claudia's right to worry. These guys may be our families, but they are dangerous. They would sacrifice us for their pride in a minute."

"Jesus, Juan, you were the one saying we shouldn't be afraid. What changed?"

"Look." He rubbed his forehead. "I don't want anything to happen to you. If it did, I wouldn't be able to forgive myself."

"It won't, Juan." Nina sat beside him. "I don't care about me. I only care about you. We can do this. Don't give up now."

Juan managed a bright smile. "Well, that's a switch, huh?"

"Yes, it is." Nina kissed him.

❖❖❖

Florence was terrified by the time Mercedes arrived. Rico filled his aunt in about Juan's disappearance. He left them to decide what steps to take. Mercedes hurried to the kitchen to make coffee. Florence refused the sweet gesture. She couldn't keep her mind off Juan long enough to do anything but worry.

"Where could he be, Mercedes?"

"What did the police say?"

"That I have to wait to file a missing person's report but because Juan is a minor they will ride around to see if he's lost or something." She wiped tears. "Which is stupid because he wouldn't be lost."

"Well, has Juan ever done this before?"

"No." Florence exhaled, rubbing her hair. "Mercedes, he could be dead. Or lying somewhere needing help."

"Flo." Mercedes rushed toward her. She guided Florence's head to her shoulders. "He's okay. You got to believe that."

"But what if he's not?" Florence checked the clock above the living room shelf.

"God, why is this happening?"

"You sit down and try to relax. Drink this coffee." Mercedes handed her the cup.

"I'm going to go call people again to see if they've seen him. Did you check with his friends?"

"I've already called them. Their parents said they came home from the bowling alley hours ago."

"He's been gone all this time?"

"I went to bed around ten, figuring Juan would be in soon. Rico woke me up and told me Juan wasn't here. Rico rode around the neighborhood but didn't see anything."

Florence sighed. "He has to be all right, Mercedes."

"He will be." Mercedes hugged her.

✠✠✠

Claudia heated canned soup while Nina helped Juan out of his clothes. When Claudia returned to the living room, Juan was in his boxer shorts with a sheet covering his legs. Amused, she passed Nina the steaming soup.

"Smells delicious." Juan sat up, surprised to see the sun beaming through the curtains. "What time is it?"

"Shit." Claudia slapped her forehead. "Nina, it's almost six thirty. We got to head to school."

"Juan, you want us to take you home?" Nina felt his forehead.

"Not really." He awaited more soup.

"Seriously." Nina grinned. "You have to contact your mother. She must be worried."

"Good." Juan played with the sheet. "It's about time some of that worry is put on me."

"I don't understand." Nina dipped up more soup.

"Never mind. I'm not going to school with the way I look and I don't want to go home." He shrugged.

"Why not?" Claudia asked impatiently. Juan lacked an answer. "You can't stay here forever."

"I don't plan to. I'll leave in a little while. I just don't feel like facing anyone now."

"Be understanding, Claudia." Nina scowled.

"Whatever. You coming to school with me or not?"

"I'm staying here. Juan needs me."

"Nina, you need to go to school. I'm fine."

"I need to be here with you, Juan."

Claudia sighed. "Nina, did your brain get sucked out when you met this guy?" They looked at her. "You don't make sense anymore, Nina. What about his mother? She deserves to know he's okay. You two are so selfish."

"I'll see you later, Claude." Nina didn't take her eyes off Juan's.

"Nina, I can't believe you're acting like this. I'm beginning to think I don't know you anymore." Claudia stomped out the front door.

"Spoiled brat. She just doesn't understand." Nina shrugged.

"I hope I'm not coming between you two." Juan sighed. She caressed his naked chest. He drew her into a tantalizing kiss. She grabbed a small tube of lotion from her purse. She spread some over Juan's skin. "Mmm." He moaned.

Nina rubbed lotion down the curves of his lean stomach. She perked his muscles up with the same treatment. The delicious-smelling lotion stayed on her hands. She obsessively sniffed her fingers to get a whiff of the sweet scent.

"I could stay right here with you, forever."

"You know I'd want nothing more." Juan sat up, demonstrating his newfound strength. "What in the world are we doing?" He sighed. "I'm so confused."

"You know we're all alone." Nina put the lotion down. The living room was lovely but she anticipated what the upstairs bedroom had to offer. "No one's going to disturb us because they don't know we're here. It's the perfect time, Juan." She planted kisses down his neck.

"Nina." He took her hand. "I know what you're doing. You're trying to make me 'feel better.' I don't want you like that. I want you when it's special. It means nothing if we do it right now."

"I don't know why I said that." She looked off. "Lately I've been having such erotic dreams about you." Juan lit up. "I feel like we've known each other for a lifetime. I want to fully be yours, Juan. I..."

"And you will. When it's the right time. Now is not the right time. Go to school, Nina."

"You sure? I don't feel right about leaving you, Juan. Besides, what will you do here?"

"I don't know." He bit his lip. "I just need to think some things out."

Nina chuckled. "How come I feel like there's something you're not telling me?"

"Go to school." He kissed her forehead. "I'll see you later, okay?" He rubbed his thumb against her smooth cheek.

"Okay. Don't forget your truck is right outside."

"I forgot you drove it over here. Maybe I should take you to school."

"No, I'm sure you don't want to see that place right now. I'll catch a bus." Nina slipped on her purse. "How do I look?" She tugged her baggy jeans and oversize T-shirt.

He laughed. "Like you got up in the middle of the night."

"This will have to do." She kissed him. "'Bye."

She couldn't tear her eyes from his. She needed to know what he did every second. Could she be obsessed? Had anyone else experienced a love as amazing as this so quickly? She left feeling better than she had in years.

❊❊❊

Juan knew everything about the Bronx Gangstas and their neighborhood. He was prepared. He didn't care about gang etiquette or the danger. He *had* to see Tajo Munez face-to-face. He risked being jumped by all the Bronx Gangstas. He even risked being killed by Tajo himself. Since Juan met Nina, he'd developed a strength he couldn't shy away from. Just seeing her lovely face in his daydreams was enough to keep him driving to Edgewood.

Juan's plan was to appeal to Tajo's human side. Approach him like a man with honor and integrity. The thing gang members valued most was respect. Juan knew that Tajo would want to hear him out just to be up on Juan's intentions. If Tajo were arrogant like Rico, he'd let Juan come in for coffee. If not, Juan would be carried home in a pine box.

The streets were empty. He expected to see Bronx Gangstas hanging from telephone poles. The neighborhood wasn't that different from his. The fact that he could have been killed just for driving in their vicinity didn't bother Juan. He wanted Nina more than life. He would do anything to be with her.

Tajo's front door flew open before Juan reached the porch. A handsome, bald, hefty man around his late twenties dumped a plastic sack into the garbage can. With one look Juan knew who he was. He reminded Juan of Nina without her feminine grace. Juan ogled the Bronx Gangsta symbols on Tajo's naked chest.

Tajo cracked his knuckles, catching sight of the stranger before him. He loved scaring people into silence.

"*Hola*," he said, surprisingly politely. He watched Juan like a lion mesmerized by an unfamiliar species.

"*Hola*. You're Tajo Munez, right?"

"Maybe." He tugged a toothpick from his front teeth.

"We need to talk. I don't care how dumb it is coming here. I just needed to see you face-to-face. I couldn't avoid it."

Tajo blocked the sun with his hand. "First of all, who the fuck are you, *ese*?"

Juan took a deep breath and spit out his name. He closed his eyes waiting for a circle of thugs to fly out of nowhere to beat him to a pulp. He waited for Tajo to throw him into the street. Instead Tajo gestured toward the door. "Come in."

Juan felt it would be better if Tajo jumped him. Now that he was off guard, he was truly frightened. He held on to the sides of his pants. Sweat trickled down his nose. He would have brushed it away but he couldn't move. "Want something to drink?" Tajo perched his nose in the air, giving Juan the intimidating look of most gangbangers.

"No. Look, I know about the feud. I know that you have no reason to like me and every reason to hate me. I know your goal in life is to kill every NYA you see. Still, I wanted you to know who I am. I wanted you to know I am not in my brother's gang."

"I know that." Tajo rested on the couch. "We're all alone so I don't mind you coming forward. I like you already, Juan. You got balls as big as Texas." Tajo laughed. "I know my boys jumped you last night. Yet you show up here with nothing to protect you. You show up here knowing how much we hate your brother. Man. In my wildest dreams, I ain't never did no crazy shit like that."

Juan nodded. "I'm not in the NYAs, Tajo. And I love your cousin very much."

"You'd have to, to come here like this. But the question ain't if you love her or not. The question is what kind of man you are. Are you a real man, *ese*?"

"I like to think I am."

"You don't know shit about my world, do you? You think you do but you don't. You have any idea how much I want to kill you right now, Juanito?" Tajo balled his fist until it turned red. "But I won't." He sighed. "I think of myself as a fair man."

"You do?" Juan exhaled.

"Uh-huh." Tajo grinned. "I should thank you. You've made my Nina happy. Deep down that's all I've ever wanted. I take care of her as best I can. I try to keep her safe."

"I'm sure you do."

"You know, when I found out she wanted to be with you it deeply hurt me." Tajo gripped his chest. "And that's not smart, Juan. You should never hurt me. I retaliate in ways you wouldn't dream of thinking about, *ese*. I am not afraid of any G on this planet. And that makes me one feared motherfucker."

Juan sighed. "I know you value respect, Tajo. As a man I wanted to appeal to that. So that's why I wanted to ask your permission to see Nina."

"My permission, huh?" Tajo bobbed his head, grinning.

"Yes."

"You don't get it, do you, Juanito? It's about family and loyalty. Now I can't grant you permission because I don't trust your ass. And I wouldn't want my baby cousin with anyone I don't trust."

"So what do I have to do to get that trust?"

Tajo smiled. "I'm glad you asked that, Juanito." He snapped his fingers. "Since you walked your ass in the door I wanted you to ask that. There is only one way you can have my blessing to see Nina. One way." Tajo's amusement disappeared.

"Tell me," Juan whispered.

"You got to be willing to do it."

"I'll do anything. I care about Nina so much. We want to be together."

Tajo sucked his lips. "Easy, dog. You got to become one of the family."

"I don't understand." Juan grimaced.

Tajo strolled around the room. He circled Juan until he ended up directly in front of his face.

"You have to become one of the family, dog. You have to become a Bronx Gangsta." He smirked.

"You..." Juan grinned. "You can't be serious."

Tajo cracked his knuckles. "It's either that or *you* take your brother's place as my favorite enemy."

"I am not, this is insane."

"Hey, hey now. I can't let my cousin date just anyone. I have to know the guy she's with is down with us. I need to be able to trust him. Either you become a G or you won't be with her. And if you continue to *try* to date her, we will kill you."

Juan waved his hands. "Tajo, this is crazy..."

Tajo ripped a gun from his back pocket. He rested the pointer on the tip of Juan's nose.

"Take it or leave it, *ese*. Ain't no side deals, man."

"This is crazy." Juan stared at the gun. "Don't you have a heart? I mean, don't you care about what Nina wants? Do you know how happy we make each other? I love her."

"I keep hearing your words loud and clear, Juanito. But there's nothing to back them up. To me, that means you're not a man but a boy. I don't associate with boys. You should be glad I haven't jumped your ass for even coming here." Tajo lowered the gun. "Now get the fuck out of my house."

Juan sighed. "I don't know why I thought you'd be different. I guess I hoped some of Nina's compassion came from her family. Obviously it hasn't."

"Did you forget what neighborhood you're in, *ese*?" Tajo massaged the gun.

"No." Juan walked to the door. "I am not my brother. I have my own beliefs, my own feelings. So does Nina. Why are you doing this? Why can't you accept that what I say is the truth? What the hell do you think I'm trying to do?" Juan rubbed his swollen jaw. "Corrupt her? See, that's funny to me. I'm not the one in the gang. *You* are. Yet you want to keep her from *me*?" He shook his head.

"Tajo, I am sick and tired of hearing about your world from my brother, you, and everyone else. It's just an excuse. You don't *want* to do better. You can't accept your own choices so you kill people. You steal, rape, and sell drugs. You do everything you can to not be held responsible for your own actions. I don't know why I came here. Now that I see you up close, I realize there is nothing in the world I could have said to give you an open mind about me seeing Nina. I really don't care."

"So?" Tajo waved his hand. It was obvious he was shocked at Juan's courage.

The more Juan looked at him, the more he felt Tajo admired that. Of course he'd never admit it.

"Do what you have to." Juan opened the door.

"See, you must not love Nina as much as you say, right?" Tajo sniggered. "You've been lying to her."

"What are you talking about?" Juan snarled.

"I know that at some point, in the comfort of her arms, you told her you'd do anything for her. But it was a lie wasn't it, *ese*?"

"I *would* do anything for her."

"Except become a Bronx Gangsta, right?" Tajo shook his head. "If you loved my cousin as much as you claimed and really wanted to be with her, there wouldn't be nothing I could throw at you you wouldn't do. That's the action of a real man, *ese*." He poked Juan's chest. "My real question is, how much do you want Nina?"

"Good-bye." Juan slowly stepped onto the porch.

"The offer will stand until I close it, man." Tajo winked. "Just got to make up your mind. How much do you want the sweet lips of my cousin? The tenderness of her touch?" Tajo laughed. "Or just the whole package? How much do you want it? How much do you *need* it?"

Juan left.

✠✠✠

Juan drove the day away thinking of Tajo's request. He had to be crazy even to consider it. The more Juan thought of Rico's insensitivity, the more he appreciated Tajo's offer. Yet there would be no way in hell Juan could pull it off. Would he have to choose between the girl he loved and his own brother? Before he knew it he stared at his mother's front door. A deep pain crossed his chest.

Cynthia sat in front of the television doing homework. Juan wasn't in the mood for her smart mouth. Lucky for her she realized he needed to be left alone. Jorge and Benny scurried from the hall with lollipops.

"Ooh!" Benny pointed at his older brother. "You're in *trouble*."

"Juan, where you been?" Jorge gasped.

"Yeah, Mamá's been scared to death. She didn't even go to work because she was so upset. She's been calling all over the place." Benny sucked the sour apple lollipop.

"Yeah, and the police have been here twice. I hope you have a good excuse."

Juan groaned. "Where is she?"

Jorge sucked his cherry lollipop. "Her bedroom, rummaging through her phonebook. She's looking for people she may have missed." Juan crept toward his mother's bedroom.

Florence sat on the edge of her bed with her back turned to the door. Sometimes duties Juan didn't expect were thrown in his path. He'd never been one to run away from his responsibilities. He knew he'd been selfish. He knew he'd broken her heart. But he didn't feel he could do any better.

"Ma?" He tapped the door. She threw the phonebook to the floor and ran to him.

"Juan." Her tears dampened his shoulder. "Oh my God. I was so scared. Oh thank you. Thank you, God. Thank you."

"I didn't mean to make you worry, Ma."

She pulled away from him. She examined the bruises on his face. Juan wondered if she tried to read his mind. Even he didn't know what he felt at the moment.

"Where the hell have you been?"

"I…"

"Answer me!"

"I'm sorry." He shrugged. "I am so sorry."

"*Sorry*? Juan, do you have any idea what you put me through? I have had the police here! I've called everyone I know! I rode up and down the streets making sure you weren't lying in the road dead. And all you can say is 'sorry'? You sure as hell better give me more than *that*. Where were you? And don't bother saying you were at school because I went there looking for you."

"Ma, it's some crazy shit going on in my head. I can't explain it. I was jumped and I didn't want to come home. I have no other reason than that."

"Who jumped you?" She squinted.

"It doesn't matter." He stretched out on her bed.

"I asked you a question."

"Some Bronx Gangstas, all right?" He covered his eyes. Going all day without sleep had drained him.

"Juan, what the hell were you doing in Edgewood? Answer me!"

"I wasn't in Edgewood, all right? They followed me."

"Did they know Rico is your brother?" She sat beside him. Juan shrugged. He didn't want to go into the real details. Whatever Florence guessed was good enough for him. "Juan, that has nothing to do with you not coming home. I'm your mother. I love you more than anything on this earth and you could scare me to death like you did?"

"I couldn't come home! I can't explain it but I didn't feel like going through the usual shit with you."

"Watch your mouth! And how dare you come in here with your head big after what you've done? Juan, you are scaring the hell out of me every day! I see more and more that you're changing and I don't like it. Where is the son that had ambition? Now all you care about is that girl." He stared at her. "Why are you being like this?"

"My actions have nothing to do with Nina, okay? I stayed out all night. It was a mistake and it will never happen again." He walked to the hall.

"I spoke to another one of your teachers, Juan." He sighed. "Your grades are slipping all over the place, aren't they? Were you going to tell me?"

"Talking about chemistry? I, uh, I flunked my last two labs."

"What?" Florence moaned.

"I've been having trouble concentrating. I can't get any rest with Rico around here. You know how he plays his music and stays up all night."

"You can't get rest because of *Nina*. Juan, I have warned you before. I told you if you and Nina couldn't handle your business then you shouldn't see each other. I can't allow you to ruin your education over some girl."

He punched the wall. "She's not just *some* girl, damn it!" Florence gasped. "She's the woman I love! She's the person I want to spend my life with. When we leave school I want to marry her. I want to have children with her."

"Juan." Florence held up her hand.

"You don't get it, do you? You've never experienced a love like ours."

"Wake up! You're only in high school. You're gonna fall in love with thousands of people after Nina."

"No, I won't. Nina is all I will ever want. She touches me in ways no one ever has. We understand each other. We have a bond that was created by destiny. We were made for each other."

Florence gaped. "Juan, you strike me as almost being obsessed with Nina."

He scoffed. "You're worse than Rico. He wants to keep us apart, too."

"I don't want to keep you two apart. But I don't want you seeing Nina if it compromises everything you've worked for."

"Tough, Ma. There is nothing you can do about that."

"The hell there isn't. What do you mean, Rico wants you to stop seeing her?"

He scoffed. "Don't you get it, Ma? *No one* wants me with Nina." Florence watched in awe. "It's Nina and me against the world, Mamá. But I'll tell you one thing, we are *not* going to let the world win." He walked away.

CHAPTER THIRTEEN

"You did *what*?" Chino accidentally knocked cereal onto the kitchen table. He ignored it.

"That's right." Tajo slapped a hamburger patty into the skillet.

"Hold on." Chino rubbed his head. "Maybe I'm fuckin' high or some shit. I know I couldn't have heard you straight, man. You offered Juan Alonso a place with us? Where the hell do you get off?"

"I didn't offer him a place. You think this is a fuckin' fraternity? You think anyone can just walk in? What I did was called his bluff. He's full of shit, so he walked off with his tail between his legs."

Chino rubbed his fist. He experienced fond memories of bashing Juan's face with it. "I can't believe that motherfucker came over here. What the fuck does it take to get through to him?" He leaned on the chair. "I should have smoked his ass. God knows I wanted to more than anything."

Tajo chuckled. "Yo, what's going on with you, dog? I know he's Rico's brother but he gets your blood boiling because of Nina, right?" Chino looked at him. "You don't have to be jealous of Juan. Nina knows what's best for her."

"Oh yeah? Then why the hell is she still with him, huh?" Chino slammed the chair underneath the table.

"You need to chill, man. I told Juan the only chance he has with Nina is if he becomes one of us. He ain't going to do that.

He's too chicken shit to go against his own family or the NYAs. He knows we will get him if he doesn't stay away from Nina. So there it is."

"There what is?" Chino scoffed.

"Your chance. You can be with Nina because you got two things on your side. You're one of my boys. And you're someone I trust. Now Nina can't be with anyone I don't trust. So stop stressing." Tajo paused. Chino turned to see Nina standing at the doorway with her backpack.

"Well, look what the cat dragged in." Chino rubbed his hands. "What's up, Nina?"

She rolled her eyes.

"Where have you been? You should have been home hours ago."

"Stay out of my face, Tajo."

"Yo, who the fuck you think you're speaking to?" He grabbed her. "Were you with Juan Alonso?"

"I was at Lisa's." She sighed. "She needed me to help her with homework. Call her if you don't believe me."

"Better be the truth." He went back to cooking.

"She lies so much, how would you know?" Chino remarked. Nina went to her room. Chino hurriedly followed.

"Get out of my room."

He blocked her from closing the door. "We need to talk, Nina."

"I got nothing to say to you." She wiped off her lipstick. "Get out of my room!"

"I could have killed your boyfriend last night but I let his sorry ass live. Don't you think I deserve something for that? You'd better realize your damn options. The game you're playing is dangerous, Nina. I didn't kill him last night because I didn't want to hurt you."

"Gee, I'm touched." She rested on the bed.

"But I *will* next time. You can bet on that. So when are you going to get smart and join the party?"

"Meaning?" She propped herself up.

"I think you know what I mean, Nina."

"Chino, let's get something straight. You and I are never going to be anything more than what we are now. I don't like you. I can't stand you." He flexed his jaws. "It doesn't matter what you do to Juan. I won't want *you*. Get over it."

"Is that right?" He sucked his lip.

"Yeah. Nothing you can do will make me turn to you for anything."

He sneered. "We'll see."

✠✠✠

School became incredibly exciting for Juan and Nina. They couldn't stand to miss a day for fear of not seeing each other. Every waking moment, every breath they took united them. They sneaked kisses in school corners. Juan spent his classes daydreaming about Nina. She spent her time writing his name on her notebook. They didn't care who knew they were an item.

They couldn't keep their hands off each other. The other students couldn't help noticing. They made a ritual of sneaking off to kiss during lunch and class breaks. The teachers noticed changes in their behaviors.

Their relationship affected everyone around them.

Juan didn't spend as much time with his friends. Nina stopped calling Claudia during school nights. They hadn't hung out in days. Nina and Juan no longer waited at the library. They used abandoned parking lots, stores, and parks as meeting places. In history class, they got bathroom passes at the same time. They ended up kissing for the rest of the period on stairwells. The more time they spent together, the more determined they were to stay together.

Nina put her painting on hold. Everything took a backseat to their relationship.

Such happiness had its drawbacks. Juan's grades continued to slip. Nina found studying a burden and disregarded the task altogether. They didn't care about the danger. Nothing disrupted their passion. The only thing that invaded their thoughts of each other was the upcoming festival.

❈❈❈

Friday nights brought anticipation from many people but nothing brought more excitement to teens than the annual Fun Time Festival. Nina scanned the overlapping crowd. Various activities occupied the park. People played video games in dark booths. Dance contests were held in large tents. A live band performed on a small stage in the midst of all the excitement.

Big, bulky seniors from numerous schools played touch football. People watched a fireworks display and a magician. Millions of blue, red, and white squiggly lines of fireworks filled the atmosphere. A top radio station hosted the event from a van in the distance. This *was* paradise. Nina made up her mind to have some fun.

"What did I tell you, girlfriend?" Claudia sucked a fat lollipop. She wrapped her arms around Nina's shoulders. Lisa and Rosa strolled behind. "We're gonna have some fun tonight, *woo*!"

Claudia howled. She wore a tank top that hit above her belly button. Tight, denim hip-huggers squeezed her firm thighs and she wore a silver chain around her waist.

"I must admit, it does look like fun." Nina watched the guys playing football. She only had one person on her mind. She wouldn't relax until she set eyes on him.

"Shit, we all look good." Rosa licked a gigantic ice-cream cone. "I'm not stopping with the festival. I plan to get dirty tonight."

"Me, too." Claudia held on to Nina. "You will too, Nina."

"Excuse me?" Nina bit into her corn dog.

"I'm talking about that hotel over there." Claudia pointed across the street.

"Get with it, girl. That's what this festival is really about. You can't finish the night off without some sex."

Rosa winked. "She's right, Nina. Now you and Juan will get your chance to put out that fire."

"Speaking of Juan." Lisa pointed past the concession stands.

A group of guys played the toughest game of basketball Nina had ever seen. She spotted Juan instantly. Perspiration drenched his naked chest. The automatic flex of his muscles enticed her. Her eyes zoomed in at will. She counted the lines of sweat dripping from his hard nipples. She went limp.

"Well, looks like you've found who you were looking for." Claudia laughed.

Nina raced toward the game.

"Come on! Come on, man," the handsome black guy behind Juan goaded.

Juan kept his cool.

Nina got as close as she could without interrupting. Juan made the shot despite being bullied by three taller guys. Dell and

Carlos held their own doing defense. Tony bent over at the sidelines, wiping his face. Juan ruled the game. Even an NBA player didn't have his cool style.

"What you wanna do, huh?" The black guy bumped Juan with his chest. Juan dribbled in circles.

"Why you on my ass, huh?" Juan chuckled. "You can't handle this, man."

"Oh no?" The black guy grinned. "Let's see what you got, man. Let's see what you got. It's not gonna be that easy." Juan did a double turn. The guy stayed on his back. "I told you it wouldn't be that easy, baby."

"Come on. Let's do this then!" Juan swiftly turned around. He juggled the ball masterfully, then passed it. Carlos did some not-so-fancy dribbling himself before passing the ball back to Juan. Juan dribbled it three times between his legs. He hit a three-pointer.

"It's your game, baby!" A blond guy wearing a Reagan High School sweatshirt shouted from the sidelines. At that moment Juan's gaze entranced Nina. He galloped toward her.

"Hey." Sweat drenched his face. Nina became woozy. She pretended he'd stepped out of a shower.

"Hey." She passed him some bottled water. "I saw you out there. You got skills."

He chuckled. "And what do you know about basketball?"

"I know I like seeing you play it." She trickled her fingers down his wet chest. "You were the fastest and best player out there."

"Right, right." He smirked. He took her in his arms. They walked down the sidewalk. "Damn." He looked at her cut-off denim shorts. Her white bra showed through her sleeveless T-shirt. "You look so good in that."

She shrugged. "Claudia told me to wear this. She said it makes a statement. I'm not comfortable having my ass all out."

"I am." Juan playfully slapped her butt.

"Honestly, are they too short?" She pulled at the shorts.

"No. You look good, Nina. I tell you, I needed to have some fun. So many things going down right now." They sat on a bench beside a girl on a cell phone. She seemed annoyed that they'd interrupted her privacy. "Nina, I've been keeping something from you for days. I did something behind your back."

"What?"

He took her hand. "You know I love you so much, right? And I would never do anything to hurt you. You know the day after Chino jumped me? When I didn't go to school?"

"'Course. I'm the one who got you, remember?" She chuckled.

"That day I went to see your cousin, Tajo." Nina gasped. "Don't be alarmed. We talked. Nothing else happened. I even think he kind of respects me."

"Juan, are you crazy? Why would you invite trouble like that?"

"I had to, Nina. I wanted Tajo to know he couldn't control me. That I was going to be with you regardless."

"What happened?"

"We talked calmly." He purposely left out the part about the gun. "I asked his permission to see you. He said he didn't trust me." Juan shrugged. "He said some things I don't care to repeat. Then I left."

"Why didn't you tell me before?"

"I knew you'd be frightened. Anyway, nothing came of it so I didn't think it was important to mention."

"But you did tonight?"

He cocked his head to the side, grinning. "Kind of, yeah. God, you are so hot." He sucked her neck. She pulled away when people passed. "Nina, do you know how good it feels when we're together? I wish we could just spend time together and not worry about anyone else."

"Me, too." She ran her hand down his sweaty arm. "Tajo's going to be gone for the weekend. How about you come to the house? You can spend the night."

Juan jumped back. "Are you kidding me?" He laughed.

"No. I'm not necessarily talking sex, Juan. But I would like to spend time with you at home. I don't want us to have to hide from people tonight."

"Nina." He rubbed her chin. "What if it leads to more?"

"Then whatever happens *happens*." She smiled.

"It will be your first time. Are you sure you'll be ready?"

"I knew it would be with you. From the first moment I saw you. I knew it. I just didn't know when. Juan, when I saw how you protected me from Chino, I knew I wanted to make love to you. You've put so much on the line for me. I want to give you something no one else can. I'm not saying it will be tonight. But if it is, I promise I won't try to stop it. You want to come?"

"I'd like nothing more. But it's too dangerous."

"No one will know. We'll be discreet as spies." She smiled.

He bit his lips. "My mom would be worried, Nina."

"Tell her you're staying at a friend's house. She won't object to that, will she?"

"I don't know nowadays. She's not too happy with the stunts I've been pulling."

"You're her model son, Juan." Nina caressed his arm. "You can talk her into anything. It's up to you."

"Okay." Juan shoved her into a kiss. The cell phone girl walked off.

"I'm going to go catch up with the girls." Nina fixed her lipstick.

"Yeah." Juan wiped his face. "I'm gonna go shoot some hoops for a while."

The abrupt, blasting thunder didn't faze them. "Let's meet up sometime later, all right?"

"Yeah." Nina agreed. They stared at each other for a few minutes, then went in separate directions.

❖❖❖

Rico stood against Nina's bedroom wall, massaging his fist. Homicide smoked a cigarette. Jelly leaned his plump frame against Nina's dresser to catch his breathing. Homicide and Rico took out serrated kitchen knives. They slashed Nina's sheets to shreds. Gil ran in with a sack of Tajo's jewelry.

"Yo, Rico, look what I found, man!" Gil held up a handful of gold chains.

"We can probably get, what? Eight hundred for this, G."

"Put that shit back. We only came here to teach that little bitch a lesson. Tajo will get his soon enough." Rico got on his knees. He ripped Nina's belongings from her drawers. Jelly scratched up the mirror until he couldn't make out his face.

"Ah." Homicide looked through Nina's schoolbooks. "It would be a shame if something happened to these, wouldn't it?" He slid the knife through the pages of her algebra book. "Oops." He laughed.

"Tear all this shit up," Rico ordered. He found Nina's underwear drawer. He'd never been one to pass up a dirty opportunity. He hadn't forgotten how beautiful Nina was. He hadn't forgotten how much he wanted to have her when he first saw her.

He closed his eyes. He pressed her soft pink panties to his lips. He swore she was still in them.

"Oh man, that's nasty!" Gil laughed. "Smelling the girl's panties!"

Rico sucked his lips. "She was something else. Shit, I might have to tell Juan to clear the way. She won't be too bad as my bitch, would she? Once she's trained of the NYA ways." He stuffed the garment into his pocket.

"You serious, man?" Homicide scraped the wall with a box cutter.

"Maybe. If she wants to fuck, why waste her time with a boy?" He grinned. "Not when she could have a man. I swear I'd split that ass in two. I'd have her begging for more."

"She sure is something. She got that nice tight ass. Smooth-ass legs." Homicide moaned.

"Firm titties I bet, huh?" Gil shook a can of red spray paint. "I ain't never seen her, but from what I've heard she must be worth some shit for Juan to go against us." He chuckled. "Hey, how about a gang bang? I wouldn't mind that one bit. We could get her after school one day. Shit, let's do that, man."

"Hell yeah. I'm up for some of that myself." Homicide shifted his hungry eyes toward Rico. Rico didn't bother to comment.

One by one, Rico shredded Nina's underwear. He left the entire drawer in rags. Gil sprayed obscenities on the walls. Jelly carved holes into the closet doors. Even Rico couldn't believe they were capable of such damage.

"Damn." Jelly held his portly waist. "Think this will give her the picture, ese?"

"It should." Rico bobbed his head. "If not, there are louder lessons we can provide, right, fellas?"

"Fuck yeah." Gil nodded. "Now what?"

"Let's go." Rico followed them out Nina's window. They'd taken great measures to hide their identities. They were disguised in black, showing no NYA colors. They'd stolen a car so no one could recognize an NYA vehicle. They headed down the street. Rico couldn't have been more content. The more he hurt people, the more he felt like a god.

The rain didn't spoil the festival. Nina couldn't remember when she'd had so much fun. She and Claudia teamed up against some girls from Kennedy High School for a dance contest. They won free movie tickets. Rosa and Lisa participated in the relays. Afterward all four of them joined up with other girls from Roosevelt to catch up on gossip and everything else girls did when they hung together.

They gathered underneath the tree by the sidewalk to see the passing cars. Claudia checked out the men that passed by. Rosa leaned against the tree with a hot dog. Lisa danced to the music from the concert.

"Why did it have to start raining?" Nina wiped pools of rain from her naked shoulder. "Why did I let you talk me into wearing this outfit, Claude? I'll be sick before we leave here."

Claudia sucked a cigarette. "Man, this scene blows."

"I'm surprised you're not having fun," Lisa teased, dancing erotically.

"Hey, where's that fine guy you were just speaking to at the stands?" Rosa asked.

Claudia grinned. "I got him to pay for my food, then left his ass over there. Damn, Nina, you're lucky. You got someone who truly cares about you."

"You'll get that too, Claude."

"Every time I think I've found someone different he turns out to be an asshole."

Lisa shook her head. "'Cause you're so damn wild. You can't be so loose, then expect them to be serious with you."

"Hey, it's not my fault I know how to have fun and others don't." Claudia eyed a cute police officer. She had no problems flirting with anyone.

He glared at her. "Make sure that's a regular cigarette," he said.

"It is, officer." Claudia winked. He walked toward the crowd. "Damn, he was fine. He was so fine I wanted to commit a crime just to go home with him." The girls laughed. Nina got on her tiptoes to see through the darkness. A flash of fireworks startled her. "Looking for someone?" Claudia moaned.

"No. What were you saying?"

"Does it matter? We know the deal. You're here with us but you're not truly here with us are you, Nina? You're looking for Juan, right?"

"Okay, I was. Is something wrong with that?" Rosa and Lisa exchanged looks but didn't speak. "If you got something to say, say it," Nina insisted.

"All right." Claudia stood away from the tree. "You're no fun anymore, Nina. You never have time to hang. All you care about is Juan."

"Claudia, that's not true. I'm here now, aren't I? I never once got on your case when you dumped *me* for a boy."

"That's 'cause I never did." Claudia rolled her eyes.

"Oh, come on!" Nina laughed. "All you do is chase boys, Claude!"

"That's Claudia, all right." Rosa chuckled.

"Okay. Let's chill." Claudia took Nina's hand. "I'm happy for you. But I'm worried, too. Since Juan was jumped I can't help but be. I love you, Nina. You're my best friend. I couldn't bear anything happening to you."

"Oh, Claude. Come here." They hugged. It was the first time things felt normal for the both of them. "Claudia, you're always going to be in my life. No one can take your place."

"Just promise me you'll be okay, Nina."

"I will. I've never seen you so frightened before, Claude. I never wanted my relationship with Juan to burden *you*."

"Something tells me Claude will get over it." Rosa pointed down the street. A black Camaro eased toward them. Four guys stuck their heads out the windows. One gazed at Nina. She immediately turned away. He was cute but she wanted nothing to do with them.

"Hey, Claude!" The guy in the passenger seat held up tattooed arms. "What's up, baby?"

"Oh shit." Claudia covered her mouth.

"Who is that?" Nina whispered.

"You don't want to know." Claudia chuckled.

"Yes, I do."

"Remember that guy I met at that pool party? The cute one that took me back to his place?"

"The one you had sex with on the plastic seat covers?" Nina gasped. Claudia laughed. "*That's* him?" Nina stared at him.

"Yeah." Claudia stomped out her cigarette.

The guy howled. "Damn, girl. You so fine, look at you. I been trying to call you and shit. How come you're never home?"

"I'm home. You just didn't call at the right times."

"Mmm." He licked his lips. "Hanging with your girls, I see?"

"Yeah. This is Rosa, Lisa." Claudia took Nina's hand. "And this is my number one homegirl, Nina."

"Y'all look fly, shit. Too damn fly to be waiting out here at this sorry-ass festival. If you want to have some real fun, get in the car. We're going to a real party."

"You guys want to?" Claudia looked at her friends. Nina sighed. Rosa nodded. Lisa waved her hand, showing she was against it. Something tickled Nina's hand. Juan stood on the other side of the tree. His fingers took hers. Nina sneaked off behind with him.

They walked to a secluded area encircled in trees. "Juan?"

He caressed her hand. "Can I have a little time with you, Nina?"

"You can have anything you want." She leaned against a creepy, lopsided tree with branches that reached out like giant fingers. "Juan, what are you up to?"

"I just want to spend some time with you."

Nina relaxed against the tree's wetness. The rain trickled down her thin T-shirt. The ragged edges of her denim shorts caught droplets of rain. Water slid from her breasts and stomach. When she got the courage to look down, she found Juan on one knee in front of her. His hot hands moved delicately up the curves of her damp body. She wasn't wearing a bra. The rain converted the T-shirt into a window.

She enjoyed his soggy lips on her stomach. He circled her belly button with his tongue. Her legs quivered. She nearly moaned, forgetting there were thousands of people close by. She didn't know what to say or do. Was this the true Nina? Was this the woman inside the teenager who longed to escape? Since meeting Juan, she was no longer appalled by sex.

She now understood why Claudia thought it was better than ice cream. She could see why teenage boys spent their lives trying to get laid.

Juan's mouth teased hers. His kisses were delicate and divine. His hands crawled toward her breasts. The rain turned into a vicious pour. Juan stood. His hair resembled a waterfall. Rain slid over the edge of his face. He stroked Nina's slippery stomach. Her hair cupped her face and neck like a black scarf.

"Nina?" Juan forced his lips to her neck. He sucked until red patches grew underneath her ear.

"Huh?" Her breasts stiffened. She rubbed her leg against his.

"Does this feel good to you?" Juan breathed.

"*Yes*." She shoved her hands behind her back, grabbing the tree. The soothing movement of his mouth grew faster. Nina felt like she'd burst from stimulation. Just when she made her mind up that she wanted another quick taste, Juan stopped. She'd never seen someone so beautiful in all her life. The rain covered his parted lips, dropping into his mouth. Then, it was over.

The girls ran up before Juan and Nina could speak. Nina's arousal turned into anxiety. Claudia howled at the sight. Lisa and Rosa grinned. All of a sudden Nina felt like a slut. The feeling left when Juan kissed her hand.

"Thanks for letting me enjoy you." He sucked rain from Nina's fingertip. Her friends nearly passed out from shock. "'Bye." He ran toward the festival.

"Oh my God!" Claudia jumped up and down. Rosa busted out laughing. Lisa was in a daze. "Girlfriend!" Claudia shrieked.

"Shut up!" Nina laughed. "I don't want the entire world to know."

"I don't believe this. Here we were thinking you two were having some boring conversation and you're over here filming '*Basic Instinct Three*'!" Claudia laughed.

"Yeah '*Basic Instinct Three: Latino Love*,'" Rosa joked.

"No, no, '*Latino Lust*'!" Claudia guffawed. "What was going on, girlfriend?"

"Nothing." Nina covered her face.

"Ah, it's too late to be getting shame now. We want details." Lisa moved Nina's hands from her face.

"Well, he, felt me up." She laughed. "I can't believe he did it!" Her eyes widened. "I wasn't expecting it or anything. He just led me here. The next thing I knew he was on his knees, kissing my legs."

"Kissing your legs?" Rosa held her hips. "That boy is too romantic. I bet he can rock it."

"Hell yeah!" Claudia laughed.

"Then he moved his hands up my stomach." Nina closed her eyes.

Lisa shivered. "Well, did he say anything? Did *you*?"

"No." Nina hooked her hands. "I don't know why I let him do it. With Juan, it's not like I plan things. He just takes me places before I know it. You know I wouldn't have done this with anyone else."

"Sure, you little ho," Claudia joked. The others laughed.

"Seriously, Claude. It means so much when you're in love."

Claudia wrapped her arm around Nina's shoulder. "Girlfriend, you've sampled the goods. You cannot stop now."

"Yes, I can."

"No, you can't." Rosa crossed her arms. "Girl, Juan's hungry. You better feed him before he goes looking for dinner somewhere else."

"Rosa's right." Claudia winked. "You got to reel him in now."

"I don't know if it's the right time," Nina protested.

"Leave her alone, Claudia." Lisa wrapped her arm around Nina. "Let her make her own decisions. She doesn't have to have sex until she's ready."

"What old-fashioned 'virgin manual' did you get that from, Lisa?" Rosa rolled her eyes.

"I don't know if it's the right time for us." Nina exhaled. "I got to tell you guys something. I've invited Juan to stay at the house with me while Tajo's gone." The girls hooted. "Come on, you guys. It's just to talk and stuff."

"*Sure.*" Rosa scoffed. "Your subconscious wants sex, Nina.

That's why you're inviting him over there. You know you want him. You'll say it'll be in control but the moment he touches you you're gonna fall to pieces. Don't fight it, girl."

"Nina, he had you pushed against a tree, practically molesting you." Claudia chuckled.

Rosa nodded. "Yeah, and you looked like you very much enjoyed it. Isn't that a sign that it's right? Girl, you've finally made it to second base, now bring it on to third!"

Rosa pretended to be a batter hitting a baseball.

"Nina, do you want to have sex with Juan?" Lisa asked.

"Of course I do. But I don't know about *tonight*, guys." She bit her lip.

Rosa grinned. "I think you'd better hurry up and *know*."

Nina took a deep breath. "And what if I *think* I know?" she whispered.

Claudia took her hand. "Then I think you should have these." She passed Nina a pack of condoms. Nina didn't know where the night would lead, but she would anticipate whatever came her way.

✠✠✠

Juan parked his truck in a remote place in Edgewood. Disguised in a scarf and cap he'd borrowed from Carlos, he raced in behind Nina to Tajo's. He studied the streets. She rushed him inside the house before anyone could see them.

"Did you call your mother?" Nina stood against the front door.

"Yeah. It took some heavy butt kissing but she agreed it was okay. I just hope she doesn't end up checking on me at Tony's." He threw his cap on the sofa. "So?" He rubbed his hands.

"So?" Nina shrugged. "Would you like something to drink?"

"Sure." He followed her to the dark kitchen. "You mind being alone all weekend?"

"I'm not alone now, am I?" She filled two glasses with juice.

"Guess not." Juan seductively sipped. She sat beside him at the kitchen table.

They didn't speak for moments, then Juan interrupted their stares. "Where is Tajo anyway?"

"He had something to, uh, take care of."

"Oh, I see. Killing someone, is he? Or beating someone senseless?"

"That's not fair, Juan."

"*Fair*? Nina, he's a gangbanger. He's a no-good punk who gets pleasure out of hurting people."

"Juan, you don't know my cousin the way you think." He scoffed. "Tajo's not like the others. He has a heart."

"Where?" He finished his juice. "Nina, I appealed to him out of respect. He wasn't hearing it. Face it. Tajo's just as bad as Rico."

She sighed. "You don't know him. Not a lot of people would have taken me in after what happened with my mother. I owe him for that. I still care about him, no matter what he does."

"You can separate that?" Juan grimaced.

"Sometimes." She shrugged. "Why do I suddenly feel guilty for loving my own cousin? You love your brother, don't you?" Juan turned away. Nina repeated the question. When he didn't answer, she let it go. "I don't want to talk about either one of them." She took his hand. "Want to see my bedroom?"

Juan nodded. "Hell yeah."

CHAPTER FOURTEEN

They started down the hallway. Nina felt ready for anything. She'd gotten to know Juan mentally and spiritually. Physically was sure to be around the corner. She instructed Juan to close his eyes. She walked backward, determined not to take her eyes off him. She didn't listen to the anxiety in her stomach. She ignored the throbbing cramps of apprehension.

Her fast heartbeat symbolized a magnetic song she would dance tonight. Her heart became the voice that led her to the next moment. She enjoyed seeing Juan helpless and at her will. He held her hand like a lost child. She pulled his fingers away from his face.

"You can look now." She opened the door. Nina gazed at him. She could tell his excitement for the moment had drifted. He looked like he would faint. "Like it?" Nina hadn't turned around. She kept her eyes on his amazed face. "That look tells me you like it."

"Nina." He rubbed his mouth. He didn't have to say another word. She turned around to face the boundless mess that used to be her room.

"Oh my God!"

Juan guided her to his chest. "It's okay." He nearly heaved when he read the NYA symbols on her walls. "It's going to be okay, Nina."

"No, it's not!" She ran into the living room. "Did you see that mess? How could they have done that?"

"With a lot of knives, I'd say." He sighed.

"This is no time for jokes!"

"I have to joke because I can't believe this shit myself. I knew this would happen! I told you we couldn't afford to reason with any of them." Juan kicked the couch. "I told you what they were capable of." He rubbed his foot through the carpet.

"Nina, what, what are we doing?"

"Juan, I don't care what they do. They are not going to keep us apart!"

"Nina, they just broke into your home and tore your bedroom into shreds! What is it going to take for you to realize we're in over our heads?"

She gawked. "What are you saying, Juan?"

"I'm saying, I don't know! Maybe this is all wrong. Maybe we shouldn't go through with this. It's my fault you're in this mess."

"No, it's not. I have a mind of my own. It's not either of our faults, Juan. What happened to that soldier in you?"

"Maybe I'm sick of being jumped. Maybe I don't want anything else to happen to you. Nina, you could have been here. No telling what they would have done to you. Is our love worth all this shit?"

She held in tears. "You truly have to ask that? Juan, I thought you loved me more than anything."

"I do, Nina. But..."

"*But*?" She trembled. "You never had a 'but' before."

"Nina, what do you expect? This is getting more and more out of hand. I thought we could handle it at first but now I don't know. I don't want anything to happen to you!"

"What the fuck are you saying? I can't understand how you can even talk like this!"

"I love you, all right!" He exhaled. "I don't want you to be hurt in any way! Can you understand that? Nina, this isn't going to work. It's just too dangerous." His eyes swelled with tears.

"I don't believe this, Juan. You're a quitter. You who spews all that political shit is a fuckin' quitter!" She punched his chest. "We swore to love each other, Juan! I promised myself to you and you can just give up?"

"I don't want anything to happen to you, Nina. God, can't you get what I am saying here? If we keep seeing each other, we will die! Can't you see that?"

"I already saw that." She frowned. "I just didn't give a shit. My love for you was more important. What about all that stuff you said, Juan? You were so strong, but now you're being a punk. I thought being with me meant everything."

"It does! But what the fuck do you want from me? I can't just be with you knowing something might happen to you!" He exhaled. "I don't care what the Bronx Gs do to me. I only care about you!"

"Juan, I don't care what the NYAs do to me." She touched his face. "Please don't end this." She kissed him. His mouth remained still, discouraging her kisses. Nina felt her heart breaking in two. Tears danced down her face.

"Nina." He pushed his shaky lips to her hands. His tears drenched her wrists.

"I can't do this. I can't put you in danger." He closed his eyes.

"Juan, I don't care. Please, all I want is to be with you. I don't give a damn about the consequences. I'm willing, baby." She forced his hand against her chest. "Feel my heart, baby." He turned away. "Don't think of nothing else. Look at me, Juan. Just look at me and remember how much you love me."

"More goes into it than that, Nina." He slowly took his hand from hers. "I love you. God knows I will never love anyone as much. But I can't let you be in danger. They have the upper hand, Nina. I was foolish to think we could change things."

"Juan." She leaned against him. "Don't do this to me. I've just learned what it is to be in love. Don't take that away. I can't stand it," she blubbered. "I won't make it."

"You will." Juan choked from his tears. "You got to, Nina. I'm sorry." He ran to the door.

"Juan, please! Don't do this to me." She shivered. "I love you too much to jeopardize your safety. Maybe we weren't meant to be, after all. I mean, not if it causes so much violence." He furiously wiped his face. "I'll see you."

"Juan, please." She continued to sob. "Please don't do this."

"I got to be a man about this, Nina. I can't, I just can't." He left.

Nina fell on the floor in tears.

***

Nina slept the weekend away. Depression fueled her soul. She hardly ate. She struggled over homework. She didn't leave the house or answer the phone. She knew her attitude was silly but she couldn't control her heart. She'd never felt so used and alone. Juan had done the one thing she hoped he wouldn't. He'd broken her heart. She wasn't sure if she could ever forgive him.

Monday morning she made up her mind to put on the biggest act in the world. She would go to school with a smile. She would ignore Juan at every chance. She wouldn't remember his sweet kisses. She wouldn't think of the sexy way he'd said her name. She wouldn't remember how great it felt when he'd held her waist. How nice he'd smelled when she touched his chest.

She wouldn't remember any of that. She'd forget she ever fell in love.

Nina found Tajo on the phone when she made it to the living room. She decided to skip breakfast altogether. She gathered her things for school. Something in Tajo's eyes told her to stick around until the phone call ended. She took a seat on the couch. She heard her mother's name mentioned twice. A sharp pain pinched the inside of her stomach. Something was wrong.

"Yeah." Tajo rubbed his face. He removed the dish towel from his shoulder. He stared at Nina as if her face gave him breath. Nina didn't care what he had to say. She made up her mind to leave when he got off the phone. "Nina, wait."

"I don't want to hear it, Tajo. I've done everything you wanted me to. I'm not seeing Juan. You should be happy about that."

"Nina, I am sorry you feel bad. But I got to tell you something."

"You don't have to tell me anything." She grinned. "You don't have to worry about me anymore. It's all over, just the way you wanted it, cousin." Tajo sighed. "Juan dumped me. And I don't plan to ever speak to him again."

"Would you just listen to me for a moment? Damn, this is serious." He threw the dish towel on the couch. "It's about Michelle, she's..."

"*Oh!*" Nina laughed. "So Mom finally called, huh? I guess you told her I was shaming you, huh? I'm sure she jumped at the chance to lecture me though she's never been there for me before."

"Nina, I'm..."

"Save it. You and my mother can both go to hell. From now on I am living my life for *me*. I am not putting anyone else's feelings above mine again. I did it with Juan and got my feelings stomped on. I won't be doing it anymore. So say hello to the new Nina!"

"Nina, something terrible has happened."

"Oh God." She slumped toward him. She slipped her backpack from her shoulder. "What is it?"

"That was the hospital, Nina." Tajo crossed his arms. "Your mom died this morning."

Oxygen leapt from her body. She couldn't breathe. She couldn't form her lips to make one sound. She heard his words repeatedly but they still didn't seem real. After convincing herself of the truth, she drifted into tears in Tajo's arms.

Claudia stood in the middle of Tajo's living room moments later. "Do you still want me to take you to school?"

"I don't know." Nina imagined Michelle standing right beside her.

Claudia rocked her like a baby doll. "It's okay, girlfriend. I'm here for you, Nina. You know that. No matter what goes down I'm here for you."

"Claudia, why does this always happen to me? How come just when I think everything's going right something knocks it out of place? I thought I'd finally learned how it was to be happy. I don't know if I can take any more knocks, Claudia."

"I know this is cliché. But when life throws you lemons, you make lemonade. Now is the time for you to really be strong and figure out what you want to do."

"Nothing seems important to me anymore. I can't paint because it reminds me of sadness. When I close my eyes I think of my mom. We were never close, Claude. I wanted so much to be close to her. Our relationship was always strained."

"Look at it from her point of view, Nina. Do you think it was easy having a baby at fifteen years old? She probably figured she could never give you what you deserved. She cared for you in her own way."

"I can't believe she's dead. It's like I close my eyes and I see her, just as flighty as ever." Nina chuckled. "The woman who everyone thought was just my sister. Hell, I certainly didn't think of her as a mother. Is that wrong?"

"No, honey. It's *honest*."

"I was already at the breaking point because of Juan. Now this. It makes me not want to care about anything ever again." She wiped her eyes. "Ever felt like that?"

"Every day of my life." Claudia sighed. "I hope this gets better when we turn twenty-one. Or else we're in for a sad life."

"A sad life without love or a mother." Nina sniffled. "I don't want to go back to Roosevelt."

"We don't have to. You know me. I live to skip school. We can go someplace fun to take your mind off of things. Or we can stay around here and talk."

"No." Nina looked at her. "I don't want to go back to Roosevelt *ever*, Claudia."

"Then, where do you want to go?" Claudia moved Nina's hair from her face.

"Remember my Aunt Lydia?" Nina sniffed.

"Michelle's half sister from Mexico?" Claudia glowered.

Nina nodded. "She's always been nice to me. She said whenever I needed her I could come there and stay with her for a little bit. I think I need her now, Claude."

"Nina, *Mexico*?" Claudia chuckled. "You can't be serious. You wouldn't make it over there. It's so different."

"Claudia, I don't know if New York is for me anymore. I don't even want to be associated with it anymore or any of the people here but you. I need to get away. Mexico can help me find myself. It will help me get back to my roots."

"Nina, this is insane. You have too much bursting out of you to leave it all behind. What about your paintings and education? Everything you've worked for over here? You're willing to give that up?"

"No. I'm willing to find myself. I need to be where I can make a difference, Claudia. I am sick to death of these gangs. And I am sick of having my heart stepped on by people who claim they care about me. At least Aunt Lydia will be supportive of me. Maybe I can do even bigger things there."

"You're not fooling me, Nina. You're doing this because of Juan. Yeah, your mom too, but mostly because of Juan."

"I'm doing this for me, Claudia. I *need* to do this."

"Nina, this is crazy."

She grinned. "Since when are you against crazy?"

Claudia shook her head, doubtingly.

❈❈❈

Nina couldn't get Michelle out of her head. She found painting her only distraction. She set up drawing paper in the kitchen. She propped the pad up against a cookie canister. It wasn't as good as an easel but it would work. Most people reminisced about things they did with their moms when they died. Nina couldn't think of anything they'd shared.

She daydreamed about things they *should* have done. She would have given anything for just one more day with Michelle. If only she'd treated her like a real daughter. Nina was convinced she'd never understand death, no matter how much she faced it. She rested her arms on the kitchen table. She dipped her index finger into blotches of paint.

She swerved her finger down the paper. She'd created a tiny streak that would be the beginning of a fantastic rainbow.

She painted nonstop for two hours. The only break she took was for the restroom. By the time Nina was done it was almost six in the evening. Her arms ached from how high she'd held them. Her fingers cramped. Her legs burned from being kept in the same position for long periods of time. The painting had evolved into something different from what she first began.

Even the beginning lines she'd created had faded into nonexistence. A gloomy, grayish-black picture resembling a stormy night stared back at her. She couldn't believe she'd invented something so creepy. She also couldn't believe the feeling she got when she looked upon it. "Fate?" she whispered. She didn't know why she'd picked that word but it proved the perfect title. But was this really fate? She sat back, baffled.

Would this be how her life would end up, like a stormy night, unpredictable, dangerous, and pitiless?

She heard the front door open. Her stomach cramped and growled but food was the last thing on her mind. She couldn't stop staring at the new painting. She looked at her fingers stained with black, blue and gray paint. She got a rag from the drawer to clean herself up. She wanted to make it to her room before Tajo came into the kitchen. She hadn't wanted to talk to him before and the feeling hadn't changed.

"Hi, Nina." She took a deep breath. She slowly turned from the sink. Chino walked into the kitchen. He had something behind his back but Nina didn't bother investigating. "How are you?"

"I was fine, until now." She took her seat in front of the painting again. Escaping it was easier to think about than do.

"Yeah." Chino sighed. His gorgeous eyes flickered as he viewed the painting.

"Jesus Christ." He reached for it.

"Don't. It's not dry yet."

"Sorry." He took a seat with his mouth opened. "It's strange, huh? It's almost like it's talking to us. It has some power behind it. Have you been working on it for a while?"

"No, I just started today. I always paint to escape. Something just takes me over. I swear, I was gonna paint some majestic rainbow but I ended up with this. I guess I don't know my own talent." Chino shrugged. He handed her a bouquet of assorted flowers. "What's this for?"

"I heard about your mom. I'm sorry, Nina. I wish I could do something for you. Something to ease your pain."

"It's funny." She sniffed the flowers. "I'm not really that sad. I'm not glad she died but I'm more angry than upset. She left too damn soon, Chino. We had so much to talk about. We had so much to..." She lightly sobbed. He passed her some tissue from the cabinet.

"When are you gonna go see her?"

She shrugged. "Don't know if I will. Tajo and the relatives will handle the funeral arrangements. I'm not even sure I'd go to that."

"Nina, you got to go. My mother died when I was ten. She wasn't perfect, either." He stared at the painting. "I didn't go to the funeral and I still feel like crap because I didn't. I just want you to know, Nina, whatever happened probably wasn't your fault. Some people are just fuck ups as parents." She laughed unexpectedly. "What?" He sat back. "Do I have something on my teeth or something?"

"No, and I didn't mean to laugh at you. It's just that the day has been so crazy the last person I expected to be having a heart-to-heart with was you."

"Maybe." He chuckled. "I care about you, Nina."

"Then why do you want to hurt Juan?" Her smile disappeared.

"I don't want to hurt anyone. It's Tajo that's making us do all this stuff. I was trying to talk him out of it."

"Really?" She scoffed.

"Yeah."

"After the way you've been acting, I can't believe that. Especially after how you acted at the bowling alley."

"Yeah, I was a jerk. Nina, how can you blame me, though? I was with the most beautiful woman I'd ever seen in my life." He shrugged. "I lost control."

"Chino." She sighed, embarrassed.

"Well, it's the truth. I just wanted to kiss you that night. I want to kiss you all the time, you know?" She looked off. "I think about you all the time. I try not to but I do. I'm not used to being around girls like you. But I know I should take my time now." He inched toward her. Her heart pounded. "It's just something about you and I can't get you out of my head. Nina..."

"Uh..." She stood. "Would you like something to drink?"

"Guess so." He bit his lip. She filled two glasses with orange juice but she slipped on her way to the table. Before Chino knew it, Nina landed on the floor, soaking wet. "Nina?" He rushed to help her.

"I'm okay!" She laughed. "God, look at this mess!" She rubbed orange juice from her arms. "God, this isn't my day, is it?" She chuckled.

"No, I guess not." He dabbed her arms with a dish rag. "Let me help you up." When they stood she slipped again. This time Chino's grip saved her. "Don't worry. I got you." He rocked against her.

"I feel like a clumsy fool. What's wrong with me?" She giggled. He touched her face. She went limp.

"Not a damn thing." His mouth took hers. The kiss was powerful but didn't compare to the electricity of Juan's kiss by a long shot. He wrapped his arms around her. His tongue obediently stroked hers. "Mmm." Chino moaned. He backed her against the table. Nina felt him pushing her down.

She opened her eyes. Whatever had taken over her was gone. He pressed his body against hers. He was roughly tender. But Nina didn't want him. She wanted Juan. What the hell was going on here? "Stop." She managed to break free from his mouth.

It gave him an excuse to start on her neck. "Stop, Chino." She pulled his shirt. "Stop, please."

"You feel so good, Nina." He looked at her. She didn't expect him to look so sincere. He started kissing her again.

"Chino, please..."

"I care about you, Nina." He sucked her neck. "No one cares more."

She held on to the table. "Stop it, Chino. Please." She pushed him off. He gaped, wiping his mouth. "I'm sorry, Chino. Just go, okay? This was just as much my fault as it was yours."

"I don't get this! I'd be a good man for you, Nina! I'd do anything for you! Give you what you want. It's best that you be with me any damn way and you want to be with a guy you can't even have?"

"What I want is none of your business, Chino."

"I love you, Nina."

"What?" She gasped.

He squinted. "I said, I love you."

"You don't even know me! You don't know a damn thing about me, Chino."

"I know I want you." He grabbed her. She pulled away.

"Go, Chino."

He shook his head. He took a paced breath. "Juan doesn't deserve you. Don't you see that what I have to offer you is for the better?" He touched her hair. "I won't back off, you know. And most importantly, neither will Tajo. So think about that the next time you're with that faggot lover boy of yours."

"Get out, Chino!"

"I can't wait until you realize you'll be better off with me." He stomped out of the kitchen.

Nina leaned against the table, terrified.

❖❖❖

By the following Saturday, Juan was completely disoriented. The days passed right by him. His mind hadn't left the last scene with Nina. He thought about her obsessively. Each moment held disappointment for what he'd done. How could he be such a fool? How could he have cut the person he loved most out of his life? It didn't matter what he'd said to her. Nina was a part of him. No one could ever change that.

By Saturday night, he'd given in to his heart and ignored his mind.

"All I'm saying," Chino strolled around Tajo's living room, "we ain't handling our business. We can't start letting the NYAs get the upper hand. We do that and we lose our place and I ain't going out like that." The others nodded. "Shit, I'm beginning to think it's time to change things around here."

"What are you talking about?" Bone muttered.

"I'm talking about how things are being run. I don't think Tajo's in this the way he used to be. I don't feel the fire he used to have when he talked about the NYAs."

"What the fuck you saying, Chino?" Shorty-Five stretched on the couch.

"I'm saying maybe Tajo ain't what we need as a leader no more."

Spider waved his arms. "Man, how can you say some shit like that? He's always had our back. The Bronx Gangstas came from his family, G. Shit, I know I ain't a real G yet, but at least I know the shit you're spitting ain't right. Tajo's our leader, *ese*. He's the backbone of the Gangstas. Maybe *you* need to go somewhere else if you think you can do better."

"First of all, if you talk to me like that again you won't be a baby gangsta. You'll be shit under the ground. You're not allowed to speak on this anyway. In fact, get the fuck out." Chino gestured toward the front door.

"Spider got a right to be here. I don't like what you're saying, either. I hope to hell you don't think we should go against Tajo."

"Come on, Juice." Chino waved his arm. "I just think we need to take action now. We can't let the NYAs get away with their shit. Hell, if I was the leader all the NYAs would be dead already. I don't take no shit." The phone rang. Chino answered.

"Yeah, what?"

Juan recognized Chino's voice right off. Rage took over his senses. What was *he* doing there? Was he there often? Could something possibly be going on between Chino and Nina? Nonetheless, Juan vowed to be civil.

"Is Nina there?" he whispered.

"She's out," Chino snapped.

"This is Chino, right?"

"Who the fuck is this?"

"This is Juan Alonso. I want to speak to Nina *now*."

"Who the fuck you think you are?" Chino grinned. "You can't call up here asking to speak to someone you got no business speaking to. If you're so bold, come over here, *ese*. I bet you won't."

"Where is Nina?" Juan clenched the phone until his hand turned red.

Chino grinned. "Shit. Why the fuck should I care if you call? It's over between you two anyway. I mean, she ain't going to even be here after tomorrow."

"What the fuck are you talking about?"

"She's moving away, homes. Oh, you didn't know?" Chino teased. "Aww! I thought you two had such a connection. Guess you thought wrong, huh? Bitch ass."

"Fuck you, Chino. Why should I believe anything you say? It's not like you want me with her in the first place."

"You don't have to take my word for it. You'll see soon enough."

"Fuckin' liar."

"Am I?" Chino hung up the phone.

Juan slammed the receiver down. "Shit."

✠✠✠

Claudia's uncle's home had become a quaint sanctuary for Nina. It was the one place that linked Juan to her so she couldn't help cherishing it. She never worried about the time when she was here. After all, it was Saturday night. She could very well sleep here if she preferred. She strolled around and ended up in the master bedroom. She studied the enticing family photos on the sparse dresser.

Suddenly Nina became lightheaded. Her eyes ached as if she hadn't slept in years. She rested on the bed. She hadn't closed her eyes for a second before she heard knocking downstairs. She couldn't fathom who it could be. Claudia had gone to a party. Rosa and Lisa spent Saturday nights at the mall. Other than Claudia's parents, no one else knew about this place.

Wait. Someone else *did* know. The same person she didn't want to see yet couldn't keep out of her mind. She went downstairs.

"Nina?" Juan tapped on the door.

She clenched her blouse. Even his voice tempted her. She'd never wanted someone so much. Still, she couldn't ignore how Juan had betrayed her. He'd turned his back on her, on their love. Could she ever forgive him? She opened the door, expecting him to pull her into his arms. Or maybe that's just what she wanted.

He kept his distance. He walked inside, using his eyes as radar to catch every emotion her body tried to veil. She could even feel his thoughts. He'd willed her forgiveness just by the way he looked at her.

"I don't want to talk to you, Juan." She shivered. Just looking at him thrilled her.

"I know. And after what I did to us, I have no right to ask you to listen to me. But I'm going to. I have to." He looked off. "I know you hate me. You have every right to. Nina, I am so sorry I hurt you. I don't know what I needed to figure out. Being away from you has been murder for me. Nina, I can't eat. I don't sleep. I don't do anything. I just stay in my room. Everything makes me think of you. I miss you so much."

She crossed her arms. "Is this all you wanted to say?"

He took a deep breath. "I know it will never be enough, baby. I don't have a speech prepared. I didn't plan to come here. I just wondered if you could give us another chance."

"If *I*?" She flicked her hair. "I wasn't the one that ended us, Juan. I don't know why you expect *me* to fix things. It's all up to you. You've got to make up your mind. Are you man enough to face this relationship or not? Or are you going to live in fear the rest of your life?"

"Nina, if we're together we'd be living in fear, wouldn't we?"

"I wasn't! I guess that's the difference between you and me. Juan, when I was with you I didn't give a shit about the violence or what our families thought. All I cared about was being in your arms, always. I thought that meant something to the both of us. I thought you loved me just as much."

"I do." He stepped toward her.

She backed away. "But you can't be afraid and be with me. It won't work that way."

"I was only afraid of what my brother would do to you, Nina. God, can't you see how this is bothering me? I've never felt like this before! I've never been so in love with someone and I got scared. I'm sorry I'm not as strong as you are. This is a new feeling for me, Nina."

"I had no problem choosing to be with you, Juan. I was willing to take the good with the bad." She turned away. "But things are different now, anyway. Look, I want to rest. I came here to be alone. Let yourself out, would you?" She went upstairs to the bedroom. She wasn't surprised when Juan barged in behind her. He'd never given up anything easily.

"What are you talking about? Things don't have to be different." He looked around at the large bedroom.

"Juan, I know you heard I was leaving. Isn't that the real reason you showed up like this? It makes me wonder if you would have come otherwise. How do I know this isn't just a ploy to get me to stay around? And why would you? So you can jerk my heart around even more? I'm not your puppet, Juan. I've been used too much in my life to let you use me, too."

"I am sorry." He knelt in front of her. "I didn't mean to hurt you baby and for the rest of my life I will hate myself for that. You know you're the only one for me. I will do anything to get you back, Nina. Let me prove myself to you."

She glared at him. "Are you here now because I'm leaving?"

He sighed. "Partly. But it forced me to see how much I needed you. I couldn't bear you leaving. Doesn't the fact that I ran over here like a fool prove that I love you? Doesn't that get any marks with you?"

"I will always love you, Juan. You've touched a part of my heart no one else ever will. But maybe you were right to break up with me. I'm not good for you. And I'm talking about your future."

"You're good for me, damn it! Let *me* make that decision! All I know is nothing else matters to me but you right now! Let's deal with this right *now*."

"How can I?"

"I don't, look, forget that other shit. I don't want you to leave. I don't want you to leave."

"I..." Nina looked into his eyes.

He held her face. He forced her eyes on his. "I don't want you to leave," he whispered. "Because if you do, I'll have nothing."

"Juan..."

He gave her a kiss that unleashed Nina's fervor in a thousand different ways. He held her waist. He circled his thumbs against her jeans. It would be tonight. Nina clamped her body against his. His eyes engulfed every inch of her face. His hands lovingly cupped her bottom. Nina moaned more deeply than she thought possible.

"I don't want to let go." Juan moved his arms toward her breasts. Nina slid her hands down his arms. His kisses nearly digested every part of her.

"*Now?*" She tingled. Juan's hands fondled her blouse. He stopped at the last button. He slipped his hands underneath her hair. He caressed her neck.

"*Now*," he whispered.

Nina stiffened. He unbuttoned her blouse until she was free of it. He gazed at her bra, then at her breasts after releasing them. She moved her palms up his chest, bringing her hands down in one swoop. Nina never imagined she'd want to take control at this moment but she wanted to show Juan just how much she wanted him. She wasn't afraid. She anticipated what making love with Juan would be like.

She hadn't realized making love began with a simple glance. She relieved him of his shirt. He smiled. It joined her blouse on the floor. Juan rubbed the back of her jeans, clenching her thighs. Before each movement he looked into her eyes to make sure she wanted it, too. He undid her belt. He slipped her jeans to her ankles.

He gazed upon her rose-patterned underwear. She knew he wanted her to undress him, too. No matter what happened from this point on, this would be the happiest day of their lives. Nina's fingers danced across his silver belt buckle. She yanked his belt, smacking Juan in the stomach.

"Oww." He chuckled. The accident lightened the mood. She loosened his pants.

She chuckled at the sight of his white boxers. "What's so funny?"

She didn't answer. She turned around to let him see her body in its pure form. "Nina, you're so beautiful."

He rubbed her hip. "It's kind of like your body is…"

"Calling your name?" She felt weird saying such a thing but couldn't have been more honest. Her back arched magnificently when she walked toward the bed. He memorized every mole and crease on her body. She flowed underneath the covers like the elegant women in old movies. She tilted her head. Juan melted into a blissful chill. He climbed into bed beside her.

CHAPTER FIFTEEN

J uan rested on his stomach. "You okay?" Nina lay on her back with her arms shielding her breasts. Losing her virginity had affected her incredibly already. At least they'd been smart enough to use protection. She leaned up to relieve the soreness in her thighs.

"Yeah." She maneuvered her body until her back dented the sheets. "Leg cramps." She wiggled her toes.

"Yeah, you get that sometimes." He rubbed her forehead. "I love you so much. And I hope we didn't go too fast."

"No. Juan, I didn't do anything I didn't want to do." She stared at his chest. "Jesus!" She laughed.

"What?"

"I can't believe I just lost my virginity in a dead man's bed. Isn't there some law against that?"

He ran his fingers through her hair. "I don't know. I've never experienced this before."

She looked at the ceiling. "God, this night is crazy. Everything's changing so fast. I hope we're ready for it. In case I forget to tell you, I thought it was wonderful."

He leaned up, smirking. "How would you know?"

She shrugged. "I know you made me feel good. You were gentle. You were patient. You let me take my time and you took yours. You didn't hurt me."

"Did you think I would?"

"Well, I expected it to hurt worse than it did. I mean, I knew there would be *some* pain. That's natural. Let's just say you made it as easy as possible for me. Sometimes it was like you were barely touching me." She became shy from his stare. "I can't believe I finally got some."

"Ha, ha!" Juan stretched. "All I wanted was for it to be special, Nina. Now it's truly official. We're together."

"Yes, we are." She pulled his arm over her breasts. "I hope I pleased you, too."

"You were great." He buried his head in her hair. "Perfect, even."

"That's a compliment coming from you, huh?" She played with his fingers.

"It's just that some girls are so stiff. It's like they're afraid to let themselves feel during sex. Like they don't realize they are supposed to enjoy it. You weren't like that. You weren't afraid."

"Oh, believe me, I was afraid." Nina grinned.

"Well, you didn't show it. You went with the flow. You didn't lie there like a victim. I didn't feel like some criminal trying to corrupt you, either."

"How old were you when you lost your virginity?"

"Thirteen." He bit his lip.

"How did it happen?"

"It was with this girl I used to always play around with at summer camp. Anyway, it was like a fluke. We didn't plan it. We were in the room alone. Everyone else was outside playing. She said she'd read some stuff about sex. She asked me if I knew what sex was. I told her yes." Nina leaned up to catch his eyes. "She told me she never saw a penis before. She asked me if I would show her mine."

"And she was thirteen, too?" Nina gaped at him.

He nodded. "It was innocent, believe me. I told her that I'd never seen a girl's, you know. So she said that she would show me her privates if I showed her mine. So we counted to ten and pulled down our pants and everything." He chuckled. "She asked me if she could touch me. I was freaking out. I didn't know what to do or say. So I just stood against the wall." He sighed. "Every part of me became stiff when I saw her. I mean *every* part. She didn't have the greatest body. She didn't even have large breasts or anything."

"But she turned you on?"

"Yes. Because of the way she touched me. She was gentle and in return I was gentle with her. We touched and explored each other forever. Then touching turned into feeling. Feeling turned into curiosity. The next thing I know I was on top of her in one of the bunk beds. And we were having sex." He sighed.

Nina wiggled underneath the covers. "Was it good?"

"Only lasted about ten minutes." He shrugged. "She said it felt funny but good. I didn't really think about the actual act. I was more surprised about seeing a vagina than having sex." He laughed.

Nina smiled. "What was her name?"

"Delores something. God, I still remember how she smelled. Kind of like lemons. I think it was her shampoo or something."

"Did you ever see her after that?"

"I saw her once in the store when I was fifteen. We talked for a few seconds. She tried to avoid me." He played with the sheets. "I never saw her again after that."

"It's her loss." Nina wrapped her arms around his neck. They kissed.

"You always care about the first time, Nina. For some reason it always sticks in your mind."

"That's what Claude says. It didn't seem as genuine coming from her lips." She giggled.

He pulled her close. "Are you staying?" he whispered cautiously.

"I love you, Juan."

"Well." He pulled her body on top of his. "I guess I got my answer, huh?"

"You bet you do. It's you and me against the world. No one is going to tear us apart. They can use all the guns they want. I don't care. I'm going to be with you forever." She laid her head on his chest.

"We *will* be together, Nina. No matter what it takes."

✦✦✦✦

Chino stared at Juan's truck from his car window. He held the steering wheel, pretending it was Juan's throat. His anger wouldn't allow a loosened grip. It hadn't been hard to find them. He vowed to have Nina even if it meant destroying the one person who stood in his way.

He took a deep, pressured breath. Juan Alonso needed to be taught a lesson. The Bronx Gangstas were the perfect ones to teach it.

Tajo rubbed his chin. Enough was enough. The last thing he tolerated was a liar. Not only would he have to teach Juan a lesson, he'd have to teach Nina that no one came before family. She'd soon realize she could never be with Juan Alonso. Not in a million years.

"Are you sure you saw what you think you saw?" Tajo exhaled.

"Fuck yeah." Chino grabbed his crotch. Tajo's eyes drifted to the beautiful bikini models on television. "I guess this place they meet at is supposed to be some little love nest and shit."

Tajo nearly crushed the television remote in his hand. "He better not be fucking her. I can't tell you what I'll do if he laid one finger on her."

"What, you think they meet there for tea? Of course he's fucking her! I wanted to run over the motherfucker, too. I would have killed him. Tajo, this shit could be over in five fuckin' minutes. Let me smoke his ass. He'll be gone once and for all."

"I gave them warning after warning." Tajo rubbed his hands together. "I told him to stay the fuck away from my cousin. And he can disrespect me like this?"

"He doesn't know who he's messing with. He's a fuckin' NYA He cannot be trusted with your cousin, or without her. The time is now, man. Juan Alonso had his chance."

"Yep." Tajo stood. "It's time for Juan to be dealt with."

"Let me smoke the fool right now."

"No. Not like that, my man." Tajo winked. "We do this in a way he will never forget. I want him to suffer. I want him to see my face and beg for his life. I gave him chances, didn't I?"

"Fuck yeah. More chances than I would have given him."

Tajo grinned. "But it's cool. We'll finally see what kind of man Juan Alonso really is."

They bumped fists.

✠✠✠

A few days later, Tajo glared at Lexi in his living room. "You sure you can handle this?" He passed her the phone.

"Yeah." She tugged on her tight spandex dress. "Shit, you already told me what to do." She popped bubble gum.

"But can you sound like Nina?"

"Shit, I can imitate anyone's voice. Now what you want me to say again?"

"Just act all sweet and shit. Then tell him to meet you at this place." Tajo pointed to the address on the paper. "And don't start grinning and shit. You fuck this up and I'm taking it out on you."

She flicked her hair from her face. "Shouldn't I be getting paid for this?"

Tajo grimaced. "How about if I don't break your neck? Is that payment enough?" Lexi dialed the phone. Juan answered on the second ring. She slapped on a little sweet talk Nina-style, then rambled off Tajo's instructions verbatim. Juan blew kisses into the phone, then bid her good-bye.

"Well?" Tajo crossed his arms.

Lexi grinned. "The stupid fucker bought it just like I knew he would."

"Good girl. You ready for this?" Tajo pulled her to him.

"Oh yes. I'm always ready to have some fun with my guys." She gripped his mouth between her lips. Before they could congratulate each other about the devious trick, Nina walked into the living room.

"What's going on here?" Nina dug in her purse for bus change.

"Nothing." Tajo wiped Lexi's cheap lipstick from his mouth. "Going to Claudia's to study?"

"Didn't I say that about ten times?" Nina rested her hand on her hip. "Why do you guys look like someone pulled a gun on you?"

"No reason." Tajo grinned. "How long you going to be gone?"

Nina looked back when she reached the front door. "Prob-ably a couple of hours. Why, you don't believe where I'm going?"

"No, I believe you. I just worry. I want to make sure you're safe." He rubbed his fist. "Have a nice time."

Nina watched suspiciously. "Yeah." She left.

"Think she suspects anything?" Lexi put her arm on Tajo's shoulder.

"Who cares? Now let's get busy." He went down the hall.

✠✠✠

"What's up, dog?" Tony cut his eyes from his favorite Tuesday-night television show as Juan hung up the phone. Juan had the brains of a college professor yet didn't have the best ability at picking out suspicious signs. He was excited about seeing Nina since she'd canceled her trip to the library. He threw on his jacket, preparing for the chilly air of fall, then headed toward the door.

"Yo, what's up, Juan?" Carlos walked into the living room with a drippy ice-cream cone.

"Got a call from Nina, fellas. You'll have to excuse me." He grinned. "But this is important. Let yourselves out."

"Oh yeah." Tony threw his feet on Juan's table. "Everything is important when it has to do with Miss Nina. Don't we get any time with you anymore?"

"Come on, why you guys tripping? You were the ones saying I shouldn't let the NYAs or Rico run my life. You said I was acting like a sucker if I gave up. Now you give me this attitude? What's up? Y'all supposed to be my boys and shit."

"We are, man." Carlos sucked vanilla ice cream from his lips. "But you need to keep it low-key."

"Nina and I are being very careful. She just wants to meet me. She has a surprise for me. I'll be back later."

"Where you going?" Tony raised an eyebrow.

"Sins Boulevard," Juan mumbled, hoping they hadn't heard.

All he wanted was to see Nina again, not deal with his friends' upcoming lectures. Carlos and Tony stared wide-eyed. Juan wasn't trying to hear it.

"*Sins*?" Carlos chuckled. "Tony, did he say fuckin'..."

"Yeah, he said it. Juan, what the fuck is wrong with you?" Tony stood. "Sins Boulevard is in Edgewood. You can't go down there!"

"I know where it is. What's the deal? I've been there before. If I lay low no one will be able to tell me from the Bronx Gangstas. It's no big deal. Nina wouldn't put me in jeopardy."

"Yo, hold up!" Carlos slammed his ice-cream cone on the table. Juan rushed to clean up the mess. "I know she jacked your ass up. And from what I can tell the ass must have been good because you're acting so stupid. I don't give a damn how fine she is or how much you love her, Juan. You cannot go to Edgewood now. They might be on to you."

"How can they be, Carlos?" Juan shook his hands, waiting for an answer. "I think I know what this is. You're jealous of what Nina and I have. You're worse than the gangs."

Tony took a deep breath.

Carlos delivered Juan a look that could make fire spread. "You've changed for that bitch, huh?"

"Carlos, if you don't watch your motherfucking mouth!" Juan curled his right fist.

"Gonna hit me, huh? So that's where this shit's leading? You spread that shit about Rico, but let me tell you something, Juanito. You don't know nothing about being a friend and you don't know shit about being loyal! All you care about is Nina! That bitch wasn't here before and I doubt she will be here when this comes to an end."

"Get out of my house, Carlos." Juan chewed his lips. "In fact, you both can get the hell out."

"Fine. We don't need this shit." Tony ripped the door open. It was barely six o'clock but dark as midnight. They stomped onto the porch. Juan regretted his words already but he hadn't the strength to rehash the argument.

Carlos shook his head. "We supposed to be boys, Juan. Remember that when Nina's out of the picture." He followed Tony.

"Shit." Juan sighed.

✦✦✦

Juan had never been to a place so quiet. Sins Boulevard wound around a church, vacant houses, and a gigantic car garage. He studied the address he'd written. He couldn't see why Nina had picked such a peculiar spot to meet. His anticipation of seeing her outweighed all risks. He parked a few feet from the garage. The decrepit front door wobbled back and forth.

When he walked inside he noticed a light shining from behind the front desk. Nina mentioned her intentions of getting a part-time job. Amused, Juan wondered if she'd become a mechanic's assistant. Scattered car parts hung on the walls. A beat-up yellow car with its hood up was parked in the corner. It appeared to have been dead for centuries.

Juan expected Nina to jump out at him from excitement. When she didn't, a strange tingle entered his body.

"Nina?"

The light behind the desk clicked off. Juan planted his feet to the hollow garage floor. He heard gentle footsteps. He made out a shapely figure. The curves of her body could not be mistaken. Her lovely frame enchanted him. She looked more radiant than in any of his dreams. He couldn't wait for her to take advantage of his flesh again. Better yet, for him to take advantage of hers.

"Close your eyes, Juan," her sweet voice commanded. He followed the order. Her soft fingers clasped his, causing him to tremble. Her breath hit his neck. She leaned him against the wall. Her hair smelled of lemons this time, reminding him of the first time he'd had sex.

"Nina, what's the big idea?"

"Shhh." Her hands rubbed the stretch of his neck. For days he'd dreamed of making love to her again. He didn't care that they were in a greasy garage. It didn't matter they were in Bronx Gangsta territory. He was with the *one* person he always wanted, *Nina*. And she loved him. She wanted him. Juan took a deep breath. Her lips spread against his neck.

She caressed his back. Her lips seemed larger, plumper. Her kisses weren't cautioned but forceful. He enjoyed the openness. Especially if he was the cause for the change.

"Let me help you," he whispered, managing to keep his eyes closed. She shoved his hands back, showing she didn't need his help.

"Does this feel good?" She rubbed his thighs until her hands crawled to his middle. Juan moaned uncontrollably. He anticipated more of her sensuous treatment. Suddenly she stopped. Her breath slowed. Juan felt her moving away.

"Something wrong?" He kept his eyes closed.

"You're so handsome, Juan." She circled his mouth with her fingers. "Do me a favor and keep your eyes closed."

He grinned. "Nina, what is this?"

"Do it for me, huh?" She tugged at his shirt. He sighed. He rested against the wall, determined not to move until his princess requested him to.

Lexi walked to the entrance of the garage with her eyes steadily on Juan. She signaled out the door. Separately, ten Bronx Gangstas strolled inside, quiet as mice. Tajo stepped in last. They formed two lines with Tajo between them. Each carried weapons of equal destruction: daggers, guns, ropes, chains, bats, brass knuckles, and towels for wiping blood they expected to splatter from the attack.

"Ha, ha!" Chino wrapped the end of the five-foot chain around his hands.

"Shut up," Tajo whispered. He nodded at Lexi. She sashayed toward Juan again. Her sweet perfume sparked Juan's arousal once more.

"Where did you go, baby?" He kept his eyes shut.

"Nowhere special." Lexi looked back at the Bronx Gangstas. They held up their weapons ready to strike. Tajo kept his gun pressed against his palm, leaving a red indention. He nodded at Lexi once more. She turned back to Juan. "Okay, you ready for your surprise?"

"Yeah." He licked his lips.

Lexi kissed him. "Okay. Open your eyes, Juan." She stood back in case he freaked from being surrounded. He didn't. She could tell from that alone that he was braver than most. It turned her on more than anyone ever had. He gazed at the hungry gang around him.

"Good job, Lexi," Tajo said. The Bronx Gangstas stalked toward Juan. "Now get the fuck out."

"My money..."

"He said..." Chino grabbed her hair. "Get the fuck out, bitch. Unless you want to attend this party, too."

"All right!" She shoved him. She looked at Juan. He got the sense she wanted to apologize. He couldn't care less. He angrily wiped away the traces of her kisses. Insulted, Lexi bolted out the door.

"Well..." Juan chuckled. "She does good impressions. She should do it for a living."

"Oh yeah? You think that's funny, huh, pussy?" Chino gripped his chain. "Let's see how funny you find what we're about to do to you. Can we start this shit now, Tajo?"

"Hold up a second." Tajo played with his gun. "Every man deserves the chance to explain things." He tilted his head in the air. A big guy like Tajo could kill Juan with one punch. Juan could only rely on speaking the truth. "So, explain things, Juanito. I'll give you that much."

"Explain what?" He shrugged. "Explain how you don't like me just because of who my brother is? Explain how I wish Nina and I could just go off together? Explain how I don't have anything to say because I know it won't make a difference?"

"Explain to me why you can't seem to understand what I mean when I say I want your ass away from my cousin! Why don't you pour some sarcasm into that, motherfucker?"

"All I can say is I love her. And when you love someone, you can't stay away from..." Juan exhaled. Two Bronx Gangstas closed the garage door. Everything went dark. Juice turned on the overhead light. Juan's voice shook from that point on, corrupting anything he wished to say.

"I told you I was a fair man, Juan. I even gave you the opportunity to see Nina. But you weren't man enough to do that. Did I once stutter when I told you to stay away from my cousin? Answer me!" Tajo roared.

"No, you didn't." Juan crossed his shaking arms. Chino played with the chain.

Tajo gave Juan the evil eye. "Do I look like a pussy to you? I mean, you think the Bronx Gangstas are a bunch of faggots? You think I'm a fool, don't you?"

"No, I don't, Tajo. This has nothing to do with you, I swear. I just want to be with Nina. Can't you understand that?"

"Talking didn't do any good with you, man." Tajo looked at the others. "And that ass whipping Chino sprayed on you didn't do good, neither. Now we got to speak louder, if you catch my drift."

"Tajo, please." Juan watched the Bronx Gangstas surround him. "I am not my brother. I am not in the NYAs. Please don't do this, all right?" Juice slapped the bat in his palm. Chino wiggled the chain. The other Gangstas played with their weapons.

"Get on your knees, motherfucker," Tajo whispered.

"I..."

"Get on your damn knees, bitch!" Chino slapped Juan's neck with the chain. He effortlessly fell to the floor. He held his neck. Blood dribbled over his fingertips. Tajo bent beside him.

"I'll give you a fair shot. Hold out your hand," Tajo said.

"Hold it out right now!" The chain rose in Chino's hands. Juan held his hands up. Blood covered the collar of his shirt.

"Since I am so fair, I want to give you this chance, Juan." Tajo placed his gun in Juan's hand. "Ever shot a gun before?"

"No, no." Juan thought he'd pass out from the pain in his neck. He looked around to make sure more guys hadn't shown up.

Tajo rubbed his chin. "Just a little bitch-ass trick, aren't you? I kind of feel sorry for yo' dumb ass. This is your chance. The deal is, you shoot me and you can go untouched. But if you don't, we kill you tonight."

Chino smiled at Tajo's haunting words.

"What?" Juan shook.

"Smoke me or we kill yo' ass. And it won't be just killing, Juanito. We'll make sure you feel much pain before you go."

"True dat." Juice held up the Bronx Gangsta symbol.

"What's it gonna be, pussy?" Tajo asked.

"Look at him. This what your cousin wants?" Chino grinned. "A little buster who can't even shoot a gat? Look at him, ol' whack-ass bitch. Motherfucker shaking and shit. He ain't gonna do it, man. Let's waste his ass."

"Shut up, Chino." Tajo jerked Juan's chin. He stared him dead in the eyes.

"You know you want me dead. You know you want Nina. If you kill me you can have her."

"How do I know that?" Juan looked up at the others. His blood reached the middle of his shirt.

"You saying you don't trust us?" Chino bellowed. "Let's kill his ass! We make no deals with NYA trash! If we don't do him, he's just gonna get his tired-ass brother. We need to stop wasting time, shit!" Chino grabbed Juan from the floor. "Let me do it, Tajo! Let me show this motherfucker what we're really made of. You have no idea how much I want to."

"You hate me don't you, Chino?" Juan squinted. "The feeling is mutual."

Chino snatched Tajo's gun. He shook it in Juan's face. "You don't get it, do you? We're the Bronx Gangstas. We were raised on hate and contempt for anything NYA. If this brings on another fuckin' war, so be it."

"You won't make it. If you kill me, Rico's going to get all of you. You have no idea how much he wants to kill you guys. I've saved you all! I stopped him from creating more of a mess than you've created yourselves."

"Oooh-weee, let me smoke him!" Chino laid his mouth against Juan's face. His breath combined with the musk of Juan's sweat. "God, let me do him, Tajo. Let me do him."

"Better yet," Tajo looked around, "I'll let you *all* do him. And do him *good*. Take his stupid ass in the back."

Chino took Juan by the arms. Two other Bronx Gangstas grabbed his legs. Juan refused to plead. He wouldn't grant Tajo any more power. It wasn't until Juan was shoved into an empty, cold room in the back that he realized his life could be over within minutes. Chino's eyes told Juan it would be more than a beating this time. They wouldn't stop until they killed him.

They dropped Juan on the floor. The sight of Tajo's big body towering over him was enough to break anyone's pride. Juan found it amusing that he wished Rico would come slamming through the doors using what Juan hated the most to help, that dumb pride.

Chino started a low chant that Juan couldn't figure out. Bronx Gangsta gibberish, he realized. One by one, the others joined Chino. Tajo slowly moved from the center of the group. The others took their place in front of Juan. Chino nodded at the others. With murderous intent, they walked toward their intended victim. Juan took a deep breath while they decided who would strike first.

Juice became the chosen one, with a steel bat in his hand.

✣✣✣

"You'll never learn, will you, girlfriend?" Claudia skipped up Juan's porch behind Nina. NYAs rested on the street a corner away. "I can't believe we're doing this."

"Just chill out, Claude." Nina knocked on the door. "And since when do you care about doing what's right?" Nina grinned. Claudia didn't find anything funny. Nina wasn't thinking with the sense God gave a rat. The more time Nina spent with Juan the worse things got.

"Hi, Nina." Cynthia stepped on the porch with a slice of cold pizza. "Want some?"

"No." Nina smiled. "Is your brother here?"

"Juan?" Cynthia stared at her pizza. "No, he rushed out earlier. But...you don't know?"

"Know what?" Nina asked. Claudia took an impatient breath.

"I was in the bedroom. I was taking a nap but I heard Juan and his friends fussing. I thought Juan said he was going to see you."

Nina looked at Claudia. "That's impossible. Cynthia, where would you get that idea? I've been at Claudia's for the last hour and a half. I told Juan I wouldn't be able to see him tonight."

"Yet we're here," Claudia mumbled. Nina crossly watched her, then turned back to Cynthia.

"I thought you called him. I heard the phone ring." Cynthia shrugged. "At least I thought he said it was you. I was in my room and couldn't hear too well." Claudia got the feeling Cynthia spent her entire life snooping.

"Do you have any idea where he went?" Nina asked in a rushed tone.

"No, I, I'm sorry. Is something wrong?" Cynthia's eyes widened. Nina couldn't bear scaring her.

"No, honey. I'll see you later, all right?" Nina waited until she went inside.

"Claude! What do you think this means? Something is terribly wrong!" Nina ran her hands through her hair. She cursed in Spanish. "Don't just stand there, Claudia! What the fuck do we do?"

"Nothing." Claudia jerked from Nina's hold. "You can't spend your life worrying about Juan, Nina." They walked to her car. "Is this what you want out of life?"

"I want to be with Juan and you know this! Why are you tripping? You act as though you're jealous or something."

"I am sick of this shit because I know how it will end. Someone's going to get hurt! I finally realize it might be you and I love you too much, Nina."

"Save it, Claudia." They got in the car. "You can't stand it that I don't depend on you for everything now. You've always wanted to be the only one with something going on. Now I got Juan and you can't stand that."

Claudia started the car. "How dare you? I bust my ass lying for you. I bring you over here though it could get us both killed. I keep secrets from Tajo though he's repeatedly threatened me into telling him what's going on. I let you hang out at my uncle's place to see Juan and you have the nerve to question me? You are so damn selfish and I cannot believe I didn't see this sooner."

"Claude, I know you care but…"

"Where you want me to take you?" she asked stiffly. Her face became void of amusement or emotion. Nina sighed. Once again she'd stuck her foot in her mouth when it came to her best friend.

"Home, I guess." Nina shook her head. "I'm sorry, Claude."
Claudia drove off without a word.

"Awww!" Juan's face hit the floor. He spit up pools of blood. Juice stood back, staring at his bat. Another Bronx Gangsta whipped Juan with a rope. The others pounced on him using their weapons on his back, legs, and chest. Juan stayed still. He prayed they'd think he was dead and skip the torture. Every so often he glanced at Tajo. He supervised diligently from the background. After the abuse, Juan nearly blacked out.

"All right, motherfucker!" Chino spit on Juan's forehead. "Let's see if you can handle what I got for your ass, bitch."

"Yo, lay it on him, Chino!" someone shouted. The pain made it impossible for Juan to move, let alone see who spoke. He braced himself. Chino yanked him from the floor.

"I've been waiting for this for a long time, sweetcakes." Chino grinned. "I've been dreaming of ways to get your ass. I couldn't come up with nothing, but then it hit me. You think you're so fuckin' special to Nina? Well, I'll let you go 'special style.' The usual killing and beating doesn't suit you, does it, motherfucker? So I'll make it something no one will ever forget."

Chino shoved Juan outside. He forced him behind the garage. Juan did his best to keep up. If it hadn't been for Chino holding him, his limp body would have crumpled to the ground. Juan noticed only a few of the others followed. Tajo marched through, shoving the others out of the way.

"I decided to let Chino handle yo' punk ass his way," Tajo said. "Now you wish you'd taken me up on my offer, huh, bitch?" Blood dribbled from Juan's mouth. He couldn't stand up without help. He retched from the pain. "I guess you don't love Nina the way you claim. She ain't good enough for you to become a gangsta, G?"

Juan managed a crisp whisper. "I, I love her more than anything."

"Bullshit! If you loved her you'd do anything for her. I thought you were such a man. My cousin ain't no ho, all right? She got a lot going for her and she don't need some punk ass like you standing in her way. Someone who can't even protect her."

"That's right," Chino added. The smell of death surrounded them. Chino threw the chain into the tree. It hooked around the lowest limb, then popped over the other side. Juan couldn't believe how fucked up they were. They were going to hang him. "Don't matter if you love her or not now. She'll have to go on without you." Chino snickered.

Juan coughed. "I never did anything to any of you. I tried to keep the peace and, I tried to change things! Nina and I never wanted to hurt anybody."

"*She* probably didn't." Chino grimaced. "But we all know what *you* wanted. You just wanted her because you couldn't be with her. Messing up my game and shit. Should have stepped aside and let a real man enter the picture. After this she'll need someone to comfort her. Why wouldn't it be me?"

"So that's what this is about? You still think getting rid of me will get you a chance with Nina, Chino?" Chino cracked his knuckles. Juan kept talking. He knew they would kill him regardless. He might as well die with dignity. "Chino, it doesn't matter what happens to me. Nina will always love me and I will always love her. She'll hate you even more."

"She'll want me."

"Oh really? No, that's what you *want* to think. It keeps you going, Chino. You're so warped. You don't know the first thing about loving a woman."

"And you do?" He shoved Juan against the tree. "Why don't

you give us a little lesson then? I mean, if you so down with the bitches and all."

"There aren't enough lessons in the world that can show you how to get Nina, Chino. And you damn sure won't figure out how to love her." Juan licked blood from his lips. "Not the way I have. Not the way she wants to be."

Tajo stepped closer. "What shit you spitting, Alonso? You trying to say you fucked my cousin? Did you fuck my cousin, mother-fucker? *Did you*?" he bellowed.

Juan looked away. "Yes, I did."

Chino socked him.

CHAPTER SIXTEEN

Tajo was nowhere to be seen when Nina got home. He'd never disappeared without telling her before. She could tell he hadn't been home since she'd left. Claudia went to the kitchen for a soda. This definitely wasn't right. Nina had a knack for smelling something fishy even if it *was* covered in a pile of bullshit.

"No, Claude. This isn't right." Nina shook.

"Well," Claudia sipped a Pepsi, "what do you want to do? I mean, we don't know where they are."

"We got to find out! I know the Bronx Gangstas have Juan. That's the only explanation. Before I left I had a feeling Tajo was up to something." Nina covered her mouth. "Claudia, they could kill him. We have to help him!"

"I'm with you, girlfriend, but we don't know where they are." Claudia held her hips. The craziest thoughts entered Nina's head.

"Hey." Lexi sashayed into the house, dangling a key Tajo had given her years ago.

"What are you doing here?" Nina squinted.

"I came to wait for your cousin to get back." Lexi checked her watch. "Shouldn't be too long now."

"You know where he is?" Nina marched toward her. Claudia recognized the fury in Nina's eyes. She'd only seen her this anxious once before. "Where is he, Lexi?"

"Step off." Lexi tried to walk past her. Nina shoved her backward. "Little bitch! Who do you think you are?"

"Believe me, you don't want to mess with me tonight, Lexi. I know Tajo is with Juan. Tell me where they are right now."

"Why should I?"

"Because I'll beat the hell out of you if you don't."

"Yeah right." Lexi laughed. Nina punched her. Lexi tumbled onto the floor.

Claudia gasped. "You little..." Lexi wiped blood from her mouth.

"Tell me!" Nina raised her fist.

"All right! I'll tell you. But don't think you can do anything about it, princess. It's your fault, anyway." Lexi stood.

"What are you talking about?"

Lexi crossed her arms. "I'll tell but if you got half a brain, which doesn't seem like it, you won't want to go there."

"I'll be the judge of that," Nina growled.

***

"Oh!" Juan dangled from the tree. Chino tightened the chain around his arms and neck. Chino had taken the abuse upon himself. With every thrash, Juan sensed pure hatred. The fact that Nina would love him no matter what provided temporary satisfaction. Still, even that couldn't take his mind off the budding pain.

"Motherfucker won't die, huh?" Chino grinned. Juan's blood covered Chino's hands. Blood dribbled down Juan's chest to his pants. Ironically he felt like Jesus on the cross. "Tajo, let's smoke this fool now, man. We need to do this because if we don't the

NYA assholes won't get the idea. They'll know they should have done more to protect their baby boy."

"What do you say about that, Alonso?" Tajo studied Juan's bruised face. His fat, purple lips trembled.

"What I..." Blood oozed from his mouth. Tajo moved back, grinning. "You gonna kill me anyway. It's worth it to you, Tajo?" Juan raised his head. "This can't go on forever. Think of Nina. You know what my brother would do to her if you kill me?"

Tajo digested the revelation. "You know, most motherfuckers would have been dead or crying by now, Alonso. You ain't cracked a tear, though. You're a soldier, though I don't know whose side you're on."

"Let's smoke his ass! Fuck this talking!" Chino took out his gun.

"You are a soldier, aren't you, Juan?" Tajo shrugged. "I might not like you but I respect you. Just the way you act tonight showed me you deserve that."

"Tajo, what the fuck are you talking about, man? Why you kissing up to this motherfucker? Let me smoke him now!"

"Shut up, Chino." Tajo sighed. "Juanito?" Juan stared at him. "I offer you the opportunity of a lifetime. You can have my cousin no questions asked. But most importantly, we'll let you live."

"Tajo!"

"Quiet, Chino, before I smoke *your* ass." Chino stomped off. "Remember that offer from before, Juan? It still stands. I offer you the chance to be one of us and be with Nina, for as long as you want to be."

"Tajo?" Shorty-Five took the toothpick out his mouth. "We got to settle this tonight. This is to show the NYAs that we still got power. It's the only way."

"I disagree." Tajo walked closer to Juan. Juan figured he'd pass out any moment from the unrelenting pain. "I know a better way to show them we got power. You know how they would feel to see one of their own as a Bronx Gangsta? You have any idea what that can accomplish? What's the choice, Juanito? You become one of us or you die."

The old Juan disappeared with Tajo's proposal. Nina had changed him. True love had molded him into a better person. He thought deeply of the happiness he and Nina could share. He wouldn't give that up for a thousand chances at life. The deal Tajo presented seemed sweeter than before. Juan's heart urged him to keep his mind on the bigger picture.

On the other hand, his heart also pointed out that Tajo's proposition could be his and Nina's only link to freedom.

"Protection, Juanito. We promise you protection from the NYAs. You don't have to worry about sneaking around. You and Nina would have our blessings." Tajo grinned. "You can be with her. You can be with her in every capacity, G."

"No!" Chino shouted. The others looked at him in silence.

"What's it going to be, Juan? Life and Nina or death and nothing?" Tajo turned toward Chino. "Remember, there's someone waiting to take your place." Juan looked at Chino. He couldn't let that happen. He couldn't bear to think of Nina possibly falling for Chino's pathetic resentment.

Juan coughed. "All my life I wanted to end things. I never understood what my brother Rico meant when he screamed 'brotherhood and loyalty.' The only person I've ever been loyal to was myself. That changed when I met Nina. I only wanted to be loyal to her. I never understood the cock-style attitude you all have. But I understand that a man has to do what a man has to do." His voice faded.

"So what's it gonna be, homes?" Tajo crossed his thick arms.

"I can't die. I got too much to live for. You want my soul for your cousin's hand? So be it." Tajo blushed from surprise. "I'll become one of you. I'll become a Bronx Gangsta and stand by your side. And stand by Nina's side."

"You got the biggest balls I've ever seen, Juan." Tajo shook his head. "The biggest." Juan rested against the prickly tree. "Get him down, Chino. He's one of us now."

"What? No way! What the fuck is going on here? Since when do we pick up stray motherfuckers? This ain't no country club! Any old pussy can't just become a part of us! We all had to prove ourselves! What the fuck you trying to do, Tajo?"

"I said, get him down."

Chino exhaled. He hesitated as if he wanted to shoot Juan first. He ripped the chain from Juan's body. Juan landed hard on the bloody ground.

"You have to prove yourself to us, Juanito. I hope you don't expect it to be easy." Tajo gestured to the blood on Juan's shirt. "Want us to clean you up?"

"No." Juan held his ribs. He slowly lifted himself up.

❖❖❖

Nina twirled Claudia's car down Sins Boulevard. Claudia panted impatiently. A deadening feeling of fear came over the both of them. Nina sped toward the garage.

"What's that?" Shorty-Five darted around the garage. He rushed back in a fit. "Someone's coming!"

"What the fuck is someone doing here at night?" Juice asked.

"Just cool it." Shorty-Five took another look. He came back with a slanted grin.

"It's Claudia's car."

"What's that bitch doing here?" Tajo shook his head.

"It's Nina, homes," Juice said. Nina charged from around the building. Claudia lagged behind. Nina's eyes caught Juan's. She nearly fainted. Her stomach tied in knots. He was draped in blood, his legs crumpled underneath him, his usually beautiful face alive with desperation.

"Juan!" She ran toward him. Before she could touch him, Chino yanked her to the side.

"Let go of me!"

"What the fuck you doing here, Nina?" His hands dug into her wrists.

"How can you guys do this? What kind of animals are you? He hasn't done anything to you! You have no right!"

"*You* had no right, Nina," Tajo argued. "And you still got no reason to be here. How did you know we were here anyway?"

"Lexi told me." She struggled. "Chino, let me go!"

"This is all your fault! Why you being such a stupid trick?" he yelled.

"Let her go!" Juan shoved Chino against the tree. Chino held up the gun. Tajo waved his hands to stop the action.

Nina huddled against Juan. She pulled his arm over her shoulder. "Just leave us alone! Why can't you leave us alone?" she screamed.

"You should be happy to know that I give you my blessings, cousin. You can be with Juan."

"What?" Nina gasped.

"It's true, Nina," Juan whispered, too ashamed to mention how it became true.

"I don't like playing games, Tajo. What are you speaking of?" Nina asked.

"Stupid bitch." Chino walked off. Everyone except Nina easily ignored his comment.

"This is what you wanted all along, right? You'd think you'd finally be happy. I'm trying to make you happy, cousin."

"I don't believe you, Tajo. Something's not right here."

"Believe what you want. The fact is we could have killed him tonight and we didn't. I have to admit you picked one noble motherfucker. He's brave, a little too brave sometimes." Tajo looked at the others. "Let's get out of here. Come on, Nina."

"I'm not going anywhere with you." She threw Claudia her keys. "I'll see you, Claudia. Will you make it home okay?"

Claudia shrugged. "Be careful, Nina."

"I will." She walked off with Juan holding on tight. The Bronx Gangstas went on their way in separate directions. Chino came back once the coast was clear. Tajo steadied his eyes on the ground, rethinking what had happened.

"So Tajo, what the fuck? What's up with you, man? How the fuck you gonna let Alonso become one of us?"

"Is he one of us yet, man?"

"What the hell you doing?" Chino bellowed. "How you gonna turn against your brothers and side with that motherfucker? He's fuckin' NYA! That means he don't deserve nothing from us! Then you let him be with your cousin! What kind of shit is that? What the fuck is going on here? You need to get your priorities straight!"

"And you need to shut the fuck up for a minute. Now, how long have you known me, man? You know me. You know I hate NYAs like I hate a dumb chick with a bald pussy." Chino shook his head. "I know what I'm doing. I hope you don't think I can't handle my business. Is that what you trying to say?"

"So this is just a setup?" Chino raised an eyebrow. "You ain't letting that motherfucker in, are you?"

"Nope, but as long as he thinks he's in we can use that to put those NYA bitches in their place. We use Rico's baby brother and he won't be able to do shit about it. Then when it's all over we smoke his ass."

"We smoke Juan?" Chino licked his lips as though a fat steak sat in front of him.

"*You'll* smoke him, fool. And then Nina will be all yours. Just the way she's supposed to be."

Chino smirked.

✦✦✦

"We can't do this, Nina." Juan waited at the front door of Claudia's uncle's place while Nina turned on the lights. She helped him inside. He tried to ignore the pain that multiplied with each step. It was impossible. He sat down, focusing on the events of the evening. "Nina."

"Quiet." She sat beside him, massaging his hands. "I won't go down this road with you again, Juan. We are going to be together, no matter what."

He rested his feet on the oval coffee table, wondering if Claudia's uncle had been rich, with such an elaborate home. "You know, being pounded in the head all night gets you to thinking." He lightly chuckled. "And I'm not giving you up, Nina. So it's going to be up to you what the next step will be for us to take."

"What exactly do you mean?" She rubbed his bloody shirt and stared at him.

"We can't keep going like this with them fighting us at every angle. So there's only one thing we can do. I have some cash saved up that Mom gives me. It's not exactly an allowance, just money I might need for a rainy day. It's enough to pay for gas, food, and lodging." He lowered his voice. "Until we get on our..."

"Juan?" She sat back. "Are you saying we should run off?"

"That's exactly what I'm saying, Nina. We don't have a choice." She looked away. "Baby, as long as we're here we can't be happy."

"But we'd be dropouts."

"Nina, we can finish high school somewhere else, that's the least of our worries." He rubbed his bruised forehead. "Our biggest concern would be making it without a job. With me being only seventeen it won't be easy to find a job."

"Juan, this is crazy. You're not even talking like yourself."

"Maybe I'm not. Hell, I may not even be myself anymore, Nina. My mom says I'm changing. And I've been thinking maybe it's damn time I did. I am sick and tired of getting leftovers, being the 'good one' when Rico and people like him get every damn thing they want. All my life I have had to sit back and take on the responsibilities of everyone else, Nina. When Rico fucked up it was me that took up the slack. He gets away with every damn thing and I never even get thanks from anyone."

"Juan, I don't want to be some pawn in this war you've got going with Rico."

"You're not." He took her hand. "Nina, I've had to share everything in my life. I have never had anything just for me. But it's different with you because I know you live only for me. You're the only thing I can call my own. The one thing no one can take away. I don't need to be around people who can't understand that."

She stood. "But there has to be a better way. Juan, we're doing so well in school these days. You may have fallen behind but you're too smart to drop out. I can't even believe you're talking like this."

"Then what the hell *should* we do? Nina, how long do we have to jump through hoops? Before, you said I was being a wimp when I broke us up. Well, now I've got an answer! You know, as well as I do, that we can't stay here and be together. You think we'll snap our fingers and Rico and Tajo will come to their senses? Look at me!" He held up his arms. "They almost killed me tonight. What's to stop them from finishing the job next time?"

"There has to be a better way, Juan. I don't want to just run off without anything in mind. This isn't a movie. We need real money and we each need to think about our future. This isn't something we should take lightly."

"I..." He exhaled into his hands.

"You know I love you," she whispered. "Don't question that. But you're not thinking clearly."

"I..."

She held up her hands. "And I understand what you mean about how you always had to handle things. Juan, I had to do the same thing with my mom. But I cannot let you make a decision you'll regret later."

He pulled her close. "I won't regret it later."

"Yes, you will. Juan, I can see us ten years from now. That bitterness that we should have done things differently will ruin what we have. I can't let that happen."

"Hey, what is this, this change all of a sudden?" He rubbed his mouth. "I'm beginning to think there's something else going on here."

"Like what?"

"I don't know. Why don't you tell me?" He crossed his arms. "Is there some other reason you don't want to leave?"

"Maybe my friends, for one. There isn't anything else. I don't want to just quit school, if that's what you mean."

"No. Is there another guy?"

"What? How can you say something like that?"

"Do you have feelings for Chino?"

"Juan!"

"I'm just asking because he speaks as if you have feelings for him."

"He's also a nut!" She took a deep breath. "Juan, there is no one in this world I want but you. Chino is completely out of the picture." She caressed his jaw. She laid her nose against his. "We just need to let things blow over. Leaving isn't the answer. But you will never know how much I want to run away with you."

"I know." He stroked her hips. They kissed. "I must look a mess." He sighed.

"And you don't smell too great, either." She laughed.

"Think Claudia would mind if I took a shower?"

"Not at all. After all, no one else is here to use it." She pointed upstairs. "The linen closet is in the middle of the hallway. The bathroom is the first thing you'll see. Uh, there's some of her uncle's T-shirts and warm-ups up there, too. I think you're about the same size."

He smirked. "Been snooping?" She shrugged. "And what will *you* be doing while I'm showering?"

She grinned. "I'll be in the bedroom making it as comfortable as possible."

"Really." He rubbed her waist. "Is there anything else you'll be doing?"

"I'll be waiting for you." She kissed him. "I love you, Juan."
"I love you, too, Nina." He went upstairs.

✦✦✦

Chino scampered through the damp grass. Fuck Tajo, Chino wouldn't wait any longer. He'd done a total of thirty-five burglaries. He hadn't regretted breaking into anyone's home and he wouldn't regret breaking into this one. He stared at Juan's truck sitting a few feet away from the front door. Chino's body went numb. He'd claimed Nina as his, now it was time to retrieve his property.

He had no problems getting inside the "love nest." The lights were off downstairs. He crept upstairs. He heard the shower. He cut his eyes to the bathroom door. Realizing it was Juan in the shower, Chino slunk down the hallway. He came to a huge bedroom barely lit by a small lamp by the bed. He peeked inside. Nina rested with her back turned to the door.

Chino would thank the moon when he got the chance. It forced its way through the window, illuminating Nina. He'd never seen anything so breathtaking. He could tell she was awake. The morbid part of him enjoyed that fact. As he watched her he became incensed. Who did she think she was? He would have given her anything if she'd given him one simple chance. Was that too much to ask? What the hell did Juan have that he didn't? That question cut deeper than any knife. He heard the shower stop. He wasted no more time. He became aroused wondering how she'd feel to find him standing over her. She lifted her head. Before she could say a word, Chino's hand covered her mouth. She furiously kicked. His eyes warned her against resistance. She blinked like an animal caught in a trap.

"Hey, Nina. I bet I'm the last one you expected to see here." She grunted.

"Sorry, this isn't a dream. I'm really here. Betcha wondering why, huh?" He gazed at her plump breasts. They lightly jiggled under her shirt. "I needed to talk to you. I'm going to take my hand off your mouth if you promise not to scream. I don't want to get rough with you, Nina, okay?" She nodded. "Okay, good girl." He uncovered her mouth.

"Chino? How did you find us?" She slid her fingers against the sheets.

He caressed her hair. "It wasn't hard, you know." He cut his eyes to the hallway.

"I tried to avoid this but you wouldn't let things be handled easily, Nina." She huffed and puffed. "Oh, what's the matter? You're afraid?"

"Yes." Her lips shook. "Chino, the smart thing for you to do is get out of here. Whatever you have planned won't work," she whispered.

"You know you hurt my feelings every time I see you?" He ran his fingers past her cleavage. He caressed the deep line that divided her breasts. "You disrespected me. All I wanted to..." Nina's eyes followed his fingers to the hardness of his jeans. "I just wanted to be there for you and protect you. Why was that so hard to understand?"

"Chino, hold on, okay?" She leaned up. His eyes stayed on her incredible body.

"Let's just put this behind us right now. Look, if I did anything to make you think I wanted you I am deeply sorry. Don't take it out on Juan. It was my doing. I swear, I had no idea you felt this deeply for me."

The rhythm of her breasts fascinated him, making it impossible to look her in the eyes. "How could you not know? Haven't I made it clear? Hell, I tried to change for you. That wasn't even enough for you, was it?" He grabbed her wrist. "Was it?" She tried to scream. He rested his gun underneath her chin before she got the chance. "I don't just love anyone, Nina."

"Please…" She sobbed. "Don't hurt me, Chino."

"No?" He rubbed her lips with the tip of the gun. "Then what should I do with you, huh, princess?" He rubbed the front of her blouse. "Maybe I should do this…"

He grabbed her breast. Nina moaned, frightened. "Is that what I should do?"

She stared at the ceiling. "Please, just don't hurt Juan. I'll do anything if you promise not to…" Her voice drifted off.

"Even now all you care about is Juan? What the fuck does he have that I don't?"

He saw her cut her eyes to the doorway. A shadow crept against the walls. Chino threw his arm back. The gun stopped Juan in his tracks. "Juanito? Did you have a nice shower?"

"Juan." Nina leaned against the headboard. He stood in gray sweatpants and a white undershirt. The wetness from the shower had been replaced by nervous sweat.

"Your lady love's gonna try to save you. I kind of expected that."

Juan crept toward him. "Chino, you don't want to hurt us." Chino stood with the gun held high. "I know you hate me, but you don't want to do this."

"Oh no?"

"No."

"I guess you don't know how much I *really* hate you, Juanito."

"Why can't someone step up and stop this?" Juan shook his

head. "Man, you want to go on living this kind of life forever? You could be so much more! You're too smart to do this shit, man, and end up behind bars. Chino, you're clever, man, you're truly clever and I hate to admit that. Man, we don't want to hurt you. All we want is to be together."

Juan glanced at Nina. "You think we're doing this to shove our relationship in your face. Well, we aren't! We don't want to hurt anyone, Chino."

"I'm clever enough to see through this bullshit. You think it's going to be this easy, Juanito? See, I know what I want and I'm not afraid to take it."

"And what do you want?" Nina whispered. She moved from the bed.

"You know what I want." He gazed at her. "I've been walking around like a puppy for you. Been standing around like an idiot with my dick in the air and you just run to Juan? You were giving it to Juan when you're supposed to be mine!"

"Calm down, Chino." Juan walked toward him.

He signaled the gun toward Juan's face. "And you are one moment away from a bullet, motherfucker! The only reason I haven't killed you yet is because I didn't want to hurt Nina." He shot her a heated glance. "Until I realized she didn't give a damn about hurting me. Both of you get where I can see you!" They stood beside the end table.

"What I want is to take you both on a little trip." Sweat dangled from his nose. "Then maybe you can see things my way."

Juan and Nina exchanged glances.

❖❖❖

"Man, I love old seventies tunes, don't you?" Chino rubbed the dashboard of his white vintage Cadillac. Juan and Nina sat stiffly in the backseat. Chino turned the radio up. Abba's "Dancing Queen" started to play. "Man, I love this song. You like this song, Nina?" He wiggled in the seat with one hand on the steering wheel.

"It's okay," she mumbled.

"Why don't you watch where you're going, man?" Juan said. He found the moonlight hitting Chino's car terrifying. "Whatever you got planned won't work."

Chino looked at Juan from the rearview mirror. "You know, you got some balls on you, boy. Here I am with my gat sitting on my lap taking you off and you still talking shit? Maybe Tajo was right. Maybe you *would* make a good Bronx Gangsta."

"I'd rather cut my dick off with an electric knife." Juan glanced at Nina.

"I see." Chino bobbed his head. He turned down a raggedy street. They ended up a ways from the garage on Sins Boulevard. He drove to a field of weeds. Suddenly the street turned into a lumpy, poorly paved road. Chino stopped the car five feet away from an old traffic sign. "Welcome." He chuckled.

"What the *hell*?" Juan looked upon the creepy area. He couldn't see any evidence of anyone for miles. Had Chino brought them out here to kill them? Juan took Nina's hand, guiding her toward him.

"Isn't that cute?" Chino held his gun. "What do you think of the place?"

"You can't be this warped. Where the hell are we? What do you plan to do?"

"This is the circle, Juan," Nina muttered.

He wiped sweat from his forehead. "The circle?"

"Yep." Chino nodded. "You know about that, Nina?"

She sighed. "'Course I do." She turned to Juan. "This is the place where the Bronx Gangstas pay their respect."

"The home of our dead homies." Chino gazed at Juan. "'Course they ain't really here but this is the designated place where we visit their spirits. Shit," he looked ahead, "sometimes I even think I hear their spirits going after that NYA blood."

"Cut the shit!" Juan slapped Chino's seat. "Whatever you think you're going to do, do it! But don't think for a minute that I'm gonna take any more of your shit. I may not be a 'gangsta' but I sure as hell am not a pussy." Chino chuckled. "So get on with it, Chino."

"Juan." Nina rubbed his hands.

"Fine." Chino held the gun toward them. He got out carefully with his eyes watching like a hawk. He snatched Juan out first, then gestured for Nina to follow.

"Over there." He pressed the gun to Juan's back. Juan smiled at Nina, then walked in the direction Chino urged. Chino kept Nina to his side.

"Chino," She tripped over sticks. He wrapped his arm around her waist. She loathed being so close to him but at this point she had no choice.

"What you think of me now, huh?" he whispered to her. "Still thinking you made the right choice? Nina, is Juan worth all this? Hey, he's caused you a lot of trouble."

They came to a clearing. Nina noticed the garage stood only a few feet away. "Stop," Chino ordered.

"Come on, man. I mean, you wanted to fuck me up and you did that. Look how good you worked me over. What more can you want?" Juan yelled.

"Oh, you have no idea." Chino looked at Nina. "Tajo wanted to wait but I had other plans."

"What do you want from us?" Nina snapped. Chino pulled her in front of him.

She stood beside Juan.

"I'm not convinced Juan's the better man. So why don't you prove it to me?" He looked around. "No one comes out here so no one will know. You'll be very comfortable. And don't worry, I won't tell a soul." He winked. "This will be between the three of us."

"*What* will be between us?" Juan swatted a mosquito from his arm.

"Well," Chino walked in a circle as he spoke, "like I was telling your lady love here, she's really hurt my feelings. I tried to figure out why she chose you over me."

"Because I fell in love with him! It has nothing to do with you, Chino!"

"Yeah, but something makes him the better man in your eyes, right?" Nina shook her head. "Let's not be coy. He's good-looking but I am, too. So I know looks can't be the reason. He ain't half as tough as me so I know that ain't it, either." Chino smiled.

"So all's left is the lovin'." He lowered his eyes to Nina's jeans. "But I need proof so I can let things go."

"What in hell are you saying?" Juan stepped toward him.

"I want to see this proof. I want to see you make love to her, Juanito."

"What?" Nina covered her mouth.

"That's right." Chino sneered. "And then this will all be over. I want to see how good it feels to be in his arms, Nina," he mocked. "How he makes you ache and call out his name."

Juan shook. "You're completely sick, aren't you?"

"Sick and tired of bullshitting, Juanito." Chino looked at the sky. "It's dark, no one's out here. The ground's pretty soft. Get started."

"You're out of your mind!" Juan lunged at him. Chino slapped him in the face with the gun. Nina hurried to Juan's side. "Let this go, Chino!" Juan yelled through his fingers. "Let this all go, please!"

"Not until I see the goods."

"Chino, please."

"No, Nina." He waved the gun. "This is how it's going to be tonight. You two wanted to be with each other. Then show me how much you want it."

Juan took Nina's hand. "Fuck you! Nina, let's go." They started off.

"Do it!" Chino held up the gun. "Or you both die tonight." Juan looked off into the distance. He figured they could make it to the garage before Chino caught up with them. The only problem was bullets were ten times faster than their legs could ever be. "Plotting, Juanito?" Chino turned around to see the street a ways back. "I doubt anyone's going to come through," Suddenly Juan knocked Chino in the back of the head. He dropped the gun.

"Juan, his gun!" Nina grabbed it.

"Give it to me." Juan snatched it.

Chino regained his strength. He laughed, rubbing his aching head. "Pretty good trick, Juanito. I didn't think you had it in you."

"Guess I fooled us all, huh?" Juan said.

✠✠✠

Florence had never been so scared but she had to think of something. Shorty-Five, Juice, Tajo, and XL, the newest Bronx Gangsta, tore through her living room. Juice crept up and down the hallway. Benny and Jorge were scrunched beside their mother on the couch.

"Ma?" Benny whispered.

"Quiet." She took his hand. "Everything's going to be all right." Something crashed in the kitchen. Tajo's hefty laughter followed afterward. "Is your sister still asleep?" she whispered.

Jorge walled his eyes. "You know Cyn can sleep through a storm." He nervously moved his feet against the carpet. "Are they going to kill us?"

"No, surely," Florence answered, not truly convinced herself. They all stomped into the living room, guns held high. She prayed Cynthia wouldn't wake up. Shorty-Five marched toward Florence. He wrapped a strand of her short grayish-black hair around his finger. "What do you want?" She scowled.

"We want to know where your son is." Shorty-Five smirked.

"Rico or Juan?" She muttered. He grabbed her neck. Benny and Jorge held each other. "You're not in the position to be smart, lady. We got business to handle. We want Rico. We intended to use Juan as bait but since the pussy ain't here, we had to come up with other options. Where is Rico?"

Tajo came from the kitchen with an apple. "XL, check the back rooms."

Florence jumped up. "No!" Shorty-Five slapped her. Florence fought to stand. "Just get out of my house!"

"Say it a little louder, honey," Juice teased. He held his gun against her chin. XL walked in with Cynthia struggling in his arms. He used the excess of her oversize nightgown to hold her.

"Mamá!" Cynthia shivered.

"Quiet. No one's going to hurt you. Cynthia, right?" XL massaged her damp brow. "Pretty little thing, aren't you?"

"Leave her alone!" Florence shrieked.

"Maybe we should teach this bitch a lesson, Tajo." Juice grabbed Florence. "Let's take the old ho with us."

"I got a better idea. If we can't use Juan to bring out Rico, we can use something else." Tajo walked toward Florence. "Tell your son we'll be at Sins Boulevard waiting on his dumb ass. We want him alone without his boys and no cops. If even *one* cop magically shows up we're killing this one." He pointed to Cynthia.

Florence shivered. "I will do that." She gritted her teeth. "And it will be my pleasure to aid him in killing each and every one of you if you lay a hand on my daughter!" She reached for Cynthia.

XL chuckled. His large, muscular body made Cynthia appear nonexistent. "She's coming with us, Mamá," he goaded. "So you'll be wise to do what we say."

Tajo threw the half-eaten apple at Florence's feet. "And make sure Rico gets his ass down to Sins in less than half an hour."

XL yanked Cynthia into his arms. He fondled her hair. "Maybe he shouldn't hurry. I might enjoy this after all."

Florence reached for him. "Don't you lay one hand on her! If you do, I'll kill you myself."

"Just worry about your son." Tajo smirked. He followed the others out the door.

Florence ran to the window with a mind to call the cops. Unfortunately she knew following their demands was the only way to ensure Cynthia's safety.

"Mamá, do you think they'll hurt her?" Jorge peeked out the window. The Bronx Gangstas sped off.

Florence turned to him. "You know where Rico is?"

"Yep, the hideout at Fifty-five East Way Street. I'll call his cell." Jorge rushed to the phone.

Florence sighed. "God, please let this end tonight."

CHAPTER SEVENTEEN

"Move!" Juan shoved Chino inside the garage. Nina watched the drama unfold with bated breath. Chino hadn't lost any of his arrogance. If anything he'd become cockier.

"It's raining." He pointed outside. Juan stood in front of him. They exchanged a look of undying hatred. Juan shivered beyond belief. He did his best to keep the gun steady.

"Shaking?" Chino squinted. "Hey, I know it must be hard since you never even held a gat before, I bet. The game isn't fun if I'm fighting a mouse."

Juan looked at Nina. She nervously bit her finger. "I'm not scared of you, Chino," he said.

Chino marched toward him. He bent down to sniff Juan's middle. "You sure, *ese*? I think I smell piss. Come on. What the fuck you gonna do? Call the police like the pussy you are? It won't stop me, G. It won't stop my brothers from getting your ass, either. We won't stop until you're dead."

"Juan, let's just go. We got the gun."

"Quiet, Nina." He exhaled. "I'm tired of finishing like a punk. You're right, Chino. This won't be over until I make it over, right?" Chino shrugged. "The only way to do that is to stand up to you. I know gangstas revere respect more than anything. You asked me how much I want Nina, *this* is how much I want her."

"Juan, let's just go!" Nina pulled his arm. He jerked away.

"Oh, I see. You think I'm scared of yo bitch ass just 'cause you flagging my piece? Come on, Juanito. We both know you won't kill me."

"But I'm in Bronx Gangsta territory, remember? You're right, Chino. This is your world. I got to be careful, don't I? If I killed you I believe I could be out of here before someone finds me. Since it's your gun, nothing would link this to me. What do you think?"

"You're bluffing."

Nina gawked.

"I'm not. I'm sick of all this shit. It ends tonight!"

Chino scoffed. He clenched his fingers until his hands turned red. "You'll have to kill *all* the BGs, motherfucker. And that's not gonna be easy."

"What will it take to knock you down a peg or two?" Juan walked toward him.

"More than what your bitch ass can come up with."

"Juan, we can't do this." Nina stood in front of him. She still hadn't blocked his focus on Chino. "If you kill him, you're worse than he is! Is being together worth all of this?"

"I am doing this for us, Nina. Who the fuck will care if we kill him?" Chino squinted. "He's the cause of this!"

"And there is a bunch of other guys right along with him! What, you gonna smoke the NYAs, the Bronx Gangstas, *and* your brother? Look at me." She held his face. His eyes stayed on Chino. "I love you but if you do this, you won't be the person I know you've fought hard to be. You'll be just like *him*." Nina grimaced at Chino.

He flicked his finger. "Listen to her, Juanito. If you pull that trigger, you'll be sorry. Your problems will just begin. My brothers would move heaven and earth to get your ass."

"Juan, listen to me," Nina whispered. When Juan turned toward her, Chino grabbed the gun. The two tussled until they ended up outside. Chino flung Juan to the ground. Nina ran behind. She viciously smacked rain from her eyes. She couldn't see two feet in front of her. "Chino, stop it!" she screamed.

"Fight me like a man, motherfucker!" Chino spit rain from his lips. "Come on and put an end to this war once and for all, Juan! Fight me like a fuckin' man. It's the only way I'll stop." Chino raised the gun.

Juan saw Nina, wet and shivering, only inches away. For her he'd do anything. He was smart enough to realize he probably wouldn't make it five minutes fighting Chino, but no matter what happened, Juan was determined it would all end tonight.

"Come on, motherfucker!" Chino yelled.

"Stop it!" Nina screamed. She ran toward them, slipping in thick patches of mud.

"I'm ready to deal with your ass gangsta style, Chino!" Juan rubbed rain from his face. More replaced it within seconds. The rain became so heavy it actually began to hurt when it fell.

Chino moved back and forth. "You think you a gangsta now, *ese*? Think I got to give in to yo punk ass? Think again!" At that moment a mysterious force entered Juan's body. He felt the presence of incredible strength, the undying strength of love. Chino slapped him with the gun. "You don't know me! You don't know shit! I'm a Bronx Gangsta, motherfucker!" Chino struck again.

"Oh!" Juan fell in the mud after a slicing kick to the stomach.

"We eat motherfuckers for breakfast around here. You think you running shit? You ain't from no set! You got nobody covering your back. You got nothing!" Chino pistol-whipped him. Juan gasped for air. "What you got to say now, Alonso? Apparently nothing." As Chino raised the gun, Nina tackled him to the ground. He flung her backward but she grabbed his leg to prevent him from going after Juan.

Juan rose to his feet. "Get off her!" He hurled Chino away from her. Juan delivered a deadening punch to his face. "You don't hold the power, understand that, Chino? There is nothing you could do to me!" Juan huffed and puffed. "So who's the better man?"

"Me, motherfucker. And you're the dead man." Chino aimed the gun toward Juan's chest.

"Juan!" Nina shouted.

Juan whipped his hand backward. He knocked the gun from Chino's hand. Chino smacked him with implausible force. A stream of blood dangled from Juan's mouth. He fell instantly.

"Come on!" Chino yelled. Juan lay on his stomach. He wasn't moving. He didn't appear to be breathing.

"Juan!" Nina slid beside him. "Juan, please." She held his face to hers. "Juan, say something." He didn't move. Nina nearly suffocated from fright. She looked up to see Chino smirking.

"Looks like it's just you and me now, huh?" He pulled her up.

"Let me go!"

He breathed roughly. "Was it exciting, huh?" Thunder roared. "Bet you loved seeing us fight over you like that." He held her waist in a strangling grip. "You like playing us against each other, don't you, Nina? It gets you off." He forced his lips to hers. Nina tried to get his gun but Chino held her too tightly. "Don't pretend you don't like it! This is what you wanted all along!"

He tried to pick her up. He slipped in the mud in the process.

"Let me go!" Nina struggled helplessly. She noticed Juan moving. Chino aimed the gun toward him. Nina slugged him.

Before she could reach for Juan, Chino threw her to the ground. He got on top of her. She used her long fingernails as tiny daggers, clawing at his face. She knocked him into the mud.

"Nina, run." Juan coughed.

"Yeah, you better run, bitch." Chino lunged for her. Nina took off behind the garage. Chino followed with his gun held high. "I'm gonna get you, you bitch!"

"No!" Juan struggled but couldn't stand. "Leave her alone, Chino!"

✠✠✠

"What the fuck?" Tajo drove toward Sins Boulevard. He heard a girl screaming. Shorty-Five shrugged. Juice struggled to see out the window. XL took a break from tormenting Cynthia. "You hear that shit, homes?" Tajo glanced around.

"Hell yeah." Juice spit out his toothpick. "Ain't that Chino's car?" He pointed as they passed the circle. "He didn't say he was coming out here."

"No, he didn't." Tajo kept on driving to the garage. "He said he was going home."

"Guess he had plans of his own, huh?" XL played with Cynthia's hair. She trembled against his chest.

"Guess so." Tajo contemplated the fact.

✠✠✠

"Stop!" Nina couldn't see Chino in the rain and darkness but she felt him on her heels. She threw her arms back to hit him but missed each time. "Leave me alone!"

"I'm going to kill you, Nina!" He pounced at her. He missed her by an inch.

"Leave me alone!" She ran into the slick street. She lost her balance. She slipped across it and tumbled into a steep, muddy ditch. She struggled to keep the rain from pulling her away. The rain landed heavily on her face, making it impossible to see. She barely made out Chino coming across the street at full speed. "Chino, leave me alone!"

"Too late for that!" He grabbed her. She struggled, knocking the gun out of his hands. The mud instantly buried it. He pressed her body against his and pulled out a knife. Nina slapped and kicked. She tried to do anything to foil his plans.

"Chino, you can't do this! You don't want to hurt me."

"Yeah, I didn't *before*." His eyes were hollow. His face was distorted with blotches of mud and streaks of rain. "But that was then!" He swung the knife toward her face. She stomped his toe. He barreled over. The knife flipped from his hands. Nina felt its blade land by her foot. She plunged her hands into the mud to find it. Chino grabbed her ankles. He swung her backward.

"Stop!" She kicked his chest. Mud flew into his mouth. As he choked, Nina searched frantically again for the knife.

�֍✦✦

Tajo snatched Juan by his shirt. "What the fuck is happening here, Alonso?"

The rain plopped against them like timber. Juan watched XL gently handling Cynthia beside the garage door. The rain made it impossible for Juan to see them once they got inside. He'd save Cynthia later. Nina's life was in danger *now*.

Juan blurted out as if he'd been in a trance. "It's Chino, Tajo! He's going to do something to Nina." Tajo looked at Juice. "He brought us out here. He's fuckin' crazy." Juan nearly choked. "I fought him. He knocked me out but went after Nina with the gun. Look, let my sister go and..."

"Bullshit!" Tajo shook him. "What did you do to Nina?"

"Nothing!" Juan coughed. "You know I'd never hurt her. You might hate me but you know I wouldn't hurt her!"

"Tajo, he's gotta be telling the truth," Juice said. They heard screaming from the distance.

"That's Nina." Juan gawked.

"Let's go." Tajo ran.

✠✠✠

"Help me!" Nina held Chino's wrist. He had her sprawled out in the mud. The knife dangled inches from her face.

"You wanted Juan, huh?" He grunted, forcing the knife closer. "Well, it doesn't work that way, Nina. He doesn't deserve you. I'd rather kill you than to have you be with him." Nina shrieked. Chino's strength became unbearable. She was overpowered at every turn.

✠✠✠

Juan and Tajo tracked through the muddy weeds. The others split up. They tried to follow the trace of Nina's screams but found complete silence.

"She ran behind the garage. They have to be around here some- where." Juan's feet were submerged in mud. It seemed like the rain would never let up. Freezing and shivering, he made it beside Tajo. "See her?"

"Nah." Tajo furiously shook rain from his face. "I don't get this shit, Alonso. Why would Chino want to hurt Nina?"

"He wants to get even with her. Hell, I don't know! All I know is he's crazy and if we don't get to Nina, God knows..." They heard screaming again.

"I think they're over there!" Tajo raced through the mud.

* * *

"Uh!" Nina pressed her hands to Chino's face. He shrieked and moaned, regaining his strength. The knife pricked her chin. He blocked her kicks. He forced her legs underneath his thighs. "Chino!"

"Don't you wish things were different, huh?" he bellowed. He brought the knife closer. "Want to make it right, huh?" He spit rain.

"Please, uh! I can't." Nina struggled to loosen his grip. He seemed to become stronger at every turn. "No one tried to hurt you!"

"You went against us, Nina. You went against *me*. I'd have done anything for you. No one goes against us, Nina. You need to learn that lesson! I told you, didn't I?"

Nina tried to lean up. She couldn't overcome Chino's strength no matter how she positioned herself. The rain came in giant swoops. She thought she heard voices. Her draining strength made it impossible for her to be sure. Chino's hand clamped her shoulder. He raised the knife swiftly. Nina closed her eyes, anticipating death.

She could feel the knife tearing into her skin before it happened. Everything flashed before her eyes. Still, after all of this, she didn't regret meeting Juan. She felt blessed that she had. She waited with her eyes shut. She wondered why she hadn't been stabbed. Chino abruptly released her shoulder. She felt him being pulled off. She opened her eyes. A large figure threw Chino on the ground. A man knocked the knife from his hands.

Rico Alonso pinned Chino to the ground. Even he wasn't strong enough to overcome Chino's rage. Chino slugged him. Rico landed on the ground beside Nina. Chino waddled in the mud on his hands and knees. He found his gun before the others saw him.

"You okay?" She gasped.

"Yeah." Rico watched her strangely. He seemed surprised she cared. He struggled to stand. Chino slapped him back down. Nina inched away. Pain from Chino's heavy body holding hers so long prevented her from standing.

Chino aimed the gun at Nina. Rico threw his leg up like a solid gate. He kicked Chino in the face so hard he tumbled backward three times. The gun flipped against Rico's leg. It plopped into the street. Chino jumped to his feet. Rico snatched his own gun from his pocket and shot three times. He hit Chino twice in the chest and once in the stomach. He fell back, groaning.

"Oh my God." Nina covered her mouth. Rico turned to look at her. She couldn't say a word to him. What she thought of saying seemed silly, but here was the most unlikely person in the world saving her life. She didn't know Rico well but knew something had changed in him. She could see it in his eyes.

"Nina!" Tajo yelled. He and Juan raced toward them.

"Rico?" Juan stopped at the edge of the ditch. He saw his brother's gun dangling from his hands. He saw Chino a few feet away wallowing in mud, rain, and blood.

"Jesus." Juan got on his knees. He pulled Nina out of the ditch.

"Alonso." Tajo looked at Rico. He stared at Chino, who could move surprisingly well after being shot. "So you *did* come, huh?"

"NYA for life." Rico held up the symbol. "We got unfinished business to take care of, don't we?" He hopped out of the ditch and landed right in front of Tajo's face.

"We sure do." Tajo groaned.

Juan held Nina in his arms. "We saw what you did, Rico. You saved Nina's life."

He scoffed. "No, I didn't. Shit, I was trying to get that bitch-ass Chino. I thought it was Cynthia out here with him."

"Right." Juan wasn't convinced and neither were Tajo and Nina. "You knew exactly what you were doing. Why did you do it, Rico?"

Rico impatiently exhaled. "You can't never be satisfied, can you, Juan? That's why I don't fool wit'cha now."

"Come on, come on." Juan lazily slapped rain from his face. "Cut the shit. Why did you save Nina?"

Rico swept rain from his mouth. "Shit, she ain't never done nothing to nobody, all right?" He marched around like a triumphant soldier. "Shit, what kind of punk would let a girl get fucked up like that? I was doing what any normal person would do."

Juan chuckled. "That's just it. You've never done anything good for anyone."

"Man, how can you say that? I've protected you all these years. I made sure no one gave you no shit. Fuck it, I ain't perfect. But shit, I do some good things."

"You did one tonight." Nina smiled. She looked at Juan. "Can't we just leave it at that?"

"We got some unresolved issues to take care of, man." Juan stepped toward Rico.

"Didn't you ever learn nothing can be solved in one night? Why you making a big deal of this? I didn't help her for you, I…"

"Yes, you did." Juan sighed. "I just wish you could admit it." Rico refused to look his brother in the eyes. "But even if you can't, thanks, Rico." Juan patted his shoulder.

"Whatever. If I got the chance to fuck up a Bronx Gangsta, you think I'd miss it? Especially when they tried to draw me out." Rico looked at Tajo. "So you called on this game. Let's get this shit started. Maybe we should walk back to the circle. Then your ass will already be there when your homies get ready to remember you."

Tajo nodded.

"No, Rico!" Juan blocked him. "It stops tonight. You two don't have to make up. I don't give a shit if you still hate each other for centuries to come, but Nina and I are out of it tonight! This is over."

"Hey, nobody said it had shit to do with you." Rico snapped.

"Yeah." Tajo clenched his fist. "You wanna be out of it, you're both out of it."

"What exactly does that mean?" Nina asked. She noticed the rain slacking.

"She can't understand that, huh?" Rico smirked. "I guess being stupid runs in your family, Tajo."

"Don't be flip, Rico." Juan stroked his soaking hair. "In plain English, what are you two saying?"

"It means what we just said. You and Nina are out of this game. But don't expect the war between the BGs and NYAs is anywhere near over," Rico said.

"But you saved my life. I know you did it because you wanted to."

Rico sneered. "You don't know shit, Nina. So why the fuck

you two still here?" He looked at Tajo. "We got business to take care of."

"Hasn't enough happened tonight?" Juan sighed. "Cynthia is safe. She's at the garage. Rico, let's just go home."

"You're out of it, little brother." Rico didn't take his eyes off Tajo. "Can't you just be satisfied with *that*?"

Juan looked at Nina. "We want it to *all* be over."

"This war's been around for years and it ain't near over." Tajo sighed. "But I ain't fucking around in your life no more, Nina. I guess that's worth something," he said.

Nina sighed. "Rico, I don't know how to thank you for what you did."

"Yeah, whatever." He acted as though being nice for one moment caused him enormous agony. "Now go take Cynthia home, Juan. Take my car." Rico threw him the keys. "Just get out of here, both of you."

"Before we change our minds." Tajo watched them closely until they were out of sight. He turned toward Rico. "So?"

"So what?" Rico stood wide-legged.

"This is off the record, all right?" Tajo tilted his head. "Now this war ain't nowhere near over."

"Hell no." Rico rolled his eyes.

"And no one has to know what happened here," Tajo whispered. Chino rolled around in the ditch. He tried to stand. "Thanks for saving my cousin's life. No matter what happens after this moment, I felt I should say that."

"Yeah, whatever." Rico watched Chino. "Better get yo boy over there. You'll need all the help you can get when we come through the next time."

"I hear you," Tajo whispered. "But he ain't my boy, *anymore*." He walked away.

"Your cousin's leaving." Juan pointed. They watched Tajo disappear into the darkness. "Can't believe they didn't kill each other."

"You think it's really over?" Nina watched Rico leave in the opposite direction. She saw Chino struggling. Blood oozed from him like water.

"The war?" Juan sighed. "I don't think it will ever be over. They're right. The Bronx Gangstas and New York Assassins are destined to hate each other. I don't think anyone can change that, not even them."

"You think they're really letting us be together?"

"I don't see why not." Juan opened the passenger's side of Rico's car. "We just have to live our own lives, Nina. At least we've got that choice now."

"I guess you're right." She sashayed toward him. "Kind of worried, though."

"How come?" He pulled her close. She fiddled with the bruises on his face.

"Since we're 'allowed' to be together now, I can't help wondering if things will be boring. Wasn't that keeping it exciting?"

"Excuse me?" He laughed. "I would never be boring."

"Well, you never know." She moved away. "Maybe I should rethink this and reconsider my options."

"Oh really?" He smirked. "Get in the car, Nina."

"Seriously." She chuckled. "I mean, maybe I need to see what someone else has to offer. I'm a hot commodity at Roosevelt." They got in the car.

He laughed. "You're something else. Don't even play like that. Let's go get my sister." He started the car.

"Who's playing?" She put on her seatbelt.

"Can't help but wonder how things will be from now on." He exhaled.

"Yeah." She leaned against the headrest. "What time is it?"

"Past midnight." Juan drove down the desolate street toward the garage. "Shit, how am I going to explain this to my mother?"

She felt his neck. "I think we got bigger fish to fry, Juan."

"Like what?"

"Mrs. Garrett. We didn't do our homework."

"Jesus Christ." Juan sighed. "Maybe we can skip school tomorrow."

She shook her head. "No way, buster. If you're gonna be *my* man, you better give it your all. You're gonna go to college, become a famous politician, and help the community. Did I leave anything else out?" She smiled.

He laughed. "It's not bad enough I got my mother working on me. Now I got you, huh? Maybe we *both* should rethink this, after all."

"Sorry." Nina grinned. "You're in it for the long haul, pal."

Juan pulled her close with his free hand, his gallant smile showing her how appreciative he was of the moment. Nina laid her head on his chest. She could believe they were free. She could even believe Rico and Tajo would one day come to their senses. What she couldn't believe was how happy she was at this moment. Happier than she'd ever been in her entire life.

THE END

EPILOGUE

Three Weeks Later

Juan wasn't sure what brought him to Chino's door. All he knew was he'd been feeling guilty for the last few weeks. He stared at the polished white door of Chino's elaborate, two-story home. This was definitely not the home of a G. Then again, Juan knew Chino wasn't anything close to what he seemed. He took delicate steps up the wide porch. He admired the fine garden and luxurious cars.

He settled within the comfortable breeze and silence that came with an upper-middle-class neighborhood. He wasn't jealous that Chino's family had more money than his ever could. Seeing this relieved his guilt momentarily. He'd spent days hoping Chino's recovery had been satisfactory. He couldn't help blame himself, though Nina tried to convince him otherwise. She simply said, "Sometimes you have too big of a heart." Whether that was a blessing or a hindrance would be figured out in the near future.

Chino's father ran a slew of Latino restaurants. He was a tall, hefty man of fifty-five. His image seeped of wealth and he wore it well. He'd provided Chino with his good looks but unfortunately not his unique kindness. Chino's father seemed like the kind of man who'd invite a homeless stranger in for lunch while Chino probably wouldn't even glance their way.

Juan couldn't understand how such a kind man could be the father of his worst enemy. He politely declined the man's offer of a snack. They chatted a few more minutes about Juan's career goals. Juan and Chino were left alone in a living room that seemed to have been customized by a famous designer. Chino appeared rather comfortable on the soft, chic maroon sofa.

He stared obsessively at a gigantic television equipped with every device imaginable. The remote looked bigger than Juan's radio! He wasn't surprised when Chino didn't speak. Juan looked out the window. He enjoyed a wonderful view of the stately homes across the street. Finally, he began his quest.

"You're not poor." Juan couldn't believe he blurted out something so stupid. He hadn't the power to not speak the obvious at times. Chino's expression stayed solid. Juan continued, "I mean, other than Rico and Tajo, I thought the others were all poor."

"Really?" Chino's voice was crisp with exhaustion. He rested his head against the sofa. Finally his eyes caught Juan's. "You thought I lived in some beat-up shack, right? Thought you'd find me sipping forties and shooting craps?"

"Yeah." Juan hated to admit his ignorance. Nina had been right. He *did* judge people on appearances. It was a habit he hoped to break before starting out in the real world. "How you doing?" He pointed to the bandages that bulged from underneath Chino's pajama top.

"I guess I should be glad I'm alive, right?" He slammed the remote on the table.

"Your dad's very nice."

Chino deeply sighed. "Another thing that surprised you, no doubt." Juan shrugged. "Why are you here, Juan?"

Juan took off his baseball cap. Caressing it made him feel less of a fool for coming in the first place. "Man, I just wanted to say I was sorry. I was hoping it could all start here."

"*What* could start here?" Chino squinted.

"Forgiveness, understanding, you name it, man."

"So I am supposed to renounce my impending sins because of what I did to you? Is that why you came here?" Chino grimaced. "You've got some set of balls. Don't ever let anyone tell you you're not brave."

"You can change now, Chino. You can leave the past behind. You could have anything you want."

Chino guffawed. "Jeez, you sound like some cheap after-school special! I can't just wish a better life."

"Why do you hang on to this persona?"

"Maybe it's all I have."

"I find that hard to believe." Juan gestured to the room. "I see fine cars, a great house, a loving father. It's hard for me to think you can't do better, man."

"You think you know everything about everyone, don't you, Alonso? The person you know least about is yourself." Juan raised an eyebrow. "Don't come over here pretending to feel sorry for me just to relieve your soul."

"I guess that's the difference between you and me, Chino. I do good deeds because I want to. You only do things to suit you."

"Bullshit." Chino tugged on the strangling chest bandage. "We are just alike. And you still don't see it. We live for the same things. We got the same strong family background. We're educated, and we would have both done anything to have Nina." He looked away. "But that's dead now, isn't it?"

Juan squinted. "You really care about her, don't you? That's why you got so mad."

"Like I told her, I don't love just anyone." Chino walled his sunken eyes.

"I didn't come to upset you. I wanted you to know that even if you don't forgive me, I forgive you, Chino. And I don't wish you to be in the pain you're in. I truly don't."

"The wounds are healing."

"I'm not talking about the wounds, Chino. I'm talking about your heart." Chino peered up at him. "No one should live their life in loneliness and sadness. You're too smart for this." Chino sat up. Juan wasn't sure if he was even listening. "That's all I wanted to say, man." He turned to leave.

"Juan?" Chino stood quite impressively. He crossed his arms like a valiant soldier. "I'm smart enough to know when it's all over. I can't change what I've done."

"But you can change your life from this point on. You got a second chance at life, man!"

"Right." He chuckled. "I got two gangs out there waiting to smoke me, man. The BGs because of what I did to Nina. The NYAs because of what I did to you. You truly see about my world now? No matter how far we go, or what we do, it's only a matter of time. I'm the enemy of both now, man. But I'd rather be that than to not stand up and fight."

Juan sighed. "Chino, if foolish pride came in millions you'd be richer than Donald Trump." Chino chuckled. "You could do something about it if you wanted to, man." Chino followed him outside. Juan turned to face him when he reached his truck.

"You did some wrong things. I did some wrong things. I'm not in any position to tell you to fix them. But you need to make it right."

"With God?" Chino smirked. "Or with the gangs?"

Juan put on his baseball cap. "Why don't you try first with yourself, man?" He got in his truck.

"Too late for that, man." Chino followed him. "You'll learn what I mean someday."

Juan nodded. "Maybe I already do." He drove off.

When he turned the corner, he noticed Chino watching him drive away. Watching wasn't the problem. But whether or not Chino had heard a word Juan said would make all the difference in the world.

FOOD FOR THOUGHT

In life we all learn huge lessons about love. In *Everlasting*, Juan and Nina learned that you can obtain everything, but until you've found true love, you really don't have *anything*.

ABOUT THE AUTHOR

Stacy-Deanne (Dee-Anne) is a bestselling author born in 1978. She is a fiction writer who began her career when she was nineteen years old. She is a certified editor, landscape photographer and model. She prides herself on writing novels concentrating on characters of various backgrounds.

Ms. Deanne is a member of the Author's Guild. She is also one of the authors profiled in the book, *Literary Divas: The Top 100+ African-American Women in Writing*. She was born and resides in Houston, Texas. Visit the author at www.stacy-deanne.net or www.myspace.com/stacydeanne, or email her at stacydeanne1@aol.com.

If you enjoyed *Everlasting*, check out another
Strebor on the Streetz title

EASTSIDE

by Caleb Alexander

CHAPTER ONE

Travon smacked his lips. "Man, you're stupid."

"Why?" Justin asked, shifting his gaze toward Travon. "Just because your brother got killed don't mean I will. Besides, it's for the hood."

Travon exhaled, and lowered his head. "I told my brother that he was stupid too, and now he's dead."

The boys continued around the side of the old red-brick school building toward the back. Staring at the ground, Justin haphazardly kicked at gravel spread along the ground beneath his feet.

"Yeah, Tre, but at least Too-Low went out like a soldier," he replied.

They were headed behind the middle school to a pair of old wooden green bleachers that sat across the well-worn football field. They could see the others standing just in front of the peeling bleachers waiting for them. Travon shifted his gaze from the waiting boys back to Justin. He started to speak, but Justin interrupted him.

"Tre, what's up with you?" Justin asked. "You ain't got no love for the hood? Your brother was down; he was a straight-up G. Don't you wanna be like that? Making everybody bar you and catch out when you step on the scene?"

Travon stared at Justin in silence. His silence seemed to only anger his friend more.

"I know that you're still trippin' over your brother getting killed, but he'd want you to ride for the hood!" Justin shouted. "He'd want you to be down!"

Travon halted in mid-step, and stared at Justin coldly. "How do you figure that?"

Like a precious family heirloom, Travon considered his brother, his brother's thoughts and wishes, as well as his memory, to be sacred. They were his and his alone.

Justin paused to formulate his reply, but one of the waiting boys shouted. "Y'all lil' niggaz hurry the fuck up! We ain't got all muthafuckin' day!"

Now filled with even more nervous anxiety, Travon and Justin quickly ended their conversation and hurriedly approached the waiting group. A tall, slender, shirtless boy stepped to the fore-front. His torso was heavily illustrated with various tattoos and brandings, while his body was draped in gold jewelry, glimmering brilliantly in the bright South Texas sun.

"So, y'all lil' niggaz wanna get down, huh?" the shirtless boy asked.

Another boy anxiously stepped forward. "Say, Dejuan, let me put 'em on the hood!"

Dejuan, the first boy, folded his arms and nodded.

Travon walked his eyes across all of the boys present. There were six of them, all adorned with large expensive gold necklaces, watches, bracelets, and earrings, and all of them had gold caps covering their teeth. They were members of the notorious Wheatley Courts Gangsters, or WCGs for short. The WCGs were one of the most violent drug gangs in the State of Texas. Their ruthless-ness and brutality was legendary.

Travon nervously examined the boys one by one. Those who were not shirtless were clad in burnt-orange University of Texas T-shirts. Burnt orange was the gang's colors, and the University of Texas symbol was their adopted motif. It stood for the location of their home, the Wheatley Courts. It was their municipality, their ruthless domain, their merciless world. It was a place where their will was law, and where all those who disobeyed were sen-tenced to death.

The Wheatley Courts was a low-income housing project where drugs and violence were the rule, and not the exception. It was also a place where many more than just a few of its occupants had made millions in their professions as street pharmacists. Perhaps worst of all, the Courts were home to the WCGs, a gang of ballers, and stone-cold murderers.

Travon shifted his gaze to his left; Justin had begun to remove his T-shirt. He looked back at the group of boys, to find that several of them were removing their shirts and jewelry as well. The festivities were about to begin.

"Let me whip these lil' niggaz onto the hood!" Tech Nine asked Dejuan again.

Without waiting for a response, Tech Nine walked away from the group and onto the football field, where he was quickly joined by Quentin, Lil C, and T-Stew. Once out on the field, the boys turned and waited for Justin.

Hesitantly, Justin made his way to where Tech Nine was waiting patiently and cracking his knuckles. Once Justin came within striking distance, Tech Nine swung wildly at him. The blow slammed into Justin's face.

"Muthafucka!" Justin shouted. He quickly charged Tech Nine and tackled him. Both boys hit the ground hard.

Lil C approached from the side and kicked Justin in his ribs. Justin cried out and rolled over onto his side. Justin tried to lift himself from off the ground, only to be met by a fist from Quentin. Justin grabbed his bloody nose.

"Wheatley Courts Gangstas, you punk-ass bitch!" Tech Nine shouted, as he charged Justin. "This is WCG, nigga!"

Lil C delivered a kick to Justin's back, just as Quentin swung at Justin again.

"Get that muthafucka!" Dejuan shouted from the sidelines.

Justin was able to roll away from Tech Nine's lunge, but had to take another blow from Quentin. He was able to make it to his feet just in time to receive another punch from Lil C. Although tired and out of breath, Justin was able to sustain the blow and remain standing.

"WCG for life!" Quentin shouted, advancing again.

Lil C swung at Justin again and missed. Justin, however, was unable to dodge a kick from Tech Nine. It landed directly in his groin.

Justin stumbled back, and Tech Nine kicked again, this time missing Justin and striking Lil C.

"My bad, man!" Tech Nine shouted. "I was trying to kick that little muthafucka!"

"Shit! Aw, fuck!" Lil C slowly descended to the ground while clutching his groin.

This brief intermission gave Justin time to recover and go on the offensive. He quickly dropped to one knee and punched Quentin in his groin, just as Quentin was about to swing at him.

"Aaaaaargh, shit! Punk muthafucka!" Quentin fell to the ground clutching his crotch.

Tech Nine maneuvered behind Justin, and threw a hard punch to the back of his head.

"Yeah, muthafucka, this is Wheatley Courts on mines!" Tech Nine shouted.

Justin rose, stumbled forward, and tripped over Quentin's leg. Tired, he hit the ground hard; this time, he could not find the energy to get back up. Tech Nine hurriedly approached and began kicking.

Justin, unable to move, curled into a ball and waited for the pain to be over.

"Punk muthafucka, fight back!" Tech Nine continued to kick brutally. He kicked Justin until he became tired, and retreated to where the others were standing.

Dejuan turned to Tech Nine. "Do you think that's enough?" he asked laughingly.

Tech Nine, sweating profusely, swallowed hard before answering. "I think he can get down. I think he's got enough nuts." He shifted his eyes to Travon. "You lucky I'm tired today, but tomorrow, I'm going to enjoy putting hands on you."